Minbak

ALSO BY ELA LEE

Jaded

Minbak

ELA LEE

HARVILL

1 3 5 7 9 10 8 6 4 2

Harvill, an imprint of Vintage, is part of the
Penguin Random House group of companies

Vintage, Penguin Random House UK, One Embassy Gardens,
8 Viaduct Gardens, London SW11 7BW

penguin.co.uk/vintage
global.penguinrandomhouse.com

First published by Harvill in 2026

Copyright © Ela Lee 2026

The moral right of the author has been asserted

The epigraph on p. vii is from Sylvia Plath's 'Parliament Hill Fields' from
the collection *Ariel*, 1965, reproduced with permission of Faber & Faber.

Lines on p. 9 from 'Funeral Blues' by W. H. Auden
copyright © 1940 by The Estate of W. H. Auden. Reprinted by
permission of Curtis Brown, Ltd. All rights reserved.

A version of the article on pp. 84–5 appeared in the *New York Times* as 'AROUND THE
WORLD; Protesters Battle Police In South Korean Capital', section 1, p. 5, 23 Nov. 1985.

This is a work of fiction. Names and characters are the product of the author's imagination
and any resemblance to actual persons, living or dead, is entirely coincidental.

No part of this book may be used or reproduced
in any manner for the purpose of training artificial intelligence technologies or systems.
In accordance with Article 4(3) of the DSM Directive 2019/790, Penguin Random House
expressly reserves this work from the text and data mining exception.

Typeset in 12.1/15.2pt Dante MT Std by Six Red Marbles UK, Thetford, Norfolk
Printed and bound in Great Britain by Clays Ltd, Elcograf S.p.A.

The authorised representative in the EEA is Penguin Random House Ireland,
Morrison Chambers, 32 Nassau Street, Dublin D02 YH68

A CIP catalogue record for this book is available from the British Library

HB ISBN 9781787303683
TPB ISBN 9781787303690

Penguin Random House is committed to a sustainable future
for our business, our readers and our planet. This book is made
from Forest Stewardship Council® certified paper.

For the mothers. For my mother.

Your absence is inconspicuous;
Nobody can tell what I lack.

Sylvia Plath, *Parliament Hill Fields*

Incheon, South Korea, 1985

The night the boy without a surname was born, the army rolled through his mother's industrial town. It was the first of November, brittle and silver. The sight of riot vans, advancing with too much intent, was not unusual; the country was under military rule. Still, resistance crackled like a bonfire, charring onto itself in sudden bursts, leaping sparks, catching.

Twenty kilometres away, having screeched into a harshly lit delivery room, a middle-aged woman was somewhat relieved for the distraction. That evening, shop shutters clattered down, windows closed. People moved unclearly, blearily, like bees feeling along a closed window. Mothers called their children inside, a lumpy football and skipping rope left beached in the street. Amidst the commotion, no one had noticed the two of them climbing into the groaning pickup, shapes in the dark, slipping away, returning as three.

The woman's bearing was humble, such that she rarely caught attention anyway. The tidy owner of the local minbak, known for her knife-cut noodles and her discretion, she conducted business without greed, earning her an abundance of goodwill. Her hands were never free and she wore her life in the folds that branched around her eyes. They arrived back home in the ochre of dawn, as the sun's yolk peeked over the weed-scattered yard. Drags of soil, smoke and salt on the breeze.

Inside, she squatted – buttocks to the floor – to place the swaddled child in her father's brown leather suitcase. Memories tightened, released: carrying the same suitcase, her infant brother straddling her left hip, as they walked from the North. The baby blinked up at her with bright, telepathic eyes and oh! Her heart barked. What to do with him? His personhood was so immediate but, to most, so tenuous. Love was blooming in colourful, exuberant rushes. She watched over him, until his eyelids drooped heavily and his bottom lip stopped suckling. Then she rose and set about the kitchen to make seaweed soup to nourish his mother, curved like a bow on her mat in the inner room.

She blew on the mossy broth, steam twirling from the spoon, before raising it to the girl's lips. Outside the window, pearls of snow started to fall, sugaring the persimmon tree, hundreds of sweet orange bulbs peeking from between the white.

Hana
하나

Sitting in the clean light of her kitchen, Hana vacantly stared into the middle distance, ignoring the phone as it shrilled over and over. It had been ringing, unrelentingly, all morning. The answering machine beeped: 'We're so sorry for your loss, such a brilliant man . . .'

Hana yanked the cable from its plug, mid-platitude. A dark mist fell. She fanned the opening of her shirt, made hot and stifled by these gluey condolences, each a statement of her new condition: widow. Life had been quite front-loaded for Hana; at forty years old, she had already been many women. But all of them, like wife, like widow, had existed outside of herself, by reference to others. A chronic cruelty, when the only thing Hana had ever truly craved was the chance to choose her own terms.

Ada curled around the door, already dressed in a black skater dress with a satin bow in her ponytail. A delicate and even-tempered fifteen-year-old, her face was clean, shaped like a plump raspberry, and her baby hairs stood around her parting like tiny exclamation marks. *Hey Mum*, they seemed to impress, *over here!* It was the last Saturday morning in June 2008, the start of the summer holidays, two weeks since they had both lost the third point of their triangulated family.

'You're up early,' Hana said in Korean.

'I couldn't sleep,' Ada replied, eyes swollen. It had been Ada who spoke to the police that terrible afternoon. The girl had banshee-screamed, Hana had moved towards the noise, towards the conclusion, to find Ada compacted on the polished oak floor, rocking knees into chest. Hana recognised the internal origami taking place within Ada ever since. That was what lessonless grief did: folded a person this way and that around loss, until they finally emerged an entirely different shape.

After a long pause, Ada asked, 'Are you going to say anything today?'

'When?'

'During the service.'

'Why would I?'

Ada pulled her chin back towards her neck. 'I don't know. I've rehearsed my poem three times this morning. It's probably too late anyway . . .'

Hana couldn't imagine trying to articulate, in English, in front of everyone, what Tim had meant to her. It would be easier to stand up there naked. She wasn't nimble with her words, and even less so with her emotions. Hana found heartache unexceptional, a test of endurance, uncomplaining sorrow as constitutional as birth and death itself. She didn't know how to communicate all this to Ada, who was still looking hopefully at her, so instead she turned away and sighed. 'What's the point?'

Ada nodded quickly, chastened. Inside, Hana begged

herself to say something comforting. To just lay her hand over Ada's. Anything but this elongated, melting silence. Right there in the kitchen however, Hana changed the topic with bustling. She wanted to believe, as tears blurred her vision, that if she devotedly wiped down the sink, tidied away all the cups, restored the buzz of domesticity, things might miraculously return to position and the girl still nodding across the counter might not have a dead dad. When Hana did finally speak, it was routine and trite: 'We need to leave soon to pick up your grandmother.'

They pulled into Farm Lane Care Home – 'the Farm' to the family – circling the weeping willow at the centre of the drive, its tendrils sweeping the windscreen. The day an unapologetic, saturated blue. Docile carers in crisp uniforms floated as if in a post-war film about a convalescence home for the shell-shocked.

Three years ago, Hana's eldest brother had called. Their mother Youngja was tripping over invisible obstacles, losing herself on paths she had trodden for fifty years, holding a remote control to her ear wondering why the phone wouldn't dial. Then, with a wide-eyed smile, she'd asked her son what town his parents were from.

'You don't work,' he had said. 'You should take care of her.' He still believed he could boss her around. All that firstborn-son Confucian cherry-picking. And then, with a defeated huff, 'You're the only one she remembers. When she goes missing, we find her at the bus stop, waiting for you to come home from school.'

Kind, altruistic Tim had sorted the best care for the progressive disease spreading like mould through Youngja's memories. He thought he was doing the right thing and

Hana didn't stop him. She sent her mother to eat jam on toast with strangers she didn't share a language with, and Youngja accepted the severity quietly. Still, they were tethered to each other as if by umbilical cord. Only Youngja knew the full of Hana. And as Youngja dissolved, Hana kept her contained at the Farm to stop the feeling that parts of herself were loosening and crumbling away too.

'Omma,' Hana reached her hand out, 'have you been well?'

'If you want me to be well,' Youngja raised her head to reply, without any sign of recognition, 'then I am.'

She didn't meet Hana's hand.

'Halmoni,' Ada said, emerging from the car and shyly bowing to her grandmother. Hana had forgotten she was in the back seat.

Youngja's face opened like a sun shower for Ada, a tiny dart in Hana's chest. She had a soft, secret need for her mother's arms. Though she'd sooner bite off her own tongue than say she needed anything from Youngja. For a pale, barely registered flash, it occurred to her that Ada might have the same yearning, but the thought dissolved as quickly as it formed.

At the entrance to the church, Hana's favourite photo of Tim on a balcony in Greece was propped on an easel, surrounded by white calla lilies. There was a swarm of suits around Gary, Tim's business partner and oldest friend. He'd wanted to be helpful, so Hana'd given him ownership of the guest list. The weeks since the accident had highlighted that she had no mummy friends from the school gates, no book-club buddies, no colleagues, no friendships welded together in beer-soaked dorms. Now, Hana could name most of the attendees, but hadn't seen them in years.

A busy hum reverberated off the granite walls and there were so many hands slapping shoulders that the funeral had the air of a school reunion. Eyes were hesitant over her. With a name like Hannah Penny, Tim's Surrey friends had expected his bride to be creamy-cheeked and impeccably mannered. But when they first met Hana, they found that she was small, with hard black eyes, and a face that was beautiful but, they'd agreed, not attractive. She was kind of sexy, but marred by a lack of ease and simplicity; an unsettling concoction to those who didn't venture beyond easy and simple. *An elopement*, they'd commented, *how Austenian*. Tim had bobbed an unfazed smile in response, his arm cradling her waist, backing his subtly sharp twenty-four-year-old Korean bride who'd appeared one day like an apparition. Privately though, she'd never forgotten that he'd scrawled 'Hannah' instead of 'Hana' on the wedding register, and, in that moment, she realised he hadn't known her well enough to marry her.

'Hannah,' Ed Malthouse, Tim's schoolfriend, approached, 'I'm so sorry—'

She nodded stoically but didn't speak.

'We can't begin to imagine . . .' The man's hammy lips faltered, searching for something to cut through the awkwardness of death. 'Do you have any idea what you'll do?'

'What?' Hana raised an eyebrow.

'I mean, where will you go? Back to . . .?'

He was so sincere, and yet so revealing, that for a horrifying moment Hana thought she might break into a giggle at her husband's funeral. She wanted to insult him straight back – tell him she'd always thought his jawline was questionable at best – but instead settled on, 'I have a passport now.'

She couldn't help but be direct. She knew English, but not *the ways* of the English. The need to cushion basic facts with fluff. Polite, but not kind. She ended up accidentally shutting down most conversations.

'Mum?' Ada said, smiling apologies to the man, one hand holding her grandmother's wrist as if Youngja might otherwise drift away. 'It's time to go in.'

A closed casket was necessary. Two weeks earlier, Tim's MG had collided with a truck carrying tiles from Portugal, destined for a bathroom renovation. His car had crumpled like an empty can under eight wheels, a forty-four-year-old man still inside. All Hana had to identify him by was the violet birthmark on his inner thigh. One of those small intimacies of marriage, born from years of comfort around each other's bodies, that only became precious after it was shared with a coroner.

Gary's eulogy brimmed with childhood anecdotes of the two boys fecklessly riding through country lanes. He wept. Guests sniffled. Tissues squeezed into damp palms. But Hana stared straight ahead, unable to lay bare her mourning. Not like this. Not so plainly. She'd long learned to weigh fear – and whatever other irritants it mixed up – down with composure. Built a fort of herself, fending off pain's constant invasions.

Then Ada rose, mild, long-lashed, floating out of the pew towards the lectern. Silence, as the freshly fatherless girl composed herself. Her world of stability so thoughtlessly thrown into chaos. She smoothed a crease in her dress, draped in a haze of diffused light, before leaning forward to recite the same Auden poem Tim read at his own father's funeral.

'"Pour away the ocean and sweep up the wood,"' Ada spoke. Dust particles hovered around her head. Her breath wavered through the mic. '"For nothing now can ever come to any good."'

The whole church held a collective breath, moved by the softness and power of this girl. There was an amorphous quality about Ada that took Hana a few years to pinpoint. The girl radiated a fullness, a spiritual wealth that humbled those around her. It was conflicting for Hana, inviting a comparison that did not favour her. Ada's frame was backlit by colourful rays of sun refracted through stained glass. Beauty persisted somehow. The rest passed in a blur. Before she knew it, the pallbearers began carrying the casket down and out to the graveyard.

As they prepared to lower Tim, a strange, physical weight pressed against Hana's ribcage. It was hard to breathe. It looked so cavernous and damp down there. He'll be so cold and wet! She wanted to crowbar his coffin open and drape a warm blanket over him. The enormous falseness of their life together something tidal, its wrongness climbing towards her, cresting, crashing. There he goes, Hana thought, with his long torso, narrow hips, straight fingers. A normal man to you, but the man who chose me, gave me claim to all the things people are supposed to lay claim to. Gratitude and guilt chased each other like a dog its tail. She had yoked herself to his offer of Hannah Penny, because Hana Park was a cautionary tale, a tragedy, a myth and a martyr all at once, depending on who you asked. And now she was sorry.

Hana blinked. Soil was already scattered over the coffin.

She'd missed it. She was terrible. People were dispersing. Gary's wife Maeve was hugging Ada tight and Hana was relieved she was getting softness from somewhere. Until she walked past and overheard Maeve saying, 'I know you feel alone, honey. You can come to ours any time, all right?'

As if Ada didn't have Hana.

Youngja
영자

It was like driving in the dark. Headlights illuminated only what was directly in front of her, while everything else fell away into a black hole. But with the scant information she had, Youngja could drive for hours. She made out blurry ghouls, moving drearily around her. Static noise blurred, this constant aural inflammation. Wherever she was, it wasn't a happy place. Youngja used to be able to spot a hare on the hillside quicker than any of her brothers, but her sight wasn't so sharp any more.

Someone took her arm. 'Omma, it's been a long day, you must be tired.'

'Are we going home?'

'Yes.'

The sound of Korean a life ring, reeling her in from the deep, back to firm ground. The woman had called her Omma so must be her daughter? But when Youngja thought of Hana, she saw a sweet schoolgirl, with a spill of hair that moved as a single, silky sheet. She saw a translucency, a tendency to slip through rooms unnoticed. She saw the two of them moving around the minbak in unison. The memories Youngja could access didn't match this refined woman in front of her, who wore naked dissatisfaction in the stiff tilt of her lips. Something between the girl Youngja raised and the woman calling her Omma was blank. Youngja zoomed into the same lips, and saw her husband's Cupid's bow, dipped like a clay bowl. The woman's skin and her own, two peaches plucked from one branch. Yet Youngja was on guard. Something didn't ring quite true.

She was being led somewhere. She said again, 'Are we going home?'

A sigh. 'Yes, Omma. This way to the car.'

Then, the woman took Youngja's hand. Their fingers bent into each other's. Hands, two half-moons, cupping together, making something whole. It was unmistakable: no matter how much the mind dissolved, the heart remained, solid and unwavering. Layers peeled away, rewinding like the film in a cassette. Backwards, backwards, Youngja went. From the squat table stowed behind the wardrobe, to the navy comforter she shared with Hana each night, and the purple plastic sieve she washed her Napa cabbage in.

My sweetheart, Youngja felt like she might burst with relief when she recognised Hana, *there you are*. She was next to her daughter, finally. How long had it been? A tiny miracle splashed inside Youngja's chest.

'Don't cry today' was a mother's parting instruction to the bride, as she tied her jeogori across her bust. 'Especially at night. No whimpering.'

Two hours later, Youngja was married. She didn't cry. The wedding was a solemn, practical affair. No such thing as the happiest day of a girl's life in 1956, when everything around them was a bleak, post-war dredge of brown. Youngja was just gone eighteen. Her tailbone-length hair graduated from a single plait to a modest bun at the nape of her neck, because she was now a married woman. The groom was three years older, taller than most at a hundred and seventy centimetres, with a tawny, impassive face. The eldest son of an eldest son, and in possession of a small sweet-potato farm which was invaluable considering the scarcity of food after the war. He clasped her hand as they drove away from her sobbing siblings, in a dilapidated Chevy with a steel panel replacing a blown-off door. Her mother's lips remained in a thin, flat line until she disappeared behind a corner.

Youngja was nineteen and twenty when her two sons were born. Swift proof of her worth. Their infancy passed in a fast gasp: babbles turned into brief grunts, and suddenly they were quick to brush her kisses off their cheeks. She was so preoccupied with the height and weight and gait of her sons that she hardly noticed her very way of life slowly unravelling. In 1961, when her eldest was four, an army general named Park Chung-Hee, with only a scuffle and no loss of life, marched into Seoul and seized power. The new president set about industrialising the country in a hurried, impersonal blur. Youngja didn't pay much attention to the brutality with which he achieved this, focusing instead on the plot of land that fed them. The farm, a fifteen-minute drive from home, was an equally weighted family member.

She fell pregnant again in 1968. When carrying her sons, Youngja was keenly aware of her body as a vector. Once exited, the boys would not be hers, but the family's. This third pregnancy however, was altogether unlike anything she had known before. It reminded her of sand mingling with sand, granite stacked atop granite, a red pine surrounded by its kin in a forest. There was such a sense of belonging, of surety that this child was part of Youngja's own topography. When the time came, it made perfect sense that she was a girl.

Youngja and Hana. Hana and Youngja. Two of the same, in different forms, like dew and clouds.

When Hana was three months old, Youngja received word that her mother, Bong-Soon, was dying. Cancer, tying knots in her stomach.

'She's a doll,' Bong-Soon croaked, smiling on Hana in the crook of her elbow. She turned to Youngja. 'I visited the fortune teller when I knew I was going to die.'

'Mother—' Youngja protested.

'I can't leave until I know what will come of you children,' she said, as if she were just going on a long trip.

'And?' Youngja kept her fear and her face discrete.

'She says the boys will all do well. She told me not to worry. The mangnae will be a writer, allegedly.'

Youngja thought of her youngest brother and, though she didn't know any writers, agreed that he had the introspective nature of one. 'I can see that. He picked the pencil at his doljabi, do you remember?'

Bong-Soon's hand landed on her arm.

'Youngja-ya.' Her mother's voice took on a tender turn. 'I called you here today because I have something important to tell you.' She bobbed her head towards the baby.

'The fortune teller said that she saw a young monkey.' She waited for Youngja to connect. 'Hana was born in the Year of the Monkey, wasn't she?'

'A lucky guess.'

'I didn't confirm or deny,' Bong-Soon went on. 'She knew

there was a baby girl, and said that, one day, she will be sent away, across seas, further than you can imagine.'

A chill rustled up Youngja's neck. Her mother was an emotionally celibate woman, who listened intently and seldom spoke out of turn. But the dying did strange things. Youngja shook the comment away, disregarding it as a fortune teller's irresponsible mutterings. The warning faded into the back reaches of Youngja's mind but pressed a fingerprint on her mothering. She clutched Hana even closer.

Only years later did Youngja suddenly grasp: her youngest brother had become a journalist.

By the time the boys entered middle school, the president was done with the straitjacket of democracy. He had served the maximum two terms but wasn't ready to leave power. Hello authoritarianism. October 1972, somewhere distant, president turned dictator. It was a Tuesday. As power was consolidating, a young couple shared their first, chaste kiss, a burst pipe flooded the local hardware shop, Youngja could name every shade in Hana's irises: copper and hazelnut and molasses. While newspapers reported a state of emergency and a suspended constitution, Youngja scrunched the pages into balls, feeding them into the firebox to heat the floor. Things of the world, but not of her world. Industrialisation accelerated to a speed that broke necks. And arms and kneecaps and spines. As the children grew, so did Incheon, doubling in land surface, the port city prodding the sea further out. Rice fields replaced with smoking factories and gleaming shipyards. Before long, the same rural town Youngja moved to on her wedding day became swallowed into a blue-collar belt, and the family's hard-earned intimacy with its soil slid out of profit or use.

Life went on. Dictators took hold elsewhere. Pinochet, Pot, Amin. In the autumn of 1979, eleven years after Bong-Soon died, Youngja was in the yard sweeping skins off garlic with a paring knife, dropping the nude cloves into the red bucket between her legs. With each flick of the wrist, she had been mulling over an emptying store shed and narrowing margins, when she heard the president had been assassinated with a bullet to the temple. The country in limbo, hope flowering, men squabbling for a seat at the table, Youngja pressing perilla-seed oil, the golden liquid dripping. One young general in particular, Chun Doo-Hwan, steadily rose ahead of the others. His only authority would be the sword. Hana was top of her year for Maths and English. Strikes and demonstrations flared. Youngja's eldest broke his collarbone and whined about his sling for weeks. The pressure was building. It would boil over in seven months' time, when the new dictator sent the military into the streets of Gwangju and made them run with civilian blood. It would be as if the country had been handed glasses for the first time, suddenly seeing clearly; democracy would have to be fought for. What followed was a state of full martial law, a ban on political activity, a censored press, mass arrests. Youngja went to the farm. She came home.

But that week, before they knew all that lay in store, Hana's father returned from the lake, triumphantly holding a pike above his head, against a ceramic sky. A softly spoken wind carried the smell of lakewater and blood. Youngja gutted the fish there and then. Its lungs still expanded as she pulled them out, full of final breath. She held one lung up and popped it like a corn kernel, which used to thrill her sons, but Hana could barely manage a smile. Youngja tossed the inedible organs and sinew to one side and, from behind the food-storage shed, came peeking the neighbourhood street cat, a white thing dirtied grey.

'Where are your babies, huh?' Youngja sing-songed to the cat.

'How do you know she has babies?' Hana offered her hand to its pink snout, the sparkly resin balls on her scrunchie knocking against each other.

'Her nipples, like taffy!' Youngja said, pointing at her belly and teats with her knife. 'She's given birth recently, no doubt about it.'

The cat settled by the discarded fish, wasps circling above, and miaowed into the sky. The edge of Youngja's knife ran along the fish's skin, scattering glistening scales. The queen kept calling. Out of the grass padded two, three, then five sets of paws. Kittens no bigger than Hana's palm. Impossibly round, cartoonish eyes. The cat guarded the fish waste as her kittens fed, a strip of light shadowing the rungs of her ribcage.

'Aygo, that wretched thing,' Youngja muttered. 'She'll starve herself feeding her babies.'

That evening, Youngja cooked the pike. Juicy, tear-dropped fillets for her husband first, then the boys. Brown, crumbled underbelly for Hana, and the head for herself. Hana's eyes darted between plates. She'd already worked it out. Silently, she swapped her own plate with Youngja's.

At the time, Youngja took it as a sign that she was raising a considerate, tender girl. Years later, the memory of that day struck like a lightning bolt. Had it been her mistake to let Hana sacrifice her own plate? Should she have encouraged her to remain confident in what was rightfully hers? Youngja was raised to be useful, not happy. To give and give and expect nothing in return. To never be fulfilled in her quest to fulfil others. And she couldn't shake the feeling – which took on the strange shape of guilt – that she had, in a series of imperceptible moments, taught her daughter to lay her wants and needs at the feet of a bigger, looming thing known as 'duty'. Youngja swallowed the shame of passing that weight down.

Oh, what did it matter anyway, all this agonising?

The woman Youngja now knew to be her daughter was staring at a big brown lump on the ground. It was grainy, with the texture of wet sand.

'Goodbye, Tim,' Hana said quietly.

The headlights strobed on, high beam. Tim's funeral. Hana began walking away, and Youngja wished she'd linger for a beat longer. Things still needed to be said. She had to tell Hana to get the video from the suitcase, before they got the barley down. Wait. She had to tell Hana to get the barley . . . she had to tell Hana to . . . she had to . . . Her brow creased. It could wait another day, she supposed.

After she left, on that awful day in 1986, Hana became Youngja's shooting star, propelled into the stratosphere, to be watched from a distance and wished upon. Hana turned nineteen, twenty-one, then twenty-four and abruptly called to say that she was getting married. She informed her parents, rather than asked. All those hard-working Korean men in England, and she'd wanted to shack up with a foreigner. Youngja hadn't known it was possible for a child to spit on her elders from continents away. If he hadn't already, her husband would have disowned Hana for such disrespect.

After a long pause, her mind wrestling, Youngja said, 'You mustn't mention it.'

'It', a handy euphemism.

A beat later, Hana replied, 'I know that.'

He had a straightforward name at least. Tim. Easy for Youngja to say. A simple name for a simpleton. Because what man recklessly proposes marriage to a woman without knowing what sort of family she comes from? She had heard that the West was loose, but that had seemed absurd. She told herself that, at the very least, he wanted to marry Hana, therefore presumably provide for her, as opposed to just sharing her bed. That was a tick in his favour.

Youngja could admit that she had been wrong about Tim. He had been a responsible husband, a tender father, and a genial son-in-law. He had always treated her with kindness, and she got the sense it was because it was in his nature to be decent, rather than because he felt duty-bound. It was a shame that no amount of integrity could keep a person alive.

Clouds carpeted the sky in a murky grey. It might rain soon. Youngja became agitated. She didn't have time for this. She needed to bring in the sheets drying outside in the yard, before they got soaked. And then she needed Hana's help to get the barley down.

Hana
하나

The letter arrived late on a Thursday morning, ten days after the funeral.

Addressed to Tim, Hana would have added it to the teetering stack of unopened post – death caused such an unceremonious amount of administration – were it not for the crimson text above their address. A faint, distant bell tinkered in the back of her mind. Nothing good was told in red. Back home, they wrote the names of the dead in red ink. Fitting. Inside, five lines, sweeping her life and marriage out from under her feet in quick, dainty strikes. The sheet slipped between her fingers and surfed the air, before whispering on the ground.

Upstairs, Hana opened the door to Tim's study. Towers of paper. His gym bag, crumpled shirt crawled half out. The lamp still shining a circle over the dust-smattered desk. Half a dozen cups dotted about. Unfinished mugs of sugary tea seemed unbearably sad to her, like childhood stickers still in the cellophane packet. She walked over to his desk, muscling sentimentality away, and began to ferret through the drawers.

It was all there: mortgage unpaid for three months, two personal loans, maxed-out credit cards. Bank balances prefixed with a minus. The Farm chasing for payment. Predecessors to this morning's letter, scarlet text increasing in size and thickness with each: *If arrears are not repaid within thirty days, we will commence repossession action.* Hana's nails scraped her scalp. There had to be some clerical error. This chafed against everything she knew of Tim, so reliable in life that the most shocking thing about him was its end.

She moved to the floor, splaying the contents of four drawers around her. The night leaked past, as Hana forensically inspected each document. At the bend of dawn, she pushed herself up and headed down the corridor, slipping into Ada's room. She leaned her shoulder blades against the wall, taking in Ada's innocence, her pillow wrapped in Tim's jumper, that central calm that had been beyond Hana's reach for a very long while now. It occurred to Hana that she was the only one who could protect Ada now. As the world woke for another day, Hana steeled herself for another awakening altogether.

'Maeve made chicken and leek,' Gary said the next day, holding out a casserole dish. 'Reckons it's Ada's favourite.'

'I have something to show you,' Hana replied, taking the dish but not thanking him. Didn't a mother have the right to her child's favourite meal? The suggestion that Ada might prefer an allegedly edible mash of beige over, say, a steaming kimchi-chigae, or bibimbap, was grating. Hana led him upstairs to Tim's study.

'Jesus Christ, Hannah.' Gary scanned the floor, which resembled the den of a conspiracy theorist. Hana handed him the letter. His jaw hinged open as he scanned it.

His response, 'Let me make a pot of tea.'

In the kitchen, Ada froze. Her arm up, mid-scooping Maeve's pie into a bowl. *Traitor.* Gary ruffled the crown of her head. He sat on the sofa and rubbed the heels of his hands into his eye sockets.

'I didn't know it was that bad,' he finally said. 'I knew you guys were having some trouble, but – I didn't realise how far it had gone.'

Hana blinked as he explained that the construction firm Tim and Gary had founded together had had their best year yet. Banks were tossing mortgages out like candy, they couldn't build houses fast enough. Tim couldn't have been doing better. Successful businessman, nice house, beautiful family. When there were signs of a downturn, he was sure it wouldn't last. What's a loan to bridge the gap? What's a few big credit-card bills? But then, the *crash.* The word spoken in a shiver, as if it were a plague chewing through human flesh. He recounted: investors pulled out, carcasses of houses left unfinished, employees laid off, the firm leveraged to the eyeballs, savings drained, mounting debt.

'Haven't you seen the news, Hannah? It's a shambles. The banks are collapsing – the big ones in the States. People are saying Barclays could go under, for Christ's sake!'

He was doing that thing. Making Hana seem so sheltered and kept. Pressing an old bruise. Of course she was aware of the crash. But in the same way she was *aware* that her house had plumbing, or her car had an engine. She felt airborne and limbless as Gary told her, his voice melting into the background, that he'd always been frugal, and Maeve's parents could help too. Meanwhile, Tim's – their – outgoings hadn't been supported for quite some time.

'Did you really not know?' Gary asked.

Hana heard an accusation. 'He didn't tell me.'

'Hannah, his hair was falling out. He'd lost so much weight. He was so stressed, not sleeping. It's a bloody global recession.' He released a disbelieving laugh.

Hana's back straightened, eyes narrowed. What did he want from her? *Had* she noticed? She wasn't sure. She could barely recall the days and weeks before the accident. It was like asking someone if they remembered whether they put the toothpaste cap back on a month ago. The unremarkable everyday was rarely registered. Each instant ticked into another, until one collided with an eternity. Or in this case, a truck.

'That's all he ever cared about,' Gary was still going, 'always wanting to impress you. He thought this massive house or whatever would do it—'

Hana held up her hand to stop him, and began to speak, but Gary overrode her.

'No. I've lost the closest thing to a brother. My best mate. He was so ashamed. Who knows, maybe that's what drove him . . .' He muffled his mouth with his palm and swallowed. They both knew what he was implying. They both closed their eyes.

'I'd help you if I could,' Gary said quietly.

'So we have to sell this house, then,' Hana said.

'You can't. Tim already looked into it.'

A vanishing anger ruffled through Hana. So, she hadn't paid attention. But she'd also been kept out of decisions. Without asking her in the first place, Tim had bought this house and only put ten per cent down.

'About six months ago, Tim refinanced,' Gary said. 'Borrowed against your mortgage. You owe more than the house is worth. You'd be in even more debt if you sold now.'

Hana thought she might vomit. Her fingers started to shake so she folded them into her palm to not give herself away. There was some commotion outside the window, and Hana followed Gary's gaze to see a black van crunching onto the gravel of her driveway.

'Probably just trying to do a three-point turn,' Gary murmured. Heavy boots thumped on the ground. Just as they looked at each other, the doorbell rang.

'Good morning, madam,' said a man with a South African accent who was stacked like a staffy. 'Is a Mr Timothy Penny home?'

A second man, who resembled a big toe, appeared.

'No, not here,' Hana managed. 'I'm his wife.'

The human toe turned around and pointed at the word 'BAILIFF' emblazoned on the back of his vest.

'Mrs Penny, we're High Court enforcement officers. We need to come in.'

'Gents, let's be reasonable. It's just his widow and young daughter here,' Gary was trying, both palms raised, but they strode into the hallway anyway. Hana pulled on a thick forearm. The man shook her off.

'I'm sorry for your loss, madam.' The staffy seemed genuine. 'But I'm afraid this is his property, and we have a court order. You can always appeal it later.'

They pushed their way forward.

'OK, hold on, just hold on.' Gary stood in front of them. 'You got all the right paperwork?'

While Gary stalled, interrogating the men on who their contractors were, and which debts they were there to collect, Hana thought fast.

'I need to get my daughter,' she murmured. 'She's in the shower.'

She guessed that the men wouldn't follow her upstairs if she mentioned that an underage girl was showering. She took three stairs at a time. Slamming her bedroom door, she lurched towards the jewellery box. Shoving her engagement ring and wedding band on her fingers first, she then stacked Tim's watches up her forearm. False tokens of wealth clanging cheaply against each other. Hana went to her side of the bed, an iron-framed antique, popped the cap off the headboard rail. Tightly rolled inside was a wad of cash. Ten years earlier, Hana had prepared to leave Tim and Ada. She had withdrawn bills irregularly until she had enough squirrelled away to last her a few months. For various reasons, she had chickened out and decided to save the money in case of emergency. And this? This was an emergency. She pulled the roll of cash out and pushed it down her underwear.

'Mum?' Ada's voice appeared behind her. 'Who are those men?'

'Come here.' No time to explain. 'Stay still.'

Hana's brittle nails folded and chipped as she clamoured at clasps and fastenings. She ran towards the wardrobes and tossed Ada one of Tim's jumpers, before clambering into one herself. 'Make sure you cover your arms, Ada. They can't see what you have on you.'

Hana reached under her jumper and dropped a few gold rings into her bra cup, then did the same to Ada. Hana pulled her chin up.

'Let's go.' Hana was out the door too quickly to see Ada's face crumple.

Downstairs, Gary looked on powerlessly as the two men walked past him on either end of their television. Fresh helplessness unfurled in Hana's chest. The staffy scooped up their desktop computer, while the toe lifted art from the walls. Outside, some neighbours Hana had never managed to become friendly with gawped. In real time, their initial concern morphed into glee at the salacious undoing of the haughty Hannah Penny. Ada's arms circled Hana's stiff waist as they towed her car.

She'd had dreams, once. Now she queued.

Each morning, the radio vexed her with more news: government bailouts, pension funds wiped, mass lay-offs. In line outside the job centre, Hana leaned her shoulder against cool brick, before laying her canvas bag down and sitting on the sun-warmed pavement. She felt silly doing so in her silk blouse and navy slacks. The morning was supple, thankfully. Behind her, the line stretched all the way to the crossing. Her stomach rumbled. She'd given her banana to the boy ahead of her, holding his father's hand, with a Spider-Man backpack and empty eyes. Eventually, she found herself sat opposite a portly man with bloodied tissue stuck to two shaving nicks on his cheek. The appointment was brisk.

'Degrees?' he asked. She gave a singular, defensive shake of her head.

Then, 'A levels? GCSEs?'

She didn't reply. He took his glasses off and put down his pen. 'Do you understand me, love? We have translators.'

'It's fine,' Hana said, biting her bottom lip as it treacherously shook, leaving teeth marks in her lipstick.

'OK.' He seemed weary. 'Experience? What jobs have you had in the past?'

A quick, popping irruption in her mind: minbak. She carefully swerved around the memory. She meekly offered, 'I was a hairdresser for a year.'

'Brill. When was that?'

'Eighty-six.'

'As in,' he paused, '*nineteen* eighty-six?'

She ran him through the various odd jobs she'd picked up during those weird, wobbly-legged first years in London: the hair salon, theatre crew, dog walking, temp retail gigs. Many jobs, no profession. All over twenty years old, cash in hand, without references.

The man mechanically handed her a pile of forms, followed by a case number. 'Fill these out. Top one is for Jobseeker's. You'll be allocated a work coach who'll be in touch within eight weeks for an interview.'

Outside the job centre, Hana calculated the sum of herself and had the sinking feeling she amounted to zero. No qualifications, no education, no money, no family, no friends. A mutual charade of a marriage. An old ache tossed and turned. Why hadn't she done more? Why had she been so passive? She'd had a baby (Tim wanted more that never came), sank underwater into that deep postnatal blue for a while. Motherhood swallowed time and sanity. Spills needed to be wiped, meals made, confidence abandoned, carpets hoovered, loneliness bloomed. She relaxed into the monotony of housewifery, as time marched on without her. No different to years whiled away at a claustrophobic desk, or skin untouched in a loveless union. Weeks that slipped into months, until it became who you were. Now, she saw her dull, sheltered life from a new angle. It was horribly, paralytically clichéd to be the kept woman who was unfulfilled, which only made her feel worse. She was holding a heavy, leathery ball of blame and had the natural urge to lob it away from herself.

She could have done more; she could have gone to university, become something. More than *could have*. No, *should have*. So how, instead, did she fail so lavishly to be of any use? The answer had been distilling for two decades, clarifying until it was as sure as the drumbeat of her own heart: Omma, Omma, Omma. Thumping back to the woman she sprang from, who sent her away, telling her to take no morsel of home with her. The woman who was, Hana believed, responsible for all her inadequacy.

Youngja
영자

It was fish-and-chip Friday.

Youngja sat in the sun-drenched conservatory at the Farm, facing the lawns, bathing in summer light. It was brutal bliss to exist in this way; void of content, the present coming, going, for her only shedding, never actualising into the past. The noise around her was lifeless and white. She rarely spoke. When she first arrived, she'd tried to make conversation, opening with a neat bow, but the others stared at her blankly, then wandered off shaking their heads. Terror had clambered on all fours inside her, as she stood alone on the spongy lino. The yellow food offered today merged into the cream plate under it. She wasn't fluent with this pronged trident the others used with ease, her fingers itching to curl around a pair of chopsticks. It was so taxing to repeatedly stab at porcelain, the clink sharp and jarring, that she abandoned trying. These days, she was only hungry for brief moments before the sensation evaporated. Still, she noticed the poverty of a steaming bowl of rice, of the crunch of kimchi, of barley tea. The vacuum of her children, all three of them obscured, as if behind a very dirty window.

Dr Hayashi saw her once a week. He scratched with his pen and asked her question after exhausting question. *Please. Speak slower*, she'd sometimes find the energy to say. Other times, even the shapes of those three words shifted. And sometimes, hot breath hitched in her throat. Fears nestled deep in a child's psyche stirred alive. The man was Japanese. She was six years old, too excited for her upcoming birthday to care much that the world was at war. Her name was Eiko in public, back then. Her mother had just that morning squatted low to remind her for the umpteenth time that under no circumstances was she to speak to, or even look at, a Japanese. They were kidnapping young Korean women and girls, sending them away. She didn't know why, only that everyone was terrified of being taken. On those days, Youngja sat unblinking and paralytic, until Dr Hayashi capped his pen and said, *Another time*. There were reviews and assessments, blood tests and scans. Even if she could understand what he was saying, she didn't have any interest. It didn't matter. She didn't expect to leave this place alive.

'Youngja . . . !' a woman all in blue, who was stick-thin with even thinner hair, exclaimed something something something. She only caught her own name. Youngja didn't know the blue woman, but she wasn't a stranger either. Youngja creaked her spine sideways, and everything came clean, the unknown became known. Today was one of those precious clear days, her thoughts unsmudged and vivid.

'Hana-ya,' she said, relieved to speak her language. 'What brings you here?'

Hana approached.

'Omma.' She sounded like a teenager again. 'I'm in trouble.'

Words rifled out of Hana and Youngja struggled to keep up. Tim, debt, centre, rings?

Hana explained that the cash she'd squirrelled, together with the pawning of her gold, covered the outstanding mortgage payments by mere pennies. Tim's watches paid the Farm bills. Youngja was sure she knew what a watch was but was having a hard time picturing the thing. The piano Ada tinkered her majors and minors on, an antique mirror Hana had driven back from France, a sixteen-piece Portmeirion dinner set, Tim's beloved first edition of *The Wind in the Willows*, all flung to the depths of eBay, their proceeds quickly evaporating into credit-card and household bills. Youngja was listening without reacting. She was finding it difficult to focus.

'I've nothing left to sell,' Hana said.

'What about Tim's parents?'

Hana reminded, 'Dead, Omma.'

'Only a little more useless than me.' Youngja laughed a sad, hollow sound. 'Still more useful than your brothers.'

Youngja was acutely ashamed of her sons. One a gambler, the other a drunk, together a reckless duo that had bankrupted the farm that had been in their family for three generations within two years of inheriting it.

'Yes,' Hana said, studying the gardens ahead. 'We're all quite, quite useless now.'

Youngja was slow to react and Hana continued, 'I went to the job centre. The man was kind, in a way.' She sighed. 'He asked about school.'

Youngja stiffened involuntarily. A faint uneasiness bothered her. Hana's eyes grew distant, like she was looking into a pool. Youngja began, quietly, 'We had no choice, Hana-ya. It's temporary, I promise. You're only seventeen, life's long, you'll get many chances.'

Hana's lips flattened. 'I don't know why I came here.' Her demeanour turned brisk. She gathered her bag and pushed her chair back. Youngja needed to pee. She couldn't forget; there had been accidents. But Hana was here, and she was telling Youngja something important about money. Both the root of, and solution to, most problems. Youngja's thoughts wouldn't make their way to her mouth. Finding the right words was like trying to capture a cloud. Her daughter needed her guidance, but she always had the feeling that her thoughts might just slide out of her head like marbles. She murmured, 'I can always step down. Getting old now. You know how to run the business better than anyone.'

Hana's back straightened.

'Yes. You should take over the minbak,' Youngja said decisively. She thought of her home and a memory bit: scrawling her address across the back of a piece of paper. 'One of us needs to be there. Just in case.'

Hana's face tilted. 'What?'

'It's good, stable money,' Youngja carried on. 'I saved our family with that minbak. Though you mustn't tell your father I said that.'

Where had it begun? Twenty-three years ago, with the arrival of 1985. On the outskirts of Incheon, an hour from Seoul. In a guesthouse that created a home for workers away from their own.

Youngja's father-in-law built the house she married into. It was a squat one-storey hanok, with a curved tile roof that swooped upwards at the corners and a central courtyard cluttered with potted spring onion and chilli plants. Damaged in the war, the joint where the new half of the building was mortared to the old was visible, the stone on one side much paler. Precious chalk striped against the cold grooves where the tops of the children's heads were once recorded.

Inside, everything wood. Wall-to-wall panels in fragrant cherry-red pine. Outside, a wooden hut boxed a cream porcelain squat toilet. Tall ceramic jars lined the exterior wall, filled with jangs: bean paste, soy sauce and gochujang. Two fallen branches were staked in the dry ground, suspending a washing line between them.

When she could, Youngja modernised the house, eventually swapping the paper panelled doors and windows with glass and mosquito netting. Their kitchen was cramped, but they were outdoor people anyway. Her husband built her a wooden platform in the yard, with a tarpaulin awning that shaded her as she spent her afternoons working. Youngja, like the factories that surrounded them, never ceased. Always shelling beans, canning corn, peeling garlic, pressing oil, planting seeds, salting cabbage. Around the side wall of the house was an outdoor laundry corner, with plastic tubs and underwear drying on criss-crossed wires. Next to it were large gas canisters, which connected to the kitchen valves. Once a month, Youngja's husband loaded the canisters into the back of his Hyundai pickup and drove forty minutes to get them refilled.

They were neither poor nor rich. They seldom went without the necessities but were always wanting more. The want ached more than the lack. They bought nothing new and threw even less away. A rag could be used to darn a bed quilt or as a headcloth. Grey water from the house was diverted to the vegetable patch. Everything was a process of exchange. When the first boy went to high school, his grandfather's watch disappeared from his father's wrist. Their second son, a small parcel of the family land.

It was to Youngja's deep shame that her sons did not seem to appreciate the sacrifice. Once graduated and visiting home, her second son had announced that their sigol hometown was backwards and dull so he would be returning to the city a few days early. His father paused, then rose. Youngja bit her lip in stress. Yes, the city was exciting, the future urban, the past inconvenient, but why did he have to reject his roots like that? Did he not realise how that condescended his parents, who worked this soil for their children's benefit? Their son had betrayed the foundation of their lives. Her husband swung his arm around his son's face.

'You bastard,' he spat, 'we gave up land your grandfather defended in the war so that you could go to school. Now you act like you're too good for us. You have no idea what this ground . . .' he faltered, no doubt remembering his own parents, ghosts of effort '. . . what this ground has done for us.'

They eventually had to break off more chunks of land to pay their debts. But the damage had been done, and Youngja's son now only came home once a year for Chuseok.

'Is this everything?' Youngja gasped, from her cross-legged position on the floor, licking her thumb pad to flick through a clip of bills that stretched less and less each week.

Her husband nodded, untucking his white vest from his waistband, darkened at the neck and pits from his efforts outdoors.

He had come home from delivering their sweet potatoes to the cooperative that distributed them nationwide. Though the farm's costs – machinery, petrol, pesticides – had soared, the wholesale price they could sell for was capped by the government. They were operating at a loss, owed mounting debts. Able-bodies had long abandoned country for city. Labour was impossible to find. The president Chun Doo-Hwan was to blame. So eager was he to appease Reagan's every wish that he undercut home-grown produce in various trade deals with the US. Wasn't that always the way? The sun rose, the seasons rolled, the moon hugged the planet, powerful men plotted their great design. Ordinary families played like pawns.

'I told you.' Her husband was gesticulating wildly. 'This government, they're lunatics. How are we expected to make a living when we can't sell our crops at a fair price?' He stared at the wall, hands on hips, breathing heavily.

'There's a meeting next week.' He hushed. 'Of cattle farmers. They've published nearly fifty pamphlets so far, criticising—'

'Don't be insane.' Youngja shot up until she was so close to his face their noses might touch. 'You will be arrested if they catch you there and sent to Namsan for God knows how long. They've tortured men for less,' she hissed. 'And then what?'

They stood face-to-face, standing off. His nostrils flared but his lips quivered, giving him the look of a stubborn child on the cusp of tears.

'I feel like a sitting duck,' he finally said. 'I can't do nothing.'

She cradled his cheek. 'We will find another way.'

'It's about the principle,' he pressed. 'We've become useless. We have to resist.'

Youngja raised an eyebrow. 'We can't eat principle.'

Men complained, women solved. The sixties and seventies saw their glorious countryside bulldozed to build factory after factory. As the economy boomed for the few, the many were asked to sacrifice for the growth of the nation. And grow it did; Korea was now a global economic power! Its progress in one generation was equivalent to a century of European development! But what did that matter to Youngja, when she was still counting coins, her days made up of worrying and saving?

There were no signs of slowing. Exports were hotter than ever. Factories churned out sneakers, soap, textiles and small electronics to be shipped abroad. Nike, Siemens and Reebok moved in to take advantage of cheap yet skilled Korean labour.

Each week, people poured into Incheon, offering their bodies at the altar of consumerism. They needed somewhere to live. Some factories provided their workers with company dorms, but there were too many to supply housing for all. Many lived in ragged, shared rooms, sleeping in shifts. Youngja had overheard the grain seller at market, who lived near one of the hakkobangs, complain that it was so teeming it was practically a shanty town. Youngja noticed a gap. Absent sons left behind empty rooms. It was decided. Between three rooms, she could charge nine people board and food. The main maru would be used to serve meals. They also had an annexe, which had originally housed her parents-in-law before they passed, that could sleep another five. They would split the buildings into male and female lodgings. The family would crowd into Hana's room together. It was the perfect solution: a minbak.

When the minbak had been open for a month, Youngja's motor began to slow. Her joints were swollen like chestnuts. The extra work sloughed excess weight from her bones. Her thoughts were always sprinting ahead, noting what hadn't got done that day, how the weather tomorrow might affect her chores. Waterlogged with exhaustion, she'd require a year of sleep just to feel like herself again.

'I need a girl,' Youngja admitted to her husband, 'I can't keep up. Maybe one of the neighbour's daughters?'

'We can hardly pay our existing labourers. We can't become indebted to our neighbours too. This is already humiliating enough.'

He meant that his wife was forced to open a second business.

'What about Soo-Ah?' Youngja suggested her school-friend who she knew was looking for work.

Her husband was startled. 'But she's an ihonmo. We can't hire a divorcée.'

It was unfair, Youngja thought briefly, but shame was as entrenched a force as money or title.

'What about Hana?' he said.

Hana was due to begin her penultimate year of high school.

'How will she juggle schoolwork as well? It's too much for her. I'd rather ask the boys to come home for a season.'

'Men must look forward not back,' he said. 'They already have the burden of army service.' Then his face changed, taking on the glint of an idea. 'Pull Hana from school.'

'You've gone completely mad, I see,' Youngja snorted. Along with many women her age, Youngja wasn't formally educated. Her schooling was interrupted when the war broke out, and by the time it ended, she was fifteen and had missed her chance. In any event, she had four younger brothers to prioritise sending to school. Her husband too, as the eldest son, had to take on the family business before his schooling was complete.

'Just until we get balanced and stable, then she can go back. What difference will a few months make?'

'How can you say that?' Youngja said. 'When you know what it means to not go to school? We have spent our lives ashamed of it.'

'It's temporary. She can go back once we have settled.'

'When have we ever grown more money? The older we get, the less and less we have!'

'Darling,' he said, his face reddening. It was a plea and an order all wrapped into one. A man had a duty to take care of his wife and family, and she was flagrantly pointing out his impotence. Instead of saying more, he turned and left. There was an implicit hierarchy between husband and wife and, this time, Youngja had been overruled. She felt unbearably lonely.

That evening, the three of them cramped on the floor of their shared room for dinner. All schoolgirls had to have their hair cut between the ears and chin and, just the day before, Youngja had whooshed scissors through Hana's lengths that had grown like weeds over the holidays.

'Your hair,' her husband noted, diving his chopsticks into the marinated anchovies.

'Yeah,' Hana smiled, bouncing on her bottom. 'Omma cut it a week early for me so that it's not so blunt when school starts.'

Youngja felt a coward. Hana was her rose, lovingly tended to, perfectly curled petals. Youngja looked away as her husband clipped her stem.

'You're not going to school this year,' he stated with punishing simplicity, as if he were simply commenting on the unseasonably mild weather. 'You need to help your mother here.'

Hana's mouth gaped. Youngja felt her daughter's gaze hot on her face.

'Why me?' Hana finally asked.

'Because I told you so.' Her father spooned a mouthful of rice.

Ada
에이다

When asked for her earliest memory, Ada tended to pick something generic about playground swings or running barefoot on Camber Sands. Even as a child, she knew not to mention to anyone that she saw, when she was maybe five or six, her mother with a duffel bag in hand, coat buttoned up, leaving their house when darkness cloaked it. The image was so fuzzy that she at times wondered if it was just the final wisp of a dream. Ada had always been a light sleeper, often waking several times at the slightest disturbance, though her parents never knew this, because she simply lay in bed, calmly gazing at the ceiling, waiting to drift off again. *So independent*, her parents crooned when their daughter went upstairs at seven sharp, brushed her teeth, and took herself to bed, *such a good girl*. They said it in a way that stoked a warm glow in her chest.

That one night, there had been some stirring, some shift in the air that had made Ada shuffle out of bed in her waffle-knit pyjamas and peek through her bedroom door, which was opposite the staircase. Downstairs, she made out Hana's hunched lines drawn by the street lamp, set against the waxy black, her slim hand reaching for the latch.

'Mummy?' Ada rubbed her eyes, clutching her purple Beanie Baby to her stomach, her bare feet cold on the wood floor. Hana froze, then looked up in surprise as if she had forgotten that she had a child. She cringed inwards, took two deep breaths in, her shoulders dropping with each. Ada couldn't figure out if this was an embellishment of her memory, which grew grander with time, taking on sinister glints, but Hana seemed to be whispering to herself. Then, she climbed the stairs, took Ada by the hand and led her back into her room. Ada returned to the warm spot on her mattress as Hana pushed her duffel bag under the bed, followed by her coat. Sliding under the covers, Hana reached around Ada's curled body.

'Your feet are ice,' Hana whispered by Ada's ear. And she held the girl's feet in each hand, warming them until morning.

The next day mostly melted into Ada's brain, as indistinguishable as any other. After breakfast, she scampered upstairs to look under her bed, finding nothing but carpet and a jelly shoe which she tidied away. When had her mum slipped upstairs to remove the bag and coat? Intuitively, Ada absorbed the secret of the night before. She saw her mother in a new light, gauzy and short-lived, like coils of incense smoke. At some point in the days following, she noticed, when she went to the freezer to get an ice lolly, that it was chock-full of neatly portioned meals in labelled Ziploc bags. Every evening after, Ada lay awake, a five- or-six-year-old vigilante night patrol, waiting for the staircase to creak. But weeks went by and nothing happened.

That night became the kernel, the foundation, of Ada's view from above. The silent house, the moonless black, a woman with a need to leave, a child's call. It planted a seed that would bear fruit in mysterious ways. It would hone an overactive empathy, a special skill to deftly read others, watching for clues of their next move. For as long as Ada could remember, all her pennies in the fountain, her wishes on birthday candles, her hopeful puffs on fallen eyelashes, were that her mum would never leave. It embedded under her skin this restless feeling. That she could be walked away from, at any moment.

'Come, sit,' Hana said gently, as Ada entered the kitchen. Her thumb clicked Pause on her iPod, halting Lily Allen mid-chorus. She tugged with the other hand on the cable, dislodging each earphone. 'I need to talk to you about something important.'

Ada straightened like a tentpole. 'What is it?'

Ada spoke good Korean, though she couldn't read or write well. Often, at the dinner table, Hana would nudge and whisper something at Tim's expense in Korean – how he couldn't handle his spice or kept dropping his chopsticks. They both giggled at clueless Tim, while the understanding of her mother's two faces slipped in underneath. It made Ada feel trusted. Mostly, though, it made her uneasy. When speaking her native language, Hana revealed parts of her native self, nuggets hidden behind the act, and inevitable edit, of translation. In Korean, Hana'd rub her groaning tummy and say with a laugh, 'Do you hear that? My stomach is trying to eat itself! A full-bellied ghost has a brighter halo.'

To Tim, she just said, 'I'm hungry.' There was a place inside Hana that howled with longing, and, as she grew older and more aware, Ada realised it was a place she had never seen or known.

'You know what's been going on,' Hana began, though she hadn't ever explained their situation; bailiffs knocking was context enough. Ada was raised to have noonchi, to understand exactly what was happening in any given situation, and respond accordingly, without it being told to her. She was used to this dance, playing catch-up to some complexity she wasn't privy to yet was expected to adapt around.

'We need to make some major changes if we're going to save the house,' said Hana.

'OK,' Ada said, feeling her vision jar. Her face quickly rearranged itself. Whenever she swallowed a resistant emotion – shock, fear, frustration – she collected a cue of approval, until doing so became a reflex. She sometimes fantasised about what a roaring teenage tantrum might feel like. The kind of vocal-cord-splitting, hormone-fuelled howl she'd seen from Mean Girl Regina George. She felt giddy just thinking about the catharsis.

'I know I never told you much about your grandparents,' Hana continued. Ada's breath held in her throat, new details to cherish. 'My father inherited from his father a house on farmland. And after farming stopped being enough, they used the house as efficiently as possible. So your grandparents ran a guesthouse – we call it a minbak.'

'OK.'

Since she lost her father, Ada had been sluggish and spaced-out. She had a permanent headache. Overnight, she had the sense of being one degree removed from everything. She'd tried to spend an hour here and there with friends in

Starbucks, burning her last few coins. But as the group collectively sucked whipped cream up through their straws and BBMed people who weren't present, Ada was underwater, separated entirely by her grief. The others sat slightly too far from her, as if she emanated the unpleasant odour of death. One girl, Emily, asked Ada what it was like to lose a parent. But try to explain the taste of chocolate, or cola, to someone who had never tried it. She resented having to make her grief understandable, and therefore bearable, for someone else, when it was so unbearable for her. She hadn't reached out again for the rest of the summer, and now her mum had sold her phone, she couldn't anyway.

At home it wasn't easier. There was this stillness. The house preserved like Pompeii, its two inhabitants in a perpetual, silent, screaming horror. It would be easier if her mother was a mess. That would give Ada the freedom to also let it all go. But Hana remained immoveable, expressionless, a permanent eleven between her eyebrows the only sign of a troubled mind. Sometimes, Ada just wanted to, she didn't know, fucking lose it! Take a sledgehammer to the silence. Slam a door so hard its hinges rattled, scream blue bloody murder—

'We have four bedrooms in this house.' Hana pulled Ada back into the kitchen. 'We'll rent them all out. I'll have to do breakfast and dinner for the guests.'

Ada's head tilted. Her mother had never mentioned her family's minbak. But she'd mentioned almost nothing about her life before. Though it was clear to Ada that there was a distinct divide, that they were the after.

'There will be a lot of changes. New people coming in and out. And we need to share a room.'

'You and me?' Ada said.

'And your grandmother,' Hana added, as if it were a minor detail. 'We can't afford her nursing-home fees any more. Halmoni will stay with us until I can figure something out. I need you to help take care of her.'

Hana delivered the news efficiently, with the presumption that Ada would adjust. There was a rattling inside her head but Ada kept her face placid and empty. Now her father was gone, she was more attuned than ever to Hana's changing emotions. Any sense of her mum's unhappiness sent Ada straight back to the top of the stairs.

The house transformed.

Hana and Ada sellotaped sheets of paper around lamp posts, advertising a furniture sale. The Andersons bought Tim's desk and chair, the Wilkinsons Hana's antique dressing table, the Patels their living-room sofa set. They'd all seen the bailiffs, they all haggled. Each bedroom was emptied, but for the bed frames, mattresses and wardrobes for the guests, and two towels folded neatly. They lugged the debris of their old life – Tim's CDs, jeans that hadn't fit Hana in a decade, Tim's map collection, unused candles, umbrellas – in three suitcases to the car-boot sale at the greyhound racing stadium and flogged it all. Tim's fingerprints pressed on a DVD that would live on a foreign shelf. He had been so excited about Blu-ray. Each time one of his books was tucked under the arm of a stranger, a pound coin in payment, a clinginess clutched in her chest. She fought the urge to run behind them as they sauntered to the next stall and wrest it back.

A return to origin meant a return to the floor. What used to be their living room was now both a makeshift storage facility and their bedroom. Ada went round the back of the supermarket, collecting discarded cardboard, and boxed up their remaining possessions. They kicked the heavy boxes against each wall, stacking mismatched furniture on top, leaving a square of bare floor in the middle. When Ada asked where their bed would go, Hana's answer was simple, 'Koreans live on the floor.'

At night, the floor space was filled by rolling out a green-and-pink padded mat for all three to sleep on. In the day, the mat was folded and stored in a cupboard, clearing the floor for sitting cross-legged, with a cushion for support. At mealtimes, they unfolded a low table to eat off that was stowed away after. The floor would take them from day to night, work to rest. One chest with three drawers housed their clothes. In three steps, Ada could travel from one side of the room to another. Everything was changing, Ada picked up by the tornado, whirling and whirling. When she got a moment alone, she wrapped her arms around herself and hugged hard.

'Mrs Penny,' the manager of the Farm, a headmistressy lady called Sonya, was hustling behind Hana as she bundled Youngja's few belongings into an overnight bag, 'a new environment will be destabilising for Youngja. We need to be careful not to upset her balance.'

Ada put her arm around her grandmother, who was wearing a dress that went beyond her knees with sweet flower buds printed on it, and a beige cardigan. She had a patch of white gauze taped on her cheekbone.

'Her condition causes a lack of coordination,' the nurse behind the glass had explained earlier, 'the legs sometimes just stop listening to the mind, so they go tumbling all over the place if you don't keep a close eye on them.'

All Ada could do was nod quickly as coldness seeped into

her cracks. The task Hana had given her, of caring for her grandmother, seeming far more formidable than she first expected.

A soft moan came from Youngja.

'Perhaps we should discuss options in private,' Sonya offered.

Hana turned to Ada and pointed to Youngja's wardrobe. 'You've got this?'

Ada began carefully folding each of her grandmother's shirts that smelled of lavender soap, as a heavy resignation curled between the women like a loyal housecat. She found unopened Heinz ketchup sachets snuffled between clothes. On the bottom shelf, a still-full mug of something furred. Fear somersaulted inside Ada's stomach. Her hand hit a dull shape. She peered into the shelf to see a shoebox.

Inside, a grainy photo of the Penny family having a picnic, edges frayed and bent as if it had lived inside a wallet for years, and a stack of letters, a dozen or so. Each envelope had the red-striped border and blue stamp of international mail. Ada ran her nail over the stack and saw that they were all unopened, addressed to Hana. She recognised their old addresses: the Pimlico flat her dad always pointed out when they drove by; the Guildford house she was born in. How did her grandmother have the letters if they were sent to her mum? Ada flipped the first one over. Her mother's crisp handwriting, *No such person at this address, return to sender.*

'Reporting for duty!' A chipper, male voice accompanied a double knock on the wall. Ada spun around to see an elderly man in a smart suit shuffling towards Youngja.

'I've been keeping these for you.' Youngja moved towards the wardrobe. Ada dutifully sidestepped and busied herself with the knick-knacks on the windowsill. She picked up a small hand-carved wooden bird, its contours smooth in her hand. She watched as Youngja reached for the shoebox, two jumpers, some orthopaedic trainers, a stack of videos and handed them to the man. Ada wanted to protest but couldn't find any reason to. And then, suddenly, Youngja dropped to a squat as if her hip sockets were optional. She was looking for something under the wardrobe? The man caught Ada's eye and pleasantly smiled as if there wasn't a balletically flexible seventy-year-old rummaging under furniture between them.

'Oh, never mind her. She leaves things in the foggiest of places,' he said, by way of explanation.

Youngja emerged, blowing dust off something boxy and silver. Ada peered closer. It was a camcorder in one hand, and a plastic-wrapped stack of CDs. What on earth? Youngja handed them to the man. Something was passing between them. Ada shook her head. Her grandmother had thoroughly lost her mind.

'There isn't much space for my things at the house, is there?' Youngja said to Ada, with surprising understanding of what was happening. 'I want to minimise my burden and leave most of my things here with Graham for when I come back.'

That seemed reasonable. Ada shrugged. The room really was bursting at the seams.

The move ended up being smooth. Youngja settled into their room harmoniously. It was peculiar to Ada, seeing her mum and grandmother together in domesticity. It changed the dynamic of the household into something altogether more ambiguous. The way they moved around each other was so fluent. Dancers in a pas de deux, footballers on a pitch, starlings in formation. It came to her in quite a startle: that her mother had once lived with her mother too.

Ada typed up advertisements for the minbak and had them printed in the library for ten pence a sheet, which Hana pinned on the local Korean church's bulletin board, the windows of Seoul Plaza and Hmart, the car park at Korea Foods. She forked out fifty pounds for a small ad in *Korea Weekly*. She also gave Ada the name of a hair salon and told her to say that Hana sent her. The owner of the salon was delighted to meet Ada, though she never explained the connection, and immediately sellotaped the ad to each mirror. In five days, Hana filled three of the bedrooms with men on transient business and had someone coming over to view the fourth. Together, they figured out that the minbak needed full occupancy for sixteen days each month to break even. When the new prospective client rang the doorbell, all three of them knew the drill. Ada closed the door to their room and settled next to Youngja. Five long seconds later, Hana swung the door open.

'안녕하세요!' she said, in her best mistress-of-the-house trill.

And each time, Ada noticed Youngja's head tilt towards the sound of Hana's voice.

Mitchell
미첼

In January 1985, the frozen air burned Mitchell Murray's nostrils. His nose dribbled and he wiped it with a saved napkin. A striped beanie protected his bald head and kept his jutting ears tucked. He cupped his hands over his mouth and blew, enjoying the brief puff of heat spreading across the lower half of his face. He wasn't used to these hollow winters, even after two decades in Korea, which, looking back, barely felt longer than a blink. The sky was pristine, set behind a row of verdant, rolling and rising mountains, dotted with clusters of orange pines. A triangle of birds soared downwind along the hillside.

Korea wasn't part of Mitch's plan. He was a college sophomore during the Cuban Missile Crisis, when he started to see bulletins to hide in one's basement when Khrushchev pressed the big red button. But he didn't have a basement. There had been a sense of apocalypse, as though all humanity could be obliterated at any moment, and the thought had made the young man feel quite hopeless. Fear dug a cavernous space in him, which he filled with the solid reassurings of religion. Junior year, the nuclear arms race waged on, Mitch chose education as his major. Then they shot JFK and Mitch sunk further into his disillusionment. He was graduating soon and had to find a way, somehow, somewhere, to be of use. So when, in his senior year, he was invited to a Global Ministries recruitment dinner and, over prawn cocktail slathered in Marie Rose sauce, presented with the opportunity to join a short-term mission programme in South Korea, he felt a new energy – be it a calling or a purpose – rustle alive.

Before then, Korea was a place that had only skimmed the edges of his consciousness on very few occasions. Many of the older guys had served missions there, flooding into and spreading across the country, opening schools and orphanages. And growing up, plenty of his friends had a father or uncle who had served in the Korean War. At Peter Lada's house after baseball practice, Mitch would study the pencil portrait of Peter's father, collared and medalled, with 'Camp Casey, South Korea, 1953' scribbled in the corner, and wonder who had drawn it. His auntie Denise, who stepped in after his mom left, had once tutted about the spectacle 'that Marilyn Monroe' had put on for the servicemen in Korea.

'Selling sex, because she doesn't have anything else to peddle,' she'd muttered as Mitch sucked the milk out of his cereal.

Mitch arrived in 1964. He had no idea what to expect. It had seemed easier to fly to Venus and bring back a chunk of space rock than to live in the Far East. He'd first landed to an iridescent, trembling iciness, cold like he'd never known before. He took in the dirt roads, the bare shelves in the shops, children hawking in the streets, daunted at the idea of calling this scrubby place home for the next few years. A little boy ran up to him, clacked his heels together, and did a serious, rigid salute. Mitch realised the boy thought he was a soldier.

He needn't have worried. Mitch was provided with a one-bedroom apartment in the missionary compound in Yongsan. A buttery slice of sixties American suburbia, his home was a Western building complete with housekeeper, security guard, gardener, and co-existence with the army's facilities. He lived alongside American missionary doctors, professors, nurses, counsellors and ministers. Hot-dogged at the canteen, Kerouaced at the library. A year later – and just as long learning the language (the mission provided a tutor and funded language school) – Mitch started in earnest to travel by bus to various towns, meeting Korean ministers, asking how he could be of service. Unanimously, they pointed him to the factories.

He ventured to a barely standing steel mill. On the drive there, first came the sprawling industrial plants with billowing smoke towers that looked like cigarettes for giants. Tucked between the landscape, rinky-dink factories that churned out pots and pans, or quilted, floral bedding. Mitch stood in the corner of the freezing factory floor in his weighty coat thinking about mac-and-cheese night back at the compound. As the men gathered, Mitch saw they were in nothing more than canvas overshirts, unprotected from the shouts of ice-wind that swept through the building. Words came short. He was stunned by his own sheltered arrogance in thinking he had any right to preach to these men about living the Gospel. A week later, he moved out of the missionary compound and into lodgings rented from a Korean family.

★

Mitch had thought his sense of right from wrong came from his faith, but he quickly learned that it was, more than anything, an American trait. His Western sensibilities were shaken by fifteen- and sixteen-year-olds, fresh from the countryside, straight into factories. Fifteen-hour days, ceilings so low the back forgot it could straighten, industrial accidents, abysmal pay. Some missing thumbs. Others so skinny he could see their food push down their throats. He had exclaimed 'exploitation!' and 'but labour laws!', before hearing how imbecilic he sounded. His optimism was this bright and colourful thing, like a child's toy, that was innocent but inherently impractical in the real world. Something he would have to grow out of. He also quickly realised that such harsh conditions were nurtured and propped up by the same America that taught him to be shocked by them. Oregonian, Pennsylvanian, Wisconsinite foremen ran indigenous workforces for runaway companies that shacked up where labour was cheap, hardship monetised, under the veil of free trade and diplomacy.

Mitch desperately wanted these teenagers, who were smart and dedicated, to believe – to know – that the only thing separating their lives in the factories from those of salarymen was opportunity. Back home, there was no such thing as enough. Money, ambition, achievement, stuff. In Korea, he found it peculiar that enough was not only encouraged, but the end goal. A thought outside the box was not celebrated. Social position was equated with personal worth. Everyone he met seemed so heartbroken. He kept going back.

Now, having stacked up two decades on the peninsula, he'd seen it transform. Overnight, it seemed, bridges straddled the Han River as far as the eye could see. Bumpy, sickness-inducing roads were smoothed over. Motorways cut streaks through land and he could top and tail the country in a day. And the other development along the way: he came to care deeply about the people he met, tenacious and tough as leather, kind and practical. So much so, that by the time he made the conscious decision to become a lifetime missionary, assigned full-time to Incheon to expand the ministry to factory workers, it was clear that his calling had been slowly delivered to him all that time.

Mitch stepped into a shock of winter sunshine, across from the house, unassuming in his tan slacks and charcoal wool coat buttoned to his Adam's apple. He felt quite emotional – proud, he supposed, to the extent a man could feel proud without being self-indulgent. He had, as of that morning, put down the final payment, registered the land as a missionary residence, and collected the keys for the plain building in front of him. A duplex at the end of an alley, its facade was chipped and falling away from the stone. By spring, the house would be operational: upstairs for mission staff to live in, downstairs as a community centre for factory workers and union leaders. Putting his teaching degree to use, they would hold high-school classes to help the teenage workers keep up their studies, and education programmes on labour laws. Only half of those that attended were Christians; many were Buddhists or committed atheists. Meanwhile, those that reaped mind-boggling profits from exploitation were prominent church figures. Conversion could not, would not, be Mitch's goal. His North Star became to live compassionately, keeping central to his ministry Jesus's teachings of social justice and fairness for all.

First things first, the house needed a small touch. He crouched down and picked up a rock, cradling it in his leather glove. From his pocket he pulled out a wooden cross and a nail he'd prepared earlier that morning, and hammered it with the rock into the front-door frame.

He had received word that John Logan was in Korea just in time.

'Following me now?' Mitch said as he returned John's call, leaning his shoulder against the wall.

'Ah! You wish,' John laughed from Seoul where he was doing his basic language course before receiving his work assignment.

'Listen, I don't know if you've heard where you're going, but I'm setting up a centre, like a YMCA, for factory workers. There're a few up and running in the region.' Where Mitch had earnestness and the best of intentions, John was a novel of a person, drawing others in.

'Factory workers?' John said.

'Trade unions are targeted by the government. The KCIA have been shutting down all group meetings. The church is the only group workers are allowed to be part of. The thinking is if you believe in God, you can't be Red.'

John was silent for a few seconds. Mitch had been around long enough to see one dictator take hold, assassinated, only for power to be seized by another. Every week, mass democracy protests roared alive, and, just as quickly as they rose, drenched limp in tear gas. Mitch suspected John didn't know much about the politics of the country, but didn't want his unpreparedness to show.

'Got it,' John eventually said.

'It could get hairy, fair warning. The police are over these workers like a rash.' Mitch felt responsible for John, even after all these years. He invoked a spin on Matthew 18:20 to relay the state of affairs, 'Wherever two or three are gathered in anyone's name, the KCIA are in their midst.'

'That much?' John asked.

'On second thoughts, it might be better for you to stay in the city.'

'No way,' John said. 'Who's gonna have your back? I'll be the muscle.'

Mitch snorted. 'Fine. You have to get acquainted with the language, quick.'

'Sí, señor!' John said. Mitch could picture John doing a salute.

'We'll stay at the local minbak, while we train staff and set up classes.'

'What's that?'

'What's what?'

'What you just said, where we're staying.'

'It's a type of lodgings. You'll see.'

He put the receiver down. John was rough around the edges, as always. He thought back to when he first met him during a furlough year in Valsetz, a company timber town a hundred miles from Portland, brawling with another boy right there in the street. Surrounded by a circle of kids, jeering and fist-pumping. Already overgrown for his age, John had his opponent's arms pinned behind his back, his face pressed into the sizzling tarmac. It was one of those days you could fry an egg on the sidewalk. Mitch intervened before the defeated boy's licence picture was ruined. When pulled off the ground, he'd asked John, bulky as a grown man but with a distinctly prepubescent scowl, what this was all about.

With a dead-eyed stare, John shrugged. 'I like to fight.'

'OK, tough guy,' Mitch clapped his hands around the boys' heads, 'go home for dinner. All of you.'

The others scarpered. Johnny stood there, aimlessly kicking the weeds sprouting between the kerb. Mitch now saw the holes in the boy's sneakers, his grungy hair and the rope that held his shorts up.

'Go on! Get!'

John looked at Mitch, squinting into the fireball sun, his hard edges smoothing.

'Don't have dinner waiting,' John said. In the boy's face, Mitch saw himself soon after his mother had left, grief punching up and through, pretending not to care. What he did next seemed entirely correct.

'Well, you better come with me,' Mitch said. 'You ever been to a church cook-out before?'

John didn't reply, just smiled, revealing a chipped front tooth.

It was an act of faith, nudging John over the years, cleaning him up, checking in regularly, but Mitch persisted in rolling that boulder up the hill. And now John was here, in the same short-term mission programme Mitch had joined all those years ago. They had a lot of work to do.

Hana
하나

In the mauve blur of five a.m., Hana blearily turned on the boiler for the guests' morning showers, before making a start on breakfast. The rooms were currently three-quarters occupied with Vincent Oh, a lanky student unlucky in UCL's housing lottery – the hakseng would stay until his father's bank wire made it across; Young-Shik Shin, a tall, middle-aged chemical engineer, awaiting approval for his work visa before he could rent somewhere more permanent; and a boisterous woman called Sun-Ok Kwon, with a strip of grown-out grey hair against box-dyed raven, in the UK for four days to drop her sons off in some Kent boarding school.

There were some dishes you could find in any Korean restaurant. And then there were dishes, elegant and comforting, made with knowing hands and nostalgic rhythm, you could only find in a Korean home. It was the simplicity of a fresh bowl of plump rice and home-made banchan that bound this ragtag crew together in the collective memory of their mothers. It sparked conversation, guests drawing distinctions (my mother never used sugar, only pears to sweeten; my mother blended potatoes as a thickening agent; my mother preferred oyster sauce instead of fish sauce). It was over pastel-yellow steamed eggs and tangled spinach namul that they learned Kim Jong-Il had reportedly had a stroke. Debate over reunification ensued. Hana secretly loved the guests' gratification over her kimchi-chigae, one sip and exclamations of *ahhhh refreshing!* The smell alone was a powerful balm for the homesick. They all ate like true Koreans: absorbedly, with annihilating pleasure.

Hana was Korean, and an immigrant, but she hadn't been much of a Korean immigrant. When she first arrived in 1986, she accompanied the family she was staying with a few Sundays to the Korean church. A buzzing tribe, replicating microcosms of home for three hours a week. They welcomed her, she bolted. Not because she was arrogant enough to think she didn't need the protection of a community, but because she had to provide a ledger of her where, when, how and why. She wondered if these smiling women who force-fed her japchae would hate her if they knew. Now, when all else was lost, it was Koreans who looked after their own. This was her life now. She woke and she served, and she made others feel at home and, at every moment, her old self nipped at her heels.

By early 1985, as her friends were buttoning up their school blouses, Hana tied a denim apron around her waist. She hated her short hair and no matter how much rice water she poured on her roots, it was slow to grow back, just to spite her. There was never a handover where Youngja taught Hana how to run a minbak. Silently, she corrected the angle of Hana's broom for maximum sweep. If Hana reached for a persimmon, Youngja glanced at the one bruised and shrinking, and Hana understood that the glossy, firm ones were no longer for her. She wondered if anything could belong to her any more.

Gradually, they settled into routine. The family rose in competition with the dawn. Hana's parents went to the farm while she served breakfast. As the guests ate, she hovered nearby like a hummingbird, materialising wants, overhearing a quotient of their personal worries. So and so was fired for asking for more pay. Did you hear who's back from the hospital? They've gone nearly totally blind. Hana couldn't relate much to the men but was particularly arrested by the women, who were only a year or two older. She found herself piggybacking on their closeness, enjoying their joking by proxy, before feeling ashamed of her need for banality. The guests all left for work by seven a.m. until evening. Some wouldn't return at all, and Hana later learned that they were forced to work overnight and into the next day if a rush order came in. When they did return, looking like walking snowmen from the accumulated textile lint and dust, they were often too tired to wash or eat before collapsing into sleep.

Meanwhile, after breakfast, Hana washed up, put away all the floor cushions and dragged the table back against the wall. Then she mopped the floors first with a wet cloth then with a dry until dinner could be eaten off them, dusted sleeping linens, opened windows, swept the yard. Then market, dinner preparation, dinner service, clean up, lock up. She was sure she wasn't anchored in any of the guests' memories. No one seemed to notice Hana. She almost didn't notice herself.

★

'Do you have any Madecassol?' an unni asked Hana one evening, gesturing to a deep scratch in the webbing between her thumb and index finger. A maroon, encrusted slash that had a damp, rotting smell like clumps of wet leaves. When she flexed her thumb, Hana could see the white elastic of her tendons straining.

'Yes, of course,' Hana nodded, 'I'll bring it to you straight away.'

She found the ointment in Youngja's medicine drawer, along with some clean gauze, disinfectant, scissors and tape, and went to the women's annexe behind the main house. Five women, who pooled their earnings to rent the space, were sprawled across the central room. One was sitting with her head tilted back against the wall, elbow resting on bent knee, nursing a nosebleed. Another lay on her stomach pressed on the heated floor, head pillowed by her arms, seemingly too tired to roll out her bed mat. Hana moved towards the unni who had asked for the antiseptic cream and sat cross-legged in front of her. She began to spray the cut, flooding it with iodine. The unni winced and covered her face with her free hand.

'I'm sorry,' Hana muttered. 'Won't be long.'

'What's your name?' the unni asked softly. Hana noticed a layer of downy fluff on her upper lip and dimples in her cheeks. 'I'm Jihye.' She introduced each of the other women who nodded or waved back.

'Hana.' A pause. 'How did you get this cut?'

The answer was simple. 'The sewing machine.'

Hana looked up confused and Jihye Unni explained, 'I fell asleep, my hand slipped. Usually, two tablets of Timing are enough to keep me awake, but they made us do two all-nighters in a row. No amount of anti-sleeping pills can keep a person awake for nearly four days straight.'

'You're lucky the supervisor didn't see you nod off,' another unni said, 'otherwise he would have clapped you around the head.'

'You might need a day to rest this arm,' Hana said, investigating the reddened, inflamed area. 'It's badly infected.'

All the women snorted. Embarrassment bulged through Hana, having clearly said the wrong thing around a group of older girls.

'My next day off is ten days away,' Jihye Unni muttered.

'Even cattle are better off than us,' the unni holding tissue to her bleeding nose spat. 'At least they get to sleep through the night.'

Jihye Unni peered at Hana. 'We want to wear a school uniform, but instead we're in a factory uniform. I go to the night hagwon run by the missionaries when I can. Even after a twelve-hour shift, I'm determined to go. A girl we know met a boy in night school and they're getting married next month. Hopefully, if I don't meet someone too, I can still graduate high school and then move to a better-paying job in the electronics factory.' She glanced at Hana's apron.

A catch in Hana's throat. She kept her eyes firmly on wrapping the wound tight in fresh gauze, round and round. They were on an unstoppable elliptical circuit, relentlessly producing and providing for other people, each orbiting their own sphere of wretched utilitarianism. There was nothing sentimental in that. It all just seemed hopelessly out of control.

On Hana's first free afternoon, she ran as fast as her spindly legs would carry her towards her best friend Sora's house, dust circles billowing behind her. She rattled on the steel-gridded window and waited, heaving cold air, but no one came to the door. Dejected, Hana turned back down the path. There was a row of ramshackle buildings at the end of the street and, as she sullenly walked past, she saw the back of Sora, in a plaid coat and brown boots, on her tiptoes, craning through the window of the middle house.

'Ya!' Hana called. 'Why are you staring like a stray cat hoping for some milk?'

Sora spun and squealed, hurtling towards Hana. They had gone from spending every day together to not seeing each other at all. Hana would be one of only a handful of girls her age not to graduate next year, and, even if she did return to school like her father had promised, she'd be humiliatingly with her friends' younger siblings. Standing across from her childhood friend, ripe-plum cheeks and eager raised eyebrows, Hana felt a decade older. Eventually, Sora would be swallowed by exams, go to work or even university, get a boyfriend, make other friends, and their lives would fork completely. Hana looked down at her third-hand boots and saw a chonsoonie. A bumpkin. She wished she hadn't come.

'If you knew what I was looking at, you'd be staring too. They're Americans! Hana-ya, you have no idea how tall they are!' Sora giddily tugged Hana towards the window where she made out two men. One had sandy blond hair that stuck up like a goose's nest, and the other was bald like a chicken's egg. Already pitting men against poultry like a market ajumma. The Americans were speaking to a group of young men and women, some of whom she recognised from the minbak. The sandy-haired one met their gaze. Sora ducked, but Hana stood gawping. The man moved towards the door.

'Hello,' he said in Korean, accompanied by a timid wave. 'Would you like to come in?' A strong accent like an out-of-tune violin. Hana's brain scrambled. 'It's at least a little warmer inside, it's far too cold out here.'

She shook her head, completely mute.

'What's your name?'

'Park Hana,' she said, formally bowing. Sora giggled from around the corner.

'My name is John Logan.' He put his hand over his chest, before pointing through the window. 'And that's Mitchell Murray.'

Hana assumed 'John' was his surname, like the Jeon sisters at school, one in the year above, the other below.

She bowed hurriedly again, then turned and ran away, leaving him alone on the path.

The girls spent the afternoon slurping ramen out of the same pot, fiery red splotches blooming on their shirts, Hana's sepia routine slowly colourising. When she made her way home in the winking starlight, her cheeks were strained from laughing, her tongue dry from all the chatter. Unlatching the gate to the minbak, she saw the sacks of surplus sweet potatoes her father couldn't sell, the raised soil beds her mother grew courgettes, squash and runner beans in, the copper water pump, the nickel basin. Just silly human things in a square plot of land. A smallness so vast it was monstrous. Breath came short.

'Hello again.' It was Mr John. Standing a few steps behind was the bald man.

'Sonnim!' Youngja called out. 'This is our daughter, Hana. She will do the breakfast service and make sure you are very comfortable.'

Mr John turned to her. 'I'm grateful to you, Hana.' His smile had the shape of a boat, wide and sturdy. Eyes like fresh bruises. A forest of a beard, though he was young. A paradox to Hana; only grandfathers had beards. It was slovenly and inappropriate for a young man to be so unkempt, and in any event, she didn't know a person could be so hairy. Hana's core leaned forward with curiosity.

She dipped her head. 'Welcome. I hope you will enjoy your stay.'

Hana didn't remember going to bed that night or splashing her face with water the next morning. She didn't know it at the time, but the molecules of her life had already begun their irruption into before and after.

By the time she met Tim, seven years later, Hana was in an entirely different skin from the seventeen-year-old girl who had scampered away from John Logan.

Now in London, Hana's days were a scraggly expanse of short-lived encounters, never given enough oxygen to gain meaning. She'd walked away from the hairdressing job Youngja had arranged for her and was working as crew in a theatre production off Fleet Street, dressed all in black and scurrying around anonymously. After curtain call each night, she made her way to the bars around the grimy language schools in Holborn, where she found a revolving door of acquaintances. All armed with a Lonely Planet guidebook and a film camera. Her only rule was no Koreans. Not all Koreans were born equal, and first interactions were evaluative. Those she met in London were internationally educated, polished to a shine, their parents' marriages carefully schemed, all bloodline pride, easy Apgujeong-honed influence. Hana hadn't finished high school. Her family were farmers. She hated the calculation of status, the tallying of education and breeding, hated the denial of being on the other side of the world but flinging an anchor back home for a smidgen of superiority.

Instead, Hana stubbornly made friends with people from

all over, seeing through their lenses the USSR's collapse, Mandela's leadership, Major's Britain. People hung around for a few weeks before settling into their new jobs or degrees. Some asked for her number, but Hana said goodbye with a conclusive smile. No one needed to know her that well.

It was the first hot weekend of summer, 1992. To the British, this alone was cause to celebrate. In an olive-green linen dress, Hana joined a Danish architect as his date to a showcase in Camden Town. She attracted those driven, creative types, who dated Asian women, but did so expecting servility and a story. The air was steaming like bathwater. The sky a ripple of lavender and marmalade. Hana tucked mini cheap Polish vodka into her bag; she knew by then that the clear stuff wiped her mind clean, while the brown brought it all back.

Her eyes landed on Tim with a healthy whack of nostalgia. He had a hay-pile of hair that made her believe for a moment that the universe had recalibrated, slotted back into centre, and brought her John. By the time the mirage cleared, Tim had clocked her fixed stare and was making his way over. She abandoned her date and took Tim back to her rented bedsit. Each surface of the common areas had a note sellotaped to it: *Hinge broken, open from this corner only*; *TAKE SHOES OFF AT DOOR*; *Leave washing machine open OR ELSE there will be MOULD*. Without so much as a second glance, she tugged on the bow at her neck, dampened by sweat, her dress skimming her body until it puddled on the ground. Tim's nostrils flared. He was unable to hold her gaze. Checkmate. She'd done it again. Another surrogate, another proxy high, another shameful comedown.

'You found me,' she breathed just before he kissed her. For their entire marriage, she went on to vehemently deny ever saying those three words. Of course, Tim took it to mean they were on two ends of a gravitational pull. A line fit for a Richard Curtis film. But it reminded Hana of some tragic inevitability. That even after all this time – even with her sincere husband and brilliant daughter – John had his muddy fingerprints all over her. She only had this beautiful life because, on that taut summer night in 1992, she had wanted to feel close to him.

Under cover of night and the daze of alcohol, she could throw her head back and imagine John sinking inside her. In the morning, Tim was irreparably different. He glanced at her whenever he spoke and apologised constantly. He was a shadow, following. She tried to be scatty and, frankly, quite rude to Tim. He referred to Korea as being in the Third World and she didn't return his calls for a month. Eventually, he turned up at her bedsit bearing a brand-new answering machine.

'But,' Hana stammered, as he thrust the Panasonic box towards her. If he really liked her, he would have bought Samsung. 'Why?'

'So you know when I've called you,' Tim said.

'No.' Hana tried to keep firm, unwilling to concede a sliver of herself, to give joy a seat at the table. 'I mean, *why*?'

He blinked at her, baffled by the question, before slouching against the door frame. 'Because,' he shrugged, 'I admire you. Being here, alone. I think you're really brave. It motivates me. Ever since we met, I'm afraid that almost everyone else is boring. And look, I don't know much, but clearly I'm not the type of guy you've been with either. Maybe change is what you need too.'

First time in seven years that someone knew what she needed before she did. She liked being someone worthy of admiration. Maybe it was finally time to let someone else take care of her. He gestured to her doorway. 'You going to let me in?'

Hana stood back and let him in. To most of it.

Tim was born to two teachers in comfortable Guildford. He went to the same school his parents taught at. Two sons, two parents, two incomes, four degrees between them. A gas barbecue. His and hers Volvos. A middle-class life that hit every beat. Tim was confident that the world was fair and people could be trusted. He saw and understood only the literal. Meanwhile, Hana was this giant biro scribble on a scrap piece of paper, undecipherable, hoping to be tossed away. He was so unversed in the kind of pain she knew, he didn't have the capacity to hurt her. In turn, for a man who saw her malaise as complexity, she made him feel a little less ordinary.

Hana had grown up being hosed down in rubber kimchi tubs in her parents' yard, until one day her father installed a shower head to the sink. She spent hours on hours in Tim's bathtub, the feeling of being enwombed in water the most relaxing thing she had ever experienced. Tim brought her peeled tangerines and glasses of orange wine. It was wonderful, delicate and temporary, being loved so sweetly.

'You've never told me about your family,' he began one day, sitting on the bathroom floor, back leaning against the radiator. He'd tried to massage her history out before, usually when her guard was down in the delirious minutes after sex, like some sort of kinky detective. They both waited, the water lapping to the rise and fall of her chest. Hana had learned that Westerners could be so candid, laying bare their intimate details for the world to see, recycling their shames into triumphs. In Hana's mind exploded memories of overhearing her parents whimper about cash, of her elderly neighbour who hadn't been right since the KCIA took her son, of a seventeen-year-old girl who wasn't worth sending to school. She saw the eagerness in Tim's face to make sense of her. It was cloying. She was protective of her family's dignity. She knew he would see their decision to pull her from school, put her into work as a teenager, as tantamount to neglect. She wouldn't throw them under the bus to give Tim the completeness of an origin story.

'What's there to tell?' she had eventually responded, swishing bubbles on her tummy. She turned her head towards him, eyes steady and unblinking. She couldn't tell him that she needed him not to ask further; that each time he needled, a cold draught swept through her and she shut down all openings to correct it.

After a long pause, he replied, 'I suppose you're right.'

That conversation seemed to have sealed a decision for Tim: if she wasn't prepared to tell him about her family, then he would become the whole of it. He proposed quickly; perhaps he saw her as a flight risk. Not long after, they were in the town hall, eloping. For Tim, a start. For Hana, an end.

Being with Tim was the safest place on the planet. Her love for him was rooted in displacement; he made her feel at home. Hana fell into his care like a giant, warm bed, and kept her secrets out of fear that that care might stop. And she could see that he too had closeted fears he'd never admit. Sometimes Hana wondered if he was with her to prove to himself something about his own complexity. Neither insulted the other by asking why they were loved, so that neither would have to insult the other by lying.

Now, she was at the mountain summit, taking in the culmination of all the half-truths and white lies that led her here, in the summer of 2008, hovering over guests, asking them how their meal was.

Ada
에이다

In late July, a teenage girl checked her grandmother's incontinence pad, before tucking a quilt under her chin for her second nap of the day. Ada had come to recognise that when Youngja's words grew fraught and her eyes lost their cheer, it was time for her to rest. As the summer turned, she'd learned to repeat herself without impatience, and to indulge Youngja's confusion rather than resist it. She didn't mind passing whole hours pretending.

'Wake me up in twenty minutes, Hana-ya,' Youngja croaked, glass-eyed as her papery cheek pressed against the pillow. 'It's a busy day, I have a lot to do. Can you take the eel fillets out of the freezer? Don't forget.'

'Sure,' Ada said, turning out the light, 'don't worry.'

It was a kindness, Ada thought as she closed the door, to allow herself to be forgotten, to take on the shape of her mother. There was something else about it too, a warmth, a syrupy sweetness in Youngja's voice when she called Hana's name that lingered in Ada's bloodstream all day. Stronger than affection, heavier than gratitude, wholly pure. She couldn't help but get towed along by all that tenderness. She enjoyed being someone, even if only mistakenly, who was so innately loved.

A stack of post shot through the letter box, which Ada picked up, already familiar with the rhythm of the bank's letters. A dizzying nausea came over her. This sickness – that made her stomach lurch out of her in waves – afflicted Ada whenever she was reminded that her dad was lying in the cold, wet earth. The wrecking-ball swung: the officer's rasp, that terrible sentence, the split-second before it registered. Knees collapsing. Screaming, screaming, all around. Only when arms wrapped around her did she realise the screaming was coming from her, a girl in her school uniform, just home from the last day of term, the pleats of her skirt fanned on the floor. She'd made toast with Nutella for a snack. The plate would sit untouched on the counter, chocolate turned gummy, for three days.

    She longed to tell her father now that it didn't matter to her that his business was going under, that he'd left them in this post-mortem mess. All that mattered to Ada was that Tim was there, day in and day out, unperturbed by the enigma that was Hana. It wasn't one thing about him that she missed; he hadn't offered pep talks or a constant supply of dated Dad jokes. Tim was insulation, padding the space between Ada and Hana. As a trio, they each had spatial awareness, understanding their positions in relation to each other. Without Tim, the balance of the family tipped like a seesaw. It wasn't necessarily that he was gone that stunned her, but the absoluteness of that fact. He was never coming back.

    'These came for you,' Ada said, finding her mum at the

kitchen counter, slicing beef away from ribs. She laid the letters down. Hana didn't look up from the meat. Her hair fell around her face, threaded with new greys.

'What're you making?' Ada said.

'Jangjorim. Mr Kim liked it last week,' Hana said briskly, wiping her hands on her apron and turning to the marinade. Soy sauce and sugar, swirling with water and ginger. Mr Kim was one of the current guests. A manager, sent from Daewoo's Korean headquarters to their European plants for quality control. He had stayed two nights in a swanky London hotel before deciding he couldn't last another day without rice and home-made kimchi. Ada dubbed him Tiger, because the entire house was subjected to his tedious boom, as he bragged about his recent hole-in-one while Hana, the still-lovely widow, cooed appropriately. It was an assassination attempt via boredom. Ada combated her loneliness with observation, giving all the guests nicknames. Whinny, for the woman whose laugh was so high and breathy it would make a pony feel at home. The Egg, who looked like someone had left an Asian Vin Diesel in the microwave too long.

Ada watched as Hana folded long spring onions in half and sliced perfect rings, noticing how lean her mother's arms had become.

'Your grandmother used to be able to do this at twice the speed,' Hana said. 'I watched her like you are now. Back home.'

Ada caught Hana's faint smile before she snatched the fondness away. She also noticed the word 'home'.

'Can I help with cleaning the rooms?' Ada offered. 'Halmoni is down for another nap.'

'Housekeeping's all done,' Hana said, setting the marinated beef over the stove where it would simmer for hours.

As Hana buzzed around the kitchen, wiping hands, rinsing knives, ticking list items, Ada watched. She waited. This woman had slightly different contours to her mother, like a rough tracing of a drawing. There was something fresh about her. Ada circled the right word. An alertness perhaps, a buoyancy? Come to think of it, even her spine stood straighter, having found the will again.

Ada's vision caught the letters she'd brought in from the hallway. Addressed to the same house, but a different person: Hana Park. Ada's pulse thumped around her head. When had her mum changed her name back? More importantly, why? It was as if Hannah Penny had vanished with her dad. Or had never been a real person at all.

They moved into this house just after the Towers fell. Tim, sunny with excitement, bustled them into the car. After thirty minutes of winding through backed-up London traffic, funnelling out of the city towards the suburbs, they pulled up to a corner between Wimbledon High Street and the Common. A house dominated the intersection, its angles and slants catching the sun in a dazzling kaleidoscope. Whimsical cream facade, sage-green shutters, gravel driveway that implied multiple cars. Passing by, men suited, women legginged, children stain-free, dogs glossy.

'Do you like it?' Tim raised his eyebrows.

Had her mum said anything? She didn't remember. Her dad pulled a pair of steel keys from his pocket and held them like a dame might hold a china teacup, his pinky sticking up in the air.

'It's ours,' he said.

'Oh my God, Dad, I love it!' Ada hopped from one foot to the other, but he didn't move, breath bated.

'I didn't know you were viewing properties,' was all her mother said.

'Surprise!' her dad said, the enthusiasm already leaking out of his pores. Ada knew her mum didn't like surprises. Tim embarked on a tour, but Ada lingered half a step behind. She could tell by her mum's staccato breaths that she was overwhelmed, so she stayed close to try to make her feel better.

Her mum kept saying empty things. 'So much space.'

Ada didn't understand. Who didn't want a house that appeared like a princess dream castle to live in? It smelled like icing sugar inside. But, as they floated through the hallway, all Ada could focus on was had her mum's shoulders been this stiff when they got into the car? Had she been this jittery all day?

Her dad pushed on. 'I know, isn't it great? Oh, a utility room! Didn't notice that when I viewed. That'll be helpful.'

Even at her age, Ada could see the joints. The house – and everything that was outward-facing – was in her father's jurisdiction. Her mother, meanwhile, had the unsettling courage to not wonder how she was perceived. As she grew older, Ada began to crystallise the fundamental misunderstanding between her parents: Tim was raised to pliantly maintain a certain life that Hana was apathetic towards. He gave her everything *he* thought she should want. That had been given to him. Her father wanted to make her mother happy. But Hana was not a happy person. Ada wondered if Hana even thought of happiness as something to have or get. She was sure Hana didn't think about happiness at all.

They stood in the middle of the empty living room. In seven years' time, Ada and Hana and Youngja would all be sleeping in here. Tim ordered pizza and, because it was a special occasion, let Ada have her own one that she could choose all her toppings for. They sat on the carpet and ate with greasy boxes across their laps, each word echoing off the walls. Ada regretted her choice of pineapple. Later that evening, Tim weaved his arms around Hana's waist.

'Promise you like it?' he asked. Ada knew that she hadn't ever said that she did.

'Of course.'

'I was thinking,' he began, 'there's a lot more for you to do around here. Lots more people for you to . . . meet.'

'What do you mean?'

'Like, other mums. To hang out with.'

'I'm not like other mums.'

Ada agreed. She didn't yet know the language for what set her mum apart, but she heard it in the way Hana pronounced *hello*.

'Friends might help you feel . . . I don't know . . . more at home,' Tim said. 'Less down.'

'Down, up, left, right,' Hana said, not unkindly, but as if explaining something very basic to a child. 'This is just life. You don't need to fix it.'

'Can you try? For me?'

Ada looked to her mother – her head was constantly turning between them like watching a rally at one of the Opens – and felt this tugging tension. Her parents didn't fit tidily together.

Ada waited for her mum to nest. To roam around John Lewis for new-home bits, because that meant a full day together and maybe they could even get lunch. But Hana simply packed and unpacked their things as if 'home' was merely a matter of location. It was Tim who took Ada out and let her small fingers run over paint cards until she landed on lilac for her walls and periwinkle blue for her ceiling. Some days later, Ada asked her father, 'Do you think Mum actually likes this new place? She hasn't said anything nice about it.'

Tim was tapping at his BlackBerry while eating a banana. 'That's just the way she is, squish.' He walked around the marble island and tapped her on the head. 'You'll eventually learn not to read into what your mother says or doesn't say.'

Ada loved her father, but that was one of the most stupid things he had ever said. He looked, but remained unseeing. Without the company of siblings, Ada grew up nestled in nooks and crannies, always observing. She saw Hana perhaps better than anyone, as a guarded, furtive animal that melted into its surroundings. Now, Ada kept a watchful eye on this newly formidable mother of hers, scraping back layers of things she didn't understand, brushing dirt from the ground, slowly uncovering a fossil. She continued to uneasily track the lean, poised Hana Park, wondering who on earth Hannah Penny had been keeping hidden.

Hana
하나

John Logan and Mitch Murray were a perplexing duo. Though Hana didn't dare call them by their names, only sonnim, which they called all the guests. They were as all-American as mustangs and cowboys. But not as she had imagined missionaries. They didn't dress in the heavy robes with the white square in the collar. They wore cotton shirts under fisherman's jumpers, straight blue jeans, grainy leather belts, scuffed workman's boots. They each had a well-constructed wool coat and a practical waxed jacket.

    Mr John especially had an unusual friendliness. He carried himself with such an incomprehensible lightness. More than once, he invited Hana to sit with them at breakfast. As if such a thing were possible! It had her brain scratching for the rest of the morning, wondering in what context such an invitation might have been appropriate. The two men were initially met with frosty side-glances from the other guests. Forty kilometres away in Seoul, students were sitting in at the US Cultural Center, protesting Reagan's support for the regime. The tide of public consciousness had turned against

American interference ever since, five years earlier, General John Wickham of the US Army approved the release of troops from the front line to Gwangju, supporting a senseless assault on civilians.

Hana overheard her father berating her mother. 'Why did you have to allow Americans in here?'

'Why? What's the big problem?' Youngja replied.

'Do you know anything? They're not our allies. They're accomplices to massacre. This butcher of a president is US-backed.' He shook his head. 'All those statesmen flying in from DC to shake hands with a dictator.'

'Shhh! You're reading too many pamphlets. You'll be taken for a Commie if you go around talking like that,' Youngja hissed. 'They're from the church. Building a community centre on the mayor's road. They're only going to be staying with us for a few weeks until it's finished.'

Her father grumbled as he shuffled away.

News of the foreigners' arrival spread quickly. *I wonder how long they're here for*, the cobbler muttered to the grocer, tossing his cigarette onto the ground and grinding it with his shoe. The grocer shrugged indifference but knew his wife, the best seamstress in town on account of being blessed with hypermobile fingers, would be interested in the comings and goings of new people. His wife rushed to tell her sisters at the bathhouse that evening. He wished, not for the first or last time, that she didn't share so much with them. The sisters didn't wait to tell their neighbours who, by the same afternoon, had told their colleagues. A small town's way of doing things.

The snow dipped away from the peninsula as winter unclenched. Clarity and energy were breathed back into the sky. Hana emerged from her brothers' lumpy puffer coats, pulling on her favourite jeans and a tan cardigan to make her daily pilgrimage to market. Cacophonous as always, stalls were built from crates stacked atop each other, selling layers of egg trays and fronted with rubber tubs of grains with plastic scoops. Youngja made her own kimchi, grew most produce and rarely served meat, but Hana bought red snapper fillets, some Chinese grain to stretch out their rice supply, and a bag of bones for soup. She spotted Mr Mitch ahead of her, the quieter and older of the two men, hands clasped behind his back. He was a thoughtful and, from what Hana could tell, respected person, rarely bothered during his strolls through town. She heard Mr John's voice before she saw him, that unending confidence carrying him further than the limits of language. He was jovially clasping hands with the tailor, before moving on to the pear seller, commenting on the recently passed frost, motioning at the skies. So expressively uninhibited. The seller said something to him, and he shook his head with a laugh.

'Hana-ya,' the pear seller waved. Mr John turned. His cheeky smile went soft around the edges. His eyes ran over her in the shape of the letter ㄹ. 'I'm trying to ask him if he has tried your mother's famous knife-cut noodles?'

Hana translated with her high-school English – she'd been consistently ranked top of her class – exercising her muggy memory, and the moment he understood, he rubbed his belly. 'Delicious! They are both talented chefs.'

'Of course,' the woman said, 'our Hana is a girl of many talents.'

She didn't translate this final comment, though her face bloomed magenta. She had no desire to draw attention to herself.

'How are you getting on with the gongsoonies at your place?' the pear seller said as she rapidly sorted twenty fruit into crates. Hana's head snapped up. It was derogatory to label the guests 'factory girls'. They were just like Hana, pulled out of school to support their families. But Hana couldn't correct an older woman either. So she said nothing.

'Anything for you, Hana-ya?'

Hana picked up a firm pear, wheat yellow, her eyes just as round. She already had persimmons for the guests. She wasn't privy to the inner finances of the minbak, but she'd noticed that the money her mother gave her was no longer enough to buy basic supplies.

'Not today.' She returned it.

Mr John watched her, before springing forward and spreading his fingers around two fruit. All Hana could think about was how his fingers flexed so wide. He paid the pear seller and said, 'Have a good day, unni.'

The lady clasped her belly and bent over with laughter, while Mr John looked confused.

Hana tugged on his elbow and they began walking. 'You shouldn't call her "unni".'

'Why not? I've heard other people saying it. It means "big sister", right? I thought I could use it for a woman older than me?'

'Only women can say "unni".' She was uncomfortable correcting him. 'Men should call older women "noona". It means the same thing, just different for men and women. Anyway, you should call her "sajangnim", as she's the owner of the business.'

'So that's what I should call your mother?'

'You could,' Hana nodded. 'But the other guests call her "samonim". It's more homely.'

He chewed his lip, bristling like a bear. 'That's so confusing.'

'I guess.' She couldn't help but laugh. English was so liberal by comparison. No one addressed by their age, gender, title and relationship, everyone on free footing.

'I have been making a fool of myself, huh?' He looked at Hana with complete seriousness, the longest time anyone's gaze had landed on her in weeks.

'It's an easy mistake to make.'

'That's kind of you to say.' They walked in step with each other. 'You're very attentive.'

Inside, she did surprised cartwheels.

'At the guesthouse,' he clarified.

'Of course.' Her face flushed. In his gaze, she saw the itchiness of her ill-fitting wool cardigan, the flimsiness of her sneakers that were so worn they could walk off on their own, and remembered she was nothing more than a domestic to him.

'Do you have any siblings?' he asked.

'Two older brothers.'

'They don't work with your family?'

'No. They moved to the city. They work in some desk jobs. I don't really know.'

'That's not fair,' he said. So casually. He couldn't know how much of a sore spot it pressed. She was learning that Americans didn't have reserve in the same way. A thought, even if it boldly criticised someone else's family, could travel into a statement without any self-consciousness. It chafed against every filter of hers. 'You don't seem to have much time outside the house.'

Tingly and embarrassed, Hana only managed a non-committal shrug in response. He noticed her, only insofar as he pitied her. He handed her the brown paper bag of pears. 'For you.'

Hana accepted with both hands, bowing deeply from the waist. 'But I don't have anything to give you.'

'That's not how this works.'

A few evenings later, Hana's father beckoned her and nodded towards the missionaries. 'Hana-ya, the light-haired one. He is asking about Korean lessons, if he could practise speaking with you.'

'That's strange.' She busied herself. It seemed dangerous to be sought out, *looked* at.

'He said he would pay for your time. So I told him you can start tomorrow afternoon.'

That was how Hana found herself in the community centre office with Mr John. The room was made of cheap plasterboard over stone, with a window that framed a yellowed patch of yard. The cold was mitigated by a space heater that puttered in the corner. There was a camping table, two foldable chairs and limp, green cushions. A steel filing cabinet, books stacked on top. Mr John rose when he saw Hana lingering in the doorway and began unscrewing a red Thermos.

'I prepared some warm tea, I know it's cold in here.' He smiled bashfully, which made her feel like a beehive had toppled over in her stomach. 'Well, I guess you'd recognise it,' he gestured to the Thermos, 'it came from your house.'

'Thank you.'

'I have a rule when we're in here,' he said bluntly. 'You must call me John when we meet.'

'I can't . . .' Hana began stammering.

'I insist. In here,' he pointed to the floor, 'I'm not a guest and you're not serving me meals. You're my tutor.' He clearly didn't understand how unusual his request was. He was anarchy. He gestured for her to sit opposite him. She realised this might be the first time she was totally alone with a man she wasn't related to. Her father must be in dire need for the extra money to allow it. He started cheerfully speaking about his week, how the winter here was much harsher than what he was used to in Oregon.

'When I stepped off the plane, the cold could've taken my nose clean off.'

'Your Korean is OK,' Hana said, almost accusingly.

'Come on,' he laughed, switching to English, 'don't flatter me.'

Hana shrugged.

'We're going to teach in here.' He leaned back, crossed his arms and surveyed the room. 'The working conditions in the factories are unbelievable. And women get paid half for the same work. We're going to have classes on labour laws, the economy, unionising. My Korean needs to improve to be able to do that. I can't be making mistakes like I did at the market for much longer. So,' he flung an invisible rod across the room, then reeled it back in, 'teach me how to fish!'

Hana giggled.

'I could teach you more advanced English if you like?'

'I thought you were paying my parents to learn Korean,' Hana said, though of course everyone wanted to speak better English.

'Exactly. Your parents are getting something for your time.' He cocked his head to the side. 'What about you?'

At first, it was just language. His and hers. He waited for her each afternoon before night classes began, except for

Sundays. The night hagwon was run by volunteer university students. Together with Mitch and John, they taught Dickens and Steinbeck, class structures, capitalism, McCarthyism and Red-baiting. For the teenage workers, they sourced textbooks and followed the state curriculum. Often, when Hana came in, she had to tiptoe over huddled bodies asleep on the floor; workers came to the centre to rest between shifts. Others were sitting in small discussion groups. They encouraged the workers to talk to each other with confidence, to interact freely. Hana hung back and watched small, significant transformations unfurl.

'Even though I am uneducated and do not know much,' Jihye Unni, whose injured hand Hana had tended to, said to her group, 'I do what I can to save money each month to send back to my younger sisters, so that they don't become like me.'

Mitch, who had been supervising, unfolded a seat across from her. He sat, then leaned forward, elbows on knees. 'No, Jihye,' he said, 'no shame.'

She coloured to her temples.

'You are not treated the way you are because you did not have the opportunity to finish school,' he said. 'It's a societal injustice. It's wrong.' He addressed everyone. 'Talk to each other about your backgrounds and upbringings. Your dreams and your hopes. But remember, we don't speak with shame or self-effacement.'

Twenty minutes later, Hana heard Jihye Unni say, 'I love watching costumes in the historical dramas. My dream is to go to fashion school one day.'

John knew a camp minister in the US Eighth Army in Pyeongtaek. Through the APO, this friend had access to, and distributed across the missionary network, otherwise censored American newspapers. Each day, they worked their way through an article. Hana drank in the grey pages, spread out like tablecloth, ink staining her fingertips, dictionary in consultation, imagining the immense world that held within it drug cartels in Colombia, a terrifying disease called AIDS, Indiana Jones, famine in Africa, malaria, Oscar nominations. She noticed sometimes that an entire page of the paper was blacked out, or missing. She found she enjoyed writing more than reading, and John asked her to draft short essays on the week's news.

'This is good,' he said when he read her first essay, 'but it's just a summary.'

'Yes,' Hana said, proud of herself for how neatly she'd copied out sentences in the articles.

'Hana, you have to write your opinion. Anyone can repeat facts. I want to know what *you* make of those facts.'

Hana tilted her head. What *was* her opinion? She hadn't given it any thought. As she began to rewrite, a small part of herself, be it her dignity or her assuredness, peeked shyly out of remission.

Two weeks into their sessions, another subtle awakening:

> **AROUND THE WORLD:** *South Korean Students Clash with Military Police*
> Students demonstrated throughout universities in South Korea today, demanding the resignation of President Chun Doo Hwan, clashing with riot police. A total of 27 universities and colleges in the capital, witnesses said. The most serious confrontation occurred at Seoul National University. Students

reportedly battled 1,000 riot policemen for three hours, hurling stones, flaming torches and gasoline bombs.

Hana was set on edge. Alarms rang in her head. It felt illicit just being in the same room as the article, and out of habit, she glanced over her shoulder. She hadn't seen similar reports in the national papers which she picked up two or three days late at market. Everything seemed blurry.

'This is how I learned to read well too,' John said, distracting her. 'My father got locked up when I was a boy. My grandparents raised me after that. Strict,' he laughed to himself, 'but I needed it. My pop served in Korea and told me all these stories about what a beautiful country it was, which is why I took the opportunity to come here. He'd spread the paper out on the porch decking and make me read it aloud. They both died when I was thirteen. Seven years ago now.'

Hana didn't know what to say. Having a criminal for a father was deeply shameful. A secret to closely guard. She couldn't understand why he was telling her.

'I got into some hot water after that,' he sighed. Now that Hana knew that he was only twenty, the distance between them narrowed. His features seemed more youthful and his confidence more boyish. She was having trouble digesting what he was saying, only staring at the slanted chip in his front tooth that gave the edge of his words the softest whistle.

What did they talk about for hours each week? As their sessions passed, Hana grew comfortable enough to kick her shoes off under the desk, John to pull his seat next to hers, their forearms connecting. He became her only friend.

She taught him Korean grammar and honorifics. The

difference between the two numbering systems. And she developed lines between her eyebrows, trying to understand why *dear* and *bear* were pronounced differently. There was the limitless, barking joy of discovering the peaks and valleys of language, a whole new universe to wander. An ear of corn! A murder of crows! Who would have thought. When it came to *your* and *you're*, he reached for her, gently tugged her scarf, fingers grazing her shoulder, and said, *This is yours as in Y-O-U-R-S*. She blanked. Later, if it wasn't for the heat pulsating in the crook of her neck, she would have thought she'd imagined it.

The time they spent together didn't go unnoticed. John, as Hana now privately called him, was the most charismatic foreigner to come through this town and that invited whispers. He was seen driving the schoolmaster's car, his wife in the passenger seat. The ladies twittered like hens, saying who would do such a brazen thing as to romance a married woman in broad daylight. Especially one with such a respected husband. And in his car, unbelievable! Until the following Sunday when the schoolmaster approached John and thanked him for tending to his wife's twisted ankle, ensuring she was returned home safely. Every now and then, a busybody aunt would happen to stop by to ask a personal question of him, but really, to peer at them. Each time this happened, the office door was wide open, Hana's head diligently down.

Within a month, Hana's English leaped and tumbled over itself. When John was busy travelling to nearby towns, he left her his books, which she kept tucked in her waistband, seizing each opportunity to devour a paragraph. Whenever she learned a new word – *stream* instead of *river*, *paddy* instead of *farm*, *lamb* instead of *sheep* – she savoured it close to her chest. She'd wait by the door each evening for John to come home, a grin so silly on her face that Youngja grumbled, *You're like a fish happy to see the hook.*

One night, Hana lay awake, which was unusual; she was normally so tired she fell asleep within the minute. A whisper sought an ear in the darkness.

'What do you think about Hana spending so much time with the American?'

No reply. Hana didn't dare breathe.

'She's such a clever girl,' Youngja worried, 'and she's learning so much from him. But a girl like her—'

'There's no need to mind her,' her father grumbled.

Youngja's sigh filled the room.

'Maybe I'm worrying too much.'

'Is he still paying extra for the lessons?'

'Yes.'

'So don't create a problem.' He crossed his arms and rolled away from them both.

Youngja

영자

The warm orange patch spilled like juice over Youngja's eyelids. She stirred towards it. Nothing more luxurious than being woken by nature's alarm. She wondered when she had last slept in past the sunrise. Her eyes flew open. What time was it? She gasped into the room. She was late. So, so late. Whipping the cover off her legs, she reached for her apron, hanging by the door. Her hand caught emptiness, cutting a streak through the air until it slapped back on her lap. Where was it? Rust red with denim flowers embroidered along the hem, Youngja particularly liked this one because it had sleeves, protecting her arms from oil splatters. Her brow creased as she tried to remember where she had left it, but she kept producing blanks. She was already running behind so gave up the search, instead pulling on the door. Wood hit wood. Hollow and dead-ended.

'Where are you going?' a soft voice called. Youngja jumped. Her husband should have left for the day by now. She turned to see a girl lying on her side, rubbing her eyes, dishevelled chestnut hair strewn over her face. She was lying on a big green . . . something. Not grass, not carpet, but . . . she didn't have time for this!

'I have to do the breakfast service! I haven't prepared, I'm going to have to rush – what time is it?'

The girl's hand landed on Youngja's forearm. 'You're not late for anything. Come back to sleep.'

'You don't understand!' Who was this insolent girl, telling a woman Youngja's age what to do? 'There's so much to get through.'

'Halmoni, please, it's taken care of.' The girl peered at Youngja for a few seconds. 'Would you like to see?'

'Please, show me!' Youngja spluttered, shaking her head. This was all slowing her down. The urgency a dictatorship.

The girl sighed up. She was wearing a giant T-shirt and tiny sleep shorts that grazed the curve of her bottom. Youngja hoped that she didn't reveal so much of her legs around their male guests. She produced a key and unlocked the door that had so infuriated Youngja earlier, opening it a sliver. 'Look.'

Youngja peered through the gap. Sure enough, she saw four people, eating at a full table. A woman who she swore was her clone – who had stolen her apron! – was hovering nearby. It was like grazing against herself, in a parallel plane, another time. A different kind of stress wormed its way upwards; her watchful eye over the foreigner and her daughter. She scanned the room for him but only saw steel chopsticks dipping into pickled radish. Steamed eggs spooned straight into mouths. No conversation, dishevelled hair, ties yet undone. The tableau slotted perfectly into what Youngja's mind expected to see. The scarlet mist dissipated. Her heart rate began to slow. The stillness wasn't peaceful, but frantic, the eye of a disaster.

'Do you feel better now?' the girl asked. And though Youngja was smarter than to let anyone tell her how to run her business, she followed as the girl led her away from the door. Warily, Youngja sat on the big green pad the girl had been sleeping on. A sense of urgency remained, but it didn't have a clear goal any more. As the seconds passed, Youngja couldn't quite remember what had upset her so much in the first place. The girl sat too and hugged her knees to her chest. She looked like Hana had spat her straight out. Pale skin, slim jaw, downcast brows. Youngja's heart wrung, squeezing out longing like a wet rag. But this girl's eyes were a deep, glittering blue like Princess Diana's ring. Youngja didn't know much about queens and princesses but thought Diana had an intelligent face.

'Are you feeling all right?' the girl said. Behind her was an abstract painting. Or was it just mess? Thick and textured shapes slurred into a jumble.

'You know,' Youngja leaned towards her, 'you're so familiar. You look, you look just like . . .' The name was dangling like a pendant swinging from a chain. Youngja's mind went to zero.

'Like Hana?'

'Yes!' Youngja exclaimed. This girl sure knew a lot about them!

'That's funny because people tell me I take after my grandmother.'

'Really?'

'Yes, it's a big compliment. Would you like me to tell you about her?'

'Tell me.'

'Well,' the girl arranged into a lotus, and took both of

Youngja's hands into her lap, 'I didn't meet her until I was twelve because she lived in a different country, but straight away I felt like I knew her my whole life. She was so protective of me, from the moment we met.'

'I bet she loves you. You're very pretty.' Youngja laughed and then lost balance for a moment, finding herself falling. She landed on her side.

'She does love me.' The girl lay next to her, so they were facing each other on their cheeks. 'And I love her.'

'What's her name?'

'Youngja.'

A flicker of mutuality. A tug inwards. The girl recognised it.

'Halmoni?'

Something was coming back to Youngja but in formless, translucent washes, like sweeps of watercolour. She peered forward. 'What's your name?'

'Ada.'

'Of course!' She laughed and feigned relief.

'Do you know why I call you Halmoni?'

'Because I'm old!'

She pointed to herself. 'Your daughter Hana? I'm your daughter's daughter.'

Youngja pulled back. That wasn't right. Hana didn't have a daughter. 'No. No.'

The girl sighed and looked away. The morning sun took on a satin, catching the serene line from the girl's forehead, slipping over the drop of her nose, meeting her full, artist-drawn lips. The familiarity was like a magnet's attraction. Basic instincts took over. Youngja was safe with her. She leaned inwards. The girl's arm scooped around Youngja and pressed their bodies together. Youngja knew they had done this a hundred times before.

The girl named Ada took Youngja out of the room. This house wasn't hers. She was being led into another room, cold under her feet. The girl pulled off Youngja's nightdress in one sweep. Round silver knobs creaked a degree. Wet wetness, all over. Was it raining? She looked up; indoors? Under her, Youngja found a body that had sagged and lumped. Soft flesh wearily attached to her frame. Quite some time must have passed, though since when she wasn't sure. There were lots of colourful bottles on the rack in front of her. She lifted one up speculatively. The writing rose and rippled.

'Halmoni, you're concentrating a lot for someone who can't read English,' Ada giggled.

'English?' Youngja asked as Ada raised the hose and water rushed over her face.

'Mmhmm.'

'Why English?'

'You live in England.'

'My daughter is the one who lives in England,' Youngja corrected. They hadn't spoken in nearly five years. She should send another letter, though her previous attempts had been returned unopened. The girl squirted something slimy into something coarse and began rubbing the foamy mixture over Youngja.

'Hana lives here too.'

Harsh, rubbing, saccharine smells. More rain whooshing.

'Do my sons know I'm here?'

'They know.' The girl switched the water off. She wrapped Youngja in a towel.

'When can we visit them? You will have to come with

me, they both live in these crazy tall apartment blocks in the city. The skyscrapers blend into each other and I can never remember which station exit is the right one. They really should pick me up. But they're young, they don't realise old people get confused.' The girl had stopped responding. A mild panic started to build for Youngja. 'Will we get to see them soon?'

'Not for a while.'

'But . . .' Hana leaving; living without her; missing her children. So much breached the surface at once, taking huge gulps of air.

'Why not?' Youngja's voice rose. 'I want to go home.'

'You are home.' The girl tried to dry the suds on Youngja's calves but she shook her away.

'No! This isn't my home! Where are my children?' Youngja's eyes scoped the door and she considered making a run for it. She began grasping her scalp, her fingers tangled in wet hair. She wanted her parents. Cold tracks of water ran down her back.

Hands firmly gripped her. 'Careful! You're going to slip.'

'I want to go home!'

The girl stood up and met Youngja's eye. There she was. Hana's blue-eyed twin. 'You live with us in London now, remember?'

A flash of a feeling: her sons fighting about who would have to take care of her. They spoke about Youngja as if she couldn't hear them. She needed the toilet, but the stress made her keep forgetting to get up. Until the warmth of her own urine soaked under her buttocks, flooding her precautionary incontinence pants. So she kept sitting in her own liquid, to the empty tune of them passing her around like a hot sweet potato. She had wished to die then. They spoke of sending her to a place called Run-Dun, to live with someone called Hana, but she didn't know where or who that was. She couldn't leave Korea when her youngest baby might come home one day. She had to stay put and wait. But each time she opened her mouth to protest, her tongue remained uncooperative.

The girl raised a cardigan. Youngja stared into a surface that had partially fogged up. A window? A mirror? She could make out the wavy shape of a woman in the condensation tracks. The woman had permed short hair, cut like a rotund mushroom head, and strong shoulders. The only thing rounder and paler than her face was the moon itself. Youngja squinted; she was sure she knew her.

'You're very pretty, Halmoni,' the girl said, meeting her eyes in the mirror.

Youngja looked back at what she now knew was her reflection and saw that time had stolen her face.

Hana

하나

Hana was feeling the inadequacy and impatience of girlhood. A lush spring arrived early, fluffy dandelions and acacias and violets pushed out from their bushes. Daylight lingered longer, leaves reunited with trees. As the world sighed into regeneration, Hana sank deeper into uncertain agony about John. When he ate in the morning, she noticed a bald patch under the corner of his jaw, the size of a ten-won coin, flexing and oiling as he chewed. She wondered if his beard would feel playful like a wiry-haired puppy, or if it would prickle roughly. They had roles – guest, helper, tutor, student – but she was having trouble understanding the intensity of this other undefined thing that whirred in between. Perhaps it could simply be explained with the fact that she was seventeen; he likely had no special interest in her. Perhaps she was just gorging herself on scant rations of attention. Or perhaps it was that, for the hour they spent together each day, Hana didn't crush herself down. More than once, his gaze tested the back of her neck, and occasionally, a vague brush of limbs. All within the realm of deniability, but, to Hana, intimacy that startled through loneliness. As she swept the yard, she thought about the nutty skin across his forearm, her pulse ratcheting up and up. As long as she didn't act on it, she resolved, there was nothing improper about what happened in the privacy of her own mind.

'That's called a broom.'

Hana spun around. There he was. Leaning against the gate, thumbs hooked in the belt loops of his 501s, looking at her like she was the very moon dangling in his sky. Which made sense because he could have been his own planet. She smiled weakly as he approached. Her eyes raced towards the kitchen. Youngja could come out at any moment.

'I brought this with me for the centre, but I thought you might like to read it first.' He held out a book, its corners flimsy with use and folded onto themselves.

'*The Grapes of* . . .' She furrowed her brow.

'*Wrath.*' He pointed. 'The "W" is silent. You could practise your writing with it.'

'Thank you.' Hana couldn't help but bow as she accepted, though he had asked her not to bow to him.

He glanced at the kitchen window. 'You'd like it. Particularly this bit, hang on.'

He stepped behind her and placed a hand under hers, using the other to flick through the yellowing pages. Cradled by his scent of Old Spice, gum, and emollient cream. Leathery and minty.

'Oh, I can't find the right section,' he shrugged. But he held his pinky, just for a single moment, on a page and Hana caught the white corner of something lodged. Then the book thudded shut, and John was already wandering down the lane.

She waited for the minutes to crawl by until she could innocuously head to the back of the house. Hidden by the shed, she held the book by its cover, flapping it until the note dislodged from its tuck. The scrap flew around, frantically carried by the breeze. Hana chased it mid-flight, groping the air. It landed not far from her foot. *Two o'clock*, it said, *meet me by the lake.*

Hana's mouth flooded with the taste of her first real secret. The note already assumed so much on his part. This feeling she had was like fire or water: elemental, dangerous. He must have known that by two in the afternoon, she would have been done with her chores, and not yet begun preparations for dinner. It was usually her time to go to market, but she quickly checked the fridge and figured out what she could make with her stores. At one-thirty, Hana rode her cream bicycle through the nettle-lined lanes, shins singing. She tried to rehearse what she might say to him – about appropriateness, and their differences – but her brain kept short-circuiting. She pedalled so hard and fast she couldn't think straight.

The lake was more like a large pond, deep in the hilly thicket at the back of town. Its surface was blanketed by a weave of lily-pads. Deep green shimmer to rival the centre of an emerald. He was waiting for her, elbow propped on the open bank, reading. No shyness in his posture. His gold-rimmed Ray-Bans and Casio watch caught glints of the sun. Hana set her bicycle down on grassy reeds and checked her reflection in the mirrors her brothers had screwed on the handlebars. Just enough time to pinch her cheeks sharply and run a wet finger-pad through her eyebrows before he looked up at her, his forehead folding into four lines.

'Hey, there.'

He was a smile, surrounded by a person. Hana approached and sat on the grass next to him. He reached across. His hand encircled her ankle like a bracelet around a wrist. Untied her laces. Movement infused with a new thickness. A brush on the arch of her foot. Excess saliva pooling on her tongue. She wanted certain bigger, better things in his presence. He took his hand away, turning towards the lake. 'I grew up near water.'

Hana shouldn't be here. He shouldn't have touched her, even if only on the foot. But was she overanalysing it? Americans were known for being more in sync with their bodies. Always hugging. She thought of clips she'd seen of Bruce Springsteen, gyrating his hips, thrusting the air, and a blush came over her.

'In Oregon,' he elaborated. 'I can't wait for you to see it.'

When could she see it with him?

'Do you like Korea?' Hana said.

'I like Koreans.' He smiled. 'The Irish of the East. That makes the Japanese the English.'

'Are you trying to insult us?' Hana didn't really know what he meant but assumed from his cheeky tone that he wasn't being complimentary.

'No.' He rolled over on his side, so they were face-to-face. 'I'm Irish.' He pointed his thumb over his shoulder. 'Got a set of Irish grandparents, on my mom's side. My Pops on my dad's side couldn't help but talk down on them any chance he got. We have a Scottish surname, I kept pointing out. Because the thing is, the Irish are resilient, like Koreans. You've got the same history. Colonisation, occupation, revolution, independence.'

Hana didn't know what he was getting at, so just said, 'I see.'

'I was just trying to say . . .' He leaned in a fraction, his shirt gaped, giving way to a triangle framing the hair that ran from his beard and spread across his chest. Hana could smell the heady aroma of his sweat. '. . . that's what draws me to you. We're from the same kind of people, you and me.'

He was drawn to her? She laughed. 'I don't think so. Look where you are. And where I am.'

'Hana.' He held her gaze and the atmosphere shifted. Everything sharpened. 'Don't talk like that. You feed and house the working class. Do you know what they're making in the factories all day?'

She shook her head.

'Office chairs that are used by companies. Car parts that get people into work. Radios that bring the news. Imagine what would happen if they didn't make those things. If your family didn't give them somewhere to sleep and eat.' He paused. 'You're part of something bigger. You contribute as much as anyone else. Don't forget that.'

Hana would have nodded if she wasn't so stunned. He might as well have told her she could taste colours or hear shapes.

'Do you understand what I'm trying to say?' John said. He was more serious, the conversation steered by a degree. What he said didn't seem to be what he meant. His eyes ran over her face. 'You're more important than you know.'

A thought lodged in her mind, producing a precious pearl: she was valuable. Possibility peeled open. Life was affirmed. He held out his hand, palm to the sky. It was a ripe peach of a day, decadent and bursting. The sun soporific as she laid her hand over his, as if comparing sizes. Her suede skin against his speckled. Slender fingers brushing callouses. They sat with the tang of lake moss and pinpricks of reflected light skimming across their faces. He curved over, lashes casting a fanned shadow over freckled cheek, and kissed the centre of her palm. Held there, the contact rushing through the length of her, heart tumbling. Then, reaching, tipping forward. Hana had never been kissed before, and mistimed her movements, bumping her two front teeth against his. He pulled away.

'I'm sorry,' he said. 'Slowly,' he reached for her again, 'we can go slowly.'

He leaned her down on her back, the sun toasting. Soft brushes on her cheek, the peak of her eyebrow, the tick of her jaw, like dragonflies landing. Red all over, pressing and cresting. That afternoon, the two of them lay open-armed and heavy-lidded, alone with just the occasional swish of a frog emerging from the lake and the underscent of still water. She loved him. She loved him and, even as he held her, she already missed him.

When they resurfaced for air, he said, 'When my time here is up—'

'You're leaving?' Hana's body, wide and languid a moment ago, seized in panic.

'Not yet, but I will have to eventually. I'm only posted here for a year. I want you to come with me.'

She shook her head, lips swollen and crushed. 'My parents need me.'

'But you don't need them. Hana,' he clutched her waist, 'it's a crime, I'm telling you, to lock you up in this backwater town. I'll buy you all the books you want. You'll finish high school. Why stop there? Who knows, you might even go to college. I mean it.'

When she heard that, she slipped out of her body and saw herself soar far, far away. Hana had been taught that luck was having a regular life. School, marriage, children. Success was the result of discipline and study. Work within the system, and it will reward you. Not for the first time, she felt the life that had been pre-packaged for her was too small. She longed to zoom out, take in more, until she had seen enough to decide what she wanted. In all her life, Hana couldn't remember being this happy. John offered something that was too good not to believe in. He cared enough about her to want more for her. To be loved was, after all, to be understood.

'We better head back,' he said.

That evening, Hana Park didn't exist. Everything had changed. Soon, there would be no farm, no minbak, no chores. More still, there would be choice. She had been stretched back and catapulted into her future at a million kilometres an hour. Yet, as she rinsed the rice until it ran clear, decanted the banchan for dinner, set the table, laid out cutlery, her happiness simmered down, and it began to feel like any other day.

They continued to meet in the centre and, no matter how much she craved to touch him – properly touch him, beyond a knee graze or a brush on the inside of his wrist – they remained coyly cautious. It would have appeared as it always had. The local girl and the foreigner, tutoring each other. Wholesome, generous. But those stilted conversations were no longer about the village and current events. He told her how his fingers were crooked because he broke them playing baseball; his grandparents couldn't afford a splint and they healed in wayward directions. She ran her fingers over the scar above his eyebrow, a receipt from a fight – *I loved to fight, before Mitch found me.* They made promises. As far as Hana was concerned, she was the ocean and he was the sun; at the end of the day, nothing could stop two from fading into one.

Ada
에이다

In mid August 2008, as the back half of the summer holiday stretched long and thin, Ada was beckoned to the kitchen by her mother, huddled over the telephone, dialling on speaker.

'Hello?' a voice crackled.

'Hello, is this the admissions office?' Hana said. 'I'm calling about my daughter, Ada Penny, she's starting her GCSE years next month.'

A deep dread that had settled like silt all summer long at the pit of Ada's belly began to stir. Earlier in the year, she had been accepted into Richmond Girls' School. She hadn't wanted to change schools, but her cooperation was taken as built in. Since everything – she still struggled to think of her father, and where he was – Ada had assumed they couldn't afford private school any more and that she would be returning to her old school where she was quiet, but knowable, and, for the most part, left to her own devices.

The man on the line said, 'Let me pull up her notes.' Typing. 'Ah yes, the entrance committee was impressed with the young lady.'

'My husband died very suddenly in June.'

Ada couldn't look at her. She could be so punishingly blunt.

'Gosh, I'm sorry to hear that.'

'And with the loss of income, the tuition fees are impossible for me to meet on my own,' Hana said. Ada knew that she was putting on her best English accent, stretching out her vowels like she was trying to catch flies, in the hope that she was imagined a damsel in distress. 'My daughter is very smart, she shouldn't lose her place.'

A non-committal murmur.

'I wanted to ask if there was any possibility for financial support. Until I can get back on my feet again.'

A steep intake of breath. 'It's a tough situation, Mrs Penny. I don't wish to penalise Ada. But I'm afraid the bursary fund has already been allocated to three other students. I don't think it would be possible—'

'Please. If you could just ask,' Hana said. Ada wasn't used to seeing her beg, but this topic had long inspired an unsettling desperation in her mother.

'Let me put you on hold and call the bursar. He's away in France at the moment, but I'll try.'

Neither of them spoke. Seconds rolled into minutes. Ada's heart rose to meet a familiar thumping interruption that, as always, traced its way back to an empty blank. A hovering question mark.

'Mrs Penny. Sorry to keep you waiting.' The man clicked back onto the line. 'I have discussed with the bursar. Another student on bursary two years above Ada's year unfortunately has divorcing parents and will be moving cities. Very sad stuff. But this does mean you can apply for the fund. No guarantees, your household needs to pass all the means-testing, etcetera etcetera. We'll make sure to expedite your application, given your circumstances.'

Hana clasped her hand over her mouth. Ada rearranged her face.

'I should add that it is results dependent. Our rankings are very important to us, so Ada will have to show strong performance in her exams.'

'Of course,' Hana was already promising on Ada's behalf, 'we won't let you down.'

By the time she hung up, Ada displayed obedient excitement.

'That's so great,' she managed a weak whisper. If she said anything more, her voice would only get smaller and smaller, before it dissolved into nothingness. How could Ada have known the still-damp wound, dormant but imposing, within her mother? A stolen schoolgirl, replaced by a working girl, replaced by a wife. Surrounded by a moat of withholding, all Ada could feel was this great weight piling atop her shoulders.

Year One, 1998. Ada's teacher, Mrs Rushton, hurried up to Hana at the school gates.

'Mrs Penny, I was hoping to catch you! Did you know that Ada can tell the time? I don't know whether you taught her that?' A swift shake of Hana's head, and Mrs Rushton said, 'We haven't covered it either. I had guessed that she had just picked it up, she's such a curious student, but even so. I wanted to talk to you about these schools,' she pushed some leaflets into Hana's hand, 'for gifted children. She's still eighteen months from Year Three but the exams are a year ahead, this January, and you know how determined some of these parents are. Who knows!'

That afternoon, Ada was being watched by a fresh pair of eyes. She kept glancing around, as Hana shifted to her knees and peered at her. She wondered if she had done something wrong, or kept a secret she shouldn't have.

'Ada-ya, where did you learn how to read the time?' Hana finally asked.

Ada scooped some Jolly Pong kernels into her mouth, her legs swinging off the edge of the sofa. 'I can read numbers, all the way to a hundred.' She nodded studiously. 'When you and Daddy say the time, I match it with the numbers on the clock.'

Hana stared at her. Her head tilted left, her ear dropping all the way to her shoulder, then right, as if searching for clues that explained this. There was a clunk of moving cogs, of a newfound attentiveness.

'Well,' Hana remembered herself, 'aygo yeoppeo.'

It meant 'how pretty', but in Korean, being pretty was often conflated with being good. Kind, obedient, respectful. Ideal. She pulled Ada's chin towards her and puckered a sweet kiss on the tip of her nose. The feeling was nothing short of exquisite.

Preparations for Hollis Grammar – the school Mrs Rushton had recommended – were fierce. A competitiveness that had lingered in Hana rose carelessly to the surface. She laid practice papers – English, Maths, verbal and non-verbal reasoning – across the dining table. Kumon, piano lessons, SparkNotes. But Ada hadn't minded, hadn't resisted, because each time Hana called her over, arithmetic workbook in hand, Ada grasped the opportunity. To be told she was pretty. To be kissed on the ball of her nose.

Ada got into Hollis Grammar. Hana took her to Pizza Express and, over dough balls glistening in garlic butter, stroked her hair and told her how proud she was. Straight away, the six-year-old forgot about the journey; it was the destination that had brought this bright, uncomplicated sparkle to her mum's eyes. Ada had done that! And while Hana basked in their joint achievement, the waft of tomato sauce and a twinkling tea light between them, Ada was thinking how wonderful her mother was when she was that happy. Deep in her subterranean, she had already learned to be loved for what she could do, more than who she was.

As the years turned, so did Hana's expectations. Tightening until Ada was on tenterhooks. She remained uncomplaining, but if her handwriting wasn't neat enough, or she hadn't managed to underline her title with a perfectly level ruler, she found she couldn't bear it. She ripped the entire page out of her exercise book and started again. Her nervous system could no longer tell the difference between a spelling mistake and being chased by an apex predator.

'The weather is so, so terrible here,' Hana lamented as Ada spent yet another Saturday indoors, studying for the eleven-plus exams. 'I need to feel the sun!'

'Why did you come here, then?' Ada said, without thinking.

Hana's head jerked. 'What do you mean?'

Ada shrugged the way kids did. 'Why did you come to England, if you hate the weather so much?'

'I actually always imagined myself in America.'

'America!' Ada imagined Disneyland, artery-gluing burgers, Hollywood starlets and couldn't imagine anywhere her mum was less suited to. But, come to think of it, she did have a twang to her English. *Sidewalk*, rather than *pavement*.

'I was supposed to go to the States. Go to college.'

College instead of *university*.

'Why didn't you?'

'Well,' she hesitated, 'your grandmother sent me here. I married your father and had you. Then it all slipped away from me.'

'That's a good thing, then,' Ada decided. 'Imagine what you'd be up to if you'd gone there. I wouldn't even exist, how weird!'

'Hmmm, yes.'

Her eyes had shone candidly. Ada shifted. Hana's words boomeranged: *I had you. Then it all slipped away from me.* Clearly, there had been two paths, and Hana had picked, or had been sent down, the wrong one. They were on their sofa in London in 2004, but her mother longed to be somewhere else, sometime else. Instead of dreary England, America. Instead of Tim and Ada, college. Then, Ada remembered that night; instead of staying, leaving.

'Do you wish you could have gone to university?' Ada asked, much smaller this time. It was a hard thing, for a child to realise their mother had long-evaporated dreams.

'I do,' Hana admitted. In those two words, Ada heard a confession. Her opponent was something far more elusive than she first realised: the riddle of maybe. The rumour of what-if.

'In America?'

'Anywhere, I guess. But yes, I thought it would have been America.'

'What would you have studied?'

'Anything.'

'Even something horrible and boring? Like, I don't know, quantum physics!' Ada laughed.

'Even quantum physics,' Hana said finally. All Ada could

see were Hana's drooping cheeks, lashes fluttering towards the ground, faraway eyes. When she came to, Hana regarded Ada as if she was looking at everything she didn't have. Ada wanted to grab her by the shoulders and say, *Where were you? What happened just then?* Although Hana never spoke about why she didn't finish school, Ada absorbed all of her mother's dashed hopes like rain seeping through soil. Felt the pain, severed from its source. She understood what she needed to do. Her mother smiled the biggest when she did well at school. If Ada could control her performance as a student, she could control the way her mother saw them. She would be enough, she promised herself.

Soon, it became unavoidable anyway. Hana never watched the news but obsessively pored over *The Times* school league tables, filling their living room with expectation, keeping each issue pristine in a plastic folder. *It will be different for you*, Hana would say. Ada wondered, different from what, though? Sure, there were always jokes about dragon mums and super-maths Asians. But this obsession couldn't be explained so neatly. Ada began to have the unsavoury suspicion that this wasn't about her education at all, not really. It was some deeper, darker wrong her mum was trying to right. But by then, the dynamic had already begun snowballing with an impossible velocity. Until Hana toured senior school grounds without inviting Ada and shortly applied to Richmond Girls'. Ada lingered nearby as her parents debated state versus private schooling. Tim, the son of teachers, a vehement proponent of the former; Hana, insistent on the latter.

'These schools are extortionately expensive, Hannah,' Tim had whispered the last time Ada overheard them speaking of it, a few months before he died. 'The cost of it, is it really necessary?'

'Of course it is,' Hana said, eyeballing him. 'Why are you worried?'

Tim made a pained face. He scratched his stubble.

When the invitation to interview at Richmond Girls' came in, Ada yet again found a thrill in Hana's approval. Then, like an aeroplane climbing through the sky, cabin pressure falling, came the fretting. *Ada, you don't understand how important this is. Ada, you're supposed to be preparing for your interview.* The goalposts shifting again. Hana outpacing her family. Ada lagging behind, breath heaving.

In the late spring, a cardboard-backed envelope arrived in the post. Buttery, thick paper, headed with an impressive crest complete with Latin motto. *We are pleased to offer you a place at Richmond Girls' School, for the year beginning September 2008.* She had done it.

Ada ran into the kitchen. 'I got in! I got in, Mum!'

Hana took the letter in her trembling hands and Ada watched her eyes scurry over the words.

'You're so lucky, Ada,' Hana said, 'to have this opportunity.'

Ada wondered what luck had to do with it. Her father kissed the top of her head, before settling on the sofa with a Peroni. Her mum laid the letter on the counter and started on dinner. Neither mentioned it again.

And that evening, Ada felt something inside herself curl up and die.

Hana
하나

Hana ended the call to Ada's school with a strange mixture swirling in her gut. Cool relief, hot jealousy. Through the open doorway into their room, she saw Youngja sitting on the floor, watching the same episode of *My Lovely Sam Soon* again, it being new to her each time. Old pain, a stain on the inside. She told herself it was about steering Ada in the right direction. But the efforts she gave to Ada's schooling were each a proof point she triumphantly tucked away to be enjoyed later: *she* would be different from her own mother; *she* would safeguard an education for her child; *she* would give and not take away.

 Hana was confident, as she wiped the guests' crumbs off the counter, that Ada would grow up to be self-sufficient. She was sure that was her duty as a mother. Ada graduating, Ada excelling in her career, Ada with her own money and pathways. So much life ahead of her. Hana condemned herself to linger behind, repackaging Ada's achievements as her own. Then, she couldn't help but wonder, did Ada appreciate the opportunities that were handed to her? What was the point of giving a child everything, if they weren't grateful? Ada was so lucky and she didn't even know it. Her life was so redeemable and revocable and wasn't that freedom just maddening? Hana's jaw tensed, her teeth ground, exercising the resentment inside herself. She did this so often that it was the strongest and biggest muscle she had.

'I'm begging you,' Hana wheedled, glancing at John lingering by the kitchen door, not crossing the threshold between guest and owner.

'Aga,' her mother said. Hana realised that she had put her in a difficult position, unable to say an outright no in front of a guest.

'It's only an hour away. I'll be back for dinner.'

'This isn't just any other school, samonim,' John said. 'It's American founded and run, in Itaewon. Very selective.'

'Yes, no doubt spaces are reserved for the cleanest children of Korea.' Youngja released a mirthless laugh that peeled back Hana's shame and spilled it all over the floor.

'I have a friend of a friend who is a teacher at the school,' John continued. 'I can get her an interview. It's an excellent opportunity. I really think Hana has a shot. What can't people achieve now, if they speak good English and have a strong education?'

'It is kind of you to care for her.' Youngja smiled but Hana could tell it was strained. It was impolite for him to insert himself into their family affairs. And downright outrageous to suggest that he could offer something better. Youngja reddened at having to spell it out. 'But we can't afford somewhere like that.'

'The school has scholarships,' John said confidently. 'For

now, I just want to introduce her to my friend, so they can establish a relationship.'

'Seoul is dangerous at the moment. So many demos, the police are everywhere.'

'That's why I'll personally escort her,' John said. He stood with his back straight, as if allergic to Hana's personal space.

Youngja's suspicion seemed to be dented. 'You need to be back for dinner.'

Seoul was hot with friction. Muggy, mottled air hung low, made the body drag. On the bus, John had covertly reached into the space between their seats and taken Hana's hand. She thought their hands fused together took the shape of a wonky heart. They stepped off the bus to a spirited spring morning, the colour of possibility and ambition. Cotton-ball clouds and cornflower blue. Back home, everyone knew the friendly, cheeky American and the diminutive, shy Hana. Here, an anonymity cloaked them both. She no longer had the sharp bob of a schoolgirl. And John, without the air of authority he held in her hometown, seemed younger. He wore a loose linen shirt, unbuttoned over a ribbed vest and high cotton trousers. He looked like a blond Richard Gere.

Years later, once Hana had travelled in earnest, she would attribute characters to cities. London was a middle-aged Jamaican gentleman who winked at toddlers, appreciated the head-to-toe of a beautiful woman, and cried alone when he thought of the birds and trees of his island. Paris (for Hana and Tim's ten-year anniversary) was an elderly Algerian professor who smelled like the fresh spray of an orange peeling and was intensely protective of the French's right to boycott the entire month of August. Istanbul (accompanying Tim to a conference) was a nomad, a vibrant storyteller, whose words rang like lyrics. And Seoul? Seoul of 1985 would live on in Hana's memory as a young humanities student on the cusp of freedom, chafing against a system built by the power-drunk, thrumming with optimism and resistance all in one. It was a place she left a part of herself behind in, which she never, ever planned to return for.

John and Hana traversed from the bus station, snaking through underpasses lined with hawking vendors. The air was grubby with petrol and exhaust fumes and cologne. There were stalls with glitzy bags strung up and laminated signs that read *Best Rolex Here*. Stockinged women strolled hand-in-hand with canvas-jacketed men. Hips rocking, lips smoking. John reached for her hand too. Distant sirens screeched and the wind carried something that made Hana's eyes run. She kept having to dab them with her sleeve. There were bigger, badder things happening in the wide city; no one would notice two more slotting into the scene.

'Let's go in here,' John murmured, before dipping through the curtained entryway of a cafeteria. 'Sit.' He gestured towards bar stools in the shik-dang opposite a large metal fan that whirred dense air onto Hana's back. She did as she was told. He signalled two dishes to the owner. With three fingers, he pulled her chin towards him. Breath left his mouth and entered Hana's.

'Yankee whore,' the owner hissed, a jowled man older than her father with a shoot of grey hair. She didn't care that he hated them. Her, specifically. A Korean girl (she thought daringly, woman?), with skin so clear you could make out the web of veins running through her arms, giving herself to an American. Why not! She enjoyed being someone heretical.

She'd give herself to him over and over. The owner's arm sliced between their bodies from behind the counter and set down two bowls of ice-cold naeng-myun. Nothing else mattered except this exact moment of time, this wooden stool, the sweat on their upper lips, her hand on his forearm, fingers on blazing skin.

After lunch, Hana got ready to meet the teacher from the American school. She went to the bathroom and splashed her face with water. She took two minutes to practise her best English in the mirror, making sure to round the words. *Hello. Nice to meet you. My name is Hana Park*. She pinched her cheeks until they flushed and put on the crisp white shirt that Youngja had ironed before she left, wrapped in silk to prevent creases. As she threaded her arms through the sleeves, Hana caught the scent of Youngja's home-made rosewater in the dingy cubicle.

They walked a few streets and she kept fanning herself with the bus timetable, eager not to arrive at the school dampened with sweat. She wished she'd saved a few sheets of paper towel for this reason. There were rusted metal signs over tunnel doorways: *Lucky Strike Bar, Dive In, Texas Hold 'Em*. The Stars and Stripes ahead draped heavily. As they approached, she could see over the steel gates a looming greige cuboid. This is it, Hana thought, remember the moment.

'Good cover, hey?' John said. Hana's head jerked towards him, just in time to catch his chuckle. 'I've thought it all through.'

A sudden snag. She froze, blinking like a deer at the barrel of a rifle. Hana felt like he had stepped on her, grinding her down with his heel.

'Oh,' John realised his miscalculation, 'I'm sorry. I thought you knew—'

There had never been a meeting. She felt embarrassed on a cellular level, as if her organs were ashamed to be indivisible from her. She wanted to cry. She was a stupid, silly little girl.

He guided her through some winding streets, and she followed, wet-brained, jaw limp. In the streets between, skinny women with bleeding lipstick and drawn-on beauty marks loitered in entrances, gazing at her knowingly. They went into an alley that dipped into a steep downhill slope, messy telephone wires criss-crossing above, crackling under the sun. The soles of Hana's feet were damp and rubbed against the canvas of her shoes. There was a friend of a friend, that part was true. The friend directed them through a door between two ramshackle buildings, into a room with brown-stained corner seams, the linger of cigarettes, layers of past inhabitants. In the room was a lonely steel bed frame, with a thin mattress. Next to it, a bedside table with a remote control and a plastic plant.

'I know it's not much,' John said, looking around. His confidence seemed to dip. He didn't seem to know what to do with his hands, raising then dropping them. 'But now we can be alone.' He took a step towards her, wringing his fingers. Her eyes slid to the window, and she noticed it was closed. She was boxed in, always had been.

'Are you all right?' He clutched her. 'Are you OK?'

The heat, her disappointment, the closeness. She willed her body to bend around his. She wouldn't be going to a prestigious international school. This man's love had to be her anchor. Amidst loss, she needed to cement what they had, to grasp as close to him as possible. Right now. She pulled at his shirt, finding clusters of moles under his collarbone. He hesitated for a moment.

'We don't have to—' he started. She kissed him hard. His body slackened, his hands bracketed her face. A groan, into her mouth. This was what people in love did, Hana told herself as they stumbled backward, the bed protesting under their weight. She was the one who wanted to be free so bad. Well, this was freedom. Texture against the grain. John's hand cupped around her breast. Her body surprised her, as it intuitively guided him. This was good, she told herself, this was enough. She looked at the ceiling, friction building, the gamey smell of mingling sweat, of nature and nudity, and went far away. It was still John with her, but not *this* John. She pictured him coming home to her in America, bands of gold around that special finger. As they moved together in Seoul, she dreamed of him telling her about his day as they slid into their clean sheets. And then, another image popped into her head. Her mother on the stoop, waiting for her to come home.

On the now-dark way back to the bus station, Hana was quiet. She was returning to the minbak, this time indefinitely. But she had found the great love of her life and she was young; she shouldn't be greedy. And yet, a grief soured in Hana's stomach. Was something she never had still loss? If a tree falls in a forest—

'Are you all right?' John murmured.

She wanted to tell him the truth. That he had disappointed her. That she never wanted to be misled like that again. Instead, she just said, 'I'm tired.'

Something caught John's attention and a mischievous smile broke across his face. 'Wait here.'

Before she could object to being left alone on a busy street, he darted across the traffic and dipped into a shop. He emerged a minute or so later, with a paper rectangle between both hands.

'For you.' He handed her the rectangle. She pulled out a purple leather notebook, with an elasticated closure, small enough to tuck into a deep pocket.

'Open it.'

She flipped the cover open and on the first page, John had scrawled, in English to avoid Youngja's prying eyes: *To my wild one, write your heart out.*

'I know you were disappointed about today, my love,' John said. 'But have faith in me. Our life is only just beginning.' He held her face. 'I promise.'

Over twenty years later, Hana sat on the staircase and turned the diary over between her palms. Ada was out studying, Youngja was napping. Its original violet leather had developed a shiny patina, the polished skin of an aubergine, holding the colour of a lifetime of lingering. Its pages long filled up. Tim had stumbled on it once, when Ada was just born. Hana was returning to it every day, and in her sleep deprivation, had become careless with where she left it.

'What's this?' he had grinned. 'Ooooh, a secret diary?'

Hana laughed and tried to snatch it from him, as playfully as she could manage.

'Oh, come on!' Tim saw the year printed on the cover. 'Nineteen eighty-five? I want to know who your celebrity crush was back then! Richard Gere, like you always say?'

Hana held her breath. She had sustained this charade for so long, her life feeling like an itchy costume. He would see John's message – *To my wild one* – and it would be time. To know about the man who had been Hana's oxygen. Tim would no doubt be strait-laced and square about it. He wouldn't accept that Hana had been a willing party, that some girls were simply more mature than others. Just at that moment, Ada had squealed with powerhouse lungs, splotchy and red from the effort. Her foghorn reverberated through the flat and Tim absent-mindedly put the diary down to attend to their baby.

Now Tim, her alibi, was gone, and she was terrified of the big, blank space he left behind. Sometimes, she imagined running into John in the supermarket, their eyes crashing between the rice and the lentils. Their bodies full of apologies. He'd be forty-three. She was forty. That their age gap was once an obstacle would now seem absurd. He'd invite her for a coffee, and they'd sit across from each other in a greasy builders' cafe, all the time rolling off them like dead skin.

'I've missed you,' he'd eventually say.

She'd nod at the table, chewing her lip. 'It's been a while.'

They'd both laugh.

They'd not know where to begin. She'd have the intrusive urge to blow a raspberry, just to break the ice.

Eventually, she'd whisper, 'You hurt me, how you left like that.'

And it'd be his turn to nod. She'd long for him to just confirm that he had come back for her, after she had already left. But instead, he'd gaze at her. There'd be the beginnings of a truce. She'd notice how deep his smile lines had become, that his beard was now wolf-grey. It would be like trying to locate a childhood home after a lifetime away. And yet, the magic would still be there, humid and combustible. What was it about him that undid her? She didn't know. Perhaps it was the power of unresolved history. She'd realise that she hadn't yet figured out how to sit across from him and not be madly in love with the illusion of him. He'd ask questions:

'Did you finish school in the end?'

'Did you ever make it out of the minbak?'

And instead of answering – of having to admit that, twenty-three years later, she still belonged to the minbak – she'd get up and walk away. They'd never see each other again. Her life had been chosen for her, all those years ago. Had she had the power to have a different life? At times, possibly. If she was honest with herself, probably. But what you didn't change, you chose. Besides, Hana wasn't raised to believe she had self-determination. She had calcified herself into this life. So, all she could do now was just keep flicking the pages of a diary, holding on to the seventeen-year-old version of herself as the gasps came and the tears fell, mourning the unbridgeable crevasse between what could have been and what was.

Ada
에이다

September arrived. School, Ada's first day at Richmond Girls', was starting. The night before, she ironed her school shirts for the week, and, by the lamplight, sewed her name labels on each piece of kit. In the morning, Ada pulled on her knitted, knee-high socks, before getting Youngja out of her pyjamas.

'Manse!' she called, and Youngja thrust her arms into the air, allowing Ada to take her T-shirt off and change it.

'Halmoni,' Ada said in a bossy tone, 'look here.' She pointed to the pink Post-it note on the headboard. Youngja couldn't read English and Ada couldn't write Korean. So, Ada drew a crude outline of a dressing gown and socks and laid both out for her on the bed. 'Remember, when you go out, you need to put your dressing gown on. OK?'

Youngja waved her away. Ada took her hand and pointed out the rest of the Post-its around the room. She used the brightest colours she could find in Poundland, in the hopes that Youngja would easily be able to spot them in their jumbled living quarters. Ada had begged her mother not to sell her iPod because it had an inscription from her father on the back for her birthday. It was now the only thing Ada could set multiple alarms on.

'I've set an alarm for noon,' Ada explained, holding up the iPod. 'When this rings, do you see that? The alarm has this blue heart emoticon, do you see? You go to the blue Post-it.' Ada pointed to it, and underneath a small bowl with Youngja's medication and a glass of water. 'You take these pills and then turn off the alarm. Remember,' Ada crouched to Youngja's level, telling her to do the very thing she couldn't, 'don't turn off the alarm until after you have done what the Post-it says.'

As Ada coached Youngja, Hana was beyond the door, serving breakfast. Ada was ready to leave but hung back a few seconds. She wanted her mum to see her in her crisp uniform. It wasn't necessarily breadcrumbs of love that Ada hoped for. Love was too big. It came with an exclamation mark. Love! She'd be happy with something neat and parcelled like appreciation, or acknowledgement. After a minute, Ada put her coat on and found enough in kissing Youngja's papery face, lingering cheek-to-cheek, praying silently that they both would be all right without the other.

Richmond Girls' overlooked the herds of deer in the park and resembled a stately home more than a school. A grandiose former manor at the end of a wide lane, mosaic clock face marking the main entrance, windows thrown open. Murphy's law that after a summer of rain and cabin fever, it was a scorching day. Netball and tennis courts were tucked in the far-right corner, next to the swimming pool. As Ada drew closer, three Porsche Cayennes, in varying shades of metallic, pulled up on the road. Girls sleepily trudged out of the passenger sides, while their mums sprang from the driver's seat, a full bunch of keys jangling from their hands, dressed in olive-coloured athleisure sets. The girls' skirts were the same as Ada's, but much shorter. And her face burned when she realised that she was the only student on the road wearing the knee-high socks. Her exposed knees like the knobby knots in a tree. Ada overheard one mum with an immaculate blow-dry ask her daughter if she was *ready for the new year, honey?* Ada thought of Hana, by now tending to her full sink, splashes on her denim apron, too busy to notice that Ada had left. A weird mixture of pride and shame flared. Already, Ada keenly felt on the back foot.

The first day was a whirlwind of newness. Numerous rust-bricked buildings were scattered around the campus and Ada struggled to find her bearings. The busyness was hive-like, each person striding with easy purpose, churning onwards. Her form tutor, who took registration and would, Ada was told, guide her through these next 'crucial' years, was Fräulein Meyer. She had a blunt bob, and didn't seem old enough to be a teacher.

'I'm new here too,' she whispered with a conspiratorial smile that made Ada feel like the sun was on her.

Assembly started the day. The headmistress, Mrs Candy, who looked salty and pinched, reeled off a list of distinguished alumnae who had done impressive things over the summer like sail an entire sea for charity or go to an orphanage in India. Photos of white girls cuddling brown babies blown up on the projector. She unveiled a wooden plaque carved with the names of the girls who went down to Oxbridge this year. All that to eventually make the point that, 'Here at Richmond Girls', we create the leaders of tomorrow. It behoves you to be extraordinary.' *Behove?* Ada wondered what ye olde world she had stepped into. It made her think of blowing out a candle and retreating to her bedchamber wondering what the morrow may bring. Mrs Candy kept saying 'we', while Ada wondered if she could ever possibly belong within that term. For the second time before nine a.m., she felt severely out of her depth.

Each teacher was intent on embodying a stereotype: Mr Pain, Physics, who assured the class that he would live up to his surname; Miss Dance, Classics, channelling anaemic Victorian child; Mrs Clark, English, giant resin pendant that could knock a teenager out; Mr Lemaire, History, resembled a mutant rat but was under thirty and therefore fancied by the boy-starved girls. The maths teacher, in particular, looked like a maths teacher. Each of them issued the same warning. Homework would increase, along with coursework. Universities would expect extracurricular participation too. *If we put pressure on you, it's only because we think you have the potential.*

By fourth period, PE, Ada had barely spoken. It became quickly obvious that the lacrosse pitch was not her natural habitat. She looked like a sprinting giraffe, sporting a netted stick in the wrong hand. The coach, Mrs Lyne, who wore a school-crested windbreaker and had blonde hair scraped into a spiky stub of a ponytail, blew the whistle mid-game to ask Ada why she wasn't 'cradling' the lacrosse stick. She beckoned a breath-snappingly pretty girl called Clarissa to show Ada, in slow motion, how to. Ada tried to keep her face neutral through the embarrassment.

'That's it!' Mrs Lyne shouted. 'There you go, caress it! Think of your lacrosse stick as your first boyfriend, that'll get you there.'

Afterwards, Ada sullenly returned to her locker. Clarissa was digging into the locker next to hers, in an aqua bra bordered with magenta lace complete with matching thong, that together screamed sex. She paused to flip open her Motorola Razr. Ada recognised the lilac special edition and saw that Clarissa had haphazardly coated the back cover of the phone with stripes of chipped nail polish. Ada couldn't help but stare; Clarissa was bronzed and supple all over, seemingly airbrushed. Ada pulled her sports kit over her head and sensed Clarissa stop moving. She clutched the top to her chest.

'What is it?' Ada said, squeezing a small laugh.

Clarissa leaned against the wall of lockers and appraised her for a second, as if making her way through a decision tree in her mind, evaluating whether to be scathing or welcoming.

'See,' Clarissa held her forearm to Ada's back, and turned to the girls across from them, 'this is too pale. I'm aiming for a dark, dark tan. Going to Cape Town for half-term and I want to be *blick*!' She mimicked a South African accent. Clarissa took a step back and scrutinised Ada.

'Where did you get that complexion from?'

'My mum is Korean,' Ada said. It sounded like a confession.

'Where?' Clarissa snorted, popping her contraband gum.

'It's a country, bimbo.' Another girl rolled her eyes playfully.

'Actually two.'

'But you have blue eyes?' Clarissa probed. Her head tilted as if she was studying a museum artefact.

'Yeah . . . my dad,' Ada said, a sharp pang between her ribs.

'Do your siblings have them too?'

'Only child.'

'Oh, gotcha!' Clarissa nodded. 'One-child policy.'

'My neighbour is Korean,' someone else chimed in, 'but she's more of the Louis Vuitton, plays golf, tiny-dog type.'

'Don't they eat dogs in Korea?' another girl tittered.

'Eww!' Clarissa exclaimed, wagging a slender finger in Ada's face. 'Gross!'

By the time Ada turned into the depths of her locker, her halfness was staring back at her in the small plastic mirror hung on a rusted nail at the back. She could go days, even weeks, immune to the fact that she was an anomaly. She didn't *feel* any different. And with her blue hooded eyes and British height, she thought she approximated whiteness enough. But eventually she was always reminded that she was a hyphenated person. Today, in the form of Clarissa, with her synthetic biscuits-and-vanilla smell and her flagrantly lacy push-up bra and her thoughtlessness, making Ada feel a sort of masturbatory self-hate. Clarissa swanned out, shoulders squared, back straight, utterly oblivious to the quickening she'd set off inside Ada. While Ada folded into herself, burning up at the edges.

At lunch, two teachers were assigned to stand at the front and end of the canteen, monitoring the girls' food intake before trays were flung into bins. Girls who only had soup or some wispy leaves were sent back for more, or *at least some ciabatta to go with your tomato and basil.* The lunch line was clumped into small groups, who would float together into preordained seating positions. When Ada got to the front of the line, with a baked potato and beans, the lunch lady gestured for her to swipe her student card.

'There's no credit on your account, love,' she said, mercifully quietly. Ada panicked and stammered with the tray in her hands. She couldn't pay for her food. Stupid, stupid. 'Just leave it there,' the lady said kindly.

Ada returned to the changing rooms and unwrapped the Spam musubi she'd packed for herself, eating it in two big bites as they collided with the huge lump in her throat. She hiccuped loudly and its echo bounced off the steel lockers. She wanted to go home. She wanted to see her dad. She wanted him to be alive. She hoped that her mum would make sure her grandmother had eaten. The bell rang.

In double History, the Weimar Republic, Germany's hyperinflation, the rise of the National Socialist Party. Every other girl had a lever-arch folder in which each sheath of paper was filed behind an appropriate tab. There was so much clicking and zipping and fluffing with every worksheet they were given, while Ada sat redundantly, without the accessories that proved she was a serious student. Mr Lemaire was the fifth teacher in one day to assert what an important year this was. *How you do in these exams will go on to shape the rest of your lives. I have no doubt you will make us proud.* The affirmations had rubbed off on her classmates, carrying themselves with a confidence that dazzled Ada, absorbing the constant assurance of their specialness without humour.

Just before the end of the day, Fräulein Meyer stopped Ada in the corridor to tell her that she had been called to a meeting with the headmistress. Mrs Candy's office was in the beating heart of the building, underneath the stained-glass dome. There were two other girls in the year, who introduced themselves as Lakshmi and Meryem. Mrs Candy opened the door and, in her plum-coloured jumper and burgundy trousers, she resembled a raisin. The three of them were ushered towards her cream suede sofas.

Mrs Candy sat opposite the girls in a plush armchair

that had a satin watercolour print. With a charitable smile, 'Game-changing, isn't it?'

None of them said anything.

'Well, don't just sit there like lemons!' She threw her head back with a laugh and they indulged her a joint nervous titter. 'I wanted to personally welcome you three specifically to Richmond Girls'. Thanks to the generosity of our donors, we have been able to support your places at the school.'

All three girls were blank-faced, unsure how to adequately display their gratitude. Ada didn't know why she, an imposter, was there.

'Sadly, we can only offer bursary places to a small number of the very deserving applicants.' Mrs Candy extended her index finger and scanned it across them like the spinner on a game wheel. 'You are the lucky three in your year. This place will transform your lives. We have provided everything, from your uniforms, to covering travel costs, and of course, besides that support, there will be no other special treatment. We hold each student to the utmost standards here.'

She smiled blandly. Ada thought a cement mixer might have more emotion than her eyes.

Youngja
영자

Youngja was getting irritated by the depression that had swallowed Hana whole since the Americans had left. The community centre was being run by a local pastor and his wife, and the missionaries had moved on to another town, as was their way. Days rolled into weeks, slipping into months, until four had passed and Youngja's patience was running dry.

September 1985, the dictator continued to discipline the country. Students, with their intrinsic belief in goodness and truth, coordinated thousands of rallies, demanding democracy. Plain-clothes agents flooded into universities, which were closed more days than they were open. Law and order were abused and undone. But Youngja could see that her child's world was cleaving apart in a different way. Hana exhausted herself, catching a tooth infection, her entire jaw inflamed and swollen. Firm styes sprouted in her lashline and, each morning, Youngja had to press a hot towel to Hana's eyes, sealed shut with a crust of pus. Ulcers pebbled in her mouth, making her speak with a soft lisp. Eventually, she looked so pitiful that Youngja took her off all food service. No one wanted to see a girl without her loveliness.

It would pass, it had to, and Youngja wouldn't indulge the pining any longer. It was a shame, of course, that after three trips to Seoul for various interviews, Hana hadn't won a place at the international school. Youngja hadn't approved of the endeavour in the first place. A person had to understand their position. Resisting it was like fighting rain. The American did Hana no good by planting seeds and watering hope in her. Each time she came close to snapping at Hana, Youngja reminded herself that she was a girl once too. She had been so besotted by her father's helper – a boy five years older than her with broad shoulders and browned muscles – that it had been all-consuming. Looking back, it was laughable. She had expected when she brought Hana into such a male-dominated environment that this sort of longing might happen. Her daughter was petite and willowy, with clear skin and a homely, honest energy. Youngja saw the way lazy eyes tracked her and, though other teenage girls might flirt and giggle, Hana had maintained a cool distance.

Finally, on a full-mooned night, four months after the Americans had left, Youngja found Hana curled under her quilt, knees folded to her chin, blinking at the wall. Youngja sat cross-legged behind her. With two careworn hands, she raised Hana's head into the crater of her lap. Fingers through her hair, she murmured, 'Aga, you have no business becoming this attached. It's time to forget about him. Guests will come and go.'

'He wasn't just a guest,' Hana whispered. A tear slipped out of her eye, as she nuzzled her face into the cotton of Youngja's trousers.

'Then what was he?'

Hana had no answer to that. Youngja was no fool; she'd noticed an overfamiliarity between Hana and the American, a looseness of laughter and a tilting of body. A lack of caution. They seemed to share nuances that were unseen to others. The truth in Youngja's mind was that her daughter had slipped in love with the man, and was heartbroken that he couldn't know.

'You won't be here for ever. But, for now, this is what we have. Be patient, Hana-ya.'

Hana gulped, unable to speak, silent tears soaking into Youngja's lap.

At last, profit. Like downpour after a parched summer: clean, honed respite. Until now, the modest income from the minbak went towards repaying their debts or upgrading the house to accommodate more guests. The local government had just announced the building of several apartment blocks to clutter the skyline, so Youngja was confident that there would be no shortage of business with all the new construction labourers coming to town. Which was why, nine months after they welcomed their first guests, Youngja informed her husband that she would be enlisting one employee. She put her foot down. Hana had paid her dues to their family and would return to school. Yes, she had lost out on nearly a year, and it wasn't a hot-shot international school in the city, but Youngja had earned the right to protect at least this. Hana would finish high school as a minimum. If she wanted, Youngja would see her through university too; she didn't care how much it would cost. The way Hana looked at her these days was already a price too great.

'Hana-ya,' Youngja called from the store shed. 'Can you help me get the barley down?'

Hana hesitated. The shed smelled of warm wood and childhood. Dusty sunlight sliced through its slatted walls. The sack was heavy – ten kilograms – and shelved high. It needed two people to dislodge it, and even then, they had fallen over many times before.

'Come on,' Youngja urged from the doorway.

Hana gingerly stood on the stool and the two of them tugged at the corner of the sack, wedged between the ceiling and that underneath.

'I've been thinking,' Youngja began. 'It's time we enrolled you for this school year.'

Hana didn't respond. She stared ahead vacantly.

'I know it's not ideal to be in a class with your friends' little brothers and sisters, but if they say anything, you just ignore them. You helped your family. You're a good girl.'

Hana kept her eyes fixed firmly on the sack, tugging a little harder. The beads shifted, then creaked like an avalanche. The sound was off-kilter, all the grain imbalanced to one side. The sack spat out towards them. Later, Youngja would wonder what exactly it was that had tipped her off. Whether it was Hana's reluctance in the first place. Or the way she jumped out the sack's way, both arms shielding her stomach. Or had it been the angle at which Hana threw herself, so that she would land on her side? Perhaps it was simply that nebulous thing they called a mother's intuition. Youngja knew. The hessian fabric had split and the grain was whooshing out.

'You . . .' Youngja said, her breath in a hold.

Hana confirmed it by looking away.

'Show me,' Youngja said. Her pulse thumped in her ears as Hana stood up and obediently turned to the side. Slowly, she pressed her loose dress around her middle. There it was. A low-slung, firm dome.

So, this was heartbreak.

'Is it his?'

Hana nodded. Youngja took a sharp step back as if Hana had spat in her face. It would have been easier if someone just killed them both.

'How long?'

'Since the first trip to Seoul. I think.'

'Does he know?' Youngja asked. 'Is that why he left?'

Hana's face took on a saintly glow. 'We're in love. He's coming back, Omma.' She cradled her belly. 'For both of us.'

Youngja cringed away, her hand clasped around her mouth. In love? What did her idiot child know about love? Was that something she thought she'd learned from the American? Love alone wasn't enough, not even close. With each second, instead of horror, instead of rage, Youngja remembered. The previous week when Hana couldn't stand the odour of the blood sausage in the kitchen. Her excuses to not go to the bathhouse together. That stomach bug that had her vomiting for days a few months ago. The time Youngja went half-mad looking for their square cloths to wrap their winter clothes in and Hana had shrugged. Perhaps these clues might have meant something if she had a different child. But not Hana. Not the child she trusted as much as the tide to foam against the rocks.

'Lift up your dress,' Youngja said.

Hana complied. Underneath, her stomach was wound tightly in the pink cloth Youngja had been looking for. Her mind fried. She wanted to rage, to call Hana a babo, a jijibae, but what good would that do? She didn't know how to act.

She finally said the only thing that came naturally. 'How have your cravings been? Is there anything I can cook for you?'

Devotion continued to flicker inside Youngja like a dusty, low-watt light bulb. She made hushed calls to a doctor who performed late-term abortions for a small fortune. Youngja would find the money somehow. Hana threatened to kill herself before having an abortion. This obstinance angered Youngja more than the pregnancy itself. So those were the headlines: Hana was unmarried; over six months pregnant with a half-and-half baby; the father was gone—

Tow the sun to light your front room, boil the ocean for a cup of tea. Both were more fathomable than raising this child as a single mother. Youngja's husband was of little use. He was a man who only spoke freely to crops and plants, often pulling his truck over if he saw ripened fruit weighing a branch down, or to untangle two trees that were hindering each other's growth. When it came to human troubles, he was as wordless as his beloved plants.

In the short term, it was essential that none of the guests or neighbours discerned Hana's condition. If the news travelled, she wouldn't be allowed to return to school, out of fear that she would be a bad influence on the other students. They'd treat her like a criminal. Their business would be ruined; no one could trust a family that kept an unwed mother. Hana would never be able to graduate, or marry anyone decent, or get a respectable job.

Each morning, the same, silent ritual. Clamping one corner of the cloth between her teeth, Youngja spun

Hana, squashing the squirm backwards against her spine. Her mind was often blank – numb with worry – until, one morning, as her hand cupped Hana's bloated belly, a distant protestation kicked her palm. A complaint about the tight living conditions. And as much as she denied herself the feeling, everything else peeled away and there was only the sharp volt of love, pulsing like a current under Youngja's skin.

When Youngja thought of what lay ahead her breath often halted in her throat. She crouched in the corner of the store shed where she first realised she was going to be a grandmother as sobs clambered out of her. Heaving and thunderous, such a relief. She had denied herself the luxury of tears when the Japanese surrendered, and, at seven years old, Youngja was a free Korean for the first time. Nor when she was twelve and the war broke out. When soldiers came to their door instructing them to evacuate, and they had to leave behind her father who had already been conscripted into the Red Army. When they walked, crunching down on snow, southward like a flock of migrating cranes. When they hid in the mountains during the occupation of Seoul, the city changing hands back and forth, bullets sparking and zipping below, and her baby brother froze to death strapped to her chest. When they came down from the mountains and saw bodies strewn like rag dolls in the streets.

Not a lot of joy had come Youngja's way. So, when the sole source of her joy turned out to be the biggest fool ever created, Youngja let the tears pour.

Two months later, when Hana was around eight months pregnant, the phone rang.

Before Youngja had the chance to say hello, her brother's voice whispered, 'Noona, are you alone? I don't have long.'

'Hold on,' Youngja said. She leaned across the counter and pulled the window closed. Her youngest brother, as coddled as if he were her own son, was the tallest of the five because Youngja had always snuck him extra milk cartons when he was a boy. She suspected that their mother was doing the same for the baby of the family. Even though he was well into his thirties, Youngja still went to Seoul every few months to deliver him home-made banchan and make sure he was taking care of himself. Now, he worked as a reporter. Solemn, straitjacketed work. She pictured his slim, elegant face on the other end of the line, smoothing his shirt even if no one was watching. 'I'm alone.'

'The army is coming.' His voice was crystal. 'The students that were arrested or expelled for protesting at the universities, they've gone underground. Infiltrated the factories around Incheon. Thousands of them.'

'What?' Youngja laughed, finding it unbelievable that well-to-do intellectuals would willingly enter a factory. 'Why?'

'I guess they realised they can't bring the house down alone. Under fake names, they're pretending to be factory workers, drumming up support for the movement. They're forming an alliance with the workers.' He paused to catch his breath. 'Noona, they're sending a thousand riot police. They've already arrested a hundred at Daewoo Apparel. Their union leader was a philosophy major, can you believe it? He was beaten almost to death.'

Youngja had bigger things to worry about as she saw

Hana out in the yard, one hand supporting her lower back, in a loose dress that concealed her bound belly, but at the stage of pregnancy where she couldn't do much about her waddle. Youngja had been keeping Hana out of sight, only allowing her out of their room once the guests had left for work. 'OK, we will stay indoors for a few days.'

'Your guests,' he whispered. 'How do you know they're not dissidents?'

'You're being crazy.'

'All it takes is for an officer to point the finger. Or for one of them to get caught up in a strike or a demo.' He muffled the phone and she heard him ask someone for another few minutes on the line. 'We don't have time for this. If you are linked to anyone that is arrested – if you're seen to be harbouring them – they might take you too. Maybe even Hana. There have been confrontations with the military all over the place. And with the women, they . . . please, be careful.'

She heard the fear in his plea.

'Noona,' he said quietly, 'I don't know my right hand from my left any more. The censor's office muzzles us. I spend my days going back and forth from the army compound, until they are happy—'

'Stop,' she commanded. Phone lines were known to be tapped. 'I know.'

'The whole office has been sent home, we've received word they're closing down the bridges and roads out of the city.'

'Will you check on Tae-Jung?' Youngja asked of her younger son. 'Tell him not to get wrapped up in any foolishness.'

'I will drop by his lodgings on the way home.'

'Stay safe, please.'

He clicked away.

Youngja's belly clenched. She had heard whispers, of course, of subversive union leaders fired. Blacklisted from working again. Teenage factory girls arrested and beaten just for asking for equal pay. She estimated from how low the baby was that Hana would deliver early. It occurred to her that the missionaries *did* have some university students helping at the night hagwon, holding classes on unionising and whatnot. And some of them had stayed at the minbak for a night or two. A solution came to Youngja. The next day, without discussing it with her husband, and without discussing with Hana, Youngja apologetically ejected her guests and closed down the minbak.

She was relieved to see, in the days that followed, the leather shop, the home-goods store, and the tailor, also pull their shutters down. Just like her brother had predicted, the army flooded into the industrial estates like an upturned box of toy soldiers. Furnished with helmets and shields, they moved with so much certainty, in a show of military might. Traders didn't come to market so the mothers stood in. They exchanged food and information: the workers were holding the fort. Four factories were now striking in solidarity, demanding the release of their union leaders. They fended off riot police with stones and iron pipes, linking elbows in human chains. Some workers commandeered heavy machinery, protecting their colleagues with forklifts and diggers. They shared around welding masks and safety goggles to withstand the tear gas. Numbers rose to twelve factories. *More riot police are coming*, a neighbour said as she handed Youngja a container of radish kimchi, in exchange for a packet of ramen, which was traded to another neighbour for a small amount of bulgogi. No one asked where Hana was. It was sensible to keep her out of sight. Police might suspect her a factory girl and take her for questioning, or worse still; they'd heard stories. But together, the mothers reminded the soldiers of their own ommas, with their perms and thickened middles and aura of protection. That way, Youngja managed to keep eyes off her daughter until her waters splattered onto the yard stones.

Ada
에이다

Ada had too many other things keeping her busy, like navigating her new school, to do anything about it. But that didn't stop her from thinking, thinking, thinking. About the time she saw her mother crying on their staircase over a notebook she had never seen before.

A week earlier, Ada was halfway to the library when she realised she'd forgotten her annotated copy of *To Kill a Mockingbird* and turned back. She snuck into the house to avoid frightening or confusing Youngja. The hallway was free of shoes; all the guests were out. A strange gargling came from around the corner. A fawn trapped in wire. A dog retching. High-pitched hiccups, then quick, stuttered breaths. Had her grandmother fallen? Ada moved towards the noise to find a shape crouched on the third step of the staircase. Hana, spluttering, gushing like a tap.

Ada wondered if she should go over and comfort her, before quickly deciding against it. Hana lifted something from her lap, Ada's pulse thumped. She turned it over in trembling hands then settled its spine on her knees. The day was browning into afternoon, giving the view a burnished, hallucinatory quality. Hana whiplashed through the pages and Ada had never seen such hunger, as if she wanted to consume the entire thing in one sitting. The flutter and flick of pages, a zebra of thick handwriting against creamy paper. From her hiding place, Ada found perverse enjoyment in watching her mother cry; it felt like candyfloss dissolving on her tongue for the very first time. Questions bottlenecked in her mind, jamming, jostling for answers. She pushed herself on her tiptoes to get a better view when a heavy hand fell on her shoulder.

'That stupid notebook,' Youngja murmured, her lips brushing the bow of Ada's ear. 'Leave her to it.'

She knew the right thing to do was to move along. Conceal, don't feel. Warehouse it in the smallest drawer in the furthest reach of the mind. But that night, as the other two women snored faintly next to Ada, the knot of words wormed their way upwards. In her imagination, the little square book grew bigger and more formidable, a loose end begging to be tugged. Honestly, it frightened Ada to see her contained mum, who had shed controlled, dignified tears when her father died, unspooling like that. Had her mum been a writer? She searched the nooks of her mind but, no, she didn't think so. It was as if one day, she had emerged from a seashell, utterly contextless, and waded into Tim Penny's life. Ada had the eerie feeling that she didn't know anything about her mother at all. That really, she was sleeping next to a stranger each night.

In Biology class, she'd learned the mechanics of the ovaries and uterus. Female babies were born with all the eggs they will ever have. The first thought that came to Ada's mind was that she'd been there all along, tucked inside Hana like a Russian doll nestled within a Russian doll, since the day her mother was born. And if she didn't know the one person she had always been a part of, then what could she know?

After school every day, Ada came straight home. She took her grandmother for two laps around the park, bathed and fed her, before settling down for her homework. Today however, the house was ghostly. She could hear her heartbeat in a sound. Youngja had a neurology appointment and she'd be with Hana at the hospital now. Ada stood still as a portrait. The rumbling energy that had been thrumming all week roiled over. The notebook had to be in here somewhere.

There were many things she didn't know about her mum, but she did know that Hana was careful. Cunning, even. The notebook wouldn't be haphazardly shoved somewhere. It was in hiding. Crouching at the bottom-left corner of the room, behind the door to the kitchen, Ada began rifling through a stack of shoeboxes, the tight jeans holding in the gut of their former life popping open. Memories whale-spouting. Hana had sold nearly everything but kept old spelling-bee certificates of Ada's, brash gold plastic medals from sports days. The next shoebox: photo albums. She recognised one framed picture because it always sat on their mantelpiece when their living room was still a living room. In it, she was a chubby baby, in a floral dress and crochet headband, sitting on a picnic blanket. Her dad lying behind her, his arm around her middle, squeezing a Capri-Sun. Hana in the corner of the rug, sunglasses hiding her face, looking at the other two with an unreadable expression. Ada shook the image away and continued plumbing.

She scaled halfway across the back wall with no luck. She checked the time. Youngja's appointment must have finished by now and they would take about half an hour to get home. Exhaustion penetrated her adrenaline and she slumped on the floor. She had been outsmarted again. Her eyes swept over the room. One corner hooked her vision. A cabinet with intricate red designs that depicted a Korean folk tale, with suitcases in front of it. Something flickered through Ada. Her mum was practical, nifty, crafty. Though their room was bursting at the seams, it had a method to its layout: heavy boxes on the bottom, clear pathways to storage. Suddenly, the suitcases blockading the cabinet seemed to radiate a red flare. Ada pounced towards them and shoved the suitcases, stuffed with spare duvets and linen, out the way, wheels careening until they bashed into the opposite wall. Her fingers gripped the cool brass handles of the cabinet.

Inside, rows of plastic folders. Ada ripped a few out. Boring shit. Council tax bills, medical records, insurance, utility bills, property information. It was all over. With a final cursory resignation, she ran her fingers over their spines. Her finger caught. She did it again. Same catch. She rose onto her knees, and with both hands, swung apart two folders. Squeezed between, pushed all the way to the back, a sliver of leather. Ada dragged a bobby pin out of her hair and clipped it onto the folder the notebook was hidden behind to mark the spot. She pulled it out. Wine-coloured, with darkened corners and a water stain seeping across the back cover. Within it, pages covered margin to margin. The curves and swoops of Hana's handwriting. At the back, loose sheafs of paper. Lined, gridded, napkins, the back of a dentist form.

*

What had Ada been expecting?

Of course, the writing was in Korean. Not the boxy, typed-up Korean with neat characters that she could sort-of read, albeit at the speed of a drunk six-year-old. Hurried words, slanting into each other, the ink faded and blurry. Brimming with legend, like long-lost war journals, hieroglyphics on stone, love letters stashed in a biscuit tin. Words that bore witness to alienation. Ada's stomach churned at the sheer volume. Her mother's thoughts unravelling like bundles of yarn. There was a rhythm to the writing, still breathing, fully in motion. She searched the pages for something familiar – any mention of herself or her dad – but the shapes didn't add up to words.

Ada's heart wobbled. When she was eleven, she had come down with a bad flu halfway through the day. Hana wrote a sick note excusing Ada from school, waiting in the car park to take her home, while Ada told her form teacher. Mrs Saunders had scanned the note and folded it in half.

'This isn't like you,' Mrs Saunders had said. 'This doesn't need to go any further if you just return to class.'

Ada's teeth were chattering, muscle aches settling in. 'Miss, I'm really not feeling well.'

Mrs Saunders had sighed. 'Very well, come with me.' Ada stood outside the headmaster's office, overhearing Mrs Saunders's complaint. 'Notice the handwriting, obviously written by a child. I wonder if her parents know that she is forging notes to get out of class.'

It hadn't occurred to them that English might not have been a parent's first language. Tim had to be called to verify its authenticity. Afterwards, they thought they were helping when they took a parent slip out of Hana's hand and hurriedly completed it for her. Hana never seemed interested in their discussions over their favourite books; why hadn't it ever occurred to Ada that reading an entire novel in a language that was not your first would be far from enjoyable? Could it really be that they'd never asked her what her favourite Korean books were? As the common ground between them shrank, in these pages, her mum's thoughts elbowed each other for space. Entire, closed worlds, privy to no one. Ada tried to imagine having to neutralise her complex inner workings through a second language. Hana was emotionally tepid but, for the first time, Ada wondered whether she herself would be able to express her deepest, most painful feelings in Korean? Or would they come out stunted, barriered, too?

Now, Ada was the one who couldn't. What sort of Korean was she? An illiterate one. An incomplete one. A half one. She spoke the language, but a puritanical, baby version of Korean. She didn't know any swear words or slang, pervasive pop-culture references or the right body-language cues. Her Korean was stuck in a censored decades-old time warp. Of course it was, when Hana was her sole nexus to her Koreanness. Staring at a language she couldn't access, Ada wondered if she had any right to call herself Korean at all.

Chastened, Ada was about to return the notebook to its spot, when she noticed something. Each page began with the same word: 요한. She knew from her basic reading skills that the first character, 요, was the sound: Yo. The second character, 한, was intrinsically Korean: Han.

Yohan.

Yohan?

'Fuck's sake,' Ada muttered to no one. What did Yohan mean? She found a page where the ink was more legible, the pen Hana used much finer. Ada grabbed her backpack and pulled out her exercise book, scribbling random deciphered sounds. Stringing syllables together, she found whole words she recognised, and then translated them into English. After ten minutes, she had a sentence and a headache. She had been concentrating so hard on decoding that she hadn't stopped to register the translation.

Every day I think it might get easier, but missing you never ends.

A great, bone-shivering fear rustled through Ada. She had been right to wonder. Possibilities raced. An ex-lover, a first heartbreak, an affair? Her thoughts expanded wider, building more architectural explanations and stories in her head. She was outraged at whoever this person was. Didn't they know Hana had a family? Wasn't that worth protecting? Most of all, Ada's long-held suspicion that she would one day lose her mum took on a real, human shape, animating from a mere inkling to a very present danger.

She thought of her father's tombstone, moss staining across it, flowers withering at its base. She knew that if he were here now, he'd just pull his mouth downwards and shrug. And that would hurt just as much.

Yunsook

윤숙

Yunsook Im's ankles were so swollen that she stood on one leg at a time like a flamingo, shaking out the other, in the hopes of relieving some pressure. Only an hour through the night shift, she dry-swallowed a rainbow of prescription painkillers, never breaking her power-stride through the ward. Her bloated-plum joints ripe to burst, her stomach growled, demanding the kimbap still wrapped in tinfoil in her locker.

Three women had come in this evening and, as the most senior midwife on shift, Yunsook was responsible for assessing each. The first two weren't ready yet. With the third patient, she inserted her gloved fingers, then removed and wiped. She could tell ten centimetres in her sleep. Time to begin. With the fluency of experience, she wheeled the patient down the corridor, an older woman trailing behind them.

Yunsook steered the girl's legs into the stirrups until she was splayed like a frog. Manoeuvred a harsh shaft of light over the exit point. Yunsook held the tops of the girl's knees and rhythmically chanted, 'Push, push, just one more time, push!' The bead of a head emerged, fawn hair swirling around its crown, which she cupped, her fingers flexing against scrunched neck. The girl bore down. Her impish face tomato red from the effort, sweat dripping down her temples, a primitive moan through tensed teeth. Her eyes rolled backwards, her breath turned ragged.

'Omma!' The girl grappled for the older woman's hand.

'Aga, you're doing well, I can see the head! Only a little longer,' her mother whimpered, as if she were in pain herself. Small intimacies between them: the mother licking her thumb and wiping tear-stains on the girl's cheek away. No man waiting outside. No ring. No excited fanfare or carefully packed hospital bag. Yunsook understood; families were as good as nude in the hospital.

At last, the baby slid out with a gush. Shiny and long-limbed like calf slipping from cow. The younger bodies tended to eject quicker. No one said anything while Yunsook clamped and cut the spongy cord. The room suspended in jelly, filled only with the girl's panting. Yunsook flipped the baby on its stomach in the palm of one hand and smacked its bottom with the other, until the first wail pierced the room and his presence was announced.

'A tall boy,' Yunsook stated. 'You did well.'

The girl tried to sit up, white-faced and leaden, then winced and unfolded flat. Judging by her plump cheeks and terrified eyes, she couldn't have graduated high school. Surely she wasn't a middle-schooler? What sadness, Yunsook thought. She very rarely saw girls this young. How did she get herself in this condition? She might have been foolish, but she didn't have the frivolous air of a thoughtless girl. It was possible that she had been raped. It was a kindness, to not ask. And Yunsook didn't like to stick her fingers in other people's messes. She carried the baby over to the basin to be cleaned up.

There wasn't much that shocked Yunsook any more.

Back in the late fifties, she'd been stationed on the outskirts of the Osan US Air Base. She could still remember her panic, as a twenty-two-year-old student midwife, at encountering her first breaching bottom. She had hurriedly rehearsed how to work the forceps, unable to concentrate because what had really shaken her was that the bottom in question was much darker than the body it came from! She had looked at the mother – a military 'entertainer' she later learned – and back at the baby's round butt cheeks, like two shiny chestnuts. Its GI father must have planted a dark seed. It had startled Yunsook, who by that age hadn't yet seen an adult of such a complexion. For the following two days, while the other nurses and midwives ignored the mother completely, Yunsook continued to use respectful, formal language towards her. As Yunsook cradled the baby's head, encouraging her to latch on to the mother's nipple, the woman quietly said, 'You wouldn't be speaking so politely if you knew about women like me, working on our backs.'

Yunsook paused only for a moment and found that this fact didn't bother her at all. The aftermath of the war had been difficult for everyone. Plainly, as she would give medical instructions, she said, 'I'm just doing my job.'

A year later, Yunsook and her new husband had been driving home from the hospital when she recognised the same mother, lingering by a fire hydrant against a brassy sunset that put in mind segments of citrus fruit.

'Stop, stop! Pull over,' Yunsook said to her husband. She

ran out towards the mother, who startled away like a rabbit, before turning back. It was definitely her.

'They wouldn't help me,' the mother whispered when Yunsook asked how she was doing. 'We had an agreement!'

She had been in a de facto relationship with the baby's father, a soldier. He gave her a secure income and living expenses, which she repaid with monogamy. The girls even referred to it as marriage. He had seemed happy that they would have a child together. Until he returned to his family when she was eight months pregnant. 'I contacted his army base, and they refused to give me any information about how to reach him.'

Yunsook had seen this many times now. The US Army promoted the use of Korean women for 'recreation' – a pressure valve for military life – but offered no financial or practical support for the mixed offspring born from that practice.

'I'm ruined,' the woman lamented. 'You service a coloured soldier once, and the white soldiers won't touch you. I can't work near the army base any more, and my family back home need me to support them. They don't know about my daughter. You saw her. They would hate her.'

Yunsook didn't know what to say to offer comfort and she didn't like to lie. She'd always been taught that the Korean people came from a single, unbroken bloodline. That they were a pure race. The word 'half' came to her mind, a grating irritation, a seed lodged between teeth.

'Social workers come into town to try and take the children living around here,' the woman said. 'They tried to convince me to give them my daughter too. I've said no but they keep coming back. They've promised her a better life in America. Why do they say it like that? Like they are rescuing her from me, as if it wasn't her father who abandoned us. They tell me she has no future in Korea. Do you think that's true?'

By the seventies, Yunsook had two teenage daughters of her own and wanted to settle down near their schools. She commuted around hospitals in the belt that hugged Seoul: Ansan, Suwon, Anyang. All industrialising like an almighty freight train without brakes. The mixed babies became fewer and further between, but Yunsook remained busy. Young boys and girls, together in close quarters for the first time, without supervision. As sure as the grass grows and flowers bloom, babies came.

There was a girl in Yunsook's own neighbourhood. Song Young-Mi. A promising university student, studying chemical engineering. The middle daughter of the grocer, she'd done well for herself. The market ladies said that Young-Mi was stocky and ruddy-faced, in comparison to her pearl-skinned sisters. *The stupid girl must have gone along with the first man who paid her any attention*, they had tutted under their visors. Easily dismissing her with antipathy and a superior comment. Yunsook wished to interrupt, as she tucked the long green onion stems into her basket, *Look to yourselves*. Hadn't several of them also been with men before their husbands? Would they consider themselves women of low morality too?

Yunsook had a soft spot for Young-Mi, who was friends with her older daughter. Though, of course, she'd instructed her daughter never to speak to the girl again, to preserve her own reputation by association. In private, Yunsook knew Young-Mi to be polite and good-natured. She was whip-smart, diligent, ranked high in her class, but lacked confidence. She had an expressive face on which all her thoughts were legible.

She was the first in her family to go to university. She flung her growing body and its cargo off the Mapo Bridge.

Yunsook never spoke of Young-Mi out loud but thought of her each time she delivered a baby to an unwed mother. She saw one girl's legs shut like a clam when she attempted an examination. Yunsook remembered her own uncle's hands roaming under her dress and understood the body's instinct to prevent invasion. Another woman was admitted on the same day, dressed in a demure cardigan, sensible leather court shoes, and had carefully rolled hair. A twenty-seven-year-old estate agent, she'd been involved with a co-worker who only later revealed that he was married. He promised to leave his wife but never did. She had no legal means to compel the father to recognise or support the child. Yunsook thought to herself, did anyone think so lowly of him as a father, in the same way they would slander the mother? And just last week, a university graduate – architecture – came in for an ultrasound at six months pregnant with her boyfriend; her family wouldn't permit them to get married because she had two older sisters who had to be married first.

And another, and another, and another. All in liminal states of motherhood. None of them would blink into the darkness, made weak by their child's sighs of safety and satisfaction. Not this time. They wouldn't convince themselves they heard an *Omma* in a babble. They wouldn't guide this child through the messy fumblings of life. Maybe one day, they'd even pass their own child on the street and not know. The thought made Yunsook shiver, as if she'd stepped out of sunlight into a stream of cold air. They entered the hospital one with their babies and would leave alone because they were told that was the ultimate sacrifice. Same old, same old, all across the globe. Women exaggerated into whores, victims or saints. Nothing changes if nothing changes.

The baby boy in the basin, his head weighty in Yunsook's palm, was pink and slimy. Under the creamy layer of mucus, she could see wisps of caramel hair. His mother – she checked the name bracelet: Park Hana – hadn't been brought in by the women from the maternity homes, so she wasn't sure what to do next. Yunsook despised uncertainty. She itched to ask the mother what her plan was.

Every week there was at least one girl. Whose belly had rounded and was sequestered away to a maternity home – by her family, by his family, by her own volition – until the time came. With those cases, there was a clear process: whisk the child away to the nurses' station as soon as it was severed, while the necessary chain of calls whipped through the systems. Yunsook liked efficiencies. She appreciated a swift checkout line, a neat shoe-rack, a key hook, a well-oiled ward, a solution to a problem. Unlike her colleagues who were pointlessly chatty and filled every silence, Yunsook never asked the young mothers about their lives. Who those girls were in the ward were smudges, soon to be wiped away. Illusions, characters that both lived on in lore and equally faded away. It had to be that way. She didn't wonder why. Some things just were.

Tentatively, Hana held out her arms. Yunsook looked at her mother first for permission, who nodded. Yunsook placed him on the girl's chest. As the baby splayed his arms wide across her, the girl looked as if she was meeting God for the first time.

'Hi,' Hana whispered, tapping his round nose with her

index finger, before inhaling the top of his head. Yunsook remembered how tactile that smell was: blood and flesh and genesis, by way of this dense infusion of love. 'Hello, John.'

Yunsook noticed the grandmother's head snap up. Eyes wide as plates.

The girl's cheeks were full of pride. 'Yohan, in Korean.'

'Are you Christians?' Yunsook asked cheerily.

'Are you not ashamed?' the grandmother gasped. 'After I have cared for you – how could you?'

Yunsook shut herself up. She recognised in the girl's self-satisfied face, as she gently stroked the baby in her arms, an elevation, a canonisation. Focus shifted. Motherhood demanded monogamy; distancing from daughterhood. The generations turned.

Hana trailed a finger along the downy hair of his cheek, whispering as if there were no one else in the room, 'I love you, Yohan.'

A muffled hiccup came from the corner. Yunsook turned to see the child's grandmother, palm clasped over her mouth, whimpering, 'I have to step outside.'

As the young girl cradled her child, Yunsook stood back and let the grandmother pass. She reached into her breast pocket, flipped open her notebook, and added both their names to her list. After ushering a nurse into the room to watch over Hana, Yunsook tucked her chin towards her chest and followed the grandmother out. It would all be resolved soon.

Ada
에이다

So, who was Yohan?

Ada got in twenty minutes before registration to use the classroom computer, tilting the screen away from the door, jiggling the mouse until the Windows logo came alive. She impatiently tapped her feet, triple-clicking the browser. On Google, now what? She typed all she had: Yohan. The first result was a Wikipedia page: *Yo-Han is the official Korean equivalent of the biblical name John. As such, it is sometimes used as a given name by Korean Christians.*

John?

She squeezed her eyes and tried to remember if her mother had ever mentioned a John. *John and Hana Park*, she typed. All she got were grainy YouTube videos of a couple's wedding.

She pushed on, searching: *Korean translator*. Then, *Korean keyboard*. Agonisingly, she matched smudged hangul symbols to the keyboard layout she found online, her typing stilted. Finally, with a sentence inputted, she tapped Submit. Total gibberish. Vintage thoughts of inadequacy returned. Perhaps there was an innocent explanation for all of this. From the frailty of the paper, the yellowing of the corners, the notebook was decades old. It wasn't unusual for people to hold on to old love letters and mementos, right? Her mother seemed too much of an emotional eunuch to conduct an affair. But then, what about the other week? Her mum on the stairs. The pages may have aged, but those tears were freshly frothed and overflowing. There was something kinetic here, snaking a path, knocking dominoes as it moved.

What else could she search? Her mum had left Korea in 1986. Where was her hometown? Ada felt embarrassed that she couldn't quite remember. It was right there in her mind but she couldn't reach it. *Cities in South Korea*, she typed. The more she learned about Korea, the further away it became. She tried to imagine walking its streets, dissolving into a crowd where others looked more like her, but all she could conjure were glitchy images. *Seoul, Busan, Daegu, Sejong, Daejon*, then, *Incheon*. Ah, that was it. Then, with low expectations, she typed in the search bar: *John Incheon 1986*. She scrolled, the results mostly in Korean. On the second page, an entry caught her eye. She clicked on it. A blogspot page loaded.

Reflections on thirty-five years in South Korea
By Rev. Mitchell Murray

She skim-read the blog, posted in 2003, scrolling, one eye on the time. It wasn't particularly useful, detailing a Christian group's endeavours in the country. Why had this come up in her search? CTRL+F: 'John'. The page shot to a pixellated photo of two white men and a group of Koreans smiling in front of a plain matchbox house, with the caption: *Over the years, many missionaries have been assigned to South Korea as our work has grown. I was joined during the years 1985 and 1986 by John Logan, in the building of a local community centre in a factory town outside of Incheon.* She scanned the faces. She zoomed in, moving the frame around, the pixels becoming boxier, the image fuzzier. She kept searching the picture. Her heart thudded against her ribcage as the penny dropped. She zoomed in even further until the frame was swallowed by her mother – her face rounder, higher, but the same mole pattern smattered across her left cheek – looking back at her. A long gaze cut through time and screen to hold Ada's, warning her that once these sands started to shift, they were liquid and uncontrollable. Ada didn't care. She had to fill the gaping hole between Hana then, and Hannah now. This was the stone in her shoe.

Ada went to Google Maps and typed in *Incheon*. Using Street View, she clicked through uneven images of the place, waiting to be smacked by *Eureka!* But all she saw were blank pictures that gave her nothing. Frustrated, and with two minutes to kill before the bell, she typed in her own address in Wimbledon. It took a few seconds to load but, as expected, there was their home, in all its tennis-adjacent, strawberries-and-cream glory. She used the white arrows to telescope the image closer. Her dad's green MG parked in the driveway, the number plate blurred out. Framed by two black iron Victorian street lamps overlooking a wide, clean pavement, the postbox at the junction. A spark raced up her spine. At the edge of the screen, shopping bag slung over his shoulder with one hand, mobile phone held to his ear with the other, was her father. Walking through life, ungrateful for it. Mid-step. Alive and well. Preserved for ever in the amber that was the internet.

'Oh,' she whimpered to the empty classroom.

What Ada would have given to be able to make him take another step. Dad, it's just a short walk down the street. Unlatch the gate. Come home for dinner.

'Ada?' Fräulein Meyer came in, a satchel dangling from her shoulder, steaming Thermos in hand. 'I'm glad I've caught you early.'

'Miss?' Ada gasped, her finger on impulse slamming the power button, her sleeve dabbing away the tears on her lashline.

Clarissa and two of her Velcro friends entered.

'I noticed that your mum didn't attend parents' evening yesterday,' Fräulein Meyer stated in hushed tones. 'Should I give her a call to update her on your progress?'

'No,' Ada said, too quickly. Fräulein Meyer raised an eyebrow. 'Sorry. I mean, please don't worry.'

Like a circling shark, Clarissa sniffed the hint of Ada's vulnerability in the air.

'Are you sure? Top set in every class, you've taken like a duck to water to the new schedule.'

'Positive,' Ada mumbled. Fräulein Meyer seemed unconvinced, and Ada knew it looked like she was holding something back. For a moment, she forgot who she was, what was real. A dimly lit escape route presented itself to her.

'My dad was working late and my mum is away so neither could make parents' evening. Don't worry, I'll update them.'

She thought of the parents' evening form, still crumpled at the bottom of her bag. What had been the point of giving it to her mum when she couldn't leave the guests for an evening anyway? In any event, Hana wasn't too concerned about the softer metrics like Ada's *confidence in class*, or her *initiative*.

'All right.' Fräulein Meyer eyed her uncertainly. She must have known Ada was lying but simply began unpacking her bag. 'I received your exam predictions yesterday.' She squeezed Ada's shoulder. Her touch, tinged with care, was startling. 'Keep it up.'

Ada breathed through the nausea in her chest. Why did she say that about her dad? She had wanted to cling to the image of him, casually walking down the street. Clarissa's audience had unsettled her. She hadn't wanted in that moment to air that she was recently fatherless. That her mum couldn't make it because she was catering to strangers in their house. The lie seemed easier than the truth.

'You're literally such a boff.' Clarissa was smirking, leaning her hip against the wooden desk, dancing on the edge of mocking and friendly. 'I'm in bottom set for *literally* everything.'

Ada made a mental note to pepper 'literally' throughout her sentences.

'But you're captain of the lacrosse A-team.' Ada's heart was tripping, her ears popping.

'So, what does your dad do?' Clarissa pushed herself away from the desk with her foot. Her eyes were a deep algae set in a perfect oval of a face. Hair like sun-dried maize, falling over her shoulder. She was still waiting for Ada's answer and raised the corner of her lip in amusement.

'Boring shit.' Ada shrugged. Ice cracking over her insides. Then, she turned to Clarissa, poker-faced. 'Literally.'

'Mine works late too. Which is fine by me. Stops him being fucking on me. So conservative – small C. *You're not applying yourself, Clarissa. You don't care about your future, Clarissa. Do you want to be the first person in our family who doesn't get into Magdalen, Clarissa?*'

'Yeah. Annoying,' Ada said.

'He's a partner in a big firm, so he's got a mega iron rod up his arse,' Clarissa continued. She reeled off a list of surnames that Ada supposed she ought to recognise. The friends tittered like a studio audience. 'What does yours do?'

'Construction,' Ada managed. For a terrifying moment, she thought she might cry.

'Jesus, that is tragic, you're right.' Clarissa sighed, her interest in Ada expiring. 'No wonder you're so emo.'

The second bell rang, signalling the start of lessons. Ada scurried away.

During break times, the girls flocked to the Junior Common Room, a sacred place as loud as a shopping centre, with tatty orange sofas, red-and-green tartan carpet. Along the back wall, a mini kitchenette with a kettle, microwave and sandwich press. There were canisters of SlimFast with their labels torn off to avoid confiscation, leaving white paper stuck to the glue stripes. Sofas in a U-shape, with purple beanbags in the middle. Filled to the edges with the constant buzz of chatter: how to self-pierce bellybuttons with a safety pin, *yeah, wear that in town and show Max what he's missing*, Ginnie McAlpine's body odour problem, Polly Gascoigne two years above got expelled for stealing her dad's prescription pad and doling out codeine pills, *Fall Out Boy* was so gay, *Green Day* was positively lesbianic, Priti Rai was off school with a supposed mental breakdown but she'd always been an attention whore. The girls slouched on the beanbags, languidly stretching their bodies. They tossed themselves on the marmalade sofas with vigorous laughter, knees open. Ada couldn't ignore their dazzling ease. These girls would happily climb on someone's shoulders during a concert. They'd have no qualms about putting elbows on both armrests on a train. They spoke over each other without restraint, unafraid to cause irritation or offence, their words bouncing like the mesh of a trampoline.

Ada wondered how. Where did this dynamite confidence come from? If someone spoke over her, Ada analysed the moment on loop, critiquing herself like scratching an insatiable itch. She had to get to the bottom of what, specifically, was boring about what she had been saying. Before she knew it, one person interrupting her sat with her for the entire day. In the end, without an answer, Ada concluded that she simply must be unengaging, evidence that she was lacking in charm, she just didn't have presence. The Greatest Hits. And although she knew she didn't *do* bad things, Ada found comfort in telling herself that she *was* bad. She didn't know where this belief that she was deeply lacking had come from, or why she worshipped it. Sometimes, an explanation – whether it was true or not – was all a person needed. So, she sat there, each break time, sipping her Options hot chocolate, observing these girls anthropologically, pitting herself against them.

A shoulder bumped Ada's. Clarissa stood over her, playing Nelly Furtado out loud.

'A bunch of us are heading back to mine tonight. Come.'

The sequence danced past Ada, and she was just happy to be there. They sat in a semicircle on Clarissa's patio, the kitchen light just enough to make out profiles. Clarissa's parents were still in the office. Ada imagined them to be industrious and important people. It was the first house she had been into since hers became a minbak. Six girls in ripening bodies.

Smooth lines and, for now, untouchable. The Arctic Monkeys played.

'I'd let Alex Turner fuck me sideways,' Clarissa announced, passing around a bottle of her father's Grey Goose. She leaned back to look up at the faint stars, the front legs of her chair lifting off the ground. Sophie Lamb, who smeared foundation over her lips so that, when she spoke, her mouth looked like an open cut on her face, began bashing the corner of her pink Sidekick 3 against the raised landscaping stones.

'These things are indestructible, I swear,' she complained. Ada was confused as Sophie's arm arced through the air, hitting the same spot again and again.

'I know,' another girl said. 'So annoying. What are you after instead?'

'BlackBerry. I *need* to be on BBM.'

No fucking way, Ada thought, as the screen of Sophie's Sidekick finally relented with a crack. The group fell into a brief silence, but for Kitty Gash pinching in a bag of Golden Virginia. The air drenched in Chloé perfume. A few sips in, Ada's brain became soluble, slowly turning to mush. She couldn't stop swinging her head around, absorbing that she was here, not looking after Youngja. She had abandoned her responsibility, and it had taken no effort at all. It felt bloody good. Like she was only just starting to exist. She covered her mouth and forced a cough, just to hide how jazzed she was.

'Hey, Lisa,' Hattie Lawson called out. A rugby hoodie slung over her shoulders, to remind everyone she had possession of a boyfriend. For some reason she was addressing Ada, holding out her hand in a cylinder shape, 'Stop hogging it.'

Ada looked down to see the Grey Goose by her ankle.

'It's Ada,' she said. She was still the new girl, she supposed. 'Here you go.'

'Yeah,' Hattie released a mushy giggle, 'but we're gonna call you Lisa.'

'Shut the fuck up, Hattie,' Clarissa snapped, still gazing up at the sky. 'You're like nowhere near as funny as you think you are.'

'What's the deal with Lisa?' Ada laughed.

'It's a joke these birdbrains came up with.' Clarissa's chair thudded back down on the patio stones. 'As in, Simpson.'

'You're, like, one chromosome away from her,' Hattie added.

Through the sluggish vodka haze, it took a moment to connect. Lisa Simpson. A punishing little-girl cartoon. A punishing yellow cartoon. And because everyone else found it funny, Ada threw herself under the bus, as she always did, and eked out a laugh. All brushed off. The girls continued chatting like it never happened. Ada's gut twisted over itself, wringing so tight it left her breathless.

Ada walked home in the dark to sober up. She chewed her lip. The two hours at Clarissa's had been a good distraction, but now she was barrelling back to her core anxiety. So her mother knew a man called John over twenty years ago. What did that really tell her that she didn't already know?

The front door to the house was open. There was someone talking to Hana, their silhouette outlined by the porch lamp. From a distance, Ada noticed that Hana's hair was combed through with young greys. The taut contours in her face shaded with a heavy weariness. She picked up letters scattered on the doorstep, before pushing them into her apron. The man, who had a broad body and wore a cargo jacket with a bursting hiking backpack over one shoulder, waited patiently. Ada immediately understood that he must be young because you never rushed your elders. She crunched up the path and he turned to look at her. He was in his twenties, boyish face with square glasses and shiny, blackened brown hair with strands straight around the crown like twigs from a bird's nest. When he saw Ada, his face spilled into an easy smile that made her insides tumble into disarray. Ada suppressed a drunk giggle. She felt conscious of her Paul's Boutique bag with textbooks poking out and school uniform, mercifully hidden by her coat. His skin tone was pale but peachy, and his eyes were the colour of tarnished brass, which made her suspect that he was mixed like her. Hana glared at Ada; she was in deep shit for staying out late. She pushed past them both and tucked herself into their room, eavesdropping as the new guy spoke with her mother.

'How long do you need a room for?' Hana's tone was a little absent and rushed.

'At least six months,' he said. His voice was soft, like he was talking to a pet. 'I'm here on an exchange programme. Do you have space?'

Ada knew Hana was startled too because she had stopped bustling, as if she was frozen in place on the other side of the door. Most guests stayed for three or four nights. The longest-staying guest was for a fortnight.

She said how much a monthly stay would be. 'That includes breakfast, dinner and daily cleaning.'

'That's fine.'

Ada wondered if her mum had totally stopped breathing. Usually, guests asked to see the rooms first. They always haggled on price.

'Cash only.'

'OK.'

'And two months upfront.'

'That's fine too.'

Ada pictured Hana's laser-vision eyeing him. 'I hope you will be very comfortable here,' she said. 'Let me show you to your room.'

From their footsteps, Ada tracked Hana leading him to her old bedroom. She pictured him, tucked into her bed, his body enveloped by the shape of hers still imprinted into the mattress. Hana pushed open the door.

'Did you hear that?' She had an enormous grin on her face. 'Six months. Six months!'

Hana gripped Ada's shoulders and she seemed to have entirely forgotten to be angry. They jumped up and down. Hana threw her head back and released a totally carefree laugh. To Ada, the sound was like a defibrillator to her brain's happy centre.

'Wow.' She wiped her forehead. 'Six months of guaranteed income. That helps,' she nodded at the floor, 'that helps us a lot.'

Youngja wandered towards them, and the three huddled, heads bowed, arms splayed across shoulders.

'수고했어, 하나야' Youngja said into their circle.

Well done, my Hana.

Youngja
영자

They – Youngja, Hana and Yohan – made it back to the minbak under cover of darkness. Her husband's rust-addled Hyundai pickup groaned over unevenness, and Youngja had never driven with such attention before, feeling every rock and pothole on the road rattle under her pelvis. A beautiful late-autumn night, above them a marble of indigo with violet streaks, if only they could forget the mayhem, both outside and within. In the days that followed, only Yohan's gurgles and slurps popped the silence. A golden boy, born wise and soulful, he seemed to understand from his pre-natal bind that he should be quiet and not fuss. He slept in the leather suitcase that had belonged to Youngja's father. The takedown of disguised students-turned-factory workers was several days in, Youngja had heard. There had been violence, but the numbers of the solidarity striking only grew in response. The minbak remained closed. What to do? What to do? Youngja thumbed the question so much she almost wore its edges smooth. Outside, snow began to fall.

She needed to report report the birth and have the child registered with the local government. But without a father to claim him, Yohan didn't have a family name he could be listed under. There was no way for him to be registered as an unmarried woman's child. No way for Hana to legally be his mother. Youngja had suggested to her husband that they register Yohan as their own son, making Hana his sister, but he had rebuked her with a blank stare, as if she had sprouted three heads, and walked away. So, for the time being, he was a nowhere boy; floating, white noise, borrowed light.

He was such a dear little thing. Youngja cradled his impossibly tiny head, making faces of extreme care, smothering the oval of his belly with kisses. She lowered him into the rubber kimchi tub she'd bathed all her children in and washed away the soft flakes that gathered in the thin folds of his neck. It was Youngja's sheer pleasure when he hiccuped in little gasps. Then, just as quickly as her joy rose, fear sent her vibrating like a leaf in the breeze. Women Youngja's age knew this country. They ploughed her fields, lost their parents to her war, sent their daughters to work, their sons to her army. Now, unable to give her first grandchild the dignity of a name to belong to, the backhand of her country smacked Youngja straight across the face.

For eight days, dirtied breastfeeding rags piled up. Youngja couldn't risk being seen buying or disposing of nappies, so her sons' old T-shirts were safety-pinned around Yohan's behind and boiled throughout the day. A meaty, biological smell – the scent of shedding – lingered. She'd been saving baby clothes in a box for her grandchildren that she didn't touch for a week, until it struck her that that was exactly what Yohan was. The stove was constantly bubbling with seaweed soup for Hana. A lack of postpartum care could affect a woman's health for the rest of her life. The broom was left idle. On the dawn of his ninth day, Yohan's irritated gurgle stirred Youngja from sleep. She peeked over the edge of the suitcase. His mouth was stretching to squeal but hadn't quite committed to it yet. To her surprise, her husband rose.

'Let me,' he whispered to Hana's raised head. 'Go back to sleep.'

He lifted the baby. Hana sagged down.

'There's milk in the fridge,' Youngja whispered. Until now, her husband hadn't acknowledged Yohan. In his mind, no matter how innocent Yohan was, the child was not a continuation of his bloodline. Children belonged to their fathers. But when she heard the door slide open and her husband shuffle his slippers on, Youngja let hope flutter in. What for, she wasn't exactly sure. Wrapping a cardigan around herself, she padded outside, creeping on the balls of her feet. Even with their own three children, her husband was an elusive, absent figure, and she wanted to be nearby in case he floundered with the needs of a newborn.

The kitchen was empty. Youngja opened the fridge to see both bottles of milk in the same spot she'd placed them the night before. Against a copper dawn, she saw the silhouette of her husband outside, blunt against the blanket of crystalline white. Behind him a trail of steps in the snow, he was looking out beyond the gate, bouncing Yohan on his shoulder. Then, he crouched on the ground and laid the bundle on the frosted grass. Youngja tilted her head. Her chest screwed into a knot. He had brought his pillow.

He lowered it on the ground, encasing Yohan, and looked away. Legs kicked and wormed under the angle of his elbow. Everything about resilience could be learned from a baby's will to live. Her husband held still, with goal-oriented focus. Youngja scrambled, her brain blanked. She felt as good as dead. Time moved like hot pumpkin taffy. She grabbed the barbecue pan, dusty with white coal ash, ran over, swinging the great weight into his side, sending him straight down. Letting the pan thump to the ground, Youngja ripped the pillow off Yohan. He was still. She pushed one finger into the fold of his neck, groping, begging for a pulse. Could she feel anything? Her brain exploding, shrapnel dispersing in every direction.

And then, the little boy flushed pink. His fists curled into balls.

'Yeobo,' her husband rasped from the ground. *Darling?* Youngja lifted Yohan, and backed away.

'Yeobo,' he whispered again. 'We will tell Hana the baby died in the night. It is common, I've seen it on the news. It is for the best.'

Youngja held her finger to her lips, filled with chest-beating fury, the dawn air chilling her forearms.

Youngja looked both ways, before zipping her coat over the baby strapped to her chest. She wrapped a scarf around her neck and camouflaged the top of his head between drapes of fabric. It was so early that she doubted anyone she knew would see her, but still, to be safe, she took the deserted path into town, her canvas trousers protecting her legs. She lingered in the bushes until she saw the top of the bus approaching around the bend. They were only at the bus stop for fifteen seconds, and she was sure there were no witnesses.

Youngja's eldest son Tae-Young lived forty minutes away in an apartment block at the top of a steep hill of concrete stairs, lined with sparse twigs for trees. Youngja took breaks every few steps to catch her breath and rest the parcels she had brought.

'Ommoni!' her daughter-in-law Hee-Jin exclaimed as she opened the door to Youngja, a film of sweat down the centre of her torso, where Yohan was nestled against her chest. Hee-Jin rushed to take Youngja's bags and get her slippers. 'What brings you here so early? I'm sorry, I wasn't expecting you.'

Youngja pointed to the bags. 'I brought you some yeolmu kimchi and some kkadugi too. Fresh, I know Tae-Young doesn't like it too sour.'

'Omma,' her son gasped, still in his sleeping shorts. Puffy crescents under his eyes. 'Is everything OK?'

Youngja unzipped her coat and their eyes settled on the baby's cocoon. Tae-Young's face screwed into an ugly swirl, like he'd sucked on a lemon, all indiscreet contempt.

'I will make some tea for you and cut some fruit.' Hee-Jin busied herself. 'Here, come sit, the floor is warm.'

'I won't be long,' Youngja began. 'I'm sorry for coming here unannounced.'

Tae-Young eyeballed her. He wasn't yet thirty but looked unhealthy, with a neck as fleshy as a pork loin, and broken capillaries all over his nose that made him clownish. His body bursting with unspent frustration. All that time spent in soju houses, squandering what little salary he made. It was hard for Youngja to watch after his wellbeing, when he rarely came home. Hee-Jin, meek as a mouse, set a plate of sliced melon and peeled orange segments in front of them.

'So she had it, then,' Tae-Young said. Youngja glared at him. She thought she'd taught her children not to judge others. She was learning so much about them.

'Would you like to hold him?' Youngja directed the

question at Hee-Jin, who glanced at her husband and then nodded. Swathes of fabric rustled as the women shuffled their arms to hand over the child. Yohan blinked, all pinched lips and marshmallow cheeks. His hair had darkened to a wet cork and coiled into one sweet ringlet. Even Tae-Young couldn't help conceding a smile.

'So small.' Hee-Jin held her index finger to his hand, which unwrinkled to grasp it. She rocked him side-to-side. Hee-Jin reminded Youngja of mother's milk, pure and nurturing. Apart from the boy's light hair, which could always be dyed, Yohan could plausibly be hers.

'I try not to interfere,' Youngja began. 'I'm sorry for saying this. But it has been three years you have been trying, and no baby yet.'

Hee-Jin's mouth dropped open slightly, which made Youngja feel terrible. Tae-Young didn't seem so anxious, but that was always the way with men. Although mothers were notorious for being tough on their myeoneuris, Youngja never blamed Hee-Jin for not falling pregnant. She always set aside money to buy them Chinese fertility medicines and expensive ginseng concentrates. She had tried to encourage Tae-Young to stop drinking, as that could affect his ability to conceive. She hoped that the care she had shown them would now pay off.

'He is your nephew,' Youngja said. 'Will you not hold him?'

Tae-Young relented and held out his hand to stroke the top of Yohan's head.

'Would you consider taking him?' Youngja asked.

'What do you mean?'

'Raise him as your own. Register him under your name. Hana can be his aunt, and we can still be his grandparents.'

'Omma!' Tae-Young stammered like a car puttering down a bumpy road. 'You want us to spend our lives fixing Hana's mistake?'

'It's not the baby's fault.'

'Darling,' Hee-Jin tugged on Tae-Young's sleeve, 'shall we discuss this in private?'

'There's nothing to discuss. I won't raise a child that isn't mine.'

'The baby needs a home,' Youngja pleaded.

'Why can't you do it?' Tae-Young challenged. How could Youngja tell him about what his father had tried to do a few hours earlier? Some things children couldn't know about their parents.

'We have the minbak, and we're getting old now. We can't provide him with the opportunities you can.'

'Darling,' Hee-Jin began again. 'Calm down, please—'

'If it were my brother's bastard,' Tae-Young snapped, 'I would concede that we have some responsibility. If he couldn't care for it, we would have no choice. It wouldn't be right for us to have a child who can continue the family name running around unclaimed.' Tae-Young was pacing and giving his speech to the wall. 'This boy belongs to his father's family. They're the ones with the legal right.'

'But—'

'How will we explain it to the neighbours? My boss? One day my wife is skinny as a rake, the next we have a baby. And look at him, a hybrid. Obviously not Korean. Do you want me to look like a cuckold? Or for people to think I'm infertile? I could lose my job. It would be impossible.' He swiped his hand through the air, through the idea altogether.

Youngja folded onto her knees, sliding forward on nylon

trousers until she reached his bare toes, begging at her son's feet for her grandson's life. 'Please. Just consider it.'

Tae-Young was silent for a moment, then turned away. 'You shouldn't have come here and asked us this.'

Youngja sat in the back row of the bus, tucked in the corner. Adrenaline crashing, hope departing. Her second son wasn't married yet. She ran through her list of siblings, cousins, nephews, nieces, who might be able to help, but no one came to mind. The baby barely made a sound, only stretching his mouth into a gummy yawn before settling again. She twined his one ringlet around her finger and puckered her lips to the velvet of his cheek. It terrified her, how obviously she loved him. Her head pounded. She needed more time. Yohan was not safe in their home. If news got out, Hana would become the local delinquent. If the family were to retain any credibility, Youngja would be forced to reject her. Even her old schoolmate Soo-Ah, who got a divorce after her husband beat her, faced stigma. People agreed, at least back then, that even if a man beats his woman to death, it's his house she should haunt. A wife didn't leave her marital home, dead or alive. Soo-Ah, owing to the divorce, lost custody of her children. She lived alone now, in the outskirts of town.

The bus trundled through a neighbouring town. Optimistic winter sun streamed into the driver's side and Youngja kept a hand to her face to shield it from the cascading light. She almost missed the paint-cracked sign. There are certain slicing points in time, imperceptible to the memory – a glimpse, a whim, a minor delay – that sever a person from life as they knew it and lead them down a completely different path, wondering for the rest of their days what had set off such a bitter chain of events. For Youngja, that moment was when she felt a cool shadow wash across the back of her raised hand, lowered it, glanced out the window and, with a catch to her breath, saw the sign for the orphanage.

Ada
에이다

In late October, the rest of the world enthralled by the race between Obama and McCain, all Ada could think about was the stamina her grandmother had, pumping her arms and pounding the path with her rubber soles. They had been walking around the Common for some time now, avoiding the horse scat left by the riding school, listening to the village go about the business of living. Ada had been lucky enough to have never thought of life and death before her father was thrown off his axis at thirty miles an hour. She used to think loss was loss. A robust, candid, exact thing. But she'd since been schooled in the wet, sloppy matter of grief. How it can come, shuddering and fast, wreaking havoc in the instant a truck hits a father's car; or how it can be the longest goodbye, stealing a grandmother away in sly, ambiguous sleights.

A mallard skimmed the pond's surface. Two red spaniels drank from its edge. The path crunched with fallen leaves, Youngja jumping with surprise every few steps. Ada waited for an entry point for her investigation. The truth was within reach – about her mum, Yohan or John, the notebook, the letters – she was sure. And it had occurred to her that day that she had been living with its source all along. If John had been in Hana's hometown, then Youngja would have known him too.

'Beef bones, stock powder, dried kelp – are you paying attention?' Youngja tugged at Ada's elbow.

'What?' Ada muttered.

'Aish!'

'Sorry.'

'What was I saying?' Youngja huffed against her scarf. She waved her hand as if trying to swat a fly. 'There was . . . we need to get . . . to get . . .'

'Beef bones, stock powder, dried kelp?' Ada supplied.

'Mmm, yes. Seaweed soup. I need to make seaweed soup for . . . this is the cheap way to do it. Without meat but with all the nutrition. I got my clever hands after the war.' Youngja smiled to herself. A sparkle of pride.

'Oh yeah?'

Youngja lifted the white of her palm to Ada's face. 'These things were skilled in the house! They had to be. We got aid rations from the Americans, my mother made me line up for hours and hours, but you never knew what you would get. Strange food, in unpredictable amounts. Milk powder and slimy red meat in cans. I was creative. I could make something delicious out of any scrapheap of ingredients.'

Ada thought of Magna Carta: Of Normans and Plantagenets. York and Tudor. The English Reformation, all six of Henry's downtrodden wives. Suffrage. Austrian archdukes, kaisers and tsars. Hitler, Mussolini, Churchill, Roosevelt.

And then what? A great big blank over the war that raised the grandmother she loved? Surely that couldn't be right. A sense of injustice, of theft, came to Ada in a quick flash.

'How old were you? At the end of the war?' Ada asked.

'About fifteen. But trust me, you wouldn't have known it. I am the only daughter of an only daughter. You can't know what that's like.'

Ada swallowed a smile, but didn't interrupt.

'We were quite affluent. My father never made it down from the North. Before we fled, we stuffed the banggorae with that year's rice harvest so that we would have something to fall back on when we came home. When some of our neighbours made it South, they told us North Korean soldiers had occupied our house. It was winter. They tried to heat the floor and burned through all our rice hidden in the smoke passages.' She stared forward. 'Not that we could ever return for it anyway.'

Ada hung on Youngja's every word.

'I had four younger brothers, and my mother worked all day long selling dried persimmons outside the train station. I had to be their second mother. I didn't go to school, to take care of them and eventually to pay for their studies. I had this makeshift wooden back carrier to fetch water from the public pump, with two galvanised-steel buckets on either side. It clattered so loudly when the buckets were empty, and when they were full of water, my shoulders! My mother had to rub balm into the blisters. I'm forty-seven, and I still remember the blisters.'

Ada didn't bother to remind Youngja that she was seventy. She could hear the empty clatter of the steel buckets, then the weight of the water on her shoulders, the burden growing heavier as the task is fulfilled. She could smell the Tiger Balm on her great-grandmother's fingers. It was strange, witnessing lucidity but only within certain timeframes. As if someone somewhere was flipping switches and turning dials, deciding when and where Youngja would resurface. If Youngja thought she was forty-seven, Ada calculated that her mum would have been seventeen.

'Surviving was a struggle, of course.' Youngja's voice took on a gravel. 'People were starving. A few times, my brothers and I were so hungry we ate handfuls of soil. Sometimes when I look at my garden,' she nudged Ada's elbow, 'you should come over some time, I grow courgettes and carrots and perilla leaves and soybeans, I'll pick you some – all I can feel is soil in my mouth.' Youngja turned a beady eye to Ada, her chin bristling. 'The taste of starvation. You can't forget it, no matter how full you are.'

Ada was humbled by her naivety.

'What about later? Did things improve?'

'I married young, three healthy children. Enough money to live. What more is there to say?'

'You miss them.'

Youngja stood back and gave Ada a once-over. 'You're too young to know that your children aren't individuals. Wherever they go, they drag the beating pulse of your heart around with them. My Hana especially—' She watched a trio of leaves whistle to the ground. 'Aygo, what's the point of going there?'

Ada steered her onto the right path. 'You think of her a lot, I can tell.'

Youngja gave Ada an uneasy look. She was quiet for a moment. 'I keep thinking it will become easier, but it never does.'

Youngja looked at Ada with plain, frank sadness. One of the first truly honest conversations Ada had ever had. When she was around Hana, or at school, Ada was stretching herself into shape. Pre-empting how to be the right kind of daughter for the kind of mother she had. An impossible task, when she didn't have a clue what kind of mother she had. She couldn't recall a time that Hana had looked straight at her, the way Youngja was now, without a shade of expectation or confusion scrawled over her face. Ada felt profoundly seen.

'To keep living without your child,' Youngja said, 'it's like carrying on with an open hole in your chest. It's not living at all. But,' she sighed, 'regret is a useless emotion.'

Ada made a small noise of acknowledgement but inside she was jolted and confused. Her grandmother was speaking as if Hana was dead. Ada remembered that, in this moment, Youngja thought that Hana was just a teenager. While Ada was fretting about her GCSEs, her mum had left her homeland. The big thumping question was why? There seemed to be many versions of the same events, all faithful and all manipulated. There was a gap in the timeline. Something happened. A vacuum begged to be filled. Ada had to turn the peg, just one more time.

'Why did she leave?'

Reluctance flashed across Youngja's face. She sidestepped the question with ease. 'Mothers generally can't understand why their children do the things they do.'

A pang of desperation. An urgent adrenaline bubbled; Ada didn't know how much longer Youngja would be lucid before she drifted away again. She had no choice but to be direct. She rushed towards the waterfall and hurled herself over its edge. 'Was it because of a man?' Youngja was walking away. Ada blurted, 'Yohan?'

Youngja froze. She started to turn, like a lumbering, prehistoric beast, the sky a stony, smudged anthracite behind her.

'What makes you say that?'

'I saw mention of him, in Hana's things.'

'You shouldn't go through someone else's things. It's asking for trouble.'

'What happened? What did he do to her?'

'Look! Look!' She grabbed Ada's forearm and pointed across the pond. 'My house is just over there, the one beyond the hill. Shall I take you? We should go, you can meet my husband. It's just a short walk.'

She was gone again. Youngja gazed at the horizon. Then, quick as a flash, her eyes shot to Ada's face, alert and bright.

'Wait, is my husband the only one home? We need to get back.' She stood up. 'Hurry! It's not safe . . . we need to get back . . . can't be alone . . .' A chill whipped around them. Youngja clamoured and pawed at Ada. 'We need to rush, hurry! Get back, we need to get back.' Ada put her arm around Youngja's shoulders as she guided them home. Darts of rain shot down. Youngja stopped in the path of the headwind, softly whimpering, refusing to move.

'It's just a little bit of rain,' Ada tried to soothe. But her fingers were sore from cold and she was on edge. Her voice came out flinty. The change in weather unsettled Youngja and she looked around herself, trying to make sense of the new atmosphere. Footsteps splashed and scurried. A dog barked. Rush-hour traffic crowded the road. Youngja stuck her pinkies in her ears, scooping with her nails. Ada tried to make placating sounds, but her presence no longer seemed to register to Youngja. People were stepping around them, heads down, minds on slipping off their wet shoes and sinking into their sofas.

'Hey, I got you, gimme a sec—'

Ada looked up to see Michael, the new young guest staying in her bedroom, pushing out an umbrella. Her hand flew to her hair, uselessly smoothing. She instinctively sucked her tummy in and smiled as coyly as possible. He had wired earphones fed through his hoodie and he nodded at her, before bowing to Youngja and guiding his umbrella over their heads. Youngja's face changed like the dawn spilling into the night. She clutched his hand as he bent to her level.

'Halmoni?' he asked, very gently tugging her towards the house.

'Aygo,' she cooed, her feet firmly stamped in the ground. Her eyes rounded, soaking him in. He fidgeted with his hoodie. Ada began to twitch. It was awkward, all three of them huddled under the umbrella. Youngja giggled like a schoolgirl, tucked her chin towards Ada, and said in a dizzy whisper, 'He's so handsome!'

Michael laughed graciously as any young man would when an elderly woman complimented them. 'Thank you.'

'You're tall, too.' She tucked a lock of hair behind her ear and batted her bald eyelids. *Oh Jesus*, Ada thought with horror, *she's perving on him.*

Michael's eyes gripped Ada's.

'She has problems with her memory,' Ada said in English.

'You're so tall,' Youngja repeated, her hand caressing his knuckles.

Michael understood to play along. 'Yes, I take after my father.'

'I know, I know,' Youngja said. What did she know? It was like watching her grandmother as a girl, falling in love at first sight. The silence was so uncomfortable, Ada wasn't sure how much longer she could stand it.

'Please, keep it.' Michael handed Ada the umbrella. 'It was nice to see you both.'

He set off down the street, rain tears staining his grey top. Youngja watched him walk away. Her chest puffed outwards as if it was filling with warm syrup. He glanced over his shoulder, catching her gaze. He raised a hand in almost a wave, then dropped it again.

Mi Hee
미 희

All the romance in Mi Hee was neutered. Ever since she started this new job, she had been sliding into disrepair. Her clothes were shabbier, the oranges in the fruit bowl lost their lustre, her face tired of all its frowning.

'You're such a cry-baby,' her brother-in-law laughed, as they sat on the lino floor late into the night, chewing strings of dried squid dipped in mayonnaise. They'd polished off two bottles of soju and were on to the rice wine. Mi Hee was living with her older sister's family, sleeping in a room with her niece, until she married. 'Consider yourself lucky. When we were your age,' he gestured between himself and her sister, 'we were in the factories, getting headaches from the fumes, going half-mad from lack of sleep. Your sister's bronchitis is still terrible. The radio on your desk probably has a semiconductor made by these very fingers!' He wiggled his calloused hand under her nose. She batted his forearm away, hiding her smile. She didn't like to reciprocate his chumminess. He was harmless, but he'd stolen her sister away and for that alone it was her duty to make him work for her affection.

Secretly, she loved being an addendum to their young family, to see the busy, warm love buzzing between them.

'Leave her alone,' her sister play-scolded, reaching for the prized squid's beak, which Mi Hee would have usually fought her for. 'What's so bad about it anyway? I can't imagine anything better than sitting at a desk all day and getting paid well.'

How could she explain to her sister, with her perfectly ordinary, perfectly whole family, what it did to her to see the children come in, their faces bloated with tears? Just earlier that day, a mother had dropped her two sons off. Her husband had fled from a gang of loan sharks, and she feared the kkangpae would go after her children to punish him for defecting. Mi Hee couldn't look away from the boys' faces, flat-nosed and heavy-browed like their mother, confused but soundless. They knew not to make a fuss. The older boy's shoulders squared, trying to fill more space in the room. He took his brother's hand. As their mother left, Mi Hee could almost feel their hearts shuck away from their shells.

Few of the children in the orphanage were orphans. Most had living parents who had turned to it as a halfway house during crisis. Divorce, financial straits, affairs, abuse. Set up by American foreign aid and Christian missionary groups in the aftermath of the war, orphanages across the country had been used to temporarily bridge the gap for families when stability was scarce. So perhaps she'd collect her sons once they'd paid back the loan sharks. Or maybe by then it would be too late. Mi Hee worried in fits all day. Tallying children in her mind, whether their families would return, what they would find if they did, kneading her anxieties until they curdled. Mi Hee was only twenty years old. Adulthood would eventually anaesthetise her. It would sweep the questions between the cracks. Just like the children.

It was a chilly November morning. A bruise of a day. Smelled like melancholy and made your nose tear up. Leaving her sister's apartment, Mi Hee regretted the thin grey jumper she had chosen and stopped to wrap a scarf around her neck. Across the intersection, she caught sight of the girls, some younger than her, heading fresh from their dormitories to the company bus that would take them to the fur factory out of town. She peered forward to see if she recognised any of them from school; a run-in would be awkward. Mi Hee was humbled by her comparatively plump, rosy face, and was equally glad that she didn't have to do a job that eroded her prettiness. She was, despite all her moral qualms, still elementally a girl, and she cared about being pretty. Her brother-in-law was right. She was lucky really.

She usually got in an hour early. Director Shim was an old-timer who liked things done a certain way. As the mangnae on the office team, Mi Hee was expected to be the first in. She naturally didn't get paid for the extra time. The 'offices' were a row of back rooms, shabby as broom cupboards. No windows and peeling, vinyl floors. They had to shuffle sideways like crabs between the four desks that were crammed in. She sat at her desk and rolled out her stiff shoulders, ten circles forward, ten circles back. She wiped down the surfaces even though she'd wiped them before she left the day before, turned on the heating, and prepared tea. Next door was an equally dingy room for the director. Being closest to the corridor, Mi Hee had the pleasure of hearing the constant grumble of his voice from morning until evening.

The morning passed by without much irregularity: illegitimates, third or fourth daughters, twins. Some coming, some going.

'The usual,' Dong-ho, who sat opposite Mi Hee, sighed.

At noon, the others got up.

'We're heading for seolleungtang for lunch,' Dong-ho offered.

Director Shim popped his head around the door. His face was swarthy, with pockmarks on his cheeks so deep he could smuggle diamonds. 'I need one of you to stay behind and help me with this case that's just come in.'

Mi Hee smiled apologetically at Dong-ho and rose, following the director to his office. There was a woman around Mi Hee's mother's age, in corduroy leggings and a blue windbreaker, sitting on his beat-up leather sofa. Her posture was queenly. Her face and hands were a dusky pink, and Mi Hee pictured her intimately, in her pyjamas at home, rubbing cold cream into her cheeks, falling asleep with the terebi on. In the crook of her arm was an apple-cheeked baby. The woman was surely too old to be the baby's mother.

'His name is Yohan,' the woman said.

She didn't offer a surname.

'The problem is,' Director Shim began shaking his head, 'we don't usually take newborns. They need to go to one of our foster homes to be nursed, and it's complicated. But I'm sure we can work it out.'

Mi Hee's eyebrow jerked involuntarily.

'Yes. Please. Just for a few weeks.'

Mi Hee occasionally padded the numbers. She had always excelled at arithmetic and was the only one who could look over the accounts without punching into a calculator. The more children they homed, the more government relief and private donations they received. The more money the orphanage had, the more likely families were to entrust their children to its care. Round and round it went, everything getting larger. An intricate ecosystem like a spider's web – each strand wispy and translucent but, zoomed out, a sophisticated structure. It made Mi Hee feel soggy. She stopped listening when the director wheeled out his rehearsed monologue about his *suggestions for the best interests of the child*. As the older woman handed the baby over to her, she smiled hopefully at Mi Hee with earnest, kind eyes.

'I will see you soon, little one.' She tapped the baby boy's nose with the pad of her finger. The woman radiated wholly, molecularly, with love for the child. She lingered for another breath, then pulled away as if an almighty magnet were tearing them apart. Mi Hee felt the same rotten sensation in her teeth that she had been working so hard to brush away. This child slotted into a real family. His fingernails and gums were grown inside a real woman. His contours were the perfect genetic mixture of two people. Her chest was expanding and contracting at once as she carried Yohan out of the office, down the corridor, towards the nursery.

He smushed his open, toothless mouth against her breast, yowling slightly, searching for a nipple and comfort. A baby boy, who knew nothing in this world besides the oblivion of his mother's hot skin overlapping with his. A sharp striking between Mi Hee's ribs. It was the good kind of pain; the kind that made the heart matter.

Hana
하 나

Hana stood on the wooden outdoor platform, overlooking the yard, wondering where her mother had got to with her baby. Youngja had developed a routine of taking Yohan out for fresh air at dawn, but it was gone noon and she still hadn't returned. The day was dead flat, breakable, with no distraction of wind or rain. Hana chewed her lip to bleeding point. Metallic cold was travelling up her shins and staining across her thighs, but she didn't go inside. She had a bizarre, restless scratching within her skin. For the rest of her life, she would be able to recall this precise feeling: the descent of twenty circling wasps; empty clusters of holes left behind by termites; lesions of cold sores breaking open on a lip. A threatening central discomfort she couldn't ignore.

Each day since giving birth, Hana was a fraction stronger. Peeing no longer felt like squeezing out barbed wire, her haemorrhoids were shrinking, her blood clots were smaller. She hadn't yet left the house; she wasn't ready for them both to exist in the daylight.

One a.m. The sky a dropped, black cloth.

Three-twenty a.m. Quick-footed wind rattling doors.

Five-fifty a.m. Chalky smudgings of morning.

Hana mad with exhaustion. Yohan suckling his way to milk nirvana. The slope of his nose! The crinkles and folds of his lips! Eyelashes! Would it ever not be a marvel to her that she grew a person with his own eyelashes, which fanned in an elegant semicircle? He was the Fibonacci spiral, the flowering of an artichoke, oozing golden honeycomb. Pure mathematical perfection. The space between the highest cloud in the sky and the final atom in the core of the earth wasn't enough to hold this new kind of love occupying her chest. She was the first person to know a sensation this colossal, an invention she had discovered all by herself. Those moments of stillness, just the two of them, mother and swaddled child, holding each other in the night, she knew he was an imperative to her. It didn't matter that she wouldn't finish school, or that it would be at least a year before she could see John again. None of it mattered. You, her body spoke to her child, I exist for you. She was his creator, but somehow she needed him more.

Six months ago, in the office where it all began, she took John's wide hand and placed it on her stomach. It took him a minute. But when John's face finally curved into one of his full-watt, crescent-moon smiles, pleasure spread through her body. She hadn't been anxious about the pregnancy. If anything, she was enchanted. There would be a baby, made of her and John; of course they would be together for ever now. What could possibly stop them? She would birth the baby, and the baby would birth her life anew. She felt true possession. The thought was so toweringly vibrant that she had to bite the inside of her cheek to contain herself.

They spent the rest of the evening in an astonished whisper. Mapping plans, plotting, giddy with the promise of a real future that had just cleaved open.

The next day, however, John's excitement took on a tarnish. He wouldn't meet her eye during breakfast, sitting instead with his back to her.

'I spoke to Mitch,' he said, when they met that evening. 'He's making arrangements.'

She heard arrangements for the three of them. He meant arrangements for himself. Less than a week later, he was packed, and Hana was still waiting on news. His hand roughly cupped her face. He said he had to leave, for her sake and for Mitch's. What they'd done was technically illegal in his state. Though he wouldn't allow anyone to suggest anything improper about their love. He couldn't bring himself to sully all of Mitch's efforts in Korea, nor could he return from a mission with an underage, pregnant bride. Immigration issues and something about statues she didn't quite understand. All valid reasons, she was sure. He'd looked straight into her soul and promised he'd come back to get them. When they held each other for the final time, their child vaulting in her belly between them, she'd whispered into his chest, 'Stay, stay, please stay.'

Because what she really meant was too pitiful for even her to bear: *Please don't leave me here.*

Hana heard the rustling of the bushes before she saw Youngja emerge from the path.

'Where have you been?' Hana called, holding out her arms. Youngja didn't reply, calmly replacing the latch on the gate. Youngja's coat was unzipped, her chest empty, face steeled, the lines around her mouth two deep troughs. An angry number eleven between her eyebrows. Shards of panic arrowed into Hana's chest. Her heartbeat spasming. The walk from the gate to the house was hideously slow.

'You have to leave,' Youngja said.

'What? Where's Yohan?'

'I've made arrangements for the baby to stay in the orphanage in Bukcheon,' Youngja said, without fuss. She didn't meet Hana's eye. 'That should give you some time to find a job in the city, and somewhere to live.'

'Why are you—'

'You have to leave by morning.'

'Where in Bukcheon? I'm going there now.'

'Leave him.' Youngja's voice impenetrable. Hana laughed in shock, but her panic was rising. A terrifying, irrational screaming inside her.

'You're crazy,' Hana muttered. This was just a menopausal mood-swing on her mother's part.

Youngja gripped the corner of her elbow. 'No, you are. What did you think would happen? That you would be able to keep your bastard here?'

Hana's eyes flared. Who was this woman? Not the doting grandmother who left this morning. Hana searched her mother's face for a sign of levity. An exercise in discipline that would soon be over.

'I said I need *you* to leave,' Youngja hissed. Hana was certain that her mother's tongue had forked. 'He stays where he is.'

'I don't understand.'

'Ya! Why do I need to explain this to you? We have to open to guests again soon. Where will a baby go? Who will take care of him? The guests will complain if a crying baby wakes them ten times in the night. We are a respectable family and you ruined that. Good people we have lived our whole lives next to will turn against us. It's unacceptable. Grow up. If you want to be a mother, then act like a parent. Go to the city, get a job. Support your child from there. Then, we can plan.'

With the distance of a generation, Youngja had the clear sight and logic that Hana lacked. But the thought of leaving Yohan behind, and going (where, she didn't know), made Hana's insides do deranged things. It stretched her to a new limit. Motherhood roared waves in her ears. Motherhood, an unrepayable debt of devotion. Motherhood a starch, keeping a woman rigid and constantly alert. Youngja nodded at her. There it was. That glimmer of concern, vulnerable meat under the shell. They packed together. All of Hana's things fitted into a small bag, and when her mother wasn't looking, Hana slipped her notebook in. A whirl of primitive reactions, all lacking shape and decision. The silence rolled off their shoulders, dropping into the dark ocean that now existed between them. Neither of them realised then how far from the shore they would drift.

Hana loitered outside, rapping the door repeatedly, until Sora finally appeared.

'Why are you turning up here like a bad smell?' Sora was ready to fight. Hana had stopped visiting when she fell pregnant. Stopped returning calls. When Sora came round to the minbak asking after Hana, she pretended she wasn't in. When, of course, she was always in.

'Sora-ya,' Hana began, feebly.

'Muh? You think you can ignore me for months?'

'Please, I need to talk to you.'

'What is it? You're too busy for me? How can a minbak girl be that busy? I have school, hagwon, university applications, you have none of that, but where were you?'

She decided on the spot to trust Sora. There was every risk she would turn away, run back into the house, tell her mother, who might spread the news of the baby around the town like wildfire. Hana placed her right hand on her still spheric abdomen. It took Sora a few seconds, too busy ranting about Hana's loyalties, for her eyes to land on the sloping shell. Sora's mouth gaped. She hustled Hana around the corner, out of the kitchen window's view. Hana was right to trust her. 'What have you done?'

'My mum gave me enough money for a bus ticket and a few weeks' rent.' Hana crumpled into her friend. 'Will you help me find somewhere to stay in Seoul?'

Sora's older sister, Soyeon Unni, was a bitch. Hana had always thought so. She used to call the friends losers for only hanging out with each other, and toyed with Sora like a puppet, enjoying the influence she wielded over her baby sister. But when she opened the door, sour-faced as usual, Hana had never been so relieved.

It took four hours of wandering lost through wet streets. Crowds bumped Hana's shoulder. Her breasts becoming heavier and more painful as the day wore on, until she had to keep one arm shelved under her chest to support them. Flashes of John taking her hand through the streets glitched around her. Smells of cigarette smoke, diesel, frying oil, muggy rain. All Hana had was a slip of paper with an address scrawled across it, along with the closest subway station and *green – line 2*. Hana was not a city girl. She dropped coins buying a subway ticket, then winced as her stomach folded in on itself as she bent down. There was a dampness between her legs and the specific smell of blood. Despite pushing a child out of herself, she still felt too embarrassed to go into a pharmacy to ask for liners, so instead stuffed her underwear with paper in the bus-station toilet, hoping it wouldn't seep through her trousers.

She unfolded the scrap of paper to show train operators and stall ajummas the address Sora had given her. They pointed in different directions. Each greying apartment block was identical to the five other greying apartment blocks that surrounded it, like a forest of tall concrete trees. When she found the right building, it was another maze to find the correct apartment among its thirty floors. In a final insult, the elevator was out of service. By the time Hana knocked on the door, she was slumped ragged against the corridor. Soyeon Unni's eyes settled on Hana's left breast, twice the size of the right and stiff as a rock, surrounded by an undignified, circular stain.

Sora had told Hana, in hushed tones, that her sister had moved to the city after being expelled from teacher training school. She didn't say what for. There was another woman, Hyuna Unni, in the apartment. Soyeon Unni boiled water and soaked two rags for Hana's now engorged ducts, scalding herself on the kettle. Hyuna Unni raced over and tenderly led her hand under running water. Hana had to blink her surprise away when she thought she saw Hyuna Unni pull the other woman's reddened finger to her lips and pucker against it. She'd never seen anything like it. In that moment, when the longing for her baby was a bottomless pit straight through her, the care between them was too much. Hana sat cross-legged on the spongy floor. As she compressed her nipples with the warm rags, sorrow twisted itself inside her. Her breath kept stopping short in her chest. She curled over the bowl. The two women didn't try to comfort. They both knew that doing so would be pointless.

Ada
에이다

His name was Michael Bauer and Ada lay awake at night, listening to his creaks through the ceiling, imagining his body turning over in her bed. Her duvet between his legs. Ever since their encounter in the rain, she'd become constantly aware of his presence like a toothache. In the mornings, she kept an ear out for his tread coming down the stairs, upon which she'd casually emerge into the hallway, orchestrating a seamless accidentally-on-purpose run-in, while the roots of her hair flushed hot. Michael quickly became a precious solace for Ada. It was a new thing.

Monday morning. Ada sleep-walked to the bus stop, mentally ticking through her tasks and chores that got Youngja through the day. She had to be the pin that held it together. The gap between the house and the bus stop was the hardest, Youngja's eyes trailing Ada as she left the room, like a puppy who didn't understand.

'Careful!' A pair of hands gripped her biceps, fingers flexing into her puffer coat.

In her grogginess, Ada had almost collided with a man at the stop. Michael. Clean-shaven, smooth like a nectarine.

'Oh,' she backed away from him, 'hi.'

'Help a guy out.' He showed her the bus timetable. She was keenly aware that their shoulders were touching. 'Does this go through Kingston?'

'Yeah, it does,' Ada replied, dismayed that they would be catching the same bus. Particularly cruel that her precious moments of fantasy would be ruined with something as drudging as a commute. She considered missing this bus and catching the next, but she'd be late for her first class.

They stood facing the wind head-on, accompanied by a silence as natural as a frog in cowboy boots. Other dreary, white-faced commuters slowly multiplied, until the pavement crowded into the gutter and Ada had no choice but to shuffle closer to Michael.

'Listen,' she began, 'I'm sorry about the other day.' She pointed over her shoulder. 'In the rain. My grandma, she gets confused – I don't know what that was about—'

He raised both hands. 'No worries.' An empty beat. 'You take care of her?'

'Try to,' Ada said, tucking her chin into the collar of her puffer.

'That's . . .' he looked into the street '. . . a lot.'

Ada cringed. She imagined the stress smeared all over her face. Then saw the pity painted over his. Before she could respond, the crimson bus pulled up, splashing gutter water over both their shoes. They jumped away, and Michael grabbed Ada's forearm to steady her, before immediately dropping it like a hot iron. He gestured at the open bus door with flattened lips in a *ladies first* fashion. She tapped her Oyster card, triggering the triple jingle of her under-sixteen pass. Mortifying. As more commuters sardined on, Ada and Michael became increasingly condensed into the luggage stowage. The bus was like a vacuum-sealed bag. Up close, his face was delicately structural, with a pointy nose, ending in a triangle chin. Slowly, they made small talk. What about? That guy looks like he's murdered at least five people, don't you think? Why else does his backpack have so many pockets if not to carry supplies? Fifteen (nearly sixteen!), fatherless. Twenty, transfer student from USC, Economics.

'My mum will, like, freak out if she knows I'm talking to a guest outside the house,' she whispered.

Michael mimed zipping his lips shut. The bus approached Richmond Girls'. The forty minutes had never passed faster.

'This is me,' she said, wistfulness seeping into her voice.

'Have a good one.' Michael smiled, raising a fist to chest level. Ada giggled, then fist-bumped him back.

Another week at school. Girls armed with highlighters, schedules, files, ready to tackle the most important thing in the world – upcoming exams – with full vigour. The first four periods, as other students homed into their textbooks with laser focus, Ada was untethered like a balloon escaping far away. In her world of secret-keepers and pretenders, what did anything matter? She drifted from class to class, before ending up in the common room at break time, gormlessly biting into a stale cereal bar.

Clarissa ambled up behind Ada and tugged on her ponytail. 'Who is he?'

She swung around.

'Who?' Ada squeaked.

'Oh shit, OK,' Clarissa giggled. She brought her index finger to her lips. 'Shhh.'

She crouched to Ada's chair level until the curtain of her hair hid both their faces. Her breath smelled like sugar, and her tongue was unnaturally red, as if she'd just had a lollipop. 'The guy I saw you with. On the bus.'

'Yeah.'

'The tall guy.'

'Oh.' Ada feigned disinterest. 'That's just Michael.'

'Who's Michael? He's really fit. For an Asian.'

'He's twenty,' Ada said. Then straight away regretted it.

Clarissa cocked her head back. 'Why won't you tell me how you know him?' She fluttered her eyelashes. 'Don't you trust me?'

'Err . . .' Ada stuttered. How could she explain how she knew him, without explaining the minbak? And how could she explain the minbak without admitting that she'd lied about her dad?

'I won't care if you're in a thing with him?' Clarissa said.

Ada looked away to hide the internal panic, which Clarissa took as reluctance.

'You *are* in a thing with him, aren't you?' Clarissa was palpably fizzing.

It was just so easy for Ada to say, 'Yeah.'

At least easier to say than, *Michael is a lodger who lives with us. Not quite a lodger, even. A client? Not in a sleazy way. A guest? But he lives with us, sleeps in my bed and my mum cooks and cleans up after him. Along with a bunch of other randoms who are living with us at any given time. Why are they there? Well, my dad died. Yes, I know I failed to mention that before. Anyway, go with me, turns out we have no money without him. So we have to rent our house out. Yes, I know your mum is an ad executive, but mine isn't.*

This is what she knows how to do. Oh, and to accommodate said strangers, I share a bed with my mum and grandmother. Yep, all three of us in one room. On the floor.

Clarissa gripped Ada's chair and rocked it until the back legs lifted. Ada's arms flew out to her sides to steady herself.

'Oh my God!' Clarissa hissed. 'Boyfriend–girlfriend?'

'Yeah.'

'This is *huge*! Who knew silent little Ada was such a dark horse.' She sat across Ada's lap, shuffling the round of her bum to balance on Ada's knees, giving her the full light of her glamorous, blonde attention. 'Tell me everything.'

'Where do I even start?' Ada pondered.

'How far have you gone? Have you done It yet?' She glanced at Ada. 'Oh my God, you *have*, haven't you! The quiet ones are always the filthiest.'

Ada backtracked. This was mutating too quickly. 'No, we haven't.' Then added, 'Yet.'

'How did you meet?'

Clarissa was schoolgirl catnip, spurring Ada on. She wanted to hold attention, to keep this delight and distraction around her.

'He's a family friend.' She tried to be vague. Where else would she, without any older brothers or a job, have met a twenty-year-old man? 'I've known him for ever, which is why it has to be a secret. My mum cannot find out.'

Clarissa pinched two fingers together and did a kitsch salute, then asked, 'How long has this been going on?'

'Not long.' A pause. 'Maybe a few weeks.'

'Gosh, it's all so romantic.' Clarissa clutched her hand to her chest. 'Ugh, you must be so, so happy.'

As Clarissa spoke, Ada *did* feel happier. It was intoxicating.

'He says he's never felt about anyone how he feels about me,' Ada found herself gushing.

Clarissa released an expired squeak, like Princess Peach. 'Has he dropped the L bomb?'

'Not yet. I definitely love him. But I'd never say it first.'

'Definitely not. God, I'm so jealous!'

Clarissa was envious of Ada. Unbelievable. She was soaring, untouchable. She couldn't help the smile creeping across her face.

Clarissa nudged her elbow. 'You're such a smitten kitten.'

'You have to promise not to tell anyone.' Ada gripped the edge of Clarissa's jumper, understanding that Clarissa saw information as power, and more so if told in confidence. Ada wouldn't deny her the pleasure.

'Obvs.' She rolled her eyes. 'Don't want your boyfriend getting arrested or something. So, Ada, you're into men not boys!'

'I guess.'

'When's your birthday?'

'June.'

'OK.' She tapped her lip, as if this was all part of her master plan. 'Not long to go until you're sixteen and freeeee.'

Clarissa bounced up, pulling Ada off the chair. She started spinning, holding both Ada's hands. Twirling and twirling like it was just the two of them in a sunflower field, frolicking on life itself.

Mitchell
미첼

More of the same for Mitch Murray. Which was the point. Consistency and unity were half the battle of collective action. In January 1986, Mitch was in the upstairs rooms of the mission home he had recently moved into, near the Banwol Industrial Complex in Ansan. Illuminated by the yellow splay from a lone lamp and the diffused smell from a basket of oranges gifted by a local pastor, he jotted down the month's schedule for night classes. Outside, the wind wheezed. He had eight house visits to make, calling on the families of workers who had been arrested and imprisoned for striking, passing on funds to support the prisoners' wives with food and school fees. And, later in the evening, he would descend to the basement of the house, with a tray of food and some books, where he was sheltering two students wanted by the authorities for 'orchestrating insurrection'.

He had to be careful. Being an American only shielded a person for so long. Twenty years ago, when he first arrived, Mitch had found the KCIA's rudimentary investigations into him rather clumsy. Plain-clothed operatives stood on their tippytoes, craning through windows, or pressing their ears to walls, during his English classes or sermons. Somewhere in the early seventies, as the dictatorship solidified, the KCIA sharpened to a razor's edge, unzipping peace with the usual tools: terror, suspicion, intimidation. Informants flooded into universities, schools, churches, factories, the civil service. Tanks and armed soldiers in position on every street. Soldiers clashed with protestors and came face-to-face with their brothers. Civil rights went down in a sinking wreck. The climate of paranoia made Mitch feel suffocated, like wearing a winter coat in the height of August.

This evolved KCIA was an entirely different beast, inspired by the doctrines of a virus or a cancer. Invasive, self-replicating, internally corrosive. Mitch was being followed. A plain-clothes agent tailed him every place he went. Mitch considered himself to have a fairly robust composition, but even his stomach churned when he began to notice wordless black-jackets slotting into his open prayer meetings, collecting names. Perceived troublemakers were abducted early morning by black Jeeps, taken for a ride to Namsan. Four or five days later, they'd be spat out at the same street corner, markedly changed. Mitch, along with everyone else, would notice their distinctive silence and withdrawn countenance. They flinched if the fabric of Mitch's jacket brushed against theirs. Rumours of torture whispered. Fear became allies with submission. Mitch's gut churned and, some nights, he had to remind himself through deep, measured breaths that the workers reflected to the truest of senses the image of Christ; Jesus and his disciples sided with the oppressed, bold in the face of persecution. Humbled by their sacrifice, Mitch believed it was his duty as a follower of Christ to stand in solidarity with the resistance.

★

Mitch was born in Pennsylvania, where his father, Angus, was a foreman at one of the country's largest steel mills. He was a quiet, observant boy. Before he could recite the alphabet, he knew angles and proportions, able to peer at a bridge with X-ray vision, understanding its skeleton. He grew up around union men, sitting on Angus's lap in barber shops, or playing with the till at the post office where his mother worked. There was a certain malaise that came with being a skilled labourer forced out of production, out-priced by Korean cheap steel and even cheaper labour. ('I mean, what the hell can you make of a country whose national dish is rotten cabbage?' Angus had ranted.) A salaryman could be laid off, an office worker made redundant. It wasn't the same. Angus had a skill he'd honed for more than half his life. He could walk the streets of any city and know it couldn't have been built without people like him. One by one, plants closed their doors, leaving behind an entire generation of workers, and their sprawling cities to rust. His father worked odd jobs: a month at a sawmill; bricklaying. Six days a week, hard labour, and the taste of austerity. And his mom still left. Mitch quickly turned into a man standing tiptoe in a boy's body.

Mitch carried the Steel Belt with him everywhere he went. He saw his father's blackhead-ridden, oaky face every day, hoped to make him proud with his work. He knew that labour wasn't some inanimate tool; it was indivisible from bodies and minds, from a human cost.

'There's someone here to see you.' So-Hyun Kim, a colleague, came up the stairs. She had such a petite frame and subtle nature that it was difficult to believe she was once a union leader. She had been arrested for coordinating a strike for equal pay at the women's garment factory and imprisoned for ten months. Upon her release, she was blacklisted from working again. Mitch glanced at his watch as his stomach rumbled. He was hungry, and it was for these brief moments that he wished he had someone who cared after the fullness of his belly. He'd never been in love, nor, as far as he was aware, had anyone been in love with him. Mitch had long learned to skirt away from primitive feelings. Love, like his father's pride, like his mother's sadness, seemed like something that entirely took over one's life.

'It took me eight weeks to find you.' A woman's voice pierced his thoughts.

Mitch nearly tripped on the final step as he caught sight of his visitor, standing in front of him, in a black wool coat over a denim house dress. Her hands patiently clasped at her belly. He immediately felt admonished by her presence, couldn't meet her eye. It hadn't been his best behaviour to have left her minbak so abruptly, when the family were reliant on the income from their lodging.

'Samonim,' he stuttered. 'It's nice to see you again. Please, sit. Would you like some tea?'

She didn't respond, but did take a seat on one of the foldable picnic chairs. There was something about an older Korean ajumma that made Mitch feel boyish. They carried themselves with such indomitable pride and straight-backed righteousness that gave him the distinct feeling of being caught elbow-deep in the cookie jar, at his ripe age of forty-three.

'To what do I owe this pleasure?' he asked.

She seemed stunned by the question, air sucked from her face, before croaking, 'A boy.'

Mitch sieved his mind quickly. He didn't want to make any

assumptions; that was a surefire way to accidentally insult a Korean. The power of implication was the hardest thing to negotiate about how Koreans communicated. Everything you said and did to a person came with a corollary suggestion about how you perceived them. An excessive housewarming present, for example, suggested that you were trying to throw your weight around. A stingy present, on the other hand, would signal that you looked down on the new home. And with offence taken so silently, it was impossible to tell where you had specifically gone wrong or why. Maybe a boy in her town needed assistance from the mission? Finally, he said, 'Excuse me?'

'He's nine weeks old now.' Perhaps it was clear to Youngja that he didn't have any idea what she was talking about because she gulped, then added, 'The other sonnim – John.' His name seemed to taste sour to her. 'And my daughter, Hana.'

It fell into position. Mitch put his head in his hands. Dizzy. He should have known. John had come to him a few months earlier and said he had fallen in love with a girl. That he was in too deep. Mitch hadn't wanted John to name names. He quickly arranged for John to return to the States. He was naive enough to think it was nothing more than a flirtation that would fizzle away once they were separated. It had never crossed his mind to think that he'd gotten a girl pregnant. He felt embarrassingly frigid.

'I'm so sorry,' was all Mitch could say. The woman's eyes were red-rimmed and tired as if men like him had thieved her of a decade of sleeping soundly. He supposed she had the right to look at him that way.

'My daughter thinks the father will return for her and the baby.' She was so calm and straightforward. 'I need you to contact him and find out if he is planning to,' she said, her voice sinking. 'In Korea, a child that is not recognised by his or her father is left hanging in the air. He has no hope for a future. Neither does the mother.'

Mitch didn't know what to say. There was one enormous problem and she went by Lori. She was a nice, if a bit dull, girl John had given a modest ring to before coming to Korea. Mitch had rushed John back to her when he admitted he had feelings for someone else. He had made a commitment to a woman, and it was only right to see it through. Shit, Mitch thought, this was heavy. No Christian way of putting it. All the blood in his body rushed to his ears. His face pulled into an uncomfortable expression, and being a woman gifted with noonchi, Youngja understood.

'I thought not.' She nodded discreetly. She quickly organised herself, gathering her bag and standing up.

Mitch's chair screeched as he too stood. It was impossible that a barely five-foot tawny Korean woman resembled his long-necked, redhead mother. And yet the two women shared a cloudiness. Dulled by the persistent knocks and scrapes of life but with the same exacting pride. Angus and Claire Murray. Present for such a small part of their son's life yet reared their heads in the most surprising moments.

'How can I help?' he said.

Youngja looked at him, face leaden. It would be fair if she didn't trust him and he hated John for tarnishing his reputation, which Mitch had always treated as his personal currency.

She considered as if taking him up on a deal. 'Can I make one request of you?'

Hana
하나

Eight weeks in Seoul, and Hana was still one raw nerve. Time lumbered, hot and sticky. She stopped caring about others.

The old Hana might have offered her bus seat for a pregnant woman. She once might have stopped to check if the halmoni labouring up the hill laden with bags needed a hand. She might have helped a young hostess get away from the disorderly businessman coaxing her into an alleyway. But now, her care was a non-renewable, finite resource, which she didn't plan on wasting. She sustained herself with dried scraps of rice, softened in water. She became quick, mine-sweeping discarded strips of meat on outdoor barbecue tables before waiters noticed. She offloaded her fear onto the pages of her notebook and ran her fingers over John's writing – *To my wild one* – when she doubted his return. Her body continued to produce for the child it had grown. If she held her breath, and squeezed her core really, really tight, it stopped the trembling for a few seconds.

Hana got a job as an assistant in an international language school. Teaching Korean to American kids, and English to

Korean kids. Children of diplomats and high-ranking civil servants. The principal thought she would be a good influence on the children uprooted from their lives after she recounted tutoring a missionary in her town. Hana the pious. Hana the reliable. She refused to visit the orphanage. The thought of seeing Yohan in there made her feel a sort of sensory violence. He would tug the threads she'd so carefully woven and this new life she was forging for them might all unravel, leaving her with nothing but a pool of tangled yarn on the ground. But she did call occasionally, speaking with a kind unni called Mi Hee who gave her brief and discreet updates. It wouldn't be long now.

On her walk to and from work, the streets palpably thrummed to the beat of young people meeting and coming together, energy elastic and building, fenced in by riot police in full combat gear. Quick, coordinated efforts to roll out posters that were torn down minutes later. DOWN WITH THE DICTATOR, CHUN DOO-HWAN. Chants rang out, THE REGIME IS ANTI-NATION, ANTI-PEOPLE. Short-lived like stars, burning bright, combusting. If she'd had the chance, in another life would she be there with them? Other futures, other paths, other possibilities, other pains, wandering out there like ghosts. By the way Hana's nose twitched like a bloodhound's, she could tell in which direction that day's protest was. Sometimes, she would have to duck into a convenience store and rub her palms into her eyes.

'Don't rub, it will make it worse. Your eyes will naturally wash it out.' The ajumma behind the counter muttered, restacking tissue packets by the till, 'The richest woman in Korea; her company's only product?'

Hana shook her head.

'Tear gas.'

★

The three women pooled their earnings and found food like they found each other. Soyeon Unni's family – Sora's family – had told her never to return home if she planned to continue her abhorrent lifestyle. The story they crafted over two bottles of makgeolli on a Saturday night was that the baby was Soyeon Unni's son. She had the most transient job as a waitress, with the fewest background checks and documentation. Whenever she started at a new restaurant, she'd say her husband was away on business. A travelling salesman or something plausible, that wouldn't invite questions or interest. Soyeon Unni and Hyuna Unni both had male friends who were like them and were willing to pose as Soyeon Unni's husband, because they needed her to return the favour every now and then.

Hana would be Soyeon Unni's little sister as they had the same regional accent, and Hyuna Unni a cousin. The landlord was illegally subletting so didn't put anything into paperwork anyway, nor did he bother to run the women's identity cards, but if anyone asked, they were conveniently all Parks. As for the issue of Yohan's paperwork, it was a risk to keep him unregistered. If he needed urgent medical care, or something happened to the women, there'd be no record of him. Not to mention it was illegal. But it would only become a major problem when he started school and they'd long be in America by then. They'd just have to carefully ride out the interim.

They agreed to coordinate schedules so that there would always be someone at home with the baby. In exchange, Hana would pay more towards rent and living expenses. It was naturally to be a closely guarded secret from the school that Hana had a child. Though they never spoke of it, because they hadn't wanted any suggestion of leverage over each other, it was understood that Soyeon Unni and Hyuna Unni would protect Hana's secret, as long as she protected theirs.

They moved into an apartment in Seongsu. Four floors up, with green streaks of damp trailing the walls. The old tenants left rubber rods out the windows to hang laundry along. The corridor leading to the apartment was unfinished concrete, so jagged it would tear any jacket that brushed against it. They spent five days cleaning the place, taking bowls of steam to the nicotine-stained walls, flossing out mouse droppings with cardboard strips in the space between the baseboards and the floor. Hyuna Unni had been stealthily stealing square face towels from the bathhouse she worked at, which she boiled and hung out the window to prepare for burping. They cleaned and cleaned until their knees were raw, their cuticles fried, pride in their house of exiles leaped.

It was all coming together when Hana had that strange intuition again. Something in her orbit was lilting off-centre. A murmur, steamy and black, tapped her on the shoulder. The last time she felt this scuffle of unease, Youngja had come home without Yohan, having left him in the orphanage. It couldn't be worse than that, she told herself all morning, but those instincts refused to simmer down. The women had planned to collect Yohan in a week's time, but Hana impulsively moved towards the phone. She couldn't ignore this feeling and, besides, what was the point in delaying? She would get him today.

Running her pointer finger down the list of numbers taped next to the wall phone, she dialled the orphanage. Mi Hee answered just as Soyeon Unni rattled through the door, a giant box of nappies under her arm.

'I can be there in two hours to collect Yohan.'

'Please wait.' Mi Hee placed her on hold. Hana was telling Soyeon Unni the new plan, hand on hip, when Mi Hee squeaked back on the line.

It was too late by the time the words left Mi Hee's lips in a thin coil and spiralled through whatever lines and leads that led to the plastic telephone cradled in Hana's hand. The tragedy had already advanced. A terrible, finger-curling groan pulled from Hana's throat. It was a sound that every parent hopes never to make. The unimaginable tearing a path until devastation is writ large across their entire periphery. Metal screeching against metal. Wood cleaving in half in slow motion. A trap closing over a mammal's rump. That noise would stay howling on the breeze, tolling through the lives of all who heard it.

'독감' was the last word Soyeon Unni heard as she prised the handset from Hana, the spring cord held taut.

The flu.

Of all things, the flu.

Soyeon Unni took control.

'Why didn't you call when he first got sick?'

'I wasn't allowed to. We thought it was just a temperature.'

'Where is the body?'

'To control the spread of infection, the director insisted we cremate it.'

What kind of people are you? How dare you? We're calling the police . . .

Hana was bent over, dry-heaving. She had lost everything there was to lose.

The voice on the line said,

'I have to go.'

Hana
하나

A child died. A woman was alone with her revoked motherhood. For a long while, her spirit was tired of tethering to her body. She was simply a collection of skin and teeth and blood pumping around a doomed loop. When she managed to drag her weight to the sink – one foot in front of the other, splash face, brush teeth – she half-expected to look in the mirror and see warts, blackened teeth, a third eye. It seemed impossible that the same face was staring back at her unchanged, when everything had changed.

Yohan's life might have stopped short, but it didn't end. Not for Hana. Guilt tortured, clinging to her every ridge and dip. She shouldn't have left him there. She was his mother; surely some internal alarm should have sounded when he got sick? She should have visited. She should have fixed up her act faster. Would it have saved his life if she could tweak any of those variables? Probably not. But that didn't stop the grieving from bartering with Death. She punished herself by imagining his last hours. Sickly, congested. Arms and legs wading through air, straining against the invasion of his body, searching for comfort on that deep, evolutionary level. Hot, damp skin, and a claustrophobic smell. The thought of her son's last breath, alone, limbs relaxing in surrender, the stillness that followed, the slow seeping of warm to cold – she rammed her fists into her eyes.

She wished she could tell someone, everyone. That she and her child had existed together in this realm for a short time was surely the only context anyone who met her needed. If she were married, she would have been allowed compassion. She would have been offered gatherings, words, prayers, instead of this intolerable, interminable solitude with loss. Without photos, or even medical records, she sometimes wondered if any of it had been real. Every ink smudge, every emboss of the page of her notebook by the nib of a ballpoint, was the only breathing proof that her son had existed, once upon her memory. Not that she needed proof; Yohan tracked her like a grief-seeking missile. As she went about her life, the rest of the world indifferent, his name whistled in the breeze. He warmed her face with the sun and shaded her with his wings. Without a proper burial, what happened to the soul after the body has died? Did it have safe passage? He was too young to remember their home, and she wasn't there now anyway. If his spirit was searching for mother, how would he know where to find her?

The first of November. His birthday. With precise intervention, Hana's body shut down. Each year, on the first of November, she was unable to move, unable to lift her head from the pillow, unable to eat or drink. She lay there, in the stuffy magnolia-walled spare bedroom, listening to the current of her breath, wondering why she was still here, a heart-raw Korean in London, taking up a slot in the world, with all the ability to *become* and none of the desire to. Meanwhile, her son's irreplaceable life, his wholly unique existence, just . . . wasn't. We all got one death, and his was spent.

And Tim, and Ada? They were there. Hana intentionally, purposefully loved them. They brought her a deep, dependable tranquillity, asking for nothing other than for her to be theirs. But even the earnest love of a good man and the peal of her daughter's laughter didn't touch the sides of that cavity inside her. Hana had to give them an explanation. She said she was sad because it was the anniversary of her grandmother's death. Maybe five years into their marriage, five firsts of November, Tim sat on the edge of the bed, and said he wanted her to see someone. 'It's called PTSD.'

She rolled away. Could he just leave her alone?

It was remarkable that the same body had grown her son and her daughter, when the person occupying the body was so changed. At a wedding not long after their own, Tim glanced at the toddler flower girls and pageboys in miniature suits, meeting Hana's eye and raising his eyebrows longingly. Dread hung like a grubby smell. The thought of another pregnancy, of labour, another child, the pressure to keep them safe, alive, made Hana buzz with panic. Eventually, she had called Youngja.

'What do you mean you don't want children?' Youngja had exclaimed. It wasn't that Hana didn't want children; it was that she didn't want *any more* children. Her mother spoke as if Yohan could simply be repeated. It was insulting.

Selective amnesia was the only way they could speak.

'I'm not ready,' Hana said. How to explain depression to

a Korean who'd lived through an occupation, a world war and a civil war?

'You have found a good man and are lucky enough that he has married you. You have to give him children.'

Hana fell pregnant with Ada within two months. Betrayed by her own body for complying so readily when she herself wasn't.

The first trimester was charmed. Perhaps this wouldn't be so difficult. She dreamed nightly of a boy, which was as conclusive as a sonogram. Wonder flowered for her second son, who wouldn't be condemned to exist only in her memory. Not to replace Yohan, no one could, but to reclaim her own motherhood through. Who she could watch grow taller, his cells working harder than ever, stretch marks cracking open across his shoulders. The baby kicked like a bucking foal. *A footballer!* they'd laughed. When Tim said he thought it might be nice if they kept the sex a surprise, Hana had agreed. She launched into pregnancy with full commitment, shunning sulphate shampoos, eliminating toxic cleaning products, fish oil capsules pushing down her throat. She had to want it enough. She had to prove to the universe that this one she could protect. It was the happiest period of their marriage, wandering Mothercare, wheeling buggies around, rubbing her swollen belly.

Until the cashier cooed, 'Your first?'

The labour was going well. And then it wasn't. Hana had been adamant that there would be no drugs, no intervention, no visitors. The labour would be her space. She wouldn't make the same mistake again of trusting anyone when it came to her child. Then, she was being whisked away, midwives shouting numbers. A sharp scratch in the fold of her elbow, something pushed into her vein. *No, no, no, no, no!* she wanted to scream but an oxygen mask was strapped over her face. This was not the way she wanted it to go. Agency was the only thing she had asked for. When her second child rushed out of her, and she heard the announcing wail, it was the first time since that awful day that her sore heart came alive. She'd glimpsed the top of a head, wet film covering a cinnamon swirl of hair, and it all slotted into place. The relief was ecstatic.

But then.

What?

A girl.

Wrong, wrong, wrong. Broken spell. Sticky redness. Wailing. Beeping machines and wires stuck to skin. Buttons pushed and questions asked and nurses faffing. Adrenaline screaming. Bright whiteness. A clammy weight placed on her naked chest. All too much. *She's in shock*, the nurse murmured to Tim, *completely normal, give her a minute*. Only in complete solitude could Hana admit that she couldn't bear to look at her daughter. The newborn felt like a changeling. It was irrational, Hana knew that. She was awful. It was unfair, unforgivable, she also knew that. But it was as real as the baby herself.

The past continued to stalk Hana's present. There was one photo: Ada as a baby, in a sundress and crochet headband, sitting on a tartan picnic blanket, staring straight into the camera. Tim lying behind her, his hair sticking up like sunflower petals, Hana in the background. A reimagining of a scene that could have been.

As Ada continued to plump into her features, it became

eerie, how alike the two siblings looked. The tips of their noses, round as a marble. Their sturdy bow-shaped legs. Their identical golden cowlick. Genetics were mad. Occasionally, when Ada gurgled at Hana, it set off a strange claustrophobic tightening in her chest. History was reincarnating itself. In those moments, it hurt to look directly at her. It made her wonder, what was different now? Why this baby, and not her first? By virtue of her marriage to Tim, Ada had the right to live. Her existence legitimised by the Midas touch of a man's recognition. Hana's own motherhood elevated from unfit to appropriate. It waterlogged Hana with anger. Anger, a hiding place where she could be protected from her wheezing heart. Something that could be expelled, could relieve the festering, could find a target. She took aim and shot it straight into Youngja for putting Yohan in the orphanage in the first place, into Tim for being so agreeable and letting it get this far. Ada in the firing line, catching stray bullets.

As she inevitably surpassed her brother in age, Ada charted what Yohan *might* have been like. Ada became Hana's clock, ticking all the time Yohan lost. What was a hovering abstract before, now tallied directly against the starkest contrast. Ada went through the terrible twos, followed by threenagerhood. With every tantrum over toast that wasn't 'toasty' enough, or grapes that weren't cut the 'right' way, Hana felt convinced that Yohan would never have behaved like this and a spike of contempt shot through her. Minutes later, when Ada did something mundanely adorable like mirror the way her mum shut kitchen drawers with a hip-bump, Hana was chastened. Loathing for herself and love for her children argued with each other all day long.

★

The years turned. Life went on. So did death. Warmth was Tim's creamy pea and bacon risotto and the squares of Ada's adult teeth pushing through her pink gums. Funny, frivolous moments happened. Like when Tim rested his hand on Hana's bum in Greece and, by the evening, a gloved tan line appeared across her behind like a branding. Ada engaged herself in her favourite only-child enterprise: shoving pebbles up her nose. They spent the night giggling in A&E, snotty rocks plopping from the girl's face at random intervals. It was delightful and hilarious and Hana's son was still dead. Parallel facts.

Or so she thought. She realised when it was already too late that no two facts in life could run parallel; they had to intersect, braid together. All joys and all losses were tributaries into the present. And the point of confluence was always Ada. Hana first became awakened to it on Ada's fourth birthday. The three of them went to London Zoo. Hana hung back as Ada sat on Tim's shoulders, steering him by the hair. In the aquarium, Hana noticed Ada with her thumb in her mouth, quietly giving way to other children who happily muscled to the front for a view of the manta rays. After a few moments of blinking at the backpacks ahead of her, Ada's head dropped as she took small steps away.

'We can see the nursing sharks instead,' she smiled bravely at her parents.

Somewhere beneath the surface, Ada had learned not to inconvenience others, to always surrender. Hana inventoried herself, of how, from birth, she'd privately been disappointed by Ada. Had Ada somehow osmotically absorbed that sensation? A beehive of shame in Hana's belly. Half an hour later, in the Reptile House, Ada held Tim's hand as she reeled off facts.

'Daddy, the oldest tortoise in. the. world. is a hundred and seventy! Iguanas have an unusually long lifespan, and a third eye! Did you know snakes smell with their tongues?'

Hana was vaguely listening when her foot caught a crack in the brickwork and her ankle curved unnaturally.

'Ah!' Hana gasped as she tugged her foot out. At the sound of her mother's aggravation, Ada stopped short, mid-reptilian-trivia. Her face that was animated a moment earlier was now even and blank. Shutting herself down. Hana was suddenly aware of her carelessness. She was blowing it. She had the overwhelming urge to reinsert Ada back into her own body and start over.

'You were saying, squish?' Tim said blithely, unencumbered by the obliterating feeling of inadequacy that was travelling between mother and daughter.

For the next year, the guilt came slowly then treacherously, like a house that gradually fell into disrepair before its foundations crumbled. It became so overwhelming that Hana wanted to set fire to the pretence that she could be a decent mother and walk away from that burning building. She was a fake. An emotional traitor. Tim and Ada were better off without her. She withdrew banknotes over several weeks and packed a compact bag; she was practised in disappearing from a life. The night she planned to leave, she tiptoed into Ada's room. She picked up the penguin figurine they had bought that day at London Zoo and dropped it in her pocket. Just as she made her way downstairs and reached for the latch,

'Mummy?'

Hana stopped dead. She looked up. Her little girl's hair, already so long, and the soap-scented pyjamas she had dressed her in just a few hours ago. Hana closed her eyes. It was all over. She raced up the stairs and bundled Ada back into her arms. She was only five then, too young to remember any of it of course. But Hana would never forget. The pure, unfiltered, otherworldly devotion that arrived like a revelation. As basic and innate as an umbilical cord. She pushed her coat and bag under Ada's bed and clambered behind her small body. Pressing herself to Ada's back, Hana matched the girl's breathing. Filling her lungs, soothing, slowing, two heartbeats held close, not a hair's width between. When Ada inhaled, Hana inhaled. As the cadence of Ada's puffs calmed and grew more peaceful, contentment trickled into Hana too. She'd stay. She would match her family's breathing. She would walk in step with them. It would be a good life. It would be enough. Everything was hard. Loving and losing, before and after, remembering and forgetting, staying or leaving. But Hana finally decided to choose her hard and choose it every day. For years afterwards, she longed to return to that moment, holding Ada, nothing but instinct between them, before actions and omissions got involved.

As Ada grew into a person that was tenuously independent of her parents, Hana was happy to see so much of Tim's big-heartedness in her. It was vindicating. *See!* she wanted to scream, *I was capable all along. I am capable.* But Ada was still half of her. There was something unsightly, some unrest, tucked deep inside herself, also lingering in Ada's gene pool. The most loving thing she could do for Ada was to keep an arm's length. As Ada grew, her bond with Tim became stronger, while Hana kept the truth of herself impenetrable.

Hana watched Ada now, blowing on a spoonful of soup for her grandmother. Everything she asked of Ada she did without challenge or question. She was never cruel or unkind or petty. Hana could sometimes hardly contain her pride. She had long ago made the choice to not pass her darkness down a generation so that Ada could remain perfect, unbroken as she was.

Ada

에이다

Ada now knew for sure that her mother was a liar. At least, she wasn't telling the truth. The two were not the same thing, she was beginning to learn. Ada too was getting intimate with the art of deception. It was, for her, an act of reciprocity. She allowed Clarissa to colonise her. In return, she welcomed her own reset. 'Ada Penny' could be whoever she wanted her to be. She did not have to be refracted solely through the prism of Hana's gaze.

Lunchtime in the common room, a few days after she told Clarissa she was dating Michael. Surrounded by two Katies and two Jennys on either side like a glitchy girl band in formation, Clarissa clocked Ada and waved. She instructed Katie or Jenny to move and make space. Ada stood a little taller as she walked over, smiling apologetically as she nestled herself into the second-in-command position. Everything had changed in one interaction. It was all a dizzying rush. A blood transfusion to Ada's life, drab concerns of money and bills and grandmothers and guests fading into background.

Ada bit into the apple she'd brought in.

'A hundred and thirty,' Clarissa said.

'What?'

'Your apple.' Clarissa gestured towards it. She held two halves of a boiled egg in her hand, the yolk previously discarded. 'Only seventeen calories. And will keep you fuller for longer.'

'Oh.' Ada let the apple limply fall back into her lap.

'What's this?' Clarissa held Ada's earlobe like a page tab. 'Your ears aren't pierced?'

'I've just never gotten it done.'

'We have to change that.' Clarissa dragged Ada out of the common room, weaving through corridors until they were around the back of the canteen. Clarissa produced a neon-green Clipper from her skirt pocket. She pulled off one of her own contraband hoop earrings and ran the flame across the post. She laid her hand over Ada's and brought the apple still in Ada's fist to her own mouth. Eyes locked as she crunched into it. A chunk creaked out of the fruit like quarry stone. It was unprecedented and erotic. Clarissa held the apple chunk behind Ada's ear, before thrusting through her lobe with the earring without warning. The soft flesh yielded easily. Ada's head exploded, and she barely felt the stake driving into her other ear. Blood rushed to the fresh holes. Her skull hot. It was over in thirty special, spectacular seconds. The most fun Ada had had in months. All because she'd let Clarissa believe Michael was her boyfriend. Everything was new and fresh. Like wading into the sea at the eve of summer, when the ocean hasn't warmed up yet. Jumping in surprise as cold water licked up her body.

Let it be known that the veneer soon tarnished. Old thoughts ricocheted. It became stressful. All week, she loitered until she heard Michael come down the stairs, timing her commute with his, to ensure Clarissa or one of her rapporteurs glimpsed them together. She even surprised him once with a quick hug that was awkward for them both, but to the voyeur looked chaste and rushed. Like all daughters, she blamed her mother. She thought of the lie she had caught Hana in today, her skin tingling, and thought, *Is it any wonder? Lying with her, I've caught fleas.*

Here was what Ada realised:

As October drew to a close, the approaching date rendered Ada a squirm of anxiety, dread rising incrementally. Because each first of November, like clockwork, her mum plummeted into a sadness that enveloped the Penny household. Retreating to the spare bedroom, Hana didn't emerge until maybe the third or the fourth. The line was that Hana was upset about the anniversary of her grandmother's death. As accepted as gravity, or the earth's roundness. *Mum's . . . I don't know . . . she just needs rest*, Tim had told Ada, one hand on the steering wheel, the other funnelling maple-covered walnuts into his mouth. Tim powered onwards as if Hana was just having a nap, or down with a bug. It helped Ada to imagine her mum being away on some mythical prophecy or quest, that she'd soon return home victorious. But really, she was just upstairs. Just behind a closed door.

Sometimes, Ada pressed, agonisingly slowly, on the handle, and peeked through the chink in the door to see a bundled lump on the spare bed, a wave from shoulder to hip. Ada murmured that she'd gotten full marks in her science test, and a gold star for her history homework, hoping to rouse her mum from . . . whatever this was. The lump didn't seem to register. Ada retreated, closing the door as quietly as she'd opened it, feeling dizzied and discombobulated. Wasn't it a bit extreme to go catatonic for a grandmother that died a gazillion years ago? (Her dad's mum, also named Ada, died when Ada was seven and Tim went to her grave with M&S lilies once a year, which seemed much more reasonable.) Maybe her mum was sick? If she was, should they call a doctor? Perhaps this was the powerful workings of a period, and, if so, Ada dreaded the day her own came. Somehow, she knew not to ask her father any of these questions, and instead they pinballed around her mind all day.

That was how she learned to lean on butter. While her mum lay upstairs, a fact that went unacknowledged, Ada – around seven or eight years old – would make herself toast with a thick layer of butter for dinner. Some frozen rice zapped in the microwave with a square of butter and splash of soy sauce. She collected stray coins and toddled to the corner shop to buy pasta for twenty-nine pence, which went down quite nicely glistening in a layer of salty butter. Tim would come home late from work to find Ada alone downstairs, hair wet, teeth brushed.

'It was a fend-for-yourself night, huh?'

Then, the heaviness would lift. The family took a deep, collective breath in as Hana emerged, unchanged, in the same black trousers and variation on linen shirt. No one mentioned it. The house returned to its fragile peacetime. It bothered Ada. This grandmother was never mentioned for the remaining days of the year. They had no pictures of her. No heirlooms. No anecdotes. And then it struck Ada like an elastic band snapping: she didn't even know this woman's name.

This year brought a fundamental change. Six-thirty in the morning, the first of November, 2008. Alarm blaring. As expected, Hana physically could not get up. She was out of battery. Luckily, it was a Saturday, and the guests usually liked to sleep in, then go out for food, on the weekends. Unlike the Pennys, Youngja did not go on as if everything was normal. In the monochromatic room, Youngja lay Hana's head in her lap. Light leaked in from curtain gaps, flattening over the cream of Hana's arms. There were whispered, cobwebby dealings that seemed to comfort Hana on some innate level. It was too dark to lip-read, their voices quiet like a prayer. Youngja's back curved over Hana, private in their shadowed conference. Whatever was passing between them, it was all knowing and feeling. Grief and love. Youngja seemed in complete possession of the situation which, only now, made Tim and Ada's fumblings each year seem neglectful. By lunchtime, Hana was on her feet, still withdrawn and puffy, but her sluggish stupor that morning already taking on the oiliness of a dream.

As the afternoon sauntered in, Youngja brushed her hair, the morning's events lost to her. She'd wanted to dress herself today and no hell or high water could stop her, resulting in a zany combo of leopard-print leggings, plaid shirt, towel headband. Her hair barely touched her shoulders, sparse against her eggshell scalp. She'd keep brushing until she was stopped.

'Halmoni,' Ada said, 'that's enough for this morning.'

Youngja laughed, revealing gunmetal fillings in her molars, bringing the hairbrush into her lap. 'Who do I have to get pretty for anyway?'

Ada rolled onto her tummy, propping her elbows up and resting her chin on her palms. She just wanted to understand. To be let in.

'Halmoni, what was your mother like?' Ada began.

'She was a hard woman.'

'In what way?'

'After the war, my mother had to provide for four children. We lost one of my brothers.' Youngja kissed her teeth. 'She became a hard, hard woman.'

'But she must have been nice at times.'

'What do you know about my mother?'

Ada tried to be gentle because Youngja had clearly forgotten. 'It's the anniversary of your mother's passing today.'

Youngja looked around herself. 'Is it really the second month already? It doesn't feel cold enough.'

Ada's lips flattened. Softly, she said, 'It's the eleventh month.'

'My mother died in the second month.'

'Are you sure?'

'I remember,' Youngja asserted, almost combatively. 'My mother insisted she be buried in her ancestral grounds, and it was so cold that the soil had frozen. When my brothers and husband tried to dig the grave, the spade bounced off the ground and hit my middle brother in his shoulder. I was lucky not to be hit. My sons were being mischievous nearby, but my daughter had chickenpox at the time. I had her bound to my chest to keep her from scratching. I had to tie socks around her hands to stop her from creating scars all over her body,' she tutted.

Ada folded, cross-legged. 'Chickenpox, how awful. How old was your daughter when your mother died?'

Youngja ground her jaw as if her teeth were loose. 'She had just had her baek-il celebration a week earlier.'

One hundred days old, Ada thought. Hana was just over three months old when her grandmother died. She wasn't raised by her. She wouldn't even remember her. A chill rustled up Ada's spine.

'It was cute in a way. Everyone thought she was crying so much because of the funeral, but she was just very itchy.' Youngja laughed.

Ada's mind spun. It was so odd. Such an innocuous, pointless thing to lie about. An elaborate deception upheld for years, without any clear motive.

'Anyway, it was definitely February because we buried her just after Seollal,' Youngja continued. 'My mother-in-law scolded me because I forgot to make red-bean porridge for my husband. Can you believe it? The day I laid my ommoni to rest. That's why mothers-in-law get a bad reputation for being so awful to their son's wives.'

Ada stopped listening. Youngja's memory might be a sieve for new information, but within certain parameters, it was agile and confident. Perhaps Ada had gotten the grandmothers confused? But she distinctly remembered her mum saying her 외할머니: her maternal grandmother. Her blood ran hot. Youngja hummed. A constellation of clues was whirring around Ada's head. The notebook, Yohan, the photograph, the anniversary of a mystery woman's death.

'Did you say it was the eleventh month?' Youngja asked, curiously, her head rising like the sun over the sea.

'Yes,' Ada said. 'The first.'

Youngja flinched. Tripped in a breath. Colour, nearness and primacy flooded into her cheeks.

Ada sat up. 'Why?'

Youngja's mouth opened, then nothing came out. Her breathing grew frightened and fast. She sat gaping, pulling air in like a fish panting out of water.

'Woah, woah, it's OK, Halmoni. Stay calm,' Ada said.

'My . . .' Youngja said, 'my . . . things . . . he has my things . . . she needs it.'

'What? What things?'

Youngja's face crunched in distress.

'Who has your things?' Ada said.

Youngja's face had gone as flat and white as an orchid. 'I gave them to . . . my things! You need to tell her.'

It came to Ada, sharp as a cat's scratch. A shoebox of letters. A stack of CDs. Youngja passing them to an elderly man at Farm Lane.

Ada was the lost third generation. Trying to envision a real place, with its flora and fauna, craters and hills, from the broad strokes of an impressionist painting. Gatherer of microscopic fragments and whispers. Witness to the ache, detached from the context. Bearer of the weight of the better life. Miner of layers and voids. Who cannot have the nerve not to strive to be the best, do the most, to squander what has been given. Who are silenced because what could they possibly understand of the dignity and indignity of pain?

All Ada knew was that heartache flowed from the woman she came from and the woman who came before her, until it trickled into a girl in London, lonely and letting another girl drive holes in her ears.

Youngja
영자

What surprised Youngja the most about her emptied nest wasn't the stillness or the boredom of her busy hands. It was the number of times she benchmarked her day against her children's. Around seven a.m., it comforted her to think about Tae-Young, monotonously heading into the office. Around noon, she wondered what Tae-Jung was up to, whether he had eaten yet. Thinking of Hana, however, was like touching a live wire, the pain quick. Choosing not to think of her equally felt cheap and lazy. The air carried the brittle smell of frozen grass. It seemed fitting that the world had iced over in the three months since Hana had left for Seoul. Soon, the rains would come. She imagined washing away, turning to liquid and spilling into the gutters, seeping through the soil, formless and free.

A few days into February 1986, a strange energy snarled around Youngja. It was the feeling of being watched. She turned to see Hana labouring towards the minbak, a dangerous and slippery lack in her eyes. Dustpan and brush clattered to the ground as Youngja ran to catch Hana's falling frame.

'He got sick so quickly. I didn't get the chance to say goodbye. Do you know – how can I – Omma! Omma!' Hana wailed into Youngja's chest, clutching at her cardigan, her fingers wrapping around fabric.

'What?' Youngja stammered. She hadn't heard. Nothing made sense.

'I don't know what to do. Omma, show me what to do!'

Youngja felt as though a horse had kicked her in the chest. Her capillaries bursting in a series of tiny explosions. She willed herself to find the words to say, but they dragged, like the haul of honey. Hana's knees pressed into gravel. Youngja looked over her shoulder, still paranoid about what some curious neighbours might glean. Since Hana had left, when asked, Youngja just said that Hana had found a teaching job in the city. She was not like the other women whose mouths were like bins, collecting waste; she had a reputation for being economical with words. If they overheard Hana now, after Yohan was lost, it all would have been in vain. She hurried Hana inside.

Hana sat on the floor, hair clumped in greasy tracks, fingernails chewed to the stump. Her shoulders sloped towards each other, skin tinged pigeon grey, lifeless, as if she willed herself to join her son. Youngja called her name, urged her to change out of her travel clothes.

'Here,' she said, 'sit close to the heater, you're freezing, put this jumper on, what can I get you to eat?'

Hana did not respond. It wasn't evident whether she was breathing or seeing or hearing or there in the room at all.

Youngja closed all the windows, doors and curtains,

warming the sealed room with a space heater like a kiln. They sat in the waning light. You could tell the difference between a woman who expected pain in the ordinary course, and a child who had yet to discover this truth. For Hana, grief was, until now, an exotic, faraway thing. For Youngja, grief was an insistent harassment. To Hana, it was a small room without windows or doors. To Youngja, it was the seven seas, the sun and all of the moons. For Hana, grief clotted in giant globules, whereas it flowed through Youngja until she wondered if she was made of it. Grief ended Hana's life as she knew it, but Youngja knew all too well that it was only the beginning.

Hana started to cry. Open-mouthed in uncompromising, unstoppable pain. Youngja reached an arm around Hana's shoulders but kept her body facing away. She couldn't stand it. The two women sat in a state of emergency. Of complete absorption. Arms mingling, toes flexing, peeling open, buckling under, straining around the incommunicable and the irretrievable.

'Aga,' Youngja coaxed the next day, holding a spoon of oxtail soup in front of her daughter's lips. Since Hana didn't have the energy to chew, Youngja decided on white rice soaked in the nutrient-dense milky broth. 'You need to eat.'

Hana stared ahead.

'Just five spoonfuls.'

'His face keeps slipping away.' Hana winced. 'I can't remember my baby's face.'

'Please.' Youngja set down the spoon. 'Why are you doing this to yourself? What difference does it make now?'

Hana's face sharpened. 'My son is only a memory. The least we can do is remember him.'

Youngja said nothing. She saw a fissure in Hana and realised that her daughter considered herself above her now; her experience elevated her into a woman who knew more, felt more.

'I need to tell him.'

'Who?'

'John. How can I get hold of him? I don't know how to contact him.'

Why didn't she realise what it meant when a man left you pregnant without a phone number or an address? Youngja was almost envious of Hana's unwavering faith. What a sign of innocence it was to be able to press belief from abandonment. It made Youngja ache. She was just beginning to see the myriad of ways John had defiled the essence of her daughter.

'You mustn't tell him,' she finally said.

'What?' A shade of hesitance crept into Hana's voice. She was at that crossroad perhaps all women came to, at the cusp of knowing so much and so little at once, equally resisting and needing a mother's guidance, neither quite tipping the scale. Youngja took her opportunity.

'What will you tell him? How will you be able to recover?'

'But he's coming back for us.'

It was a defeat, seeing your child love the wrong person. Youngja looked back at her parenting. It was not the done thing for children to bring their problems to their parents. It was just not in their nature as Koreans to be effusive with their affection. Had she not openly told Hana that she was loved? Had that pushed her to fall for some man's empty declarations?

'I have something for you.' Youngja rose and left the room. In the front yard, she made sure no one was passing by on the path, and then reached under the ceramic pots. She had placed an envelope here a few days earlier, in the hope that her prodigal daughter would soon return. She went back inside and handed Hana the bulging package.

'Make sure to separate it,' Youngja said. 'Put some in your shoes, your bag, your underwear too. Keep some in plain sight. Where no one would think to look.'

Hana released its top lip. They were silent but for the scratchy rustling of paper. She gasped. 'Is this all your savings?'

Youngja didn't respond. Hana had little grasp on the finances of the minbak. Even after working in its beating heart, ensuring each limb got the resources it needed, Hana didn't actually know how much they charged per night. What the discount was for long-staying customers. What commission they paid to the factory foremen who sent workers their way.

'Omma,' Hana said again, 'what is this?'

'I've made plans for you.' Youngja pressed their foreheads together, her breath a shiver. 'Do you remember my cousin Sang-min? My second aunt's boy. You probably don't, you were very small when you met him. He moved to England. He's the one who used to send you the Toblerone bars and the yellow-haired Barbie you always carried around. I have contacted him. I have told him about your diligence, how hard-working you are, and he has got you work in a hair salon in exchange for a room in his friend's house, so you can get a visa. This money is for your flight and your first few weeks. I heard it is more expensive there—'

'Omma! Stop. I'm staying here and waiting for John.'

That was when Youngja said the irredeemable. She needed Hana to listen. She needed to get her child as far from that man's grasp as she possibly could. Later, Youngja would tell herself over and over and over again that betraying Hana was the cost of protecting her. Youngja let her voice run as cold as the Yalu River and said, 'Do you think he will forgive you?'

Hana snapped back like a trap closing.

'Who do you think you're fooling with that look? He is coming back – if he comes back – for his baby first, you second. How do you think he will react when he realises his baby is gone? Think about your father and how different he was with your brothers. Men care about their sons, it's in their psychology.'

'You think he will blame me?'

'Who will he have to blame but you?' Youngja let that sink in. 'That's why you mustn't ever go looking for him, do you hear me? You want to leave him with the happy days, not know you like this. If you really love him, you will spare him the pain.'

The blood drained from Hana's cheeks.

'Go,' Youngja pleaded and pressed the envelope firmly in her hand. 'Take this. You speak good English now. Forget about this year. Nothing good will come of remembering it.'

Hana's head moved in a tiny nod.

'Hana-ya.' Youngja would cling to this moment, because once Hana left, it would be nineteen years before she saw her again. She pulled away and gave Hana a box of tablets. 'And take this.'

'What's this for?'

Youngja wanted to grab her close. Snug their bodies together like the two halves of a walnut.

'It will stop the milk.'

Ada
에이다

Ada had never been grounded. She'd never been given a detention. She'd never been warned not to skip school or lectured on the dangers of drugs or alcohol or cigarettes or unsafe sex. She was a Good Kid. Which was why, when she coughed into her elbow and theatrically shivered, wrapping a scarf around her neck, nobody thought it might be a performance. When she asked Fräulein Meyer if she could please be excused from afternoon periods because she thought she was coming down with a bug, she was trusted without hesitation, Fräulein Meyer's hand squeezing her forearm, *I hope you feel better soon.*

A few hours stolen, to return to the Farm.

Briskly walking towards the building with her school uniform stuffed into her backpack, her mother's heavy wool blazer over her shoulders, Ada was tense, her insides spinning like a top. On the bus, she'd fished from her bag a pot of Maybelline Dream Matte Mousse and smeared it over her cheeks. She'd twisted her hair into a low bun, swiped on some lipstick. As a visitor, the Farm had seemed as idyllic as a windmill or a cottage. But now, Ada just saw a sprawling pebble-dashed building, with oddly high fences and vomit-coloured carpet. The sharp smell of disinfectant tingled her nostrils. At the reception, a dark-haired woman with alert eyes looked up. Ada fought the urge to flatten her lips into an awkward smile and apologise for bothering her. It was a mistake to come here. She caught a glimpse of her ashen, painted face in the reception glass and saw how effortful she looked in her ridiculous costume. She was overall ridiculous. When she opened her mouth to speak, a voice that wasn't hers came out.

'Hi there, I called earlier, I'm here to pick up some of my mother's things that she's misplaced,' Ada said. Inside, she fluttered with how confident she sounded. It was thrilling. 'Her name is Youngja Jang.'

'I can help you with that,' spoke a voice that had so much gravity it could be the earth.

The man ambling towards her had a head full of sheet-white hair. His back had curved like the handle of his walking stick, but from the length of his legs she could tell he was once very tall. He was the man Youngja handed the shoebox to.

He moved like an ancient turtle on a deserted beach. 'I'm afraid I don't have much speed on this engine any more.' He held out his hand. 'Graham, pleasure to meet you. Your old lady spoke about you so much I feel like I already know you. Shall we?'

He held out his arm for her, while turning over his shoulder and winking one navy eye at the receptionist, who scoffed endearingly. His touch sparkled with generosity. They serenely paced a long hallway. The walls were covered in green pinboards scattered with leaflets. There was an astringent, clinical smell that later Ada would recognise in GP waiting rooms and pharmacies and would associate forever with this day. They passed rooms each with a handful of residents, doing the paper's sudoku or watching *Countdown*. The building had a fragile quiet, like a glass box that could crack at any moment.

'My late wife Kalpana got to know Youngja first,' Graham said as he turned the handle to his room and held the door open for her. 'She never could stand seeing people alone. And thought it was an awful thing that she was here but unable to speak English.'

Of course, Youngja couldn't speak English. How terrible it must have been for her to be here and unable to connect with anyone, at a time when the rest of her world was already fading away. Hana seemed needlessly cruel.

'I'm so grateful to you both,' Ada said.

'Kalpana was the most beautiful woman I ever saw. Fell in love instantly. Saw her in the hotel lobby, tailed her for fifteen minutes before she turned around and whacked me with her handbag. Told me to either ask her out or bore off. Christ,' he chuckled, 'that woman.'

Ada listened, happy to hear the man's love of his wife.

'August fifteenth,' he announced. 'The day Youngja and Kalpana first started talking. India and Korea have the same Independence Day, though you'd already know that. Those two were inseparable after. They didn't speak much but played cards. Your mother taught her hwa-too and they were at it all day. Friends, until the end.'

He paused, then looked at her with a sad half-smile as if trying to reassure her that Youngja was all right. Ada's throat swelled. So much life lived, all whizzed past in a few seconds. She felt a pang of affection for Graham and Kalpana. She was being unfaithful to him, pretending to be someone he could trust. Before she could reply, Graham creaked at the waist and pulled out of his cupboard the box she had come for. It had become frayed at the corners in storage, and a layer of dust was smattered over the lid.

'Et voilà!' He presented the box to her. 'I believe this is what you came for. Did you want the coat and shoes as well?'

'No, no,' she patted the top of the box leaving fingerprints in the dust, 'these will help with refreshing her memory. She'll be happy to be back with her mementos.' The jumping fleas in Ada's stomach settled slightly. She was about to thank Graham for his time and race out. She wanted to rip off her disguise like an overheating costume as quickly as possible. Just as she took the box under her arm, Graham leaned forward, two fingers held her elbow.

'I know you and your mother weren't on the best of terms. Don't worry, I don't know the ins and outs,' he said. 'But I just want to say that I'm so glad you're taking care of her now.'

There it was, the canvas on which she was painted.

'It was so terrible,' she found herself saying. 'It was hard on us both.'

'My dear, of course it was. That's family. You fight, you make up.'

She huffed dramatically in the way she'd seen carpool mums do. 'I'm not sure about the making up.' Then added, 'Because she's so disoriented.'

'Ye of little faith!' Graham exclaimed. He reached for the top drawer of the writing bureau by the door and lifted something out. Ada only saw a metallic flash before it disappeared into his palm. A lighter? A lipstick? 'This will help you get there, I hope.'

He fiddled with the object between his spindly fingers. 'This took a long time, it was really draining for her. I hope Youngja is happy with it.'

Ada couldn't make out what it was until he handed it to her. A steel USB stick. Only when her body gasped for air did Ada realise she had been holding her breath.

'I don't understand,' Ada said.

Graham floated towards two wicker chairs by his window. He gestured to the chair next to him. The rattan weave stretched as she sat back into it. Between them, an empty vase. Beyond the window were the gardens below. A young family with a blond retriever on a leash were walking with their resident relative. A squirrel ruffled itself in the fountain. The padded sounds of doors closing and feet shuffling around them.

'It's a terrifying thing,' Graham said, 'losing yourself. You spend your prime fretting about material possessions, small fires. Problems that aren't problems, they all come out in the wash. And the next thing you know, you're reminiscing on the glory days.' He turned to look at her. 'Or you can't remember your own child's name. You can never say everything. Not at the end.'

His face was still and accepting, and Ada had the sense he was trying to tell her something. It was getting dark, the room tinting to navy. Ada's pulse thumped under her neck.

'Youngja still had so much to say. To you. It was bothering her so much it was making her sick.' Graham stretched his arms out and gestured to the gardens. 'Well! We have so much time here, and you can only do so many laps of the premises before you feel like a hamster on a wheel. So we decided to get it all down with our trusty old camcorder. "The Project", we called it.'

Ada held up the USB stick. 'This?'

Graham nodded.

'To be honest, even after all the time we spent together, I couldn't understand a word of Korean so I'm not sure what she was saying. Wait, let me see, an-yong-ha-seh-yo. See? And gam-sah-ham-ni-da!'

'Bravo!'

'I'm better as a supporting character anyway. I handled all the tech bits, spent a helluva lot of time on YouTube trying to figure out how to get a video from this,' he pointed to the camcorder on the windowsill, then to the USB stick in Ada's hand, 'onto that.'

Ada felt light-headed. It came back to her now. Youngja scrambling under the wardrobe, pulling out a camcorder. Ada had assumed she was just being loopy but she was ensuring her story made it to Graham before she left the Farm.

'Anyway, it took us a long time because we could only record on days she was lucid,' Graham continued, 'and even then, it was so tiring for her she'd always need a lie-down afterwards.' He paused. 'It matters. A whole lot.'

Anticipation spread over Ada's body in a hot rash. Graham faced her, his chin resting in his palm.

'We all have our stories, every single one of us.'

Youngja
영자

Graham fumbled with the Record button, which would translate to a static scratching when Ada later played it. He shot Youngja double finger guns. In the few minutes it had taken to set up, Youngja felt soupy, like a window staining with fog. Soon, she wouldn't be able to handle chopsticks or enjoy an orange segment bursting on her tongue or speak at all. So, she would try today to speak the truth. And if it didn't come, then she would try and try until she could. Not to absolve herself; she was long past that.

She closed her eyes and imagined she was talking to Hana directly. She inhaled deeply, savoured the moment, then opened her eyes, and, staring straight into the lens of the camcorder, she plunged.

'Hana-ya. If you are watching this now, it means that I am no longer with you. I'm running out of time, and I have a lot to say. I'm not sure there will ever be the right moment. I have been a coward, waiting this long.' The folds of her mind stretched and narrowed like an accordion, unsure where to begin. 'I know you have never recovered from losing your child. I pushed you to have another when you weren't ready. If you had known, maybe things might have been different.' Her breath unsteady. 'The truth isn't mine alone, it's yours too. Aga, I don't have the right to ask. But I hope you can forgive me.'

In a hospital on the first of November 1985, Youngja witnessed Hana earth a boy and name him after the man who abandoned her. Crushing. Only when she scuttled out into the car park, and slumped against a concrete pillar around the side of the maternity wing, did Youngja realise her whole body was chattering. She put her hands on her knees, head hung between her legs. Blue-and-red sirens howled. She didn't know how long she was like this, staring at the tarmac, entirely still while emergencies erupted around her. Footsteps approached.

A practical, middle-aged voice said, 'Soon, this difficult time in your lives will be behind you.'

Youngja straightened. Her eyes took a second to focus. It was the midwife. Youngja had been so busy blotting Hana's brow, holding her hand, feeding her ice chips, that she almost didn't recognise the woman. Her name tag read *Yunsook Im* and she was standing a respectful metre away.

Yunsook had a flat, open face which Youngja searched to understand what on earth she meant by 'behind you'. The child was less than thirty minutes old. The arduous road was very much ahead, not behind. Yunsook handed Youngja a business card. 'The mother is a minor. So, they only need a family member's signature.'

Youngja glanced at the card, the door to an entirely new path flung open. Her brain steaming with too much new stimuli. She stuffed it into her pocket and didn't think about it again for eight days. Not until the dawn her husband brought his pillow over a swaddle in the frosted grass. Thundering pressure in her ears. A few hours later on the same morning, her son turned away from her pleas to take in the child. By noon that day, Youngja had entered a depressing four-storey orphanage where the director – who looked like a beanpole in a suit – led her and Yohan into his office. There, Director Shim made the same suggestion Yunsook had, gesturing out the window to the neighbouring, identically drab building. Youngja had shaken her head no. Yohan would only be in the orphanage temporarily until she could scramble together a plan. Stepping back into the street, leaving Yohan behind, felt at the time like the very worst moment of her life.

The evening after she dropped her grandson at the orphanage and her daughter had left for Seoul, Youngja sat cross-legged, the business card, now frayed at the edges, on the floor in front of her. It was a preloaded gun; all she had to do was pull the trigger. She stared at it, hoping for some divine intervention or sign.

'Has she gone?' her husband interrupted.

Youngja made an animal noise.

'Where?'

'Seoul.'

'Who with?'

'Do you care?'

He had the audacity to look surprised. Youngja wanted to knock over the cabinet he was leaning on and yank him by the hair. Chase him out of the house. She wanted him to disappear.

'Don't look at me like that,' Youngja said. 'You caused this.'

'Hana caused this.'

'She's just a girl.'

'Yeo-bo,' he started but Youngja's head snapped towards him and he decided against whatever he was planning to say. How would she continue to live with this man? He finally said, 'What about the boy?'

'His name is Yohan.'

'Where is he?'

'So you can finish the job?'

He sighed. 'As long as no one finds out.'

He made towards the door, cigarette dangling in the corner of his mouth.

'I hate you,' Youngja whispered. 'I hate you for what you made me do.'

He paused between steps for only a split-second, then continued on.

She needed to find the father first. She went to the community centre the Americans had established, now being led by a local pastor and his wife. They welcomed her into a plasterboarded room that was cold, unfinished with open wires still poking out of socket holes, but clean. A shiver rushed through her as she entered the room where her Hana slowly became a stranger, not two hundred metres from home. She told the pastor that the missionaries had left behind some belongings that she would like to return to them, would he be able to provide a forwarding address?

Pastor Noh wasn't sure about the young fellow, who was a short-termer anyway, but Mitchell Murray was still in Korea, working now in Ansan. They didn't know which specific industrial estate, and he hadn't written or called yet with an address, but they'd ask around for her. With her days and nights tied to the reopened minbak, she couldn't aimlessly walk around Ansan searching for him. She had to be patient. But the idea that this man was out there, not very far away, lacing his shoes, brushing his teeth, heating soup, all the while possibly holding the keys to her child's future, was maddening. She needed to find him to confirm whether the father of the child was really planning on returning for his family. If he was, then Youngja would support Hana and Yohan until he did.

When she found Mitch, all it took was his awkward expression for her to privately understand she had been just as foolish as her daughter to hope. The father wasn't coming back. All options were lost. She had no other choice. When she got home that evening, she reached into her dresser, where she had tucked the business card next to her creams, and pulled it out.

Now, Youngja was in a deep squat, rinsing the crack-lipped pots that sat along the garden ledge. She had to refill them with gochujang and fish sauce today. Her arms trembled and her balance wasn't what it used to be. She kept scrubbing to keep her mind on her stinging cuticles and sore arms. It was baby Yohan's baek-il last week; the day yawned by without the celebrations and festivities that should have been. Youngja called the number Hana's friend Sora had sheepishly handed her on a slip of paper, then hung up before anyone answered. This happened often and Youngja wondered if Hana knew that her omma called even when she didn't have the right words to say.

If she lingered for a moment too long on Hana, the rawest

feelings sprouted through and overcame Youngja. She'd left the outdoor tap running, rainwater flushing over clay, staring at the wall, asking how Hana could have been so cruel. It was expected that girls would experiment with independence, talking back, drinking too much. And still, they never took it past the point of no return. Even the mothers Youngja knew to be constantly critical of their girls had managed to keep them close. So why her Hana, then? Was it too much to ask that she live a normal, respectable life? Youngja had tried to be a good person. A good wife, a good citizen, a good child, a good business owner, a good neighbour. A good mother. Her love for her daughter was the opposite of the sun's warmth that disappeared each day; it was the moon's faithfulness. And still, all this. There were few greater sins than bringing this much shame to one's parents.

'Samonim?' a docile voice called.

Youngja startled, dropping the clay lid in her hands. It clanged on the ground, but didn't break, instead rolling down the path before spinning to a stop. She turned off the outdoor tap. Mitch approached. Hands by his sides but flexed outwards, as if she were feral. The gochugaru in the tub next to her must have wafted towards him because he sneezed three times in quick succession.

He rubbed his palm in circles over his head, cringing. Youngja briefly thought it was a shame that his subtle face was so creased with worry. 'I've made some calls through different groups. A family in a congregation in Oregon. A young couple, Christian. No existing children.'

The rag she'd had in her hand had been compressed into a squashed ball. He had done as he had promised, when they last met in Ansan. She told him the only solution – put in her path by the midwife and the orphanage director – and Mitch had agreed. She had made only one request of him: find a family for the boy. She couldn't just let him go out into the world with all its innumerable cruelties, without knowing what kind of family he would end up with. Missionaries had access to networks that she didn't. Forces, large and omnipresent, had determined that what someone else could offer Yohan was more valuable than what they could. She had a secret need to implicate someone else, to share a portion of this extraordinary weight. Otherwise, she was sure she'd go utterly mad. To her horror, tears gathered freely. She had never in her forty-seven years cried in front of another person.

Yohan lay like a cocooned caterpillar on her lap. They were sitting in an administrative office. Youngja wondered whether the 'administration' being spoken of was that of shipping babies away. Mitch and Youngja were escorted from the orphanage to the adjacent building the director had pointed out to her when she first dropped Yohan off. Fluently, as if they were simply water running through pipes. Business as usual. She kept glancing around herself, hoping for an obstacle to slow this all down. Everything was so streamlined. When they arrived in the administrative office, she offered Yohan her finger and he unsprayed his hand wide, before curling around it. Her liver-spotted skin against his velveteen. She felt sick. Could she really do this? She had to. It was a comfort to Youngja to repeat to herself that sacrifice and sorrow, of limitless degrees, lay central to the female condition.

 She scooped the boy to her face. The fuzz on his cheeks tickled hers. His heady preciousness so close. Her chest rippled at the thought that he might never know how much they loved him. That he might grow up to think he was unwanted. What was taking them so long? They were giving Youngja so many warm and liquid minutes with him. She lowered her nose into the V of his neck and bottled his scent in her memory. She prayed she'd never forget it. He scrunched his face and opened his mouth into a gummy yawn. When he wailed, Youngja joined in. That was the last thing they did together. Mitch stepped out of the room.

The door clicked and two sombre care workers entered. One had a face like an elephant's knee, and the other looked as though he had been born in his cardigan. Utterly unremarkable. You'd pass them at market, sit next to them on the bus, and not remember their faces. They did not deserve this insurrection roiling in her chest. Youngja couldn't bear the thought of these happiness sponges taking Yohan. Instinctively, she held him closer.

'I've made a terrible mistake coming here,' she began. 'I think I have wasted your time, I'm so sorry.' She went to stand up, cradling the baby's head. The others stood side-by-side and didn't react. 'I don't think I can do this,' Youngja said, more assertive.

The cardigan said, 'Please consider this carefully.'

'I have and I—'

'What is your plan, may I ask?'

'What do you mean?'

'What do you think this baby's future will be like? Koreans will not accept him. You know that. Same for his mother; no one will hire or marry a mihonmo. How will he and your daughter live? With ridicule and rejection in every aspect of life.'

'Your hesitation is normal,' the other worker said. 'Almost everybody experiences it. But they all make the right choice in the end. He'll be taken into a nice home, a wealthy family. He will have a good education. He will grow up to be very prosperous and successful.'

They made it seem so simple. A luckless life traded for a lucky life. But it seemed obvious to Youngja that school and food and money couldn't replace a mother's cool hand on a hot forehead. Simply incommutable. Land and sea. Fire and water. In Youngja's mind came the squeal of chicks in spring, waiting in the nest. Of the neighbourhood cat, feeding her kittens. Every living being wanted to rear their young. When did humans become so preoccupied with outcome?

'This way, everyone gets a second chance,' the cardiganed worker continued. 'Your grandson will receive the gift of two loving, committed parents. Your daughter, a fresh start; no one needs to know. And most of all, you will be giving a childless couple the gift of a family.'

Youngja bristled. Her grandchild wasn't a parcel, to exchange hands and bring value. One family's fulfilment, built on another family's loss. An innocent child at the heart of this twisted, Solomonic affair.

Yohan's bottom lip suckled against her chest. The agency worker was right and she hated that. Hated that their love wasn't enough. Hated that, for him to be seen as a person in his own right, all those that came before him would be erased. This boy with the apple-red cheeks came from a real girl, who had twenty shades of nut in her hair. His mother was both a marvel and an enigma to her own mother, who was likely the same to her mother too, and so on and so forth all the way back through the generations. Youngja thought of herself, crouching among the spiky succulents on the mountain's edge, hearing guns rifling in the city below, and of her blistered shoulders as she ferried water each morning for her siblings. If it weren't for those torn shoes that padded the mountain path, or that jerry-can water carrier, this boy wouldn't be here, in her lap, in this office, in this specific fold of time. And that thought made her shiver with fear at the idea of having never known him, and envious of all the other versions of herself that didn't know the pain of losing him. They had beaten fate and chance to both be here, together on earth, and that in itself was a miracle. Now, all too soon, they had to let each other go.

In the end, Youngja couldn't manage anything besides a nod. Something was signalled between the others. They laid a piece of paper in front of her. No one said anything. It was as if the room had been muted. Her eyes scanned the paper.

> Statement of formal relinquishment. I hereby irrevocably consent to the emigration to the United States of PARK YOHAN, a minor, for the purposes of his/her adoption by suitable adoptive parents. I am hereby releasing my right to the custody and guardianship of this child.

She reached for the pen first, flipped the paper over, and scribbled a message in a desperate surge, for the boy to one day read: *Son, this is your mother's name, your father's name, your grandparents and where you were born. This is your mother's identity card number. This is our address. This is our number. Call us one day. We'll wait for you. Live well, be good to your parents, be happy. Forgive us.*

She reached for her dojang and dabbed it against the red ink-pad.

She pressed the seal to the documents. The rubber peeled away from the paper like treacle.

They lifted him from her arms. Muffled, damp words

about how he'd return to the orphanage until the immigration paperwork and medical tests were finalised.

She didn't open her eyes until she heard footsteps leave, and the door close.

A week later, Hana would return to the minbak. She would reach halfway up the path before her knees would jerk away from beneath her. Youngja would catch her in her embrace and she would howl.

'He got sick so quickly, Omma! I didn't get a chance to say goodbye! I don't know what to do. Omma, show me what to do!'

Youngja would quickly adjust her reaction. She was shocked. It was, Youngja assumed, a ruse to ensure certainty of custody. This wasn't part of the plan, but perhaps it was for the best this way, a clean cut. Sterilise Hana's past, scalpel it straight out of her story and allow her to move on, without looking back. Youngja would push the envelope of cash Mitch had delivered to her a few days after she signed the statement – his personal savings, he'd said, to help the family – into Hana's hands and beg her to use the money to go to England. She would not mention where the money had come from. As Youngja held Hana against herself, she would look beyond her shoulder into the nettle bushes in the distance, her raised vegetable beds, the storks soaring in the sky. She'd wonder if the baby boy had been safely delivered into the waiting arms of his new family.

Go well, son, Youngja would whisper behind Hana's back.

Sujin

수집

Sujin Kim was having a very long day. Not only had her mother called for the third time this month to berate her for going into 'Social work? What sort of job is *social work*? Your father already has angina!' but she had the defeated feeling that her mother was painfully right. Which, no matter your age, was the cruellest form of cosmic correction.

She hung up. She couldn't quit now. She wouldn't be able to stand their smugness. Yes, the pay was bad, especially considering how lucrative the work was, and no, it wasn't as respected as other professions that had been open to her. But money and prestige had never been atop Sujin's priorities. She knew this job wasn't right for her because she couldn't quieten the obstinate part of her brain that insisted on asking questions. It had often gotten her in trouble. At school, her English teacher taught them to say 'yes' as 'yusseu', which hadn't sat right with Sujin. She kept raising her hand, bothered by the instruction to mispronounce such a basic word. Even if she was right, to repeatedly point out a teacher was wrong? It was insubordinate and disrespectful and arrogant and violating, all wrapped into one. She was disciplined at school, and then again at home. Her mother made her kneel in the corner with her arms outstretched above her head for twenty minutes, before inviting her to come have dinner. Her mother said as they ate, 'Sujin-ah, you can't get a reputation for being unruly in class. From now on, when the teacher tells you to do something, you do it.'

'But why? He was wrong!' Sujin sniffled, vexed by a child's notions of justice and unfairness.

'Because that's the way of the world!' her mother cried out. 'Just accept things as they are. You have to do as you're told.'

All these years later, Sujin's inner questions frequently rubbed shoulders with her outer conformity. She sighed at the mound of paperwork ahead of her that seemed to multiply each time she blinked. She didn't imagine she'd still be doing menial paper-pushing at twenty-five, but she couldn't afford to stop.

'The faster you work, the less expenses are incurred, the more money we have to pay our employees,' her boss had winked. Still, the target he had set that month would require her to work at super-speed, plastering smooth intricate details in the rush. Just as she'd finished with one file, two more came in. Sometimes, he stood behind her desk, hands clasped behind his back, the pressure of his gaze watching her hand skate across the page. She felt like a racehorse. *Faster, faster, faster.* Crack, crack went the whip. The same questions kept agitating her. Why did she feel like a customs officer, processing an export, like radios, quilts or sneakers? Where was this constant supply of children coming from? And how can some of these people have so much money? Administrative fees, legal processing, visas, flights, foster homes, cash zipping through all. Each application she processed brought in, by her rough currency conversion, thousands of American dollars. She kissed her teeth when she realised that the agency made more with one case than her entire year's salary.

Sujin was recruited as a fresh graduate into the International Processing Division, and, to the envy of her colleagues, her English degree gave her a better desk next to the heater and more lenience from the director to travel home for Chuseok and Seollal. He'd approached her on campus and promised that her language capabilities made her a sought-after jewel. Though she hardly felt that way as she reached for the top of the fresh pile that had been delivered to her desk by the mail room.

Files. That's what they said. *How are you getting on with today's files? Bring me this or that file. We need to get through a lot of files this week.* So vacant and procedural Sujin almost forgot 'files' was shorthand for babies. The first had a label across the Manila front cover: Ahn Eun-ji and a paper-clipped photograph of a baby girl propped against a large cushion in a frilly dress, blinking sweetly into the lens. Sujin scanned the information inside. Born on 16 March 1985, to an accountant mother, and a corporate salesman father, both thirty years old. They were not married but had been dating for a year. The father ended the relationship when he learned of the pregnancy, leaving the mother solely responsible. She didn't want the stain of illegitimacy on her child, interfering with marriage or job opportunities. There were a few additional lines of information, including contact details should the child wish to get in touch in the future, but, just then, the director walked past with a box of doughnuts and a stern expression, so Sujin looked busy.

Sujin was automatic. It was quick work to disappear a person:

> *Mother: unknown.*
> *Father: unknown.*
> *Date of birth: 16 March 1985.*
> *Place of birth: unknown.*

Next. A toddler boy named Kang In-Ho. DOB: 30 December 1983. Mother's name: Kwon Kyung-Sook. Father's name: Kang Min-Cheol. Place of birth: Cheonan. The parents were divorced and the father brought the child in for adoption, only his signature on the relinquishment papers. Sujin knew that it was possible that the mother didn't even know her child was being sent away, having no parental rights following divorce. A few months ago, a desolate divorced mother sprained her wrists banging on the agency's door, demanding information about where her child was. Sujin had watched from the second-storey window as her colleagues locked the doors.

> *Mother: unknown.*
> *Father: unknown.*
> *Date of birth: 30 December 1983.*
> *Place of birth: unknown.*

Next. This one a little older. A five-year-old girl named Seo Soon-hee, who had spent a few months in the orphanage. DOB: 15 March 1980. The Ides of March, Sujin thought. This child was already registered: she read the hojeok inside the file. When a new birth was registered, a child entered the record of an existing family, nestled among their relatives, a fresh branch on an old tree. Her mother was a widow. Relinquished by her grandfather out of concern that a young child would preclude his daughter from a chance of remarriage.

> *Mother: unknown.*
> *Father: unknown.*
> *Date of birth: 15 March 1980.*
> *Place of birth: unknown.*

Next, an infant mixed boy, relinquished by a Jang Youngja. DOB: 1 November 1985. A bluster of handwriting was on the back of the paperwork. *Your mother's name is Hana Park. Your father is an American from Oregon named John Logan.* These surrendering women, like all the others, clung to the margins of Sujin's mind. She replied to these handwritten pleas:

> *Mother: unknown.*
> *Father: unknown.*
> *Date of birth: 1 November 1985.*
> *Place of birth: unknown.*

Next. Next. Next. Next. Until Sujin's hand cramped, her back ached, and she had to lower her head to the desk. She wasn't sure she could bear it much longer. *I'm just doing my job*, she excused herself. But her job was to flatten these children, fragment them from their families. Turn their parents into ghostly, wispy figures. She was no longer the person she once was, sure of herself, outspoken. Sujin now peered outwards with cynicism. Because of what she did each day, removing people from their most sacred of bonds, from their very own personhood, nothing could be certain. This was who she was now. Someone who, between the turn of a page, removed a child from their context. Paper-orphaned. Untraceable.

At lunchtime, she separated the old and new files into different stacks. The original files were to remain at the agency, evermore the gatekeepers. The new stack of reports Sujin created, each child stripped to the bare, would be couriered to the local district office where they would be registered as the only member of a brand-new, fabricated family. As if they had hatched from an egg. The machine would manufacture a new person. The district office would issue an 'orphan hojeok', mass-produced and identical but for the names and date of births, officially erasing all of the child's known history. No family, no origins, no ties. Therefore, available.

Once the requests were rubber-stamped, the agency could then apply for the visa documentation that would allow them to put those children on a flight out of the country. The applications were always approved. Sujin had never encountered a follow-up question.

The rain clattered on the tarpaulin sheet extended over a gathering of plastic stools and tables. The weight of the rainwater made the sheet sag in the middle.

'One tteokbokki, one odeng, one ramen, one sundoobu!' the ajumma yelled out from behind her steel stall.

'Coming!' Sujin's low ponytail swung as she leaped up and brought the food over. She laid four polystyrene plates on the rickety table. Her puffy coat protected her torso from the vigorous cold, and she'd soon have a soju layer keeping her warm.

'Hey!' her colleague, Ha-Jeong, called out to the stall-owner's son, playing a Game Boy in the corner, waiting for his mother to close for the night. She pulled out a bill. 'Run to the convenience store and get us two bottles of soju. You can keep the change.'

He nodded with a huge, gap-toothed smile.

'Don't give him any ideas,' his mother tutted as he ran off into the rain. 'You better return all the noona's change, do you hear me!'

The women's chopsticks dove onto the food.

'I fucking love ramen,' Ha-Jeong laughed brashly, before blowing on the curly strings hanging from her chopsticks, steam wisping into the air. 'Do you remember when we were little? How good ramen was? It was all I wanted to eat.'

Sujin nodded. 'I once made it in secret in the middle of the night and burned my mother's stainless-steel pot. Oh, how I got a beating the next morning.'

The boy returned with a blue plastic bag, two bottles clanging inside.

'Your change,' he said sullenly.

Ha-Jeong pushed his hand away and whispered with a wink, 'Go buy yourself candy, or some manhwa, I won't tell.'

Sujin smiled as the boy scampered away. 'You seem to like children.'

'Of course I do,' Ha-Jeong replied, without qualm. 'You have to, in this job, don't you think?'

Sujin shifted uncomfortably. The two women had frequently eaten lunch together, and had drunk in the evenings a few times. But Sujin still wasn't sure how much Ha-Jeong had swallowed their agency's party line.

'I need to ask you something.'

Ha-Jeong picked up a sauce-smeared fishcake. The way she ate was the wildest thing about her, smacking between bites, chewed-up food in her molars. 'What?'

'Where do the babies we process . . .' Sujin struggled to find the right words '. . . come from?'

'So, when a man and a woman like each other, they may want to get closer,' Ha-Jeong jibed, miming her finger penetrating her fist.

'I'm serious.'

'The agency has ties with hospitals and maternity homes in the area,' Ha-Jeong replied, unfazed. A shawl of wind encircled them and she pulled the collar of her jacket closer around her neck. Breath ribboned from her lips.

'Ties?'

'Founded them. Others we donate to. I worked in the maternity home at the end of the road for six months last year. Capacity is around fifty pregnant women. Many of them have been turned out by their families, so need somewhere to go. They sign the paperwork ahead of time so that we have legal custody of the child before they're even born. Smart, huh?'

A cold trickle ran through Sujin. She compelled herself to nod.

'Then it's the midwives and gynaecologists on our books too, who pass on the names of women who are pregnant or who've given birth recently. They're mostly single mothers, but it could be anything. Maybe they had an affair with the father or just can't afford another child.'

Sujin's head tilted; her brows came together.

Ha-Jeong leaned forward. 'We pay the mother's medical fees or help her access government healthcare if she agrees to give up her baby. The midwife who calls us gets something too. That way we get the best ones. Newborns. So we can do our best to fulfil adoptive parents' requests. Some of them can be so picky.'

'What about the older children?' Sujin asked. She felt ashamed that, until now, she hadn't stopped to zoom out, to take in the wider picture she was only a brushstroke in.

Ha-Jeong shrugged. 'The orphanages, mostly.'

'Next door?' Sujin gasped. She knew that an orphanage was on the same site as their agency, and for some reason hadn't interrogated that fact until now.

'One of our feeders. We have others too. Two fifty, three hundred maybe?'

'What happens when the parents come back? After the child has . . . you know.' Sujin gestured into the darkness.

'*If* the parents come back,' Ha-Jeong corrected. 'Doesn't matter. The orphanage director has custody of the child. He can place them into adoption.'

'Without telling the parents?' Sujin wanted to stop talking. It was better to remain blissfully ignorant. Her mother's words echoed: *It's just the way of the world!*

Ha-Jeong pointed her chopsticks at Sujin. 'They *left* their child. I mean, these people are broke, or single mothers, or divorced,' she threw her hands up, 'even if they do come back, how will a child fare with parents like that? If anything, the child will probably grow up resenting their parents for *not* letting them be adopted.'

'Maybe they just need a little help,' Sujin said.

'If we don't process the child, another agency will.'

Rain plopped onto the tarp, an inexorable drumbeat, the well-oiled machine she was a part of coming into sharp focus.

'But—' Sujin gulped another mouthful of soju. She wasn't a frequent drinker and could already feel the heat spreading to her cheeks. There was something that had been needling her for months. A worming, crowded question that she hadn't been able to isolate from all the others until now. It came to her in a colourful and definite way. 'These children aren't orphans. They have living parents.'

Ha-Jeong looked confused. 'What do you mean?'

'Why am I processing them all as orphans? Tens of them every day. When we all know – you've just told me – their parents are still alive.'

Ha-Jeong paused, not quite understanding the question. 'For a child to be adopted, they have to be legally ruled an orphan.'

Sujin furrowed her brow.

'You're a little slow to be in the fast lane, aren't you?' Ha-Jeong teased. She used the clean end of her chopstick to demonstrate a diagram on the table. 'America, and the other countries we send to, have immigration requirements. For a child to be adopted into America, they must be legally deemed an orphan. It's just a formality.'

'A fiction,' Sujin murmured.

'Sure,' Ha-Jeong said, 'I guess. If you want to call it that.'

'But . . . but . . . nothing comes from nothing.'

'That's real deep. More?' Ha-Jeong topped up Sujin's soju glass.

'What if they want to find their parents when they're older?'

'You're missing the point!' Ha-Jeong exclaimed. 'It's better for everyone involved. The adoptive parents want to think they're getting an orphan. It's more powerful. They want to think they are saving a child.' She clutched her hands around herself. 'Which they are in my view. And they want to know that no one is going to come out of the woodwork later down the line. If there are no parents to find, then the children won't go looking. Once the child gets on that plane, it's final.'

Sujin was troubled. She didn't know what the alternative was; she certainly couldn't imagine how someone could raise a child alone. Yet it was too dark, too nebulously amoral, tasted too bitter. What no one at her work seemed to consider was that children grew into adults, searching through a hollow dip of information for a new contour, a new detail about where or who they might have come from. A person couldn't be reduced to a convenient label and a slip of paper. Everyone deserved to be known in their uniqueness. Everyone needed, from time to time, to look backwards to see forwards.

Ha-Jeong sensed her discomfort and said, this time softer, 'You do the easy paperwork, Sujin-ah. You don't see the mothers, girls as young as my sister, fattened with babies. They can't do it alone. Giving up their child is the ultimate sacrifice. It's brave. This is for the best.'

A wrong leapfrogging straight into a right, with some simple affirmations. Sujin didn't know what to say. She thought she was helping children find parents. It seemed instead that she was helping parents find children. She was, she realised with a thud, the distance between being an orphan and being orphaned.

Ada
에이다

It wasn't that Ada wanted to die. It was that she shouldn't have ever been born.

She slumped against the acrylic chair. Iron radiators clanged and creaked alive. Teachers clack-clacked down austere corridors. Smell of freshly printed paper and whiteboard markers. Ada, tucked into the far corner of the computer room, USB stick, well, stuck into the machine. One other kid on the opposite side of the room playing Doodle Jump, disinterested in the head-spinning discovery taking place just a few metres away. Ada watched jagged clips of Youngja crudely edited together, the window behind her framing sleet, sun, rain tracks and a palette of heavy blue. Her hair frizzy in some, scraped back in others. A chorus of near-Youngjas and almost-Youngjas. Ada played it through twice, brain splitting. So many names, places, gaps to leap. But this much she had managed to understand: her mum had had a child named Yohan long ago; she believed him to be dead.

Her grandmother had given the child up for adoption. He was still alive.

Yohan was her brother. Ada's heart skipped. She had a brother.

Well, she thought, hi.

The truth had been buried. Another word for a series of underground explosives was 'landmine'. Ada looked back to see all her missteps, her full weight on triggers, a sequel of detonations in her wake. Year Five. Learning about the origins of the census, the class was asked to compile their family tree. Her friend Kiran was round at the Pennys' that afternoon and Ada, without thinking, asked Hana to fill out her side of the diagram. Hana's eyes rushed like a squirrel guarding a chestnut.

'What an odd assignment,' Hana said, shivering slightly as if a breeze rustled through her. Her expression turned sharp, angry, in an instant. As if the entire History curriculum and Ada's corresponding homework had been designed to somehow taunt her.

'It's not way back, Mrs Penny,' Kiran said cheerfully, 'just your parents' parents. Ada will fill out her aunts and uncles and cousins and stuff.'

Ada looked down ashamed. She realised in that moment that it wasn't normal to not know her mum's siblings.

'Will she?' Hana said coolly, before turning away and leaving the room.

'You shouldn't have said that,' Ada hissed, annoyed at Kiran's stupidity. Didn't she know that mums were delicate beings, capable of pulling away at any moment? The absence of aunties and uncles, cousins to grow up parallel with, had never struck her as odd before. Her dad wasn't close with his brother either. It was as if the three of them had sprouted from a bulb in the ground. The family-tree task made Ada wonder for the first time whether that was possible. It seemed like everything was connected.

Later that evening, Hana didn't come down for dinner. Tim and Ada glanced at each other, eating their microwave lasagnes like naughty children. Just before she dipped into her room for bed, Hana pulled Ada aside.

'You share too much with that girl,' she said.

'Kiran? Why?'

Hana held her fingertips over her eyelids. She turned away, and Ada got sick of being ignored.

'Jeez,' Ada muttered, loud enough for Hana to hear. 'What's your bloody *problem*?'

Hana whipped back around. Ada panicked. She'd never used a bad word in front of her parents before. But, to Ada's alarm, tears sprang on her mother's lashes.

'You think it's so simple, don't you? That you can just list everyone in a cute little drawing. I'm ashamed to have such a narrow-minded daughter. What about the bark that falls away, the roots that reach out in the soil doing all the hard work, the leaves that drop and disintegrate into the soil? Just because they are gone now, are they not part of the same tree?'

She sounded like a fortune cookie. Ada blinked, unsure if Hana expected an answer to her question.

Hana's nostrils flared. She spoke to a corner of the landing, to a ghost. 'It's not that simple.'

Ada wanted to say, *Then explain to me!* But Hana had already hardened. 'I don't want that uppity girl coming round any more. Kiran's life is hers, and ours is ours.'

Ada fell into a troubled silence, not understanding the need for secrecy. What was she hiding? Why? Still, as always, she complied.

'OK. Goodnight,' Ada had said.

Hana was staring at the floorboards, physically on the landing, but distant and vague. Then she remembered herself. 'Sleep well. Goodnight.'

Yohan and Ada had shared a womb. And bizarrely, because there was no logical reason for this sensation, she missed him. All this time, there had been a fourth member of their family, taking a seat at the dinner table, sitting next to her in the people carrier. And though Ada had never known about the absence of her brother, he was written into the lines across her palm, imprinted into her genes. Abstract feelings she'd so far struggled to name took shape. A real person, with leg hair and an American accent and cold sores. She tried really, really hard to picture him but all she could muster was a stock image of 'a man'. The kind a five-year-old might draw of their male relatives. Where one question was answered, others pushed out like ticker tape: What was Yohan like? Was that still his name? Did he know about them? Would he be happy about a sister? Had he ever been to London? What weird, unexplained quirks would they share? Did she have nieces or nephews?

And just as her mind crowded with hypotheticals, the here, the now pushed itself forward. That same, dull, soreness. Her worst suspicions about herself made manifest. Long ago, an assured voice had been lodged into Ada that, over time, grew more insistent until it became a constant, internal chatter that told her she wasn't enough. That somehow, somewhere, she had not been wanted, fallen a hair below adequate to the woman who made her. *I know you have never recovered from losing your child. I pushed you to have another when you weren't ready.*

Then, for the first time, she took it a step further. She didn't need to exist. More than anything, Ada hoped that there was a version of her mother in another, parallel universe that got to be happy. Her mum who wasn't her mum, finishing school, going to America with her baby, getting that degree. Her mum who wasn't her mum, raising a child that is never taken from her. Ada squeezed her eyes shut and willed all this into the other dimension. She didn't have to be born, and she would trade it all to give her mum back what she'd lost.

The truth had held on for twenty-three years, criss-crossed the globe in thousands of miles, clung like a barnacle to minds and hearts, and now was interrupted again by a fifteen-year-old girl.

It all happened quite unconsciously. Two or three turns in a decision maze, which went as such: Youngja had never intended for Hana to see the recording until she was either dead or beyond the precipice. What Youngja did was a profound, irreparable wrong. And yet, Ada couldn't help but think of how, each morning, Youngja peered at her, a papery hand cupping Ada's cheek, and said, *Thank you, Hana-ya.* Too much love for a teenager to know what to do with. No, Ada couldn't betray her grandmother's wishes. Anyway, what good would come out of dredging up all that history when there was no way of knowing where her brother was now? Surely, giving Hana false hope was fresh cruelty?

At least that was what Ada told herself. But from an unguarded sliver, in her unseen, fear escaped. Fear that Hana would pack a bag and leave to find her son. That she'd been biding her time anyway. There was evidence that under-pinned that theory – a seam of insecurity that stitched all the way back to a night ten years earlier, a little girl's cold toes flexing on the landing. Ada had already come close to losing Hana once, her father was in the ground, and her grandmother was slipping out of grasp. For now, her instinct was preservation. It wasn't the right time. She knew it was selfish, but she was bad. She would hold the truth. Or she would hold a lie. She didn't think the difference mattered any more.

The bell rang. She rose and slung her satchel over her shoulder. Clarissa saw the look on Ada's face and hooked their arms. They headed to class together.

Hana
하나

At the same time her daughter was across town at school, unplugging a USB stick from the computer furthest from the door and weaving through corridors to get to her first class, Hana handed the final plate to be dried to her mother. They'd done this together a few times, tentatively at first, then automatically.

'Ya, did you check the change box?' Youngja croaked. 'Do you think we have enough left over to serve mackerel at the end of the week? The guests need the healthy fats if they're going to avoid accidents at work.'

She was still back there. She never left.

'If not mackerel, then I'm sure we could at least get some mudfish,' Hana sighed.

In March 1986, Hana boarded a plane for the first time. It had been a four-week blur since Yohan's death, how long it took to get a passport and organise her visa. For every agonising minute of unfamiliar announcements and women in dress-up uniforms and rules, she wanted to tear out of this deathtrap and run home. As the plane pulled away from the only ground she had ever known, she unmoored. Scar tissue forming around her centre, her soul swallowing, as she watched her homeland – that held her mother's barley scent and her baby's ashes – grow smaller and smaller, until it disappeared beneath a canopy of clouds across a lingering pink sky. A bare, oesophageal sound escaped from her chest. The seventeen hours in flight felt Odyssean. For such a young person, she'd already been so many women: schoolgirl, minbak girl, John's lover, Yohan's mother. Now, she was none of them. Society was so adamant it knew who Hana was. A mother with a dead child was a Tess Durbeyfield character, an ethereal, tragic heroine. Meanwhile, a teenage single mother was an irresponsible rebel, promiscuity used to fill some other gaping hole. Out of everyone, Hana wasn't allowed to say who she was. Not that she knew; she was eighteen.

A few hours after thudding on British soil, Hana huddled under the steel awning of a suburban train station, dribbles of rain plopping on the pavement. Gone was the imagination of teetering red double-decker buses, teddy bears in window displays, elvish women in stockings and glossy green front doors. Behold instead a wetland that pelted the face with wind. She followed her instructions, copied diligently into a pocket spiral notebook, to a cul-de-sac. The house was red-bricked, terraced and twee. Tarmac driveway and mossed fence. A fox darted across the road.

'Hana-ya,' Bokhee Unni opened the door in a striped dressing gown, 'we've been expecting you.'

She had a disarmingly cute smile, complete with dimples, and her husband stood a metre behind with an equally amiable face. It was late, and they were both in loose, night-time clothing.

'I'm sorry to keep you waiting, I was delayed by the District Line.' First person in her bloodline to say that combination of words.

'Come, come.' Bokhee Unni placed an arm around Hana's shoulders as if they really were sisters. 'It's too cold, isn't it?'

Hana stepped into the tiled hallway and untied her shoelaces, increasingly stressed about the droplets of water cascading off her jacket. She kept bowing and apologising.

'Aygo, aygo,' Bokhee Unni helped Hana's jacket off her shoulders and fussed about, 'you'll catch a cold. We need to warm you up.' She handed Hana a pair of comfortable, soft trousers and bustled her towards the bathroom. 'Change quickly! I've been preheating them on the radiator.' That cute smile again.

By the time Hana changed, Bokhee Unni had already bundled her wet clothes into the washing machine and mopped the hallway of any raindrops.

'In here,' she called from the kitchen, stirring powdered hot chocolate into boiling water, and inviting Hana to sit at the small, wooden table. As Hana's fingers curled around the mug, heat began to rush through her. Bokhee Unni was talking to her about the bed arrangements. Hana was to sleep in their daughter's room, she'd had a long trip so they didn't expect her to start at the salon straight away, maybe in a week's time? Hana thanked her, all the while taking in the yellowing wood veneer kitchen cabinets, greige tiles, faded furniture and net curtains held by elastic rods. The bathroom had maroon-brown or brown-maroon tiles. Every now and then, the faint slush of passing cars. Gratitude came in small jackpots. Steam rising from the rice cooker, colourful magnets on the fridge holding up a child's timetable, three sets of fluffy slippers by the doorway along with the fourth new pair, still in its plastic, the hot chocolate warming her palms. This was a home full of care.

Youngja called regularly, at great expense. Hana couldn't answer. One word in her mother's voice would spin her back to the wet-soil smell of their yard, the row of green rubber clogs lining the doorway, stacks of mismatched plates and collections of used jars, the sounds of knives hitting chopping boards, and of women berating their men. She longed to roam through her hometown unseen like a broad wind, to smell the woodsmoke on the air. She dodged her mother's calls with ease, leaving Bokhee Unni to reassure Youngja that Hana was coping well.

Three months after Hana arrived in London, a cardboard box littered with postage labels arrived for her. She tore it open to find dried squid, home-made gochujang and a plastic bag of her region's rice. Her childhood in packets of Choco Pie, Ace and shrimp crackers. Ginseng concentrates and vitamin powders. Hand-roasted seaweed and dried anchovies in old biscuit boxes. A note tucked under the fold of one: *Don't skip meals, stay warm.* Each item wrapped in newspaper and tape. And – the garlic smell alone made Hana's chest exhale open even though it was wrapped in an entire roll of cling film – one Tupperware of Youngja's kimchi. Glistening scarlet bundles of a mother's love. She carefully made a bowl of rice and sat at the narrow kitchen table. Laying a perfect piece of kimchi on a mound of rice, Hana took a bite. From a world away, her omma was in the room, holding her. Hana cried soundlessly as she finished the entire bowl.

Over a year later, Hana still hadn't spoken to Youngja.

For nineteen days in June 1987, Hana and Bokhee Unni's family sat glued to the television, watching coverage unfold of mass protests against the dictator's government, roaring and united on a scale unlike anything they had ever seen before. It seemed all of London's Korean diaspora had crowded into Mrs Kim's restaurant with a satellite television, to watch their country tip over the cusp of democracy. The last time Hana had seen a crowd of enamoured Koreans like this was for the '86 World Cup, when Maradona's Argentina beat South Korea. The loss hadn't stung; to play the team that went on to be reigning champions was a sign of better things to come. In December 1987, a people's election was held.

Meanwhile, Hana had forgotten the word 'appointment'. It was at the front of her mind, squashed between the jostling Korean words that insisted on sitting on her tongue. After three torturous seconds of stammering, Hana settled on 'You have a haircut?' She now knew how to wash, trim and blow-dry in thirty minutes. She could deliver a classic perm sported by all the local ajummas. She was, by all accounts, hard-working and trustworthy. The trouble was, she only knew how to cut Korean hair. Pin-straight as if determined to reflect its rule-abiding owners. She only had Korean customers. She only ate Korean food and only spoke with other Koreans. In London, her English-language ability had gone backwards. So, as she stood face-to-face with the first English customer in a year, and forgetting the word for 'appointment', she felt the immense falseness of it all. The fraudulence of running from her country for a fresh start, only to melt back into her own people. Was this why she couldn't be with John? If she was going to live with this gaping hole in her chest, the least she could do was make her 'freedom' worthwhile. She had to leave. And, in doing so, left the last place she ever felt at home.

Until now.

When Youngja first moved into their home, 1985 hooked Hana's soft flesh and tugged her backward. Hana placed Ada as the buffer between them. She'd been in charge of herself since she was eighteen, kept afloat, given birth and raised a girl, had the sincere love of a good man. She'd never relied on drugs or alcohol or pills. As far as Hana was concerned, she'd earned the right to her anger, guarded it like a lion its kill. It was the one vice she permitted herself.

Then Ada started at Richmond Girls' and Hana was alone, properly, with Youngja. It was hard to believe that this frail woman who brushed her teeth with shaving foam if she wasn't supervised was the same person she'd been so furious with for so many years. When Hana's feet bloated from cleaning the house top to bottom, Youngja rattled around the room, emerging with a laundry tub. Somehow, she filled it with warm water and told Hana to sit down. Hana didn't have the heart to tell her that she'd drizzled sunflower oil into the tub instead of soap. Youngja creaked into a lotus, and led each of Hana's feet into the warm, oil-slicked water. Youngja repeatedly thumbed the arch of Hana's foot.

'I'm so proud of you,' Youngja said plainly, cupping her hands and scooping water up and over her ankles. 'I'm sorry you're not at school right now; it won't be for ever, I promise.'

A thick sorrow rasped in Hana's chest.

Hana found herself whispering, 'Omma, why didn't you stop Appa? Why didn't you protect me?'

Youngja reached behind herself and dried Hana with a T-shirt instead of a towel. Hana didn't know if she would reply or she had simply forgotten the question. Eventually, Youngja said, 'Everything I did, every choice I made,' she paused to swipe a swathe of hair away from her face, 'might not have been right. I have to live with that. But I had to save you from yourself.'

'Do you see what has become of me?' Hana couldn't stop herself. 'I didn't go to school so I achieved nothing—'

'Take some responsibility for your own life, Hana-ya,' Youngja said, with calm, cleansing clarity. 'If you lie down and spit at the ceiling, it will only land on your own face. You're hurting yourself when you blame others.'

'But . . .' Hana started. She needed this. She needed Youngja to recognise the harm done. '*You* stopped me from going to school. You sent me away. I could have been—'

'What?' Youngja raised her eyebrows. 'What could you have been? A man who wanted to sleep with you said you were amazing. So what? If you had ambitions, you could have faced them. But you chose to sit on the sidelines until you wake up and you need someone to resent. And don't forget the choices you made too.'

'Choice!' Hana retorted. 'Choice was the one thing I didn't have!'

Youngja sat back on her heels.

'Is this how I raised you? To be unable, or unwilling, to see the impact of your actions on anyone but yourself? The risks you put our family in. You covered us in shame. Your father was changed. I was changed. You didn't call us once. Not once. Not until you needed me again.'

Their longest conversation in twenty-three years. The lucid, whip-smart Youngja reappeared like a magic trick just to take Hana by the shoulders and shake her out of her multi-decade inertia. It was a knotty feeling, to be chided as a grown woman. To be slapped with her own failings when she'd intended to hammer home someone else's. She was a coward.

Youngja softened. 'Hana-ya, it's the same for everybody. Did it never occur to you that I may have wanted something different for myself too? It's not something that happened only to you.'

Youngja reached with the corner of the T-shirt between each of Hana's toes. A simple intimacy fell between them, the beginnings of a truce. Anger started falling away like meat off a tendon. Something inside Hana took its jacket and shoes off, climbed under the covers and rested.

And, as she mellowed towards her mother, something else changed. In her mind's eye, John's sun-bleached hair turned to straw, his words soured from honey to vinegar. False hope and bluffed promises were the potent ingredients of that romance. Heat and vitality and imagined potential mingled into something enchanting. It had made her existence seem on the cusp of ripening. Had it even been love? Or had it been the same old tale of sex then abandonment? She had been too arrogant, bitter and stubborn to see it clearly. John had asked her to stop bowing to him. He must have thought he was being modest and agreeable. But baked into his request was the assumption that she was bowing to him because he was superior to her, when it was just the standard Korean greeting. He never came to the table believing they were equals. Hana imagined the uncompromising incandescence she would feel if a man treated Ada the same way. She thought of Tim. The imperfect victim of the Park family saga. How, how did she get it so monumentally wrong?

'Oh, oh, oh,' Hana whimpered. She tucked her damp heels under her pelvis and covered her face with her hands. Grief came in a geyser. Yohan, Tim, Youngja, Ada, herself. Hana cried for them all. She felt a complete, prismatic sense of confrontation.

Youngja sat kneeling in front of her. 'You needed this.'

After some time, Youngja muttered something about preparing dinner. She took Hana by the elbow and led her towards the kitchen sink. She pointed at the tap. Youngja made the children wash their faces after they cried, saying it was no good to wear your tears all day. Hana splashed her face, her eyelashes clumped together in thick spokes. A renewal was born. She didn't expect they would speak about 1985 in full, ever lay it all out on the table. But what family did ever speak openly about the uneasy weight of the past? No, instead, people quietly returned home and slotted themselves back into place.

Youngja

영자

A floury mandu wrapper in her palm. A pink brain of meat at its centre. Youngja turned to her left and saw a girl first, separating the wrappers, then a woman filling them, and then her own hands. Memory stored in her fingers came alive. She began making intricate folds, her hands moving in concert, though she couldn't begin to imagine what for.

'Omma?' The woman nudged her with her elbow.

'Oh yes, give it to me.' Youngja took the next wrapper. She tutted. 'You're using too much meat. You're only feeding guests. You should use mostly vegetables. Meat is too expensive at market these days.'

'I get the meat on clearance,' the woman muttered sullenly. The specific sheepishness in her voice confirmed that she was Youngja's daughter.

'You're filling them too much, Hana-ya,' Youngja sent one back, 'they will split.'

'Yes.'

There was a metallic shape. She picked it up. Squelchy.

She read the letters in front of her three times over, without being able to understand them.

'What is this?'

'You can see it's kimchi,' Hana muttered.

'You're buying kimchi now? What next? Buying cooked rice? Have you forgotten how to run your own household?' It was so natural to fall into patterns of correction.

'I don't have time, Omma.'

'If you came home more often, you know I would set aside kimchi for you.' Youngja's voice was wounded. Hana didn't reply.

'How is my son-in-law?' Youngja tried to make conversation. 'Make sure you are feeding him well; he is far too skinny, like a fighting dog.'

The girl opened her mouth but Hana nudged her. 'He eats until he is full,' she said. 'What more can I do?'

'Aygo, what are you talking about? A husband should be eating bowl after bowl of his wife's food.'

Another pair of footsteps entered.

'Oh,' a man's voice said.

Youngja's fist automatically clamped the dumpling wrapper, squeezing the mincemeat into the underside of her finger creases. The man was in shiny, tight black clothes, and his arms glistened with sweat.

'I'm sorry, I just came back from the gym, I didn't mean to interrupt.' He bowed to the women.

'Michael sonnim!' Hana trilled.

Youngja's body drained of energy. She was sure she knew him. The words trailed from her lips. 'Where are you from?'

'Me?' He laughed a little. 'My mom is Korean, my dad is from the States.'

A Korean mother, American father. He was around the right age. Youngja stared at him. Those features, like a composite sketch, were exactly how she'd imagined. A jagged, chopped scene resurfaced: seeing him in front of the house, holding a black rain tent over her head, her breath halting in her throat. A strapping, strong young man, taller than she'd imagined. Like the perfume of a past lover, the sight pulled forward a borrowed vision: Hana's baby doesn't remain an infant but grows into a man. Wrinkles smoothed, resentment softened. Could he be their Yohan? The years had never sandpapered away her hope that he would one day come back to find them.

Son, if it is you, will you please nod?
If I call out your name, will you just look at me?
But it can't really be, can it?

She was being tickled to death, pride and love clambering up and through, sprinting towards the grief of knowing the tricks of her mind.

'How can I help?' Hana asked Michael, wiping her hands on her apron. Youngja couldn't ignore this urgent pressure in her chest.

Before he could reply, Youngja's arm raised towards him. 'But, but . . . you're . . . you're . . .'

'Ada,' Hana's voice was steel, but with a strained smile plastered on her face that gave the impression of a very well-behaved manic episode, 'can you take your grandmother inside?'

The girl was Ada! The last time Youngja saw her, she was just a grainy baby in a picture. Logically, she knew that it was impossible that Ada and Yohan could exist together in the same room. He was an illusion. And yet, she was transfixed. She couldn't tear her eyes from his tall frame, the lighter-than-Korean brown hair, while he nervously shifted from foot to foot.

'No,' Youngja mewled. 'No . . . you . . .'

'Ada.'

Youngja wanted to scream. *I used to be a businesswoman! Don't treat me like a baby!* Ada took her arm. Youngja's mouth undulated wordlessly. In a desperate bid to make herself heard, Youngja blurted, 'Yohan!'

Hana turned with an expression of watching a glass fall to the ground in slow motion. Ada looked to Hana, who looked at Youngja. Statues for a moment. Then, Ada pulled her away. The door closed. The boy gone.

Some minutes, or hours, later, someone came into the room.

'Can you leave us?'

'But—' The girl with the jewel eyes had some papers scattered across her lap. 'I'm in the middle of my homework.'

The woman shot the girl a warning look Youngja recognised well. The girl shuffled herself up. Just before the girl left, the woman held her forearm and said, 'What your grandmother said earlier, ignore it, she's just confused.'

The girl's expression was blank. She nodded, before slinking out. Youngja wondered whether dinnertime had passed. She looked out of the window to see floating circles of light. So, it was evening, maybe. A woman sat cross-legged in front of her. She was naked! Were they in the bathhouse? She blinked a few times and realised the woman was wearing a tan T-shirt that blended into her skin tone.

'How long until dinner?' Youngja asked. She rubbed the crescent rolls that had taken shape around her midriff. 'Or is my mouth just bored?'

'Yes. That's it.'

She watched Youngja with a hopeless longing. She wanted something she didn't expect to receive.

'Hana-ya?' Youngja leaned forward. It was a question because she was guessing. Youngja nodded a few times to reassure the woman that she was trying. 'Sweetheart?'

'Yes, Omma.' Something like relief raced across the woman's face, though Youngja struggled to read expressions the way she used to. The woman clamped her hand over her mouth and turned away. Youngja's eyes slid across the room. So much clutter, she felt she was living within a pointillist painting. Her brain couldn't make sense of where one thing ended and another began.

'Omma,' the woman whispered. 'I know it's hard for you. But you can't do that.'

Youngja chuckled. 'Do what, honey?'

'You bothered a guest – you called him—' Hana stopped herself.

Youngja didn't have the loosest sense of what she was talking about, but a hot ember choked alive in her gut. An alarm ringing in the distance, even though she couldn't place the danger it was warning of. 'I would never bother a guest, my dear!'

'Omma. I'm sorry. Just please don't,' Hana whispered.

Youngja whimpered. Sheer, white noise. She didn't even know what she had said, but she knew from this heavy pressure across her organs that it had been wrong. She felt useless, mechanically broken. 'I'm just getting a little confused.'

Hana crouched next to her. Their shoulders pressed together. 'You can't mention him in front of Ada. She doesn't know.'

Clarity bloomed. Everything dipped in colour and context.

'But—' Youngja started. Now was the time to blurt it out. That it *could* be him. That he was out there, somewhere. Words were trudging through sludge to reach her.

Hana stopped her. 'The man you were talking about is a guest. A stranger. He is irrelevant to you.' Hana reached out and stroked Youngja's head. 'Omma, you're so tired. I'm sorry you're having to live like this. It won't be for ever. I promise you.'

Hana pushed herself up and left.

Some time later. Youngja lay awake in bed, not daring to move a muscle until she heard the others' deep, exhausted breathing. She usually slept in short and frequent bursts. She lay on her back, brows furrowed. *It could be him*, she thought. Then, *Stop it, escape this fantasy*. She begged her mind to absorb the instruction. But the possibility of the impossible continued to thrum, an agitation in her core.

Something was amiss. She couldn't trust who was who, what was what, any more. Her body floated up. Under a spell, she moved through the darkness like a sprite. Swallowed by a big black hole, sucked into the galaxy. Gravitating towards the slice of light leaking under the door, she kept her footsteps precise like a ballerina. She saw a staircase and wasn't sure where it rose to but ascended anyway. Both racing and lumbering, her legs effortful as if wading through quicksand. All she knew was that she had to speak to him. She had so many questions. Son, where have you been all this time? Are you happy? I know it doesn't matter; it doesn't change what I did. Is it fair for me to say we grieved for you? Did you know that you have the slanted tip of my nose, north of your mother's Cupid's bow?

Do you know that every day that we had you, and every day since, we have loved you?

Can you ever forgive me?

She reached the top of the stairs and stared at four closed doors around her. She didn't know where he would be, but his energy was around her, pulling her forward. She reached for the first doorknob she saw, directly in front of the staircase, and turned it. Ah, there he was. The crescent moon's glow bounced off his broad chest and slim face. Comfort washed over Youngja. How he had grown! She was so proud. She was on her knees at the side of his bed, appreciating her grandchild sleeping safely, tenderly caressing his face. She remembered doing this with her sons; they used to tire themselves out playing so hard during the day that even fireworks couldn't wake them. Their peace was her peace.

Then, his eyes flew open. He choked on his own breath. The magic started to shatter. He pulled his sheet over his naked chest and scrambled away from her. Youngja was smiling, her eyes wide, hoping, madly, that he might recognise her. But he was jumping out of bed, leaping like a flea to the other side of the room.

Ada
에이다

She didn't have a choice, she had to confess. Five days a week, Ada went to school and cemented herself further into someone she didn't recognise. It was all her badness, rising to the surface like a bloated drowned body. She didn't want to do it any more. She had to stop herself, before it became who she was. Before she couldn't tell where Ada the character and Ada the person accrued into the same.

'What are Christmas plans chez the Pennys?' Clarissa asked, materialising a nail file and shaping her index fingernail. They had skived double Science to sit in the car park under Sainsbury's, on benches littered with energy-drink cans, condom wrappers and cigarette butts. Ada sat sitting forward, and Clarissa lay across the bench, her head in Ada's lap, sun-dyed hair rainbowed around her face. Under her school shirt, she was wearing a lemon-yellow, lace-frilled tank top from her weekend job at Abercrombie.

'Not much,' Ada deflected. 'Your holidays will be much more fun than mine.'

'Antigua.' She sighed as if deeply inconvenienced. 'You been?'

And because it had become habit, Ada said, 'Yeah, last year.'

It didn't matter where Clarissa said any more. Koh Samui. Val-shitting-d'Isère. Saturn. Ada would have said yes. She began to panic that Clarissa would ask Antigua-specific questions.

'It's funny cos, like, my parents can't be around each other. The fucking rows they have. I can't even. Last year in Barbados we barely left the suite. It's like, guys, it's *boring*.' Clarissa's jaw softened. 'Doesn't help that I'm expected to share with my sister who's spewing her guts up every five minutes. It's cos of her "allergies".' Clarissa air-quoted and exaggeratedly rolled her eyes.

It was that overactive empathy that made Ada see past performative nonchalance. She'd never seen Clarissa eat anything more substantial than fruit or half a rice cracker. She wouldn't tip over fifty kilos soaking wet.

'You haven't, like, tried it, have you?' Ada asked, imitating Clarissa's drawn-out eye roll.

'Ugh, no way,' Clarissa dismissed. 'It's soooo bad for your teeth. And I like *begged* my parents for Invisalign. Plus, you don't always have a running tap and a bathroom, you know? Better to cut the supply at the source.'

Ada reached for Clarissa's hand. Clarissa stared at the concrete ceiling, covered with spikes to stop nesting pigeons, squeezing Ada's hand back. Quietly, 'Our mum used to stick a candle in an apple for our birthdays. Idolises Kate. Thinks bread is the devil reincarnate. But,' she sighed, glassy-eyed, 'neither of us have got our period yet so I guess that's a plus.' She tried to grin but her trembling lips couldn't quite comply.

She bolted upright and turned her torso back to face Ada. 'Swear on *your life* you won't tell a soul.'

'Bible,' Ada said, borrowing from the Kardashians. She didn't have MTV or Sky any more, but reality TV vocabulary swept through a girls' school like nits. Clarissa lay back down. Ada thought of all the times she had stared at Clarissa's stretch-mark-free thighs and her concave stomach with envy and felt like a hobgoblin by comparison. She had longed to be smooth and skinny just like that. Nothing was as it initially seemed. It wasn't fair to predicate their friendship, Clarissa's trust, on a false version of herself. Ada was all too intimate with the consequences of caring for someone you didn't know.

'I've never been to Antigua.'

Clarissa didn't miss a beat. 'And your dad died back in June.' She gazed up at Ada, mossy eyes impassive.

'How – how did you know?'

'I mentioned we were hanging out to my parents last week. They recognised your surname and told me to look out for you. The accident was in the paper.'

'You're not mad?'

Clarissa sighed and looked back at the ceiling. 'I figured it was your prerogative.'

Ada was stunned. Acceptance was such a simple thing. She could let go of it all. 'And . . . well . . . about Michael. That's not true either.'

'Well yeah, thanks, Captain Obvious,' Clarissa laughed. 'I'm not as dumb as the teachers think I am.'

'You're not dumb at all.'

'No,' Clarissa said in a small voice. 'And you don't have a dad or a boyfriend.'

'No.'

'Glad that's cleared up.' Clarissa held Ada's hand the entire time. She would never know how monumental this permission was. No one had ever suggested that it was perfectly fine for Ada to come as she was.

'OK,' Ada said.

On the way home, cradling her newfound self-actualisation, Ada concluded that she may not have been the child Hana wanted, but she was exactly the daughter Hana raised. She listened closely to the gaps, because what family meant was rarely what they said. She'd learned from her mother, who'd learned from her mother, that everything people did to the ones they loved involved some twist of deception. It was almost a relief to see that now, a way to understand the world around her.

Michael had left quickly that morning. Bundled his sparse items into the one backpack he arrived with and, shooting Ada a brief, apologetic look, strode out of the house. It was very reasonable of him to not demand an immediate refund on his outstanding rent, though Hana made him write down his number so that she could get in touch to pay him back when she could. This time, Ada fought the urge to check on Hana, to gauge her reaction from the shifting of her shoulders, the tautness of her brow. To tell her not to worry, they'd find someone to replace him. She no longer felt the need.

She wandered upstairs to her old bedroom. Her thumb sought a familiar groove on the banister. Her toes remembered the uneven ridge in the floorboard. The brush of jute carpet under her feet took her back to when her dad was on the other side of his study door. Rushing, rushing, between meetings, to go fill the car's tank, to make parents' evening, trailing a waft of musk and coffee through the landing. It seemed unreal. The family a mere illusion. She nudged the door open to her old bedroom, starkly empty. Michael had been good enough to even strip the bed before he left, leaving a bundle of sheets in the corner by the door. She couldn't truly remember once having this room as her own.

The room was L-shaped, and as she moved further in, she saw a ball of clothing and limbs on the floor. Youngja, back rounded like a turtle, forehead on the carpet, hands splayed, as if in a temple, bowing to a deity. Ada pulled down and fire-blanketed her. She heard soft panting. They melted into each other. Youngja raised her head and let it nestle against Ada's shoulder. Hot, wet breath on Ada's cold-flushed cheek. Youngja smelled like Clinique and the faint, dry whiff of urine. Ada held her as the sun submerged, the carpet pressed crosshatches into their knees, and the room was swallowed into an inkblot.

After some time, Youngja said, 'He's gone.'

'Yes.'

A reckless, thick sound came from Youngja's chest.

'It's been so long, so many years, to see him just once more,' Youngja whimpered. 'All this time, it's had to be enough, just to know he was living under the same sky.'

Ada nodded, her cheek brushing the carpet. All she could do was give Youngja the room to mourn what she thought she'd lost for a second time. It didn't matter that Michael wasn't who she thought he was, that her brother was still out there. One day, when Youngja was gone, Ada would tell her mother the truth. One day, maybe they'd find him, and he'd plug all the holes in their family and stop them seeping. Or maybe not. Maybe families were like waterfalls, always full, never complete. All she knew for sure was that there was a grandmother and her granddaughter huddled together on the carpet, and one could help the other.

'You have to know I did my best,' Youngja said.

Ada let her instincts guide her. It was clear what her grandmother needed so desperately, and why withhold it? It seemed petty now to not give her peace. Ada gave herself permission to, finally, take control.

'You did the right thing, Omma.'

Twists of deception.

Youngja froze. The room perfectly still. Then the taut shell of her body slackened, as if she'd been keeping her body tense, upholding a great weight that was now lifted. Ada reached out and brushed her fingertips along the back of Youngja's hand. A small, but almighty forgiveness.

'I just wanted to give you a chance.'

'I know.'

Youngja bowed her head, pressing her forehead against Ada's, awash with gratitude and atonement.

'You took care of everything all this time,' Ada whispered. 'I've got it from here.'

She didn't know what, specifically, she was promising, but Youngja's breathing slowed and, after a long while, Ada managed to coax her up. There was so much more that could be said, but at the same time, none of it was needed. So much had criss-crossed past the three of them already. Ada led her grandmother back to their room in the half-light of the house. Nestled her into bed and pulled the quilt to her chin.

'Are you sure?' Youngja looked at Ada searchingly.

'I'm sure.' Ada kissed Youngja's forehead. She knew she would have to forgive her on Hana's behalf again tomorrow, and the next day, and the day after that.

Sang-Soo

상수

Everything Sang-Soo ate came wrapped in foil. Kimbap mainly. Cheap, filling, delicious cold, and required no utensils or washing-up. When he was with Sumi, they ate out. He had no choice but to become a rich man to keep her happy, and he would have let her bleed him dry with a smile on his face. None of that mattered any more. Her parents blocked the engagement, displeased with his grubby profession, reporting on all the unsavoury parts of society, jeopardising their good friendships with government officials. Now, alone with his kimbap, he hated them, and he hated her.

Once every few months, his sister came to the city, let herself into his apartment while he was in the office and cleaned the place top to bottom. Occasionally, she rearranged furniture. She brought two big bags full of little containers of her banchan. She aired the place out and beat dust from the curtains. Sometimes, he'd come home to find her on her hands and knees, rubber gloves to her elbows, scrubbing the carpet. Each time, he made a big show of insisting she shouldn't clean up after her fully grown baby brother, and she made a fuss of promising she wouldn't again. Then they went out for barbecue, and she'd insist she wasn't hungry, urging him to eat most of the meat. He'd lie and say he'd had a big lunch, pushing the meat towards her. He felt so lucky to have her that his heart welled up. He whispered thank you. And the seasonal cycle continued. He measured time by the stuffy, closeted atmosphere in his apartment and the accumulated smell of soup. It must have been at least three months since her last visit.

Sang-Soo spent his days at a Formica-topped desk with his word processor, hostage to censorship, keeping vigil with the last scrapings of truth. When he died, he imagined an autopsy would reveal him split straight down the middle: lofty notions of integrity and anarchy flooding through his left, taking residence around his heart; practicality and an effective dose of fear holding firm in his right. He barely could sleep through the night, and when he did, it was a held, cloying sleep, occupied with images of troops and pairs of running legs and collapses into spirals and big boxes of black.

The choreography of line-toeing was simple. Articles were drafted on the facts of the day's demos, sit-ins, strikes, civilian clashes with the police, arrests, injuries, fatalities; driven to the censor's office in the military compound for review; returned to the office with the substance of the article redacted; amended. It was tedious and insulting. As if the newspapers' silence made anyone ignorant to the fact that the country was rising up to meet its voice, gaining inexorable momentum. He was a fraud. A ventriloquist's dummy. Just last week, he wrote that ~~10,000 demonstrators took to the streets~~ dissidents caused chaos, disrupted the peace, and by the next day, ~~numbers rose to 30,000~~ order was restored.

Sometimes he intentionally left blank gaps in his sentences, like unfinished thoughts trailing off, or a double space, to signal to the reader that something was being concealed. They all kept copies of their uncensored drafts hidden – in a false drawer, or, in Sang-Soo's case, behind a loose vent in his ceiling – for posterity.

In his spare time, Sang-Soo was working on a bigger story. It pursued him with a doggedness that tangled him in his sleep. Sang-Soo was piecing together its fragments, a process akin to chipping through a tunnel with a teaspoon. Chasing echoes that led to closed doors. Accidental concessions from sources who wouldn't go on the record but put a saddle on his enquiries. Each time he thought he had identified an isolated case, another connected one sprouted, then another, like a mutating octopus. He chronicled each tidbit on index cards and pinned them across the longest wall in his apartment.

It started with a request from his boss. Editor Choi was from a wealthy closeted-bohemian family, degreed overseas in the States, friends in dizzyingly high places. He had had dinner with a friend who worked at the US Embassy.

'He mentioned in passing an exodus,' Editor Choi hushed, leaning over Sang-Soo's desk and tapping it with a rolled-up poster. 'Of *children*.'

'Mmm?' Sang-Soo murmured.

'He's issuing adoption visas. *Five hundred* a month. His actual words were: "It's fucking biblical."' He put on a New York accent to mimic his friend. 'And that's just to America. Imagine how many are going to other countries. A story will probably get blocked, but look into it, will you?'

Sang-Soo first went to the Ministry of Health and Welfare where he found laws, establishing four government-licensed adoption agencies, authorised to place children in homes overseas. Straightforward. He went back for two subsequent days for more information about quotas, minutes, guidelines, regulations, ombudsmen. They were emigrating infants, after all. His search was not fruitful. When he finally managed to speak to a clerk, after waiting for three hours on a wooden bench so uncomfortable it would put a rock to shame, he was redirected back to the laws he'd found on the first day. By this point, the story hadn't yet ensnared Sang-Soo. Adoption was widespread, so what? Hardly a juicy exposé.

Quitting the search at the Ministry, Sang-Soo decided he needed to approach the issue from the other end. With the phonebook splayed across his desk, he dialled an adoption agency, trailing each number with his index finger. The first receptionist who answered could have worked for a corporate headquarters, or a dermatologist's office. Businesslike but blank. Sang-Soo introduced himself as a reporter.

'Please hold.' The line cut to Vivaldi's *Four Seasons*.

A moment later, an older, more assured voice. 'How can I help?'

Sang-Soo reeled off his introduction again. 'I'm researching a story on international adoption, I was wondering if I could speak with your director?'

The line went quiet. Sang-Soo's interest grew.

'I'm afraid the director is unavailable.'

'I'm happy to organise a time?' Sang-Soo offered, reaching for his calendar. 'Perhaps later this week?'

'The director is fully booked,' the woman stated. 'An appointment won't be possible.'

Attention morphed into suspicion. Sang-Soo's eyes narrowed. Why the stonewalling? They were a government-licensed agency; with that came an expectation of transparency. Sang-Soo pushed. 'I understand. Would it then be possible to talk with another member of your team? I am interested specifically in discussing the numbers of those sent abroad, and how so many children came to be in your custody.'

The woman's breath tripped. After a three-beat pause, she said, 'Due to privacy laws, I cannot provide you with the information you're looking for. Thank you for calling.'

She hung up. Sang-Soo felt a line of sweat trickle down the knots of his spine. He hadn't asked for any personal information – names or case numbers or addresses – so her claim to be bound by privacy laws didn't make sense. Some people were just standoffish, he concluded, before turning the pages of the phonebook to the next agency on his list. By the end of the day, Sang-Soo had called every adoption agency in the phonebook in a series of brick-thick shutdowns.

Nothing else for it. Sang-Soo made an appointment at the biggest agency, Hall Global, posing as a father prepared to relinquish a fictional child. There, the social worker asked him, 'When was the child born?' He was about to provide his own birthday, so that he wouldn't forget it and slip up later, when the social worker added, 'Or is the mother still pregnant?'

Sang-Soo's face came to a halt. The social worker's demeanour was brisk and impatient. She made clear she was in a big rush, and she didn't notice Sang-Soo's shock.

Out of curiosity, he murmured, 'Pregnant.'

'OK.' She didn't even look up. 'If you can bring her to one of our maternity homes, she can remain there to ride out her pregnancy. You'll agree to relinquish the child on entry. That way, we take legal custody of the child before birth.'

The word 'our' was odd. Did the agency *own* maternity

homes? It discomfited Sang-Soo. An agency in the business of sending infants abroad, simultaneously housing pregnant women? A supply chain began to take shape. Above them, a wall of framed photos of young children flanked by smiling white parents.

Sang-Soo asked, 'You have maternity homes?'

She reeled off a list of homes, in various locations. She acted as if this was a garden-variety interaction, as commonplace as filling a cavity, or renewing a licence.

Sang-Soo pressed, 'And if . . . er . . . my girlfriend doesn't agree to go to a maternity home?'

His tone must have been off – a little too piqued perhaps – because the social worker met him with a cool, guarded suspicion. He could almost hear the shutters clatter down. 'I'm sure she will.' She stood. 'Excuse me.'

There was something here, Sang-Soo was sure, a gnawing splinter under the skin. He became consumed with breaking it wide open. For eight weeks, index cards multiplied across the wall, the picture clicking into focus. It made his head roll. At the widest aperture, what he saw was an evolved, sprawling infrastructure, all leading to the same goal: selling children. There was nothing else to do but write. Stripping away the fireworks of rhetoric, the tide of narrative, the arrogance of style, Sang-Soo wrote and struck out and amended his first draft all through the night until the morning stopped him and he had to go to work.

It was a rainy evening. Sang-Soo had picked up two rolls of kimbap – tuna and sausage – which he tucked into the pocket of his anorak. He saw the purple rubber boots in the footwell of his apartment. It would be wonderful to spend this cold evening with his sister and her warm glow. Sang-Soo was eleven when their mother died, and he was too young to remember their father. His sister had taken on the role of both parents without hesitation or complaint.

'Noona?' Sang-Soo called out.

Silence. He moved further into the apartment and saw a small figure in the noir. Rain spilled down the windows in pearlescent streams.

'What's all this?' Youngja asked, standing in front of his wall of index cards, hands behind her back. Sang-Soo cocked his head to the side. By now, she would have coddled him thrice over. Told him he wasn't dressing warm enough. That he'd lost or gained weight. That his skin was especially sallow or bright. She stumbled a little when she looked at him.

'Just a story I'm working on,' he said. He peered into the kitchen and saw a giant stockpot simmering on the stove. Sweeping back towards her, he saw his stack of papers – the article he had begun to draft – had shifted from the left side of his desk to the right.

She swallowed hard.

'Tell me, Sang-Soo-ya,' she pointed at a pink index card, gulping fast, as if she was putting on a brave face, 'is this true?'

He took a few steps forward until he stood next to her and read his own scrawled handwriting. *Children sent away, usually with all identifying family information erased from their paperwork, listed instead only as orphans.*

Youngja
영자

Summer. Lazy afternoons. All doors wide open. Hana lying in the maru on her tummy, in the path of the airflow. Flicking through an old magazine, bright flits of light across the backs of her legs. Her crossed ankles swaying side-to-side. Blink. Just an empty room.

Mosquito coils burning in the yard. The heady fragrance of citronella swirling. But still: raised, raw bites all across Hana's back. They had a taste for her sweet blood. Youngja licked her thumb-pad and pressed it on each bite. Everyone knew that spit neutralised the itch. Blink. A coil dish. A pile of ash.

Footsteps down the lane and the rustle of a plastic bag. Heat that kept streets empty. Hana and Sora bringing home three chuchuba, blue-soda flavour. *You shouldn't have got me one*, Youngja said, *don't waste your pocket money on me*. Hana said, *Hurry, before they melt!* Youngja squatting next to the girls as they sucked on their sugary ice pops, tongues tinged electric blue. The back of her knees slick with sweat. Blink. Both girls, gone.

DRAFT
Orphan Exports: the nation's profit-driven adoption industry
A report by Jang Sang-Soo

The hottest day of the year. Twists of hair stuck to foreheads. Usually, they'd eat samgyetang. Now, she wasn't hungry.

> Gimpo airport. A Northwest Airlines 747-400 is taxiing down the runway carrying passengers of the largest emigration movement in our country's history. Onboard, you will not find professors, nurses, construction workers or skilled craftsmen. There are no optimistic students or newlywed couples hoping to start again on new shores. Instead, the flight is ferrying a crucial national export. Eleven babies, to be adopted into the United States.

'You take after me.' Said on an August evening, with a small opening of pride. Seeing herself, her silly mannerisms and random habits, reflected in the mirror of her daughter.

> The first international adoption programs were established in the 1950s, as Western aid and Christian missionary groups flooded into Korea, responding to the countless children orphaned in the war or fathered by US or UN soldiers. [MORE. Nationalism. Sovereignty. Population reduction. Mixed kids and the hanminjok.] However, three decades later, adoption has evolved from its origins in humanitarian efforts into a lucrative economy that trades in one product: our children.

The waning of autumn. Half-asleep at dawn. Rolling over and expecting to feel a girl's form. To slide warm legs together like a dovetail joint. Finding cool empty space. Feeling cavernously alone.

Women, complaining. Their daughters can't find decent matches, and they're not even trying! They'll stay at home for ever at this rate and they can't even cook a decent broth! Youngja listened silently, filled to the brim with things she cannot, must not, say. This is my punishment, she thought. Listening to the ungrateful, unaware of how precious their girls were. It made her feel homicidal.

> Hall Global is the country's leading adoption agency, still bearing the name of its founder, ~~Christian fundamentalist religious zealot born-again Evangelist~~ missionary Jim Hall. Often credited as the 'father' of Korea's foreign adoption system, Hall introduced streamlined processes and inventive measures that maximized the scope of international adoption to its vast proportions today. In the last half-decade, one in every hundred children born in Korea was sent for adoption.
>
> Hall Global is a family-run ~~business~~ enterprise. After Jim's death, the baton passed to his daughter, Matilda Hall, who stated: 'My father dedicated his life to saving the unwanted children of Korea, working tirelessly to ensure they join loving, Christian families. Led by God and faith, he revolutionized the concept of the family itself. It is my goal to continue his remarkable legacy and extend the hand of his pioneering charity. During the holidays every year, we receive sackfuls of cards from parents whose lives we have touched – from Minnesota all the way to Maine – with outpourings of thanks for the gift of their children.'

Hundreds of guests. Not a single day away from the minbak. A view from the sink.

> 'From Minnesota all the way to Maine', Korea is now the largest supplier of babies into the United States, begging the question, where do these children come from? Our investigation has found that an integrated system of institutions – maternity homes, hospitals, delivery clinics, foster homes, orphanages – act as extensions of the adoption agencies' reach, together securing a continuous supply of healthy, newborn babies.

Elections. Democracy.

The Eight-Eight Olympics. Seoul duly whipped into shape.

> Just a stone's throw from Hall Global's headquarters is the White Carnations Maternity Home, responsible for providing Hall Global with up to one hundred babies a year. Speaking with the matron, Yoon Ok-Soon, I was told that most mothers in her care 'come to regret their irresponsible decision to bring an illegitimate child into the world. Due to financial and social ostracization, they have no viable options. Here, we help them overcome their unfortunate past and secure a better life for their child. Do we receive donations from the adoption agencies? Of course we do. But really, the donations are for the good of both mother and child.' An inquiry into land registry records revealed that Hall Global LLC owns the White Carnations building.

A girl they called Ada. Brand new, yet a culmination of whispers of actions that came before.

Money grazes all facets of this ecosystem. It is common practice for midwives, gynecologists, obstetricians and doctors to receive payments for detecting single, expectant mothers and steering them into adoption agencies. It is estimated that over 70 percent of children sent for adoption were identified at, and relinquished in, the hospital in which they were born.

One source, who worked at Hall Global for a year, and wished to remain unnamed, said, 'We never could meet the demand. Our numbers were always falling short. It was like a factory. We had to compete with other agencies over the same pool of babies. So when a doctor or midwife sent babies to us, we paid them commission.'

Photographs of the little girl arrived. Nine months old, sitting on a picnic blanket in a floral dress and crochet headband, with Tim lying behind her, and Hana in the corner, her expression hidden by sunglasses. How lucky Ada was to have such a doting father! Look how fancy her sunglasses were! Look how plumply kissable that child's cheeks were!

> Currently, the majority of birth mothers are unmarried women facing a hostile landscape of stigma and discrimination. When asked, a soon-to-be mother staying at White Carnations Maternity Home, who wished to remain anonymous, said, 'I hoped to raise my child, even if alone. But the staff here have persuaded me that it would be impossible, that life would be too difficult. It doesn't seem like there is any other option.'

> Two months later, I met with her again in a tearoom near Itaewon where she told me, 'The adoption agency must have been notified as soon as my waters broke because they were at the hospital waiting for me. A few minutes after my daughter was born, they took her. I didn't know what was happening. I didn't even see her face. I asked for some time with her. They said my father had already signed the relinquishment papers and my daughter was already legally in their custody. I suppose my father was considering my future, but I feel so empty.'

Words screamed past, beyond her reach. Her hands shaky, her vision faded. Old age and hard work, they dulled your sharpness. Life forced you to slow down.

> Adoption agencies also support orphanages in exchange for priority over the most desirable children. Director Shim of the Hope Orphanage in Bukcheon stated, 'Yes we work closely with the agencies. It is naturally in the child's best interests to be adopted into a stable, loving home with two parents, where they can prosper, than be raised in an incomplete family or in an orphanage. I am glad to play a part in safeguarding an abandoned child's happy future.'

> But are they abandoned? Last year, over 8,500 babies [double check] were sent abroad, most citing 'abandonment' on their papers. Upon further inspection, it is apparent that these documents are fabrications. Family severance is a key part of the commodification process. Most adoptions today involve 'orphanization', through which children are

sent abroad with papers listing them as 'orphans' or 'abandoned', with their family and birth information erased. [ADD: Mass production. Consumerism. Human rights??]

A morning like any other. Except Youngja, for the first time in her life, forgot to switch on the rice cooker. One of the guests called out, 'Samonim, when will we get our rice?'

At the same market she had frequented for thirty years, the large plastic buckets of banchan were suddenly indistinguishable. The marginal differences in shade and shape that used to indicate freshness and quality, now meaningless. Youngja stood gaping, while the banchan stall owner said, 'Tae-Young's omma, are you all right? Do you want the usual?'

> Louise Moore, an adoptive mother in New Jersey, believes in the benefits of the current system. 'We had been trying for so many years for a baby when a friend told us about the work of Hall Global,' she said, cradling her eighteen-month-old son, Christopher. He was adopted by the Moores at three months old. 'We're big on family values. We tell him every day that love is what makes a family. He knows his birth mother loved him very much, but she couldn't care for him. That was why she abandoned him at that police station, to give him a better life.'

The dusty fork of the road. Left or right? She spun around, trying to place where she lived in relation to the hill in the distance, the faded yellow house on the right, the brick well behind her. The air was so wet. Her lungs were drowning.

Her skin allergic to her clothes. A loud car horn rang out behind her. Commands not reaching confused feet. The horn becoming angrier. Legs snapping back into action, scattering out of the way. Deep breaths. Left.

> However, Kwon Mo-Sae, an international student who volunteered on an 'orphan flight' in exchange for a three-quarters reduction on his airfare, expressed discomfort: 'Looking back, I regret taking part in removing those children from their homeland and into a nation where they might face discrimination and alienation from their culture. I was assured they would be happier in their new homes, but I'm not sure how the agencies can promise that'.

Driving the truck to the farm, the distinction between the kerb and the tarmac blurred. Her foot catching the step between the yard and the front gate. Propelling face-first into the gravel.

Using tweezers and a red plastic hand mirror, Youngja carefully picked shards of gravel from her cheekbone, while her husband read the paper in the corner.

'I think there's something wrong with me,' she whispered.

He sighed.

Her cheek stung. 'These changes aren't normal.'

'Of course they are.'

Her nostrils flared. 'What?'

'A woman of your age? Hormones are wrecking your body.'

Her husband interrupting her in the middle of a task to ask where she had tidied his belt away. 'What do you mean you don't remember? I need it. You must be able to remember.'

This demand is driven mainly from the United States. [Add: abortion/contraception/infertility = not enough children available domestically in the US.] The ~~dystopic~~ process works by proxy measures, invented by Jim Hall, obviating the need for adoptive parents to travel to the country from which they are adopting, resulting in what Boyd Harding, an INS officer at the US Embassy in Seoul, described as 'mail-order babies'.

Harding goes on to state that, 'The numbers are concerning. Several hundred children each month. That's incredibly high. It represents the movement of big, big bucks. It's inevitable that there will be some under-the-table dealings. Kickbacks and such. On that scale, I don't think it would be possible to take a case-by-case approach to the individual needs of each kid. It's far too systematic. Call it as I see it, it's an export business'.

Their fortieth wedding anniversary, Youngja grilled mackerel, its burnished colours glistening. Her husband expertly pulled the fillet off the skeleton and ferried it to his bowl. Then cracked the fish's head and dropped it in Youngja's. The final fragment of patience unmoored. She flipped the squat table they both sat cross-legged under, rice and fish hitting the wall, utensils clattering to the floor.

'After all this time, I've raised our children, provided for this family,' she screamed, 'at this age, must I still eat the fish's eyeballs while you take the fillet all for yourself?'

He looked dumbly at her, eyes bewildered and stupid. He finally said, 'I thought you ate the head because you liked it.'

Their eldest son Tae-Young and his wife never conceived a baby. Their second son, however, did marry and have a little mouse. His wife was Chinese and far from her family, so Youngja decided to close the minbak for a month, for the first time since the coups of 1985, and travel to Busan where they lived to take care of her and help with the baby. Her husband grumbled, his permanent cigarette tucked in the corner of his mouth, about her departure even though she had spent the entire week batch-cooking a month's worth of meals for him.

'Why do you need to go so far, did they even invite you?' he said.

'I want to support them. She is our only grandchild in the country.'

'You women are so obsessed with your grandchildren.'

Her right eye twitched. She never knew if he said these things purposefully to irritate her.

'You have rice portions frozen and galbi-tang in the containers in the fridge,' she said, putting her coat on. She registered a puddle of water under the leaking fridge, which she'd nagged her husband to fix all week. She wouldn't remind him again. She closed the door behind her and began walking down the path, the dirt crunching under her feet. Just as she reached the gate, she heard him shout out, followed by a tumble. A large weight thumped on the ground with a hollow thud. Then, silence. She froze, hand still on the gate. She waited for a moment, scanning the perimeter, to see if there was any more noise. It was eerie. Without thinking, her hand pressed on the gate's latch. She floated onto the street and continued on her trip. She would forget this soon. And whatever she would find on her return had already happened.

And what of government ~~complicity~~ oversight? Add:

- Quick-fix social welfare
- $15–20m USD revenue py. Valuable foreign currency.
- Managing Director of Hall Global = retired military general. Over 30 government personnel hired. De facto gov-run institution.
- **<u>Careful</u>**

Vast blanks. Drapes of heaviness. Sparse expanses of . . . what was she saying? Flares so bright. Notecards. Pages. Words. Holding her grandson. Regret. She fell asleep thinking about a woman's plight and so on and so forth.

Hana
하나

These days, Hana felt a part of herself – the hard, round bead in her centre – detach from her whole. The day was a headache, overcast in an unforgiving, blank grey. In the garden, the bushes were naked and skeletal. Winter was only just hitting its stride, and she sighed at the prospect of the gaudy lead-up to Christmas. She noticed herself revving her motor, trying to jump-start the same annoyance that had fuelled her for so long. *Come on! Your mother drove your highest-paying guest away! Your most secure form of income.*

But it wouldn't get going. She no longer had the energy to feed it.

It didn't occur to her until she heard Michael screaming upstairs that leaving home included leaving her mother behind. She had just assumed that things plodded on, same as they ever were. Hana remembered the afternoons she spent with Youngja, collecting mussels by the rock pools, ripping sweet potatoes fattened by the ground, mornings braiding her hair into intricate Dutch plaits. She paused, her hand cool against the marble countertop, waiting for an excuse to come to her. A silver bullet that made her own pain trump all. She glanced petulantly around the kitchen as if she might find it in one of the cupboards next to the mugs. That night, pulling Youngja away from Michael's bed, Hana had hissed in her ear, 'Are you insane? What the hell are you doing?'

'I just want to talk to him,' Youngja had whimpered. 'He needs to know I'm sorry. He needs to know.'

Hana's cheeks had reddened as if she had been slapped. After everything else that had loosened in her mind, Youngja's guilt remained fleshy and insistent. Hana crouched beside her. Youngja's nightdress was billowy and loose, like a rudimentary ghost costume put together last minute for Halloween. Ada lingered in the doorway. Michael was rubbing his eyes and covering his bare chest. Before she knew it, Hana looped her mother's arms around her own neck. Ada hustled next to them and joined, taking the other. Together, they scooped Youngja up. Even though they slept on the same mattress each night, Hana had never found it easy for their bodies to be so close. As if any physical touch indicated a thawing, an opening, that she wasn't ready to concede. Carrying Youngja down the stairs that night, jelly-legged, Hana felt the tiredness of lugging around the past lift. Mainly, a swell of relief. She had really missed holding her mother.

Five minutes into cleaning Michael's room, the Hoover choked. Something had clogged its motor. Hana stuck her finger in the hose and groped its sides until a small piece of plastic came loose. Into her palm fell a sea-green pen cap from the set of gel pens Tim had bought for Ada's twelfth birthday. How studiously and responsibly Ada had kept the entire set together, not scattering loose pens all over the house, or losing half of them within a few weeks. Ada through and through; keeping it together. Hana had known it for so long that she'd forgotten to notice it. She remembered the obvious. This wasn't Michael's room, but Ada's. She wondered if she could take a small, safe step towards rebuilding.

She thought about it for about an hour or so. Word of Hana's minbak had spread far and wide, and it was such a powerful tool that she had begun turning away guests. She was already making her way downstairs before she made her decision. In their cramped room, she gathered Ada's things. It was quick work, as Ada had two designated drawers and one shelf. Consistently folded T-shirts; exercise books that weren't tattered at the corners; schoolbooks that had been neatly annotated and colour-coded. Hana didn't have time or money to repaint the bedroom back to its original colours, but she could surprise Ada this evening with a night in her own room again. It wasn't much, she knew, to offer a fifteen-year-old a closing door and a single bed. But it was her way of acknowledging Ada's sacrifice. It meant more like this, than if she just said it. Small steps.

She retrieved from the attic Ada's Laura Ashley bedsheets. Fluffing the bed, it already looked like a teenage girl's room again. Hana pinched her eyebrows together, trying to remember whether Ada had any posters on her walls, or trinkets on the windowsill. She couldn't picture anything enshrined besides her school timetable and the Korean alphabet chart pinned into a cork board. Hana wondered if Ada let herself have any fun. She carefully hung everything Ada owned, staging a homecoming. She raised Ada's spare backpack and emptied it: a Twirl wrapper; lip balm; body spray. She absent-mindedly reached into the back zippered pocket and felt a stiff piece of plastic. A folder. Inside, letters she hadn't seen for a lifetime. Her mother's writing pleading, her own hand rejecting. A quick, terrifying pain clattered through her ribs when she saw that they each, one by one, were still sealed shut. And one more thing. A steel USB stick. She would have thought it contained Ada's coursework, or some presentation she had to give at school, but for the fact it was with the letters. Its presence was growing in the room, pulling her attention, making her feel more awake than ever.

Later that afternoon, after her daily run to the shops, Hana floated into the public library, sitting at the computer banks, pulling the USB from her pocket. She shuffled herself close to the screen as the file crackled alive.

The first time she watched it, she reared back, the chair squealing against the floor. Her brain short-circuited. A loud, irate confusion started coiling and compacting. This had to be some barbaric trick of her mother's illness. The musk of the library was heavy around her face and she wanted to retch. Inarguable truths reckoned with other inarguable truths, which made them seem like lies, and everything was blurry. The structure of the past twenty-three years of Hana's life buckled, like an enormous glacier crumbling into the sea. So, she watched it again. Then again. And then again. Realisation inhaling and exhaling.

She could have sat there all day and night. Her son had died. He died an infant. Stomach lurching from conclusion to conclusion, she took in that her baby had grown into a man without her. A twenty-three-year-old man. She tried to picture him, the image swaying. That there was a real person, her child, made of muscle and joints and lipids and pores, with interesting thoughts and internal bewilderments, who had probably loved and been loved, whose life had been existing alongside hers all this time, was so dizzyingly high, so far away from what she knew, she thought she might collapse. Not a lot of conscious processing was happening. A sheath of light flared over Hana's face.

Hana let her tailbone tuck under her hips, curving herself until she was slumped against the back of the chair. Her hands fell to her sides. It was too much to absorb at once. She was a cluster of nerve endings. Her mind telescoped in and out. She would go home and scrounge together every penny and get on the next flight back to Korea. She would pound down the doors of the agency that had taken her child. She would roam the earth to find him. She realised she couldn't 'start' searching for him because she had always been finding him in the breath of the breeze, in an errant ray of sun on a dark day, in the pages of a notebook. My son, her heart wrenched. My son, I'll find you.

And then just as the ante was upped, it plummeted. She couldn't leave yet. What about Ada? Ada and Yohan; the scales settled in a moment of balance. She had two children. Two. She was replaceable everywhere but with them.

Hana sat in a long moment of silence. Slowly came the sinking realisation that Ada must have stumbled upon this half of her story first. She shut her eyes. Her daughter had seen the deepest part of her underworld, and instead of sticking her finger in it, swirling it around and making a mess, she'd closed the lid and accepted it all just as it was. Ada accepted Hana, just as she was.

And as for her mother? The video was paused and, in the snapshot, Youngja was in a striped shirt on a beige armchair lit by the glow of a floor lamp. Hana's one constant. All that devotion. All that loyalty. All those lies. All that betrayal. All those years. Two women, hands forced by their place in history and time. And at the end of the road, when all Youngja had was a clutter of memories and a flickering flame, she still made sure the truth wasn't lost with her. Hana understood that now, through her video, Youngja was offering her own life for Yohan's.

'Omma,' Hana wailed, piercing the empty room. The whoosh of her breath lifted a layer of dust that floated around her face. Hana put her head in her hands, the computer screensaver bouncing blue light over her knuckles.

Ada
에이다

'Hmm,' Ada pondered aloud to her new-old room.

She hadn't slept well. The night had been restless. She was shivery, and no amount of wrapping the duvet around her shoulders could compensate for the loss of two bodies' heat. She kept fading in and out of sleep, until the sherbet morning lulled in. Ada, half-conscious, cast her arm about the mattress for Youngja's bony hip, or Hana's wall of back. She had startled awake at the feeling of emptiness, before realising where she was and, with some disappointment, lying back down. Through the gap in the curtains, the sky was a single, pensive shade of cerulean. She was back in her childhood room, in a single bed as vast as the desert, a small desk by the door, and a wardrobe opposite. It was exposing.

She could hear the guests coughing around her, mouthwash gargling, Capital radio, drawers pulling, bags zipping. It was icky being one of the people upstairs, like she had abandoned Hana and Youngja. She wondered if, downstairs, they missed the shape of her as much as she missed them. She should go down and check on Youngja. But maybe they were fine without her now. She groaned as she covered her face with her forearm. Birds – Ada didn't know which kind – sang to each other. She remained this way until the shuffling past the walls around her died down, and the front door opened and closed four times.

Shortly after, a small knock before Hana entered. Her mum knocking? That was new too. She shut the door behind her and came over to the bed. Wordlessly, Ada lifted the corner of the duvet and Hana shuffled in next to her as if they were at a sleepover. She really was a woman of two halves. Within a chasm of words, Hana spoke with gestures and physicality. She rustled in her apron pocket and pulled out a stack held together by a hair tie. Ada recognised the red-striped borders immediately. Hana laid the bundle of Young-ja's letters on the duvet between them. Ada bit her lip, not daring to look at Hana. They had been in her backpack; so her mum caught her snooping red-handed and was here to discipline her.

'I . . .' Ada began weakly 'I found them at the Farm – I didn't know—'

'Let's open them together,' Hana said. 'Your grandmother is still sleeping.'

Ada was shocked. She had not been expecting that.

'OK.'

They mulled the sealed letters over one last time. Pandora and her box came to Ada's mind. Hana reached for the first one. Ada remained perfectly still as Hana ran a bare nail under the envelope seal. The aged glue peeled open with satisfying elasticity. Hana peeked inside the triangle, then pulled out a pad of cash about half a centimetre thick. The notes were a mixture of green and yellow. They both stared.

'How much is that?' Ada said. Another small prickle,

invisible to the eye. How could she be familiar with the currency of the country she'd never visited?

Hana counted the bills between her thumb and forefinger so quickly her joints practically went rat-a-tat. 'About three hundred pounds now. Worth a lot more in,' she checked the postage stamp, 'nineteen eighty-nine.'

'Is there a note?'

Hana flipped the letter upside down and shook it. 'No.'

'Open the next one.' Ada nudged her elbow.

Hana looked at Ada helplessly as she pulled out another stack of green and yellow. She resembled a mob wife, clutching fans of cash in each hand. They had crisp edges and still had that new-paper smell, which made Ada picture Youngja calmly waiting in line at the bank to withdraw fresh bills. The next envelope was embossed with a square groove. Under her fingertips, Ada felt a slim piece of cardboard like a matchbook. With furrowed brows, she opened it to find a flawless coin, fresh from the mint. *Seoul Olympics 1988*, engraved in a semicircle across the top, with the image of the stadium in the centre. Youngja had been sending Hana carefully rationed glimpses of life.

Dispensing with caution, Hana rounded her shoulders. The bills fluttered over the bedspread as her hands unfurled. Heavy, fat tears fell onto the sheets. There were still nine more unopened envelopes. Even if only half were filled with money, the cost to Ada's grandparents would have been significant. And yet, Youngja never resigned. She never opened the returned letters and used the money elsewhere. She never lost hope.

Ada raised a third letter to the window and saw it didn't contain money. She passed it to Hana. Out dropped three glossy photographs. The first was a black-and-white group, sitting on a stoop, a row of shoes by their feet, a straw hat hung on a wooden post. The date stamp in the corner read *09.75*.

'That's Halmoni.' Ada pointed at a woman in a cotton hanbok with her hands in her lap.

'Those are my brothers,' Hana said. Ada saw two young men in buttoned jackets and ramrod posture on either side of Youngja, sitting with their palms resting on their knees. She had never seen her uncles before. And standing to the side, a girl in striped trousers and a wool coat. Hana's nail appeared next to the girl. 'That's me.'

The second photo was stamped *08.83*. A snapshot of a young girl with a clean bob and plain T-shirt, hands reaching upwards into the branches of a persimmon tree. The third didn't have a date stamp but showed two girls, both in identical white short-sleeve shirts, black A-line skirts and ankle socks, standing on the steps leading to a big building with black-gridded windows.

'Sora,' Hana whispered, picking that photo up and holding it so close to her face it seemed like she wanted to climb through it. 'Sora and me.'

She turned to Ada. 'This was my best friend. I owe everything to her and her sister. This was us in front of our middle school. This was the tree my grandfather – your great-grandfather – planted. It was so plentiful that my mother sent me round all the neighbours with boxes of persimmons. And this,' she raised the photo of the group, 'I was five years old when this was taken. I don't remember it. But this was all of us, except for my father, at home. The minbak, before it was the minbak.' Her voice broke into a throaty whisper. 'I never thought I would see it again.'

They sat shoulder-to-shoulder. How many times had the

world shattered between them? Ada wondered what her mother would do over, if time was hers again. Would they still find their way here, next to each other?

'Mum.' Ada felt selfish for what she was about to say. 'Did you want me?'

'What do you mean?'

It hit Ada with a crackle in her chest. If Hana found the letters in her backpack, she would have stumbled across the USB stick too. Had she watched it? They didn't have a computer at home, did her mum even know of the wonders of the USB? Ada tested the waters.

'Did you,' she fiddled with some loose skin on her cuticles, 'want to have another baby?'

They both heard her say *another*, but the only reaction from Hana was an infinitesimal stiffening of her lower half. It had been wrong of Ada to try to hide it. Yet another victory for shame. Yet another gap for silence to grow into. Her brother had always been, and would always be, a part of their lives. The prospect of continuing to deny it exhausted Ada.

Hana turned to face her, eyes candid and deep breathing. She knew. And she knew Ada knew.

'I love him with all my heart,' Hana said. Ada's hope sank at the mention of *him* being the one Hana loved. 'And I love you with all my heart.' She shrugged with a defeated, faraway smile. 'You are both my children. You're my home.'

Was this the first time they had both been wholly honest with each other? It was all Ada had ever wanted. Home wasn't a place. It was your people. It was where your spirit was last whole. It was the locus that lay central to everything. From which you came and to which you returned. Youngja sent these photos to Hana all those years ago to remind her that, no matter the miles and seas and continents that separated them, she had a home. That she had a connection to a life before now. They suspended an innocent time, before their inhabitants had to live with the certainty of decisions that couldn't be undone. Precisely in their simplicity – a tree, a school, a home – they held a motherland. A thousand words.

An hour later, the three of them stood in the kitchen, Ada and Youngja leaning over a pot on the stove.

'Doenjang chigae,' Youngja said. 'For me?'

'Yes, that's right,' Ada said, dropping chopped half-moons of courgette and onion to fry in the pot. Hana watching, breathless. Youngja smiled serenely. Her eyes blank and glassy. Hana took a few steps to where Ada and Youngja were standing by the stove and stretched her arms around them. The triplet bent to each other's curves. There was still so much to eventually say, so much to mend. But Hana would have to start cooking soon to make dinner for the guests in time. They returned to their positions. Time would have to do its thing. Winter would make its entrance. Christmas would come. The past would continue to reopen itself in shy and inventive ways. There would be remorse. There would be joy. No more, no less.

In mid February 1986, the director of the Incheon branch of Hall Global raced down the corridor. He needed this problem like he needed a hole in the head. Screeching around the corner, he slammed a scrap of paper, with numbers scrawled across a torn edge, on his junior Sujin's desk.

'I need you to find these files,' he barked. 'Bring them to my office as soon as you do.'

Sujin sighed; he was often so brash that she no longer took offence. She used her fingernail tips to flick through the steel filing cabinet. They said computers would make all of this obsolete, and the day couldn't come soon enough. It took her half an hour to track down the files pertaining to the eighteen numbers. Children, she corrected herself. Eighteen children. She smoothed the wrinkle in her pencil skirt down and took the files to the director's office.

'The documents you asked for, sir,' she said.

He flipped the covers over.

He grunted. 'What I expected.'

'Sir?' she asked, even though she knew what was in each folder.

The boss pulled his glasses off and rubbed the nose-pad imprints left on his face. His office had the gloomy tang of stale cigarettes and coffee, the smell somehow exacerbated by the creaking light bulb and the bleak yellow walls to match. 'There's a chartered flight leaving tomorrow. These are the children going.'

'Is there anything I can help with?' Sujin said, unsure of what the issue was. There were flights nearly every day. She hadn't noticed anything unusual in the files.

The director pushed his breath out. 'Some of these children have since become . . . unavailable.' He sighed. 'There's been an outbreak of the flu next door. We don't have time for this.'

Sujin's teeth ground against each other. Ever since her conversation with Ha-Jeong under the rain-weighted tarp, Sujin's ignorance had been unseated, replaced with something closer to bitterness.

'Should I set about starting new applications, sir?'

'Of course not,' he snapped, as if his patience simply couldn't handle her question. 'We can't charge the client twice for the administration fee, the visa, the flight. It would all take too much time and cost.'

He closed his eyes. Then, slowly, opened them. Sujin was unsure what she was supposed to do.

'That's all, Sujin-ah,' he said.

Sujin realised she was dismissed and left. She had a lot of work to get through and it was already noon.

Four souls left their bodies in feverish, sweaty half-sleep, in the flu episode. Two girls, two boys. A lack of vaccinations and close quarters gave the virus dominance. Three of the dead were already processed for adoption. Replacements had to be found. The dominoes started to fall, clacking into each other, one by one. Across the network, calls were made, babies were switched and shuffled around, connective tissue flexing and moving in unison. Three children were sourced and given the names of the dead.

There was a very brief skirmish when one teenage mother had called from Seoul, wanting to collect her son, who had, unbeknownst to her, already been signed away for adoption by his grandmother. The director, in his indifference, gave instructions to tell the mother her child had succumbed to the same flu. Neither cross-checked the child's name with the names of the two dead boys.

When the time came, eighteen children were present and correct, nestled into white cardboard boxes, cushioned with a beige waffle cloth. Seat-belted onto a commercial flight to Portland International. Five adults would accompany the babies, feed, burp and change them, in exchange for a two-third reduction on their airfare. Upon landing, all eighteen were unloaded and processed. It was the busiest year on record for the agency, with flights nearly daily. Shooting paper orphans out like paper planes.

On the tarmac in Oregon, hopeful faces with eager, fearful smiles were set against a vibrant day, awaiting the plane's arrival. A young woman, in a taupe trench coat, French pink on her nails, and leather court shoes. Her husband, in a smart grey suit and sensible lace-up shoes. They'd dressed up for the occasion, Olympus camera at the ready. The woman erupted into relieved, happy sobs as a social worker carrying a plain white box approached her. Her husband sported a proud expression, rubbing his wife's lower back supportively.

And stapled to the side of the box was a brown Manila tag that read:

Park Yohan, 1 November 1985.

Afterword

On the morning of 12 December 1979, my mother, then twenty-two years old, headed to her first day of work as a newspaper reporter. At noon, the editor-in-chief asked her where she lived, then abruptly sent her home. She returned to her apartment, crossing the Han River, wondering if she had somehow made a terrible first impression.

Unbeknownst to her, the editor had received word that the city's bridges would soon be blocked by the military. Conflict was erupting downtown, eventually spreading across the capital. An up-and-coming army general named Chun Doo-Hwan was staging a coup. By the following morning, he had taken hold of major state functions, assuming de facto rule. Though he would eventually instal himself as President of South Korea, he would be remembered by a different term: dictator. My mother later learned that her best friend, a kindergarten teacher, had walked for hours in tears, to her home across the river.

While South Korea's military regime remains infamous today for the brutal characteristics common to most dictatorships, it is less well known for another act of state violence: creating the most efficient and deregulated adoption industry in the world, motivated by foreign policy, economic ambitions that viewed adoption as the cheaper alternative to domestic child-welfare systems, and population reduction goals. A full account of the history of international adoptions from South Korea is beyond the scope of this novel, and I refer below to only a small quotient of the important scholarship on the subject. More than 200,000 children have been adopted from South Korea since 1953. What originated as a response to the aftermath of the Korean War had become by its peak in 1985 an unchecked network of institutions competing to source and send abroad unrestricted numbers of children. South Korea is historically the largest and longest provider of children placed into international adoption.

The stories of Yohan, Youngja and Hana are fictional but, in the words of Margaret Atwood, 'If I was to create an imaginary garden, I wanted the toads in it to be real.' Many sources have been central to my research and understanding. Eleana Kim's *Adopted Territory: Transnational Korean Adoptees and the Politics of Belonging, Transnational Adoption and (Im)Possible Lives, My Folder Is Not a Person: Kinship Knowledge, Biopolitics, and the Adoption File, Producing Missing Persons: Korean Adoptee Artists Imagining (Im)Possible Lives*. Arissa Oh's *To Save the Children of Korea: The Cold War Origins of International Adoption*. Kyung-Eun Lee's *The Global 'Orphan' Adoption System: South Korea's Impact on its Origin and Development*, and her thirteen-part *Korea Times* series on the topic. Tobias Hübinette's *Comforting an Orphaned Nation: Representations of International Adoption and Adopted Koreans in Korean Popular Culture*, and *Korean Adoption History*. Yuri Doolan's *The First Amerasians: Mixed Race Koreans from Camptowns to America*. Francisco Pilotti's comparative study *Intercountry adoption: trends, issues and policy implications for the 1990s*.

I circled Hana's character for a long time. She was private and hidden, even from me. I knew what might have happened *to* her, but spent a lot of time ruminating on her mornings and nights. What was it like to be a young woman experiencing love, loss and personal crisis in a dictatorship? Was she proud or ashamed? Birth mothers are a notoriously taciturn group in South Korea, silenced by a long history of discrimination against unmarried (including divorced and widowed) motherhood. Like Hana, it was not unusual for women to withhold their prior experiences from the husbands and families they later went on to have. I am profoundly humbled by the women who shared their stories with me. I have done my utmost to honour them.

I also learned much from: Hosu Kim's powerful book *Virtual Mothering: Birth Mothers and Transnational Adoption Practice in South Korea*; Mi-Jeong Lee's report *Reviewing Issues on Unwed Mothers' Welfare in Korea: Intercountry Adoption, Related Statistics, and Welfare Policies in Developed Countries*; Hye-Young Kim's report *Korean Public Opinion Survey on Unwed Mothers and their Children*; Gretchen Sisson's *Relinquished: The Politics of Adoption and the Privilege of American Motherhood*; and *I Wish for You a Beautiful Life: Letters from the Korean Birth Mothers of Ae Ran Won to Their Children*, edited by Sara Dorow. Youngja's lament that she had to be content with knowing that Yohan was living under the same sky is taken from the words of one of these mothers. I also highly recommend the films *Resilience* by Tammy Chu and *Between Goodbyes* by Jota Mun. I am grateful to the following people for giving me their time: Hosu Kim, Im Ae-Duck of Aesuhwon maternity home, Kang Young-Sil of Aeranwon maternity home, Jeon Hyun-Sook of TheRUTHtable, Yu Mi-Sook of the Korean Unwed Mothers Support Network, Kim Min-Jung of the Korean Unwed Mothers' Families Association, and Kim Yukyeong of Banet.

Mi Hee and Sujin's scenes at the orphanage and adoption

agency respectively are imagined. Little is known about the inner workings of the adoption agencies and their wider networks. Lax paperwork, spotty records, active falsification and privacy laws obscure our understanding of day-to-day procedures, and information was often shared informally. Personal (mostly anonymous) accounts of former adoption agency workers were particularly illuminating. I am grateful to Helen Noh for sharing her experiences as an agency worker with me. I also referred to Hyun Sook Han's memoir *Many Lives Intertwined*, as well as Frontline and the Associated Press's important documentary, *South Korea's Adoption Reckoning*.

Many adoptees have uncovered falsified, inconsistent or heavily redacted paperwork in their adoption records, including the systematic practice of 'orphanisation', culminating in a structural concealing of their biological families. Children recorded as 'orphans' or 'abandoned' often had living parents who, in some cases, had not consented to the adoption. Adoptee-led organisations have advocated tirelessly for access to their records held by adoption agencies. At the time of writing, the transfer of over 250,000 vital files from four private adoption agencies to the government's National Center for the Rights of the Child is under way, though adoptees have raised concerns over the suitability of the storage facility for fragile paper documents and are still waiting for access.

Attentive readers might have noticed that the novel is told in a total of eight perspectives, none of which is Yohan's. This followed a great deal of reflection and discussion on the fine line between representation and appropriation. In deference to the nuanced voices of the Korean international adoptee community, and their continued advocacy for rights and recognition within Korea, I have chosen not to write in Yohan's perspective, in the hope that this book will instead direct readers towards their first-hand accounts. Many adoptee-led organisations, such as the Global Overseas Adoptees' Link (GOA'L) and the International Korean Adoptee Service Inc. (InKAS), work on the ground in Korea, facilitating a bridge to the country, language, culture and heritage as well as assisting with birth-family searches.

Despite having similar origin stories, Korean adoptees are widespread geographically and were adopted over a seventy-year period. Therefore, like any diaspora, they have diverse experiences, paths and relationships with their adoption stories. A constellation of organisations specific to each receiving area exists to support adoptees, and the International Korean Adoptee Associations (IKAA) seeks to facilitate collaboration among these networks, hosting International Gatherings, including the triennial Korea Gatherings. In these spaces adoptees come together, build community, share their lived experiences, generate dialogue, and collaborate on advocacy causes such as access to records on a global scale.

I started writing this book in early 2021. In 2022, the government's Truth and Reconciliation Commission launched its investigation into South Korea's adoption practices, after the tireless campaigning of adoptee-led organisations for an inquiry. I am grateful to Peter Møller of the Danish Korean Rights Group, who also heads KoRoot, for his valuable insight. In March 2025, as I was proofreading the final draft of the novel, the TRC published its findings, acknowledging widespread systematic failures, inadequate oversight and insufficient legislation, resulting in malpractice for profit. It concluded that the state had violated the human rights of Korean children. The inquiry has triggered parallel investigations in receiving countries such as Norway, Sweden and Denmark. It remains to be seen how these findings will result in tangible remedies or reconciliation for adoptees.

I encourage anyone who is seeking to understand more about this unique experience to refer to the following moving books: Nicole Chung's *All You Can Ever Know: A Memoir of Adoption*; Jane Jeong Trenka's *The Language of Blood: A Memoir*; Lauren J. Sharkey's *Inconvenient Daughter*; and Katy Robinson's *A Single Square Picture: A Korean Adoptee's Search for Her Roots*. I also highly recommend the work of documentarian and film-maker Deann Borshay Liem, in particular the following films: *Geographies of Kinship*; *First Person Plural*; and *In the Matter of Cha Jung Hee*.

Sang-Soo's draft article is loosely based on Matthew Rothschild's 1988 article *Babies for Sale: South Koreans Make Them, Americans Buy Them*, published in the *Progressive*.

Mitch and John exist only in the pages of this novel. However, Christian missionary groups have long been prolific in South Korea, their numbers dramatically rising following the end of the Korean War, playing a significant role both in the national democratisation movement and the origins of the adoption industry. Almost all adoption agencies, orphanages and maternity homes share their roots in a foreign Christian organisation. Presbyterians, Seventh-day Adventists, Methodists, Catholics and Protestants were all active at the time, which is why I do not assign a specific denomination to Mitch or John. The following contemporary missionary accounts informed my depiction of both characters: *More Than Witnesses: How a Small Group of Missionaries Aided Korea's Democratic Revolution*, edited by Jim Stentzel; *Our Lives* in *Korea and Korea in Our Lives* by Dorothy and George Ogle; *South Korea: Dissent Within the Economic Miracle* by George Ogle.

Minbak only skims the surface of the democratisation movement of the 1980s, as I had to remain faithful to the inner lives and experiences of a teenage girl and middle-aged woman of the time. Words like 'dictatorship', 'authoritarianism' and 'revolution' often overshadow our understanding of daily life under such circumstances. Seung-Kyung Kim's *Class Struggle or Family Struggle? The Lives of Women Factory Workers in South Korea*, Hagen Koo's *Korean Workers: The Culture and Politics of Class Formation* and George Katsiaficas's *Asia's Unknown Uprisings: South Korean Social Movements in the 20th Century* were deeply illuminating as to the workers' democratisation movement, including the student infiltration of factories that is depicted in the novel.

The Korean Image Archive was also a brilliant resource, compiling contemporary photographs that helped bring the setting of 1980s Incheon and Seoul to life.

Although I have relied on the above listed sources, any historical licences, departures or errors I might have made are my own.

Some additional notes:

Hana is described as seventeen years old, but under the Korean traditional ageing system, she would have been considered eighteen. I have kept her age consistent with the international standard to avoid confusion.

There are two types of boarding houses in Korea: a minbak-jib and a hasuk-jib, largely overlapping in services, but the former being akin to a bed-and-breakfast, while the latter is for longer-term stays. The business Hana runs in 2008 is a minbak, whereas Youngja's 1985 business could resemble a hasuk-jib more closely. For the purposes of the narrative, I have called them both minbaks.

In Youngja's opening chapter, her condition is described as 'driving in the dark', an expression I drew from novelist E. L. Doctorow's beautiful metaphor on writing.

As a final note, I say the above because, though I have only written a novel, I will be pleased if I have been able to direct readers in some small way towards this part of Korean history that continues to reverberate today.

London, October 2025

Acknowledgements

To my agent, Hellie Ogden: your unwavering guidance, near-daily WhatsApps, and dogged support are not taken for granted. From the first time you emailed me in 2021, you've continued to change my life. To my editor, Katie Ellis-Brown: you've shaped and championed my writing with unending generosity and care. I appreciate you so much. To Anouska Levy and Claire Cheek: thank you for your capable insights and passion for this story.

Thank you to Ma'suma Amiri, Liz Foley, Kate Fogg, Cassie Browne, Ellie Auton, Mia Quibell-Smith, Mairéad Zielinski, Lucy Beresford-Knox, Yeti Lambregts, Sarah-Jane Forder, Graeme Hall and everyone at Harvill, Vintage and WME, the real MVPs.

I owe a huge debt to multiple wise people who spoke with me, either in person or over video call, sharing their expertise and answering my questions about the machinations of the adoption industry, the social climate for women in 1980s Korea, life under military rule, the democratisation movement, and the work of missionaries.

Eleana Kim: thank you for laying the foundations of my understanding, sending me resources, patiently imparting your knowledge and dedication to the field. Arissa Oh: within five minutes of meeting, you dove into assessing the historical accuracy of the unfolding events in the book, and I was blown away by your sharp intuition and infectious energy. Hosu Kim: your research and oral histories of birth mothers is inspiring and invaluable, thank you for graciously sharing it with me. Kyung-Eun Lee: your books have informed me so much, while your homemade muguk and banchan warmed my soul. Oh Myo Kim: you thoughtfully guided me through so many intricacies that I had been ignorant to, thank you for your clear-eyed insights. Peter Møller: for the nearly three hours I spent in your offices, I couldn't write notes fast enough, thank you for meticulously explaining your work. Helen Noh: our conversation bolstered my understanding of how adoption agencies operated, and I'm so grateful that you generously made the time (until 10 p.m.!) to speak with me. Bastiaan Flikweert: thank you for a robust conversation that was very much needed. Rick Allen: I feel lucky to call you a friend. Jenna Lee Kim: I could have talked with you for hours, if only we could for once be in the same place at the same time! Kara Rickmers and Tommy Gentzler: thank you for sharing the work of adoptees on the ground. Rylee Meyer: another wonderful conversation, thank you so much. Chae Heuer: meeting you and your mother felt so poignant, thank you for spending time with me during your short trip to Seoul. Philsik Shin: I've referred to the notes you wrote in my workbook over udon and kimbap countless times, thank you for your essential assistance. Im Ae-Duck: meeting you at Aesuhwon in Jeju was one of the most energising conversations I had during my fieldwork, thank you for your dissertation, and for the oranges. Kang Young-Sil: thank you for opening the doors to Aeranwon, and for the warm hospitality. Kim Min-Jung, Kim Yukyeong, and Yoo Mi-Sook: thank you for sharing your remarkable work with unwed mothers. Jeon Hyun-Sook: I have done my utmost to honour your words in the novel. My thanks also to Father Donal O'Keeffe and George Katsiaficas for their generous insights into the democratisation movement. Above all, I am immensely grateful for the candour, patience and encouragement of the women who spoke to me during research trips to Korea, often about very personal and painful memories; I am so moved by your resilience. Meeting you has enriched this novel and my life immeasurably.

I am lucky to have friends and family who generously read early drafts, provided rigorous comments and intelligent feedback: Alexia Syrmos, Zoe Li, Lillian Brown, Amelia McGrath, Bec Galloway, Mark Galloway, Rae Breidahl, Harry Breidahl, Genevieve Liston, Zahra Mashhood, Christopher Lillywhite, Ella King, Callie Kazumi, Liv Matthews.

Bo, you don't know what a book is, but you helped me get the words down every single day.

To my mother, who spoke to me every day in her mother tongue and made sure I knew my heritage and culture. A former reporter from whom I must have inherited a love of writing, she was my first teacher. To my father, for being steadfast in his support and love. I have always been able to rely on and look up to you, which is the quietest gift to give a child. To you both, I am because you were.

To my husband Pete, after a total of some 150,000 words written and deleted, I fall short of finding words that can adequately convey how much I love and appreciate you. When we first met, you heard my nascent, self-conscious ambitions to be a writer, and in countless ways since, have adjusted our life to make sure I could achieve them. Thank you for everything.

About the Author

Ela Lee was born in 1995 and studied at the University of Oxford. Her debut novel *Jaded* was an Amazon Best Fiction Book of the Year. Lee has been named a Spotify Breakout Author and has also been selected for Forbes 30 Under 30, class of 2025. *Minbak* is her second novel.